The Guest List

Books by Fern Michaels

Fear Thy Neighbor
Santa Cruise
No Way Out
The Brightest Star
Fearless
Spirit of the Season
Deep Harbor
Fate & Fortune
Sweet Vengeance
Holly and Ivy
Fancy Dancer
No Safe Secret
Wishes for Christmas
About Face
Perfect Match
A Family Affair
Forget Me Not
The Blossom Sisters
Balancing Act
Tuesday's Child
Betrayal
Southern Comfort
To Taste the Wine
Sins of the Flesh
Sins of Omission
Return to Sender
Mr. and Miss Anonymous
Up Close and Personal
Fool Me Once
Picture Perfect
The Future Scrolls
Kentucky Sunrise
Kentucky Heat

Kentucky Rich
Plain Jane
Charming Lily
What You Wish For
The Guest List
Listen to Your Heart
Celebration
Yesterday
Finders Keepers
Annie's Rainbow
Sara's Song
Vegas Sunrise
Vegas Heat
Vegas Rich
Whitefire
Wish List
Dear Emily
Christmas at Timberwoods

The Lost and Found Novels:

Hidden

The Sisterhood Novels:

19 Yellow Moon Road
Bitter Pill
Truth and Justice
Cut and Run
Safe and Sound
Need to Know
Crash and Burn
Point Blank
In Plain Sight

Eyes Only
Kiss and Tell
Blindsided
Gotcha!
Home Free
Déjà Vu
Cross Roads
Game Over
Deadly Deals
Vanishing Act
Razor Sharp
Under the Radar
Final Justice
Collateral Damage
Fast Track
Hokus Pokus
Hide and Seek
Free Fall
Lethal Justice
Sweet Revenge
The Jury
Vendetta
Payback
Weekend Warriors

The Men of the Sisterhood
Novels:

Hot Shot
Truth or Dare
High Stakes
Fast and Loose
Double Down

The Godmothers Series:

Far and Away
Classified
Breaking News
Deadline
Late Edition
Exclusive
The Scoop

E-Book Exclusives:

Desperate Measures
Seasons of Her Life
To Have and To Hold
Serendipity
Captive Innocence
Captive Embraces
Captive Passions
Captive Secrets
Captive Splendors
Cinders to Satin
For All Their Lives
Texas Heat
Texas Rich
Texas Fury
Texas Sunrise

Anthologies:

In Bloom
Home Sweet Home
A Snowy Little Christmas
Coming Home for Christmas

Books by Fern Michaels (*Cont.*)

FERN MICHAELS

The Guest List

KENSINGTON
PUBLISHING CORP.

www.kensingtonbooks.com

KENSINGTON BOOKS are published by

Kensington Publishing Corp.
119 West 40th Street
New York, NY 10018

All Kensington titles, imprints, and distributed lines are available at special quantity discounts for bulk purchases for sales promotion, premiums, fund-raising, and educational or institutional use.

Special book excerpts or customized printings can also be created to fit specific needs. For details, write or phone the office of the Kensington Sales Manager: Kensington Publishing Corp., 119 West 40th Street, New York, NY 10018. Attn. Sales Department. Phone: 1-800-221-2647.

The K logo is a trademark of Kensington Publishing Corp.

ISBN: 978-1-4967-3664-2
First Trade Paperback Printing: August 2022

ISBN: 978-1-4201-2880-2 (e-book)
First Electronic Edition: August 2000

10 9 8 7 6 5 4 3 2 1

Printed in the United States of America

Prologue

John Evans stood with his hands jammed into his pockets in the open doorway of his wife's hospital room. He was instantly aware of two things: first, that his wife looked as if she'd been *arranged* in the bed. She wore her frilly bed jacket, and her long golden hair had been placed just so over her shoulders. Lipstick and rouge were evident, as though she were waiting for a special visitor. He sniffed. Perfume, too. The second thing he noticed was the silence, a little like the first ten minutes before Mass got under way at St. Gabriel's.

He didn't want to go into the room and make conversation with his beautiful, unloving wife. He didn't want to be the one to tell her the bad news, but the doctors insisted he do it. They thought Harriet would accept it better coming from him.

They didn't know Harriet.

No one knew Harriet, except maybe his brother-in-law, Donovan. This past year John had come to realize that Donovan knew Harriet better than he did. If John had known two years ago what he had learned since, he never would have married her. His only explanation—and Donovan agreed with him—was that she'd cast a spell over him with her beauty, her wit, and her charm. Who but a fool wouldn't have been smitten?

John's eyes narrowed. The still form in the bed hadn't so much as twitched. If her hands were folded across her chest, she would look like a mortician's handiwork. He thought about the ten-and-a-half-month-old baby at home with the sitter. Baby Mallory looked like him, with her dark eyes and dark hair. He adored her.

Harriet tended to the child, but as far as he could tell, she'd never bonded with her. She never cuddled her or rocked her, never played with her. She saw to the baby's needs, but that was all. All the loving and cuddling had to come from him. He did it all willingly because he loved the child.

A voice behind him hissed in his ear. "Is she dead?"

John twisted around. "Jesus, Donovan! Don't sneak up on me like that." He put his hand on Donovan's arm. "Let's go out to the waiting room."

Donovan Mitchell was a tall man, sandy-haired, rugged, with an open smile. For a big man, he carried his 180 pounds with athletic grace. His wife, Harriet's sister, Emma, had died in childbirth. He'd tried to warn John about Harriet—that she was mean and hateful just like Emma—but John had been too smitten to listen.

"You look like hell," Donovan said with concern. "Was it a hard delivery?"

"Ten hours. Longer than the doctors expected." John raked his fingers through his hair. "I've been here all night. I think I drank two gallons of bad coffee and smoked two packs of cigarettes."

"Who's watching Mallory?"

"Mrs. Lascaris."

Donovan narrowed his eyes. "There's something wrong,

isn't there? Harriet looks fine, so it must be the baby. Don't look at me like that, John, what's wrong?"

John shook his head, unable to speak.

Donovan clapped his hand on his friend's back. "C'mon, tell old Donovan what's wrong."

"Why don't I show you, instead? Then you tell me. You didn't go to the nursery, did you?"

"Nah. I came straight here when I got your message. I know where it is. The nursery, I mean."

They walked in silence until they came to the nursery window. John tapped lightly on the glass. A nurse looked up and smiled. She moved to the far end of the nursery to lift a small pink bundle from the crib. She was still smiling when she held the infant up for inspection.

"Shit!" Donovan gasped. "What the hell is that? Is it going to go away? Jesus, John, what is it?"

"A birthmark. The doctor called it a port-wine stain. I don't know if it will go away or not. She'll have to go to a specialist at some point. It's really deep. It's the whole left side of her face, Donovan."

"I see that. Listen, modern medicine . . ." His voice trailed off as he stared at the baby.

John's shoulders slumped. "Harriet is never going to . . . Children are so cruel. . . . Jesus, Donovan, what if it can't be removed?"

Donovan hooked his thumbs into his belt loops. "Listen to me, John, this isn't the time to be thinking along those lines. Is she healthy? Will that mark make you love her any less?"

"She's perfect in every other way. And, hell no, it won't make *me* love her any less," John said, rallying to Donovan's question. But then he thought about Harriet. "Harriet doesn't know yet. She's going to be . . ." He sighed. "To make matters worse, she was expecting a boy."

"A boy. A girl. Babies are babies."

"God, Donovan, what *am* I going to do? If I know Harriet, she won't want anything to do with a less-than-perfect baby." His voice softened as he stared at the baby through the glass. "Look at all those golden curls. I didn't know babies could have so much hair. Mallory was bald for six months." He turned away from the window, and the two of them started back down the hall toward Harriet's room. For John, each step was harder to take than the last. "I don't know what to say to Harriet. Where's the money going to come from for the operations? Insurance will only pay so much if they pay for something like this at all. I can't work any more overtime. As it is, I'm killing myself taking care of Mallory and working seven days a week. You know the construction business. What happens if we hit a dry period?"

Donovan put a hand on John's shoulder to halt him. "It'll all work out," he assured him. "I've got a healthy little nest egg. I'll help you."

The corner of John's mouth lifted in a semblance of a smile. "Thanks, buddy, but we both know that money is only a small part of this problem."

"Yeah, and you and I both know the solution to all this bullshit is for you to take the kids and walk out. It's never going to get any better between you and Harriet. I never thought I would say this, but divorce is your answer. Harriet won't give a shit one way or the other. Trust me on that, John. She's just like Emma. Hell, I can even tell you what she's going to say the first time she sees the baby."

"I don't want to hear it, Donovan."

"You need to hear it, so you're prepared," Donovan persisted. "She's going to tell you to put the baby up for adoption or farm it out to foster care. She's not going to want anything to do with that child."

John's face contorted with anger. "You're wrong. Harriet would never say something like that." But she would. He knew she would. What he didn't know was why he was defending her.

"Ten bucks says I'm on the money," Donovan said, then waved his arm as if to erase what he'd said. "Oh, forget it. I can't take your money. It was a bad joke, and I'm sorry." He punched John's arm. "Listen, buddy, how about I go over and pick up Mallory and take her to my house so Mrs. Lascaris can go home? It'll cut down your sitter bill. I'll clean her up and put her to bed." When John started to shake his head, Donovan cut him off. "Don't argue with me. You stop at Tony's on your way home and pick up a large combination pizza. We'll pound a few brews and think about what to do. You can even spend the night if you want. Okay?"

Defeated, John nodded.

"Tell Harriet I said hello." Donovan waved his arm. "Nah, forget that. Harriet thinks I'm the spawn from hell. See you later, buddy."

"I'll be over later," John said to Donovan's back as Donovan walked down the hall. He watched his friend until he got into the elevator. Donovan was right—about everything. Even about Harriet hating him. Actually, it was their friendship Harriet hated, probably because it was the only thing he refused to give in on. In everything else, he let Harriet have her way. It made life easier.

Before he knew it, John found himself back in his wife's doorway. Nothing had changed. She still looked *laid out,* and he was still as jittery as he'd been twenty minutes ago. *Just tell her,* he told himself. *Get it over with. Cough, shuffle your feet, shake her shoulders. Blurt it out and get the hell out of here.*

He did all three at the side of her bed.

Harriet opened one lavender-shadowed eyelid. "Oh, John," she said wanly. "Have I been sleeping long?"

John cleared his throat. "I don't know. I just got here a little while ago."

"Did you see our son?"

"We don't have a son. We have another daughter," he said, practically running the two sentences together.

"A daughter! That can't be. I wanted a boy! I was going to call him Christopher Matthew. There must be some mistake. Hospitals are always making mistakes. You need to check on that, John, and you need to do it right now before it's too late. Go. Quickly." When he didn't move, she asked, "Why are you still standing there?"

She was an amazing woman, he thought. She had more arrogance than any man he'd ever known. She'd wanted a boy, and she'd taken it for granted that she would have a boy. It never even occurred to her that God might have something else in mind.

"I'm standing here because I don't know what else to do. Our daughter is wearing her ID bracelet with our name on it. There is *no* mistake."

"It's your genes, John. This child was supposed to be a boy. I wanted a girl *and* a boy. That's the way it's supposed to be." Harriet turned her face to the wall.

"I'm sorry, Harriet, but in spite of what you wanted, this is the way it is, and there's nothing either one of us can do about it. I happen to love little girls. A son would have been nice to carry on the Evans name, but a girl is just as nice." He bent his head and mustered up his courage. "I need to talk to you about something, Harriet."

"For heaven's sake, what is it?"

"Aren't you going to ask how Mallory is?" he asked, hedging from what he'd meant to say.

"Mrs. Lascaris is very capable even though she's a nosy old biddy. Mallory is in good hands. Giving birth is very traumatic. I'm here to rest. There's absolutely no need for me to concern myself about Mallory."

Gathering his courage, John moved around toward the window. "Look, there's no easy way to say this except to say it," he said, shoving his hands into his pockets. "Our new daughter was born with a birthmark on her face."

"What!"

"They call it a port-wine stain," John explained, determined not to break down. "It covers the whole left side of her face and neck. The doctor feels at some point it can be removed, but I don't know when that will be. She would need a specialist. She weighs seven and a half pounds and is twenty inches long. Her head is covered with golden curls. She's beautiful, Harriet. Aside from the birthmark, she's perfect."

Harriet reared back into her nest of pillows. Her carefully made-up face turned hateful as she spit out the ugly words that would ring in her husband's ears for the rest of his life.

"Are you saying I gave birth to a *freak?*"

Part One

Chapter One

Edison, New Jersey—1981

John Evans sat at the kitchen table, a pile of bills in front of him, consumed with worry about how he was going to pay everything and still have enough money left to take Abby to the specialist in New York. He pushed the bills aside as Abby ran to him, tears rolling down her cheeks.

"I want to go, too, Daddy. Mama said no. Can you take me?"

John's stomach started to churn. It was like this every damn day of Abby's life. He had a strong urge to smash something or better yet to pummel his wife, but instead he reached for the curly-haired little girl, lifted her onto his lap, and dried her tears with the edge of a paper napkin.

"Daddy, Daddy, how do I look?" Mallory shouted as she danced into the kitchen.

John stared at the fairy costume that had cost him half a day's pay and winced. He struggled for a light tone. "You look just the way a fairy princess is supposed to look." *Too bad you don't act like one,* he thought.

"Do I look *bee-yoot-e-full?*" Mallory asked, turning left, then right, so he could see her from every angle.

"You look—"

Harriet's high-pitched, nasal voice stopped him from answering. "Come along, Mallory, or we'll be late. The star of the play has to be on time." Harriet stuck her head into the kitchen. "She looks magnificent, doesn't she, John?"

"I want to be a fairy princess," Abby said, sobbing anew.

Mallory twirled around on tiptoe. "You can't be a fairy princess. You're an ugly witch!" she said spitefully.

John jumped to his feet, Abby in his arms. "That's enough, Mallory. Tell your sister you're sorry."

Mallory flew into her mother's arms. "I'm not sorry. I'm not," she wailed loudly.

John ignored the whiny little girl. "I can't believe you're doing this, Harriet. Why can't Abby go to the play?"

"You know very well why she can't go. This is Mallory's night. There is no place for beautiful and ugly in this discussion."

John stared at his wife in utter disgust. "What kind of a mother are you that you can be so cruel to your own child?"

"If you remember, John, I didn't want to be her mother. I only took her home from the hospital because you insisted." In a double swirl of skirts, Harriet and Mallory turned and went down the hall.

John cradled Abby in his arms, crooning soft words of love that he hoped would replace Harriet's and Mallory's hateful ones. "I have an idea, honey," he said, turning the little girl around to face him. "Let's walk across the yard to Donovan's house and see what he's doing. I bet we can get him to make us ice-cream cones. With chocolate sprinkles."

"Okay, Daddy. But first I have to get Bailey." She never went anywhere without the cuddly stuffed dog, a gift from Donovan.

"Ah, my two favorite people in the whole world!" Donovan Mitchell shouted, as John and Abby walked across the lawn and up to the patio. "I bet you're here for ice-cream cones. Good thing I remembered to buy sprinkles." He held the screen door open, then knelt as Abby stepped inside onto the porch. "I got you something else today, too. Something you've really wanted."

"You bought me a present?" the little girl squealed.

Smiling, Donovan nodded, then pointed her in the right direction. "Go into the living room. It's in the big white box by the sofa."

As soon as she raced off, Donovan popped an iced beer for his friend and pulled out a chair. "I told you Harriet wouldn't take Abby with her."

John slumped into the chair Donovan offered. "I know." He sighed and turned his face toward the street. "It's just so damn hard for me to believe a mother can be so cruel to her own child. It's not natural. It's sick. Mothers are supposed to . . . Ah, hell!"

"Yeah, that pretty well sums it up," Donovan agreed.

"And on top of everything else," John went on as if he'd never stopped, "she's teaching Mallory to be just like her." He set his beer down on the floor and rubbed his hands over his face. "I don't know what the hell to do anymore."

"Lookee, lookee, Daddy! It's a fairy-princess dress just like Mallory's!" Bubbling with excitement, Abby draped a filmy net creation over her father's leg. "Can I put it on? What do fairy princesses do, Uncle Donovan?"

A wide grin split Donovan's features. "They wave their magic wands and say abracadabra!"

"That's what magicians do," John said, grinning in spite of himself. Donovan always made things better. He was a hell of a friend and a one-man support group. John picked up the frothy little dress and helped Abby into it. "Fairy princesses do nice things for people and make them feel better when they're sad," he told her, then patted her bottom and sent her away to play.

Once she was out of sight, he sighed and looked at Donovan. "Thanks. How did you know?"

Donovan shrugged. "I have eyes and ears. Yesterday when I was mowing, the girls were playing in the yard. I heard Mallory bragging to Abby about her dress. You don't need to be a rocket scientist, John, to figure out which way the wind is blowing. Mallory is turning into a spiteful, miniature Harriet, but then you already know that. Anyway, I called Carol and asked her to pick up the costume on her lunch hour today."

John thanked God for a friend like Donovan. What would he do without him? "I'll have to remember to thank her. You need to snap that woman up, if you ask me. Women like Carol don't come along very often. She's perfect for you."

"Maybe a little too perfect," Donovan said, chuckling. "Nope. Marriage isn't for me. I tried it once, and that was enough. Things are fine the way they are. It works for Carol, too. You know what they say—if it ain't broke, don't fix it."

Abby came running back. "Look, Daddy, Bailey has a costume, too. I love this. I love this," the little girl squealed as she dipped and swayed the way she'd seen Mallory do. "Am I still ugly, Daddy?"

Donovan reared his six-foot-four, 180-pound bulk out of his chair so fast, John was left breathless. "You are the prettiest fairy princess I ever saw!" he boomed. "And I've seen a lot of fairy princesses in my day. Ask your daddy."

John hauled Abby into his arms. "Uncle Donovan is telling you the truth, honey. You are the prettiest of them all."

"As pretty as Mallory?"

"Prettier," both men said in unison, then laughed.

Abby tucked her chin into her chest. "Then why wouldn't Mama take me to see the play? I promised to be good."

"You aren't old enough," John lied. What else could he say? He couldn't tell her the truth. He pressed his lips to her temple. *Who am I kidding? She isn't deaf. She heard the truth from her mother's own lips.*

"It's a silly play," Donovan added, feeling out of his depth. "You wouldn't have liked it." He reached down and touched the tip of her nose. "I have an idea. Why don't you and Bailey go into the living room and practice a play for your daddy and me. When you're ready, come out here and perform it for us. You can sing us one of the songs you learned in nursery school. Afterward, we'll have ice-cream cones smothered in chocolate sprinkles. What do you say, Princess?"

Abby's eyes brightened. "My name isn't Princess. It's Abby." She giggled.

"Oh, I forgot. I guess I must have called you that because you look like a princess." She giggled again, then skipped off.

As soon as she was out of earshot, John swigged from his beer bottle, gulping down half the contents without taking a breath. He sat back, leaning the chair on its hind legs. "I can't take it anymore, Donovan. I think this play thing was the last straw. I know what you're going to say, but how can I leave? I can't afford to maintain two residences, pay alimony and child support, and pay for whatever treatment Abby needs." He rotated his neck, trying to relieve the tension. "Just before I came over here, I was trying to figure out where I was going to get the extra money to take Abby to New York to a specialist the pediatrician recommended."

"And?"

'There is no 'and.' We only worked ten days this month. Who knows if the rain is going to let up anytime soon. June, July, and August could be just as bad."

"You could tell that wife of yours to get off her skinny, regal ass and get a job," Donovan drawled.

John gave a humorless laugh. "I tried that once. It didn't work."

"She's so much like Emma, it's scary," Donovan said, shaking his head. "Their mother did one hell of a job on those two girls. Emma thought just the way Harriet does, that the world owes her a living and man was born to be her slave. I knew I'd made a mistake the first year of our marriage. Like you, I hung on thinking it would get better. If Emma hadn't gotten pregnant, I was going to get a divorce. I still have trouble believing she really had a heart attack on the delivery table and that the baby was stillborn. I wanted that kid. I really did, but everything happens for a reason. She would have been the same kind of mother Harriet is."

"It is what it is," John said. He thumped his empty beer bottle on the wrought-iron patio table.

Donovan sat down across from John. "There's something I want to talk to you about. I've been kind of waiting for the right time. I think this is it. I've been offered a partnership in a construction company in South Carolina. Building is booming there, and the weather is pretty good all year round. I've got enough capital to buy in and enough set aside if things don't work out. I paid off this house right after Emma's death, and with property values being what they are now, I should get a pretty penny for it."

At John's look of confusion, Donovan explained. "I used Emma's insurance money. A hundred thousand dollars. I guess Harriet didn't mention it. Probably because it's sticking in her throat. She told me I should give it to her—or at least half of it." He leaned forward. "Listen, I'd like you to come with me. We make a good team. I know Harriet wouldn't object to your taking Abby. In fact, she'd probably be relieved never to have to see her again. She'll fight you for Mallory, though, but that's a choice you'll have to make. Abby will be better off with the two of us since we both love her. It's not that I don't love Mallory, I do, but in a different way. She's not a kid that lets you get close to her. She's like her mother—prissy, arrogant, and cold."

When John nodded, Donovan went on. "I've given this a lot of thought. At first we could rent a house with a yard. Later, when we're settled, we could buy." He paused. "If you need an incentive, think about this. This company does work overseas. If things get dicey with Harriet, we could both do a stint in Asia." John's look of interest spurred him on. "I'm going to be leaving in a few days to check things out. I'll probably be gone a week. If you want to get away from Harriet or you just want some peace and quiet, feel free to stay here. There's plenty of food and beer."

John rubbed his hand across his chin. "I don't know what to say, Donovan. It sounds great, but if I tell Harriet I'm leaving her, she'll . . . Christ, I don't know what Harriet will do."

"I'll tell you what she'll do. First she'll act shocked. Then she'll act sweet, *nicey-nice*, and try to get you to make love to her. If that doesn't work, she'll start making all your favorite foods, and when you've eaten your fill, and you're at your most vulnerable point, she'll try again to entice you into her bed. And you'll go. She'll play her little game for about two weeks, at which point the devil in her will sprout wings. She'll get you where it hurts, with Abby." He stopped to take a breath and regroup. "Emma did the same thing. I'm not a seer or clairvoyant or anything like that. I lived it. Think about it, John. You know I'm right. This is your chance, my friend, to make a clean break."

John let his breath out in a loud *swoosh* and shook his head. "It's too much, Donovan. You've always been generous, but this is going too far. I'll be like an albatross around your neck."

"You're my friend. There isn't anything I wouldn't do for you, just like I know there isn't anything you wouldn't do for me. I was taught never to take friendship lightly. My old man used to say you could be dollar-poor but emotionally rich if you had one good friend. I'm not looking for a payback, John. I just want to help, to see you and Abby happy." Donovan's voice turned gruff. "Besides, I don't want to lose you two. You're family."

"Christ, Donovan, I don't know . . ."

Donovan raised his hand to stop him. "Take some time to think about it. I'll call every other day or so to check in, but as soon as I get back I'm going to put this house on the market. School will be out in another week. We could be out of here in ten days . . ."

"Ten days," John echoed. "That doesn't give me much time."

Donovan ignored John's worried look. "The only reason not to consider going is if, in spite of everything, you really love Harriet."

John pulled another beer out of the cooler. "Love her? No, I don't love her. At least, not anymore. I can't even remember the last time Harriet and I had sex. Certainly not since before Abby was born."

"Do you think you could leave Mallory behind?"

"I don't know. I—I suppose I could. . . . It's not that I don't love her," he insisted. "I do. It's just that I've never been able to get close to her. God knows I've tried but . . . She's so like her mother; she doesn't seem to have much use for me."

"Well, then?"

"Daddy, I'm ready," the golden-haired little girl called as she came out onto the porch.

"So are we, baby," John answered in return.

John stared at his beautiful wife, trying to find one thing he liked about her. Dressed now in a frilly robe with matching mules, her makeup model-perfect, she glided toward the refrigerator to pour orange juice into a crystal wineglass. John watched her with clinical interest. Two little quick sips, then a longer sip, and then she drained the glass. She set it in the sink, knowing he would rinse it later. He waited. If he took Donovan up on his offer, then his cleaning-up-after-Harriet days were just about over.

"Mallory was enchanting this evening. She took two bows. She was really quite mature about the whole thing. Her costume looked so professional, not tacky like the others."

John said nothing, Donovan's offer ringing in his ears. In ten days, he and Abby could be out of there and on their way to a new life. His shoulders stiffened when his thoughts shifted to Abby and the last words she'd mumbled as she drifted off to sleep. "Will I be pretty someday like Mallory, Daddy?" He'd wanted to cry. Shit, he wanted to cry right now, but couldn't risk Harriet seeing how upset he was. *Be cool like Donovan,* he told himself. *Be a goddamn man for a change. Stand up to this bitch the way Abby's father should.*

Harriet really was beautiful, with a model's thin body that wore clothes to perfection. He was homely by comparison, with his thinning sandy hair and wire-rimmed glasses. Unlike Donovan, who was thirty-five—eight years his senior—and an in-your-face person. John had always been laid-back, easygoing, never confrontational. How often he'd wished he was more like Donovan. Then again, if he was like Donovan, they probably wouldn't be friends.

"I suppose you're going to be in a snit for the next week or so over me not taking Abby to the play," Harriet said. "Get over it, John. I hate taking that child anywhere. People stare. They talk behind your back. It isn't good for Abby, and it certainly isn't good for Mallory. Mallory is *normal* in case you hadn't noticed."

Her eyes flashed, and he could see her lips moving, but the only thing he could hear were the words he'd been practicing in his head. "I'm leaving you, Harriet, and I'm taking Abby with me," he blurted, startling himself. For Abby's sake and his, he forced himself to make a quick recovery. "I'll be out of here in less than two weeks. After that, you can do whatever you want."

Harriet looked incredulous. "What did you say?"

"What part of *I'm leaving you* didn't you hear?" he asked in a tone he'd never had the courage to use with her before. "I'm leaving, moving out. I no longer want to be married to you. I'm divorcing you." There, he'd said it, and it felt good. Damn good.

Harriet threw her head back and laughed. "We'll just see about that. There will be no divorce in this family." Her voice was so cold it could have frozen ice cream.

John stood his ground. "That's what you think. And when a judge hears how you've neglected and mistreated Abby, there won't be any contest about who gets custody of her. I'll have so many witnesses testify on my behalf, your hair will turn gray." He swept his arm in front of him. "You can have this house along with the mortgage payments. You can have both cars with both car payments. You can have all the maxed-out credit cards. In short, Harriet, you are going to have to get off that skinny, regal ass of yours," John said, parroting Donovan's words, "and get a job to support yourself and your fairy princess of a daughter."

Harriet waved her beautifully manicured hand in dismissal. "This is absurd, John. We've had our ups and downs, but things haven't been *that* bad." Her eyes narrowed in suspicion. "This is that bastard Donovan's doing, isn't it?"

John felt his insides return to normal. "This has nothing to do with Donovan. I've been thinking about divorce for a long time."

"Stop talking like a lunatic, John. This is all because of that crazy Donovan. My sister must have been insane to marry him. He was happy when she died so he could collect her insurance. He preys on women. I've seen the parade of women who go in and out of his house. He has a different one for every day of the week. If he was a woman, I'd call him a slut."

"He doesn't have a very high opinion of you either, Harriet."

"So you want a divorce," she said, walking away from him. "You'll have to pay alimony and child support, you know."

"We'll let the judge decide what's right." Now that he'd gotten past telling her, he felt more confident.

"I know what you're doing. You're trying to get even with me for not taking Abby to the play. We've been down this road before, and I have no intention of traveling it again. It's late. You have to get up early to go to work."

"There's no work tomorrow, Harriet. The site is water-logged." He picked up the stack of bills he'd been sorting through earlier and jammed them into her hands. "You might as well take these because I'm not paying them. They are now officially all yours."

John saw naked fear in his wife's eyes and knew he finally had her attention. A smile tugged at the corners of his mouth. He waited for what Donovan said would come next. It came sooner than he expected.

"Be reasonable, John. Let me get you a cup of hot chocolate and let's sit down and talk about what's troubling you."

"No thanks, Harriet. I'm not in the mood for hot chocolate or any other food or drink."

Harriet unbuttoned the first two buttons of her robe. "All right then. Let's just go to bed, John. It's so much easier to talk in a relaxed atmosphere."

"Relaxed atmosphere? You mean seductive atmosphere, don't you? I don't think so, Harriet. Whatever feeling I had for you died a long time ago." He straightened his shoulders. "This is the way it is now, Harriet. I'm leaving you. That's the bottom line, so you better start getting used to it."

"You're just going to throw it all away? Just like that!"

It was his turn to laugh. "Throw what away? We don't have anything to throw away. All we have are bills," he said, flipping the paper edges with his finger.

"Go to hell, John Evans!" Harriet shouted, as her high-heeled mules slapped the tile floor in her haste to get out of the kitchen.

"Right again, Donovan," John said, his fist shooting in the air.

Donovan Mitchell stared across the yard. "John, John, why did you marry that bitch? I tried to warn you. Now look where it's gotten us."

He was glad he had said it to himself when he saw his curious but good-hearted neighbor looking at him over the bushes. "Lovely morning, isn't it, Mrs. Lascaris?" he called.

"Indeed it is," she replied before she went back into the house. "I only wish that kid would stop working on his car."

Ninety minutes later, at 11:45, Donovan Mitchell strode down the concourse of Newark Airport. He hoped he was doing the right thing in accepting the new job. He felt so good it had to be right. He thought about Carol as he handed his ticket over to the flight attendant. He wondered if she would mind giving up her teaching job and joining him in the South. Did he have the right to ask her to join him without giving her a commitment? Probably not. He liked her, even cared for her, but he wasn't in love with her. Maybe he would be better able to make up his mind after this trip, when his mind was clearer.

Donovan buckled his seat belt. In a way he felt guilty. He shouldn't be taking up Carol's time if he didn't plan on marrying her. He should cut her loose and let her find someone who would love her the way she deserved to be loved. Was he willing to do that? Once his seat companion was buckled in, he leaned back and made himself comfortable. Closing his eyes, he brought Carol to the forefront of his mind. She was tall, just a few inches shorter than he, with wonderful, warm, laughing brown eyes, an infectious smile, and a great body. She had a great sense of humor and liked to experiment in bed. She could cook up a gourmet meal in no time and give Heloise some housekeeping hints. She was a giver all the way around, and she loved kids and animals. She'd taken to Abby right away and Abby to her. She was everything he'd ever thought he wanted in a woman so what was his problem?

Maybe John had inadvertently hit on it when he said Carol was perfect for him. His first thought had been that she was too perfect. He shook his head, putting it out of his mind. Nobody was perfect. Everybody had flaws. Even Carol. Though, admittedly, he had yet to find one.

Maybe a new environment would do the trick. Once he was away from all the memories of Emma, their stillborn child, the house, and Harriet, he'd be able to get his old life back. The life he'd had before he met the Lambert sisters.

As he dozed off for the ninety-minute flight to Charleston, Donovan Mitchell wished he had a fairy princess who would wave her wand and make him feel better.

Chapter Two

Construction-site coffee has to be the worst coffee in the world, Donovan thought as he sipped from the Styrofoam cup. His gaze swept the work crew over the rim of the plastic cup. He itched to pick up a hammer, but fought the urge.

"So, Donovan, are you in or not?" Steve Franklin asked as he rolled up a set of plans. He opened the trailer door and stepped outside, signaling Donovan to follow him. "As you can see, we have almost perfect weather."

"What do you do when hurricanes come along?"

"Inside work. That way we never miss a day. It's all in the way you schedule, but then you know that." Steve handed the plans to his foreman, then took Donovan's elbow and walked him toward a pile of lumber. "We've got contracts up the kazoo and more on the way. You can build your own crew and bring anyone aboard you want. I'll give you the whole Sun Blossom development in Seabrook. It's yours to run with no interference from me. Oh, I almost forgot, you get your own coffeemaker."

Donovan didn't need to think about it. He'd known he was going to accept the moment he set foot on South Carolina soil. He liked this cousin of his even though he'd only seen him every five years or so at family reunions. Steve was honest, ethical, hardworking, and didn't cut corners. He built quality housing at affordable prices, and his reputation was sterling. "The coffeemaker cinches it. I'm in," Donovan said, extending his hand.

"So when can you start?"

"A week or so. First, I'll have to find a place to live. That shouldn't take but a few days at the most. For now, a rental will do. I told you about John and his little girl. Three bedrooms are important. A couple of bathrooms, too. Little girls like to take bubble baths."

Steve pushed his hard hat farther back on his head. "Tell me about it," he said, grinning. "I have four girls."

Donovan rolled his eyes. "As soon as I rent a house, I'll head home, find a realtor for my house there, pack my stuff, and come back here. So . . . yeah, I think we're looking at a week on the outside."

Steve nodded.

"Were you serious about my own crew because if you were, I have four guys besides John I'd like to bring down."

"The more the merrier. If we ever get caught up, maybe you can build my house on Edisto."

"Sounds good to me." Donovan glanced down and checked his watch. Five o'clock. "Okay then, if there's nothing else, I'm outta here. I'll check in with you when I get back to Jersey. Thanks for the offer, Steve. It came in at just the right time."

"Hey, Steve!" a voice bellowed from the site trailer. "There's a phone call for Donovan Mitchell."

"Go get it, buddy," Steve said, slapping Donovan on the back.

Donovan seemed surprised. "I can't even imagine who

would be calling me here," he said, then loped toward the site trailer. "Mitchell here," he barked into the phone.

"Donovan. It's Carol."

He turned around to face the open door. "Carol, what's wrong? You sound funny. Are you okay?"

"I'm fine, Donovan. But—Listen, there's no way to tell you this except to blurt it right out."

"Jesus, you aren't going to tell me my house burned down, are you?"

"I'm afraid it's worse than that. I just heard it on the news when I was going to the cleaners. Harriet and John are dead."

He held the phone in front of him and stared at the handset, then put it back to his ear. "Have you been drinking, Carol?"

"Donovan, listen to me. As soon as I heard, I drove over to John's house. The police were swarming the place. Evidently Mallory and Abby had been playing at a friend's house, and when they got home, Mallory went upstairs to find her mother but couldn't wake her up. She ran crying to your neighbor, Mrs. Lascaris, and she checked it out, then called the police. They found John downstairs, sitting at his desk. He was dead, too. I'm calling from Mrs. Lascaris's house now."

Donovan sat down in the closest chair. "Jesus Christ. How? How'd they die? What happened? Was it carbon monoxide poisoning?"

"Nobody seems to know yet, or if they do, they aren't saying. I think you need to get back here just as soon as you can. I'll pick you up at the airport if you call me and give me your flight information."

"Yeah. Okay. Sure," he said automatically. "I'll head back to the hotel right now. I'll call you from there about the flight." He paused. "Carol—The girls—Are they okay?"

"They're right here with Mrs. Lascaris and me. They have no idea what's going on, but they're confused and scared."

"Yeah, me too," he said. "Take them to my house, Carol. I'm the closest relative those girls have, so the authorities shouldn't give you any trouble about taking charge. If you need to, mention my hefty donations to the Police Benevolent Association. John would—" His voice broke. "John would want me to take his kids." He paused, took a deep breath, and stood up. "I'll call the police myself from the hotel. I don't believe this. John dead. What do you think, Carol?"

"I don't know what to think. We'll have to wait to see what the police and coroner have to say. I'm so sorry, Donovan. I know John was like a brother to you."

"John was more than that. He was my best friend. Look, I have to get out of here, Carol. I'll call you with the flight info."

Sweat dripped down Donovan's face. At least he thought it was sweat. He knuckled his eyes, then glared at the man who'd called him to the phone before he stomped his way from the trailer to the rental car parked at the entrance to the building site.

Donovan got into the car, turned on the ignition, and let the engine idle for a few minutes. His thoughts turned to Abby and Mallory. What would happen to them? he wondered. Would the courts want to put them in foster homes? "Over my goddamn dead body!"

Rain beat down on the green-canvas tent. Donovan tried to listen to the minister's words. He heard phrases like pillars of the community, caring individuals, and loving parents. He couldn't help but wonder where the stoic-looking minister had gotten his information. Or did he have a generic script that he went by? Did he ever deviate from the flattering words? Donovan did his best to remember what the minister had said the day he buried Emma and their stillborn child, but he couldn't remember a single word.

He looked around, astonished at the turnout. All the guys from the construction company were there, probably because it was raining and there was no work. Everybody liked John, but Donovan knew in his heart the crew wouldn't be there but for the rain. How strange they all looked in their suits and white shirts and ties. He probably looked strange to them, too.

"Ashes to ashes . . ."

Donovan cringed. Carol reached for his hand and squeezed it. Carol had been a rock these past three days, taking care of him, the girls, and handling all the funeral arrangements. He didn't know what he would have done without her.

It was almost over. He had to hang on. He couldn't lose it with everyone watching. What he wanted more than anything was to run like hell and not look back. He clenched his jaw as he led the small procession past the two bronze Springfield caskets and dropped a single rose on top of each. Mallory followed behind him, but when it came time for her to put her roses on the caskets, she refused to part with them.

"Put them on the caskets, Mallory, like everybody else," Donovan said between his teeth. He wanted to smack her. She must have sensed his anger because she screwed up her face into the prelude to a tantrum.

Carol stepped between them. "I'll take care of this, Donovan," she said, pointedly, then bent down to Mallory's level. He didn't hear what she said, but whatever it was, it worked because next thing he knew Mallory was putting her flowers with everyone else's.

"What's in the boxes, Uncle Donovan?" Abby asked as she laid her roses on top of the caskets.

It only just occurred to him that he hadn't done a very

good job of explaining things to her, to either of the girls for that matter. *Way to go, Mitchell*, he thought.

Abby tugged on the hem of his suit jacket. "What's in the boxes?"

"Ashes," he blurted as he grappled for the right answer. That's what the minister had said. Ashes to ashes . . . But it didn't make any sense. The bones remained intact for hundreds of years before they turned to—*Not even ashes*, he thought. *Dust. The bones turned to dust.*

"Dust to dust . . ."

He wasn't sure how long he'd been standing there staring at the caskets, but when he looked up, all the mourners were heading back to their cars.

Holding Mallory's hand, Carol joined him and put her free arm through his. "Come on. It's time to go."

"No, I can't do this," he said suddenly. "I can't put John in the ground. It's . . . John didn't want to be buried. He wanted to be cremated. I just now remembered." He gave Abby over to Carol and ran to find the funeral director. Rain sluiced over him. Within seconds he was drenched to the skin. "Wait!" he shouted. "I changed my mind. I want to have . . ." He forced himself to calm down. "I've decided to have the bodies cremated instead of buried. I don't care what it costs, just tack it on to the bill."

"Twenty-one straight days of rain," Carol said as she climbed into Donovan's car. "I'm sick of it."

"It's sunny in South Carolina. I saw it on the news this morning," Donovan said inanely, water dripping down his face. He wiped it away, then reached for Abby and set her on the seat beside him.

"How long do you think the reception will last?"

"An hour or so. Everyone will have a little something to

eat and drink, they'll say nice things about John and Harriet, then leave. I don't expect more than a dozen people to show up. Everything is ready. We really don't have to do anything but circulate," Carol said. "Then, when everybody is gone, we're going to talk about why you did what you just did."

Donovan nodded. He could tell Carol didn't approve of his sudden change in plans. Probably because of the added expense. *To hell with the expense,* he thought.

He looked in the rear view mirror at Mallory. She looked lost, forlorn. In spite of what she'd done at the gravesite, he felt as sorry for her as he did for Abby.

"We're going to drop the girls off at the Barkers' house," Carol said a moment later. "Mrs. Lascaris is sick. The Barkers' daughter, Marie, is going to watch them until . . . until it's time to . . . to bring them back. Oh, and don't forget, you still have to talk to Harriet's aunt and fill her in on the details."

"Until you told me you found her name in Harriet's address book, I didn't even know she had an aunt. Emma never mentioned her to me, and neither did John."

"She sounded elderly but sharp. I think she said she was eighty-six. She wanted to know how much insurance there was and if she's mentioned in the will. She said she doesn't want . . . any responsibility."

"When can we go home?" Mallory whined.

"We don't have a home anymore," Abby informed her sister. "Isn't that right, Uncle Donovan? We're going to live with you now, aren't we?" Abby said, throwing herself sideways against Donovan.

"I want to go home," Mallory whined again. "All my stuff is there. I want my stuff."

Carol glanced behind her. "We have to wait for the police to tell us we can get your things from the house, Mallory. I'm sorry, honey, but there's nothing we can do until then."

"I'll share the toys I have at Uncle Donovan's," Abby generously offered.

"I don't want *your* toys! I want *mine*. They're way better than yours."

"Mallory!" Donovan said in a stern voice. "That's enough of that. You girls are going to have to get used to sharing for a while."

"I don't want to share with Abby."

"Oh, yes you will, young lady, and I don't want to hear another word about it. You will both be responsible for making your own bed, putting your clothes in the hamper, and picking up your toys. That's the way it's going to be. Crying and whining will not make me change my mind," Donovan said in his new parental voice.

"Mama always made my bed and picked up my clothes and toys," Mallory said, starting to cry.

Donovan didn't want to hurt Mallory more than she was already hurting, so he chose his words carefully. "I know, honey. But your mama is in heaven now with your daddy. Abby will show you how to do it. Abby makes her own bed when she sleeps over." Donovan glanced at Carol and saw her staring at him in a way that said, "this is not going to be easy."

"Mama said I was a princess and princesses don't do chores."

Donovan didn't know what to say to that. Mallory was a brat, but this wasn't the time to discipline her. "We'll talk about it later, all right?" he said, tight-lipped. His hold on Abby was fierce. The rest of the drive to the Barkers' was made in silence, as Donovan squirmed in his soaking-wet clothes.

"I feel so sorry for those girls, Donovan," Carol said after the girls had gotten out of the car. "What in the world are you going to do?"

"John's will appointed me executor of the estate and the girls' legal guardian in the event of both his and Harriet's deaths, so I've had my attorney petition the court for custody. He seems pretty sure no one will contest it. I'm afraid Harriet's aunt won't see a penny. What money is left after the bills are paid and the house is sold will go into a trust for the girls." Donovan took Carol's hand and squeezed it. "Later on, after the girls have adjusted, I'd like to look into adopting them. I don't even know if the courts would consider a bachelor, unless, of course, I wasn't a bachelor, but a stable, married man." He drew a long breath. "You want to get married, Carol, and make me a stable, married man?" He intended to spring the big question on her later, after the reception and before the girls came back, but instead, the words had just popped out of his mouth.

"If you're looking for a stand-in mother and housekeeper, you've got the wrong girl, Donovan Mitchell," Carol said, dashing his hopes. Then her expression changed, and a warm, loving smile lit her face. "However," she lowered her voice a few octaves, "if you're looking for a loving wife and a helpmate who'll nurse you through the flu and rub your feet, I'm at the top of the list. If the kids are part of the deal, that's okay. I love Abby. I honestly don't know if I can learn to love Mallory. She's a spoiled, willful little girl. I'd like to think with love and discipline we could change her, but . . ." She shook her head.

"So what's your answer? Yes or no?"

Carol appeared to give the question serious thought. "I need you to say the magic words, Donovan."

"The magic words? You mean, I love you?"

"Well, do you?"

He looked at her out of the corner of his eye. "I think I do. I've got all the symptoms. You can rattle my cage like no one else. I love the way you cook. I love the way you look. You make my blood boil when I think about spending the night with you. You're great in bed. We're great in bed. As in together. If you weren't in my life, I would miss you. If that's love, then I'd have to say I'm in love with you." He flashed her a boyish grin.

She grinned back. "That was quite a testimonial."

He dropped his hands from the steering wheel. "Look, Carol, I don't know if I'm marriage material or not. I didn't do so well the first time around. The girls are going to be a handful. I don't know if I have the right to ask you to take them on. We'll be a ready-made family. I'd want you to be a stay-at-home-mom, cooking and baking and all that wifely and motherly stuff. That's not to mean you can't work if you want to. You can." He shook his head. "I don't know what the hell I'm trying to say here."

"All I asked for were the magic words. I don't want you to say them if you don't mean them. It wouldn't be fair, Donovan."

"I love you, Carol." The minute the words were out of his mouth, Donovan decided he truly meant them. "I do. I really do."

"Then I accept."

He stared at her, hardly believing his good luck.

"Will I like living in the South?" she asked.

Donovan took a deep breath. "Probably not in the beginning, but it grows on you. I grew up in Louisiana, so I'm partial to it. Weather is great except for the humidity and the hurricanes. Stays green all year. People are gentler, more mannerly. It's a laid-back way of life."

"Sounds nice."

"I hope the kids will adapt to all the changes. They're so young that it shouldn't be too hard on them. I'm not so worried about Abby, but Mallory . . ."

"You're going to have to work on hiding your feelings

from her, Donovan. It's obvious you don't like her and that you adore Abby."

"It's just that Mallory is so much like Harriet, it's goddamn spooky. She makes my skin crawl, and I hate being around her. How do I overcome that?"

"By working at it. She might need some therapy. I'll look into it once we get settled." She took his hand and squeezed it. "So when do you want to tie the knot?"

"The sooner the better. How do you want to do it?" Donovan asked, his voice filling with panic.

"A justice of the peace would be the simplest. We could do it here or on the way to South Carolina."

"I'm no good at that stuff, Carol. You . . . you take care of it. You're good with details . . . and stuff. You know?"

Carol smiled. "In other words, tell you when it's all set up."

"Yeah. Yeah, that's good. Let's just get through this next ordeal, then we can do some serious planning. I asked my lawyer to stop by tomorrow. He's coming around three and bringing a social worker to see the girls. If we're lucky, we might be able to wind things up here in a few days and be on our way." He turned the corner to his street. There were cars everywhere, but his driveway was clear.

"I know I asked you this before, but won't there be any kind of an investigation into Harriet's and John's deaths?"

Donovan cleared his throat. "I thought I told you already . . ." He pulled into the driveway and turned the key.

"No. No you didn't."

"Jesus, Carol, I'm sorry. I don't know where my mind is these days." He shook his head and gave her an apologetic look. "The police finished their investigation yesterday afternoon."

"And what did they conclude?"

"The coroner determined that Harriet died of a heart attack and—"

"Did he do an autopsy?"

"No. He didn't feel a need. There was no evidence of foul play."

"But people her age don't just up and die of heart attacks!" Carol argued.

"Generally speaking, that's true, but Emma died on the delivery table. Only after I demanded an autopsy did they know she had a rare heart condition. They thought it was probably hereditary. And since Emma and Harriet were sisters . . ."

Carol gasped. "God, I forgot about that. What did they say about John? Did he really shoot himself?"

"Evidently," Donovan said. "John wasn't what you'd call a religious man, but he believed that suicide was a sin—a one-way ticket to hell. I don't see why he would go against what he believed in, but he left a typewritten suicide note explaining everything. He said he told Harriet he was divorcing her and taking Abby. When she couldn't reason with him, she tried to seduce him. He pushed her away and all of a sudden she started gasping for air and holding her chest. By the time he thought to call for help, it was too late. She was dead. He made it clear that he blamed himself for her death and he couldn't live with knowing what he'd done.

"If I hadn't pushed John to leave Harriet and go to South Carolina with me, none of this would have happened. If I hadn't interfered . . ."

"Don't go blaming yourself. You offered him a chance at happiness, that's all. John was weak. You know that. He must not have been thinking straight; otherwise, he would know that he wasn't to blame for what happened. He knew about Emma's heart condition, didn't he?"

"Yeah. I told him a long time ago. Like you, he must have forgotten." Donovan turned in his seat. "You know, I keep thinking something isn't quite right. I figured after our little heart-to-heart last Friday night, John would go home, wait for Harriet to come home from the play with Mallory, and tell her then and there, while he was still fired up. But the coroner says they both died sometime between ten o'clock and noon on Saturday." He thought a moment. "What time was it that I called you?"

Carol's left eyebrow rose a fraction. "Ah, let's see. You called me Friday night after John left and told me everything you and he talked about. And then you called again Saturday morning to remind me to pick you up and take you to the airport."

"That's right. My flight was at noon, so I must have called you about ten-thirty or so."

"No. You called at nine-thirty to remind me to pick you up at ten-thirty. So what's the problem?" Carol asked, her face a mask of curiosity.

"I remember looking out the window while I was having my coffee and remembering seeing John and Abby leaving for swimming lessons about eight that morning, and then Harriet right behind him, taking Mallory to her gym class. Everything was as it always was. It just seems odd to me that John would wait all that time to tell her . . . and that Harriet would try to seduce him later that morning."

"She must have been desperate," Carol said, sighing. "He probably didn't want the children in the house. If you think about it, it makes sense."

"Yeah. She must have been."

"I'm a little surprised nobody heard the gunshot," Carol said, changing the subject.

Donovan shook his head. "It wouldn't have sounded much different from a car's backfire. The kid down the street has been working on his hot rod every weekend for a couple of months. Every time he starts it up it backfires. What does surprise me is that John never told me he had a gun. I didn't even know he knew how to use one."

"There's nothing to using a gun," Carol said, shrugging.

"I guess not, but I just never figured him for owning one. The police said it wasn't registered, so he must have had it a long time."

Carol consulted her watch. "Speaking of time, we'd better get in there before our guests arrive."

Donovan looked at his new wife and then at the list in her hand. It was only eight A.M., and she was already organized and ready to go.

"Let's go over this one more time," Carol said. "I don't want to get to South Carolina and find out I screwed up somewhere along the way and one of us has to come back here." She glanced down at her list. "Let's see now. You're meeting with the real-estate agent in an hour from now to sign the listing agreements on both houses. The Goodwill is going to pick up all of John's and Harriet's stuff and that big pile of your stuff at three this afternoon. All the bills are paid. All the utilities, except for the water, have been turned off. The Barkers will see to it that the lawns are mowed and watered until the houses are sold. The last of the trash was picked up this morning. Copies of John's and Harriet's death certificates have gone out to everyone requiring one. Their bank accounts have been closed. A trust fund has been set up for the girls. Harriet's aunt waived any rights she might have to the girls. The paperwork making us their legal guardians is in my briefcase, along with their medical, dental, and school records. I called and got us set up with a post office box until we have a permanent address. Now, did I forget anything? Jeez, yes, I did forget. I wanted to tell you that I packed up two boxes of John's and Harriet's personal stuff for the girls. We'll take it in the car with us, and when they're older or the time is right, we'll give it to them. There isn't much."

"I think that's just about everything," Donovan said, exhausted just listening to her. He'd known she was organized, but my God! The woman didn't miss a thing. She reminded him of a general, plotting strategies, barking orders, and following up. And she did it all without a single complaint. "Wait a minute," he said suddenly. "There's something I forgot." He pulled a letter out of his pocket. "It seems Harriet had an insurance policy just like the one Emma had." He handed Carol the piece of paper. "Mallory is the sole beneficiary." Carol looked at it, then at him. "It's for a hundred thousand dollars. I just assumed John was the beneficiary, since he was always complaining about the premiums. I think it was shitty of Harriet not to put Abby's name on the policy, too."

"Think of it like this: We won't have to worry about Mallory's financial future."

"Speaking of Mallory, where is the little . . . darling?"

"Sulking in her room. Probably trying to think up new ways to torment Abby. I'm sorry, Donovan, but I don't like her. Not even a little bit. There's something not quite right about her, and I don't mean her nastiness. Maybe she's one of those bad seeds they always make movies about."

"She's a little girl, Carol. She needs her bottom paddled a time or two, and she needs to know that you and I are united in our efforts. I know in my gut that Abby doesn't tell us half of what Mallory does by way of tormenting her. As soon as we get settled, I think you should carry through with your idea of getting her into therapy. If that doesn't work, we'll pack her off to boarding school. I won't let her ruin our lives."

"Donovan, are we taking on more than we can handle?"

"I wish to God I knew. Only time will give us the answer to that question."

A horn sounded in the driveway. "The movers are here," Carol said as she hurried off to greet them.

Donovan ran upstairs to check on the girls. He blinked at the sight that greeted his eyes. Mallory was rocking sedately in a chintz-covered rocking chair, spewing words of hatred at her sister, who was trying to gather up some marbles that were rolling every which way. In the blink of an eye, Donovan lifted Mallory out of the chair and put her over his knee. He whacked her bottom until his hand hurt. Then he stood her up in front of him. "I'm only going to say this once, Mallory. If I ever hear you talking like that to your sister again, I'll confine you to your room for a month with no television. If you sass me, it'll be two months with no television and no toys. You will apologize to your sister, *now*."

"I hate you. I hate *her*, too. I want my mother. I want to go home," Mallory cried.

Donovan raked his hair with his fingers. He had to remember that she was only a child. How could a child become so mean and hateful by the age of six? His gaze went to Abby, who was pulling the drawstring on the bag of marbles. She wiped at her tears with the back of her hand.

"What happened to the marbles, Abby?" Donovan asked.

"They . . . they spilled," she choked out.

"Is that the truth or is it a lie?"

Abby's eyes filled again. "It's a lie," she whispered miserably. "I'm sorry."

Donovan reached for the bag, undid the drawstring, and dumped the marbles on the floor. "Pick them up, Mallory. And don't you miss a single one. I'll wait right here till you're through. Get Bailey, Abby, and go outside and find Carol."

Donovan sat down on the edge of the bed, his eyes on the little girl in the starched white pinafore. He'd never seen her in anything but dresses that were starched and ruffled. Abby, on the other hand, wore ragged shorts and coveralls. When she did wear a dress it was one of Mallory's castoffs that wasn't starched and didn't fit properly.

One by one Mallory picked up the marbles. She was about to hand the bag over when she stubbed her toe and fell forward. The marble bag shot out of her hands, the marbles scattering everywhere. Donovan watched in horror as she shoved the chair against the wall, the spindles on the back jutting half-in and half-out. "See what you did," she screamed. "You made me drop them. I'm not picking them up again!"

Donovan sucked in his breath. In a voice he barely recognized as his own, he said, "Oh, yes you are, and you'd better make it quick before the moving men work their way in here. And because you broke that chair and sassed me, you're going to spend the next few hours sitting on the steps until we're ready to leave. If you even dare to get up, or if I hear one word out of you, I'll spank you again." He leaned toward her. "Let's understand each other right now. I will not tolerate your temper tantrums, and if you ever talk to your sister like that again, I'll—"

"I don't care what you do. I hate you, and I hate Carol, too. And if you spank me again, I'll tell."

Donovan's blood ran cold. He tried for a light tone. "Who are you going to tell?"

"Those people who said I have to live with you."

Donovan raised a hand into the air. "Okay, fine, but first you have to pick up the marbles."

Mallory stood firm and stared at Donovan with bone-chilling intensity. "I'll tell that you do bad things to me—that you . . ."

"Carol!" Donovan roared. The sweat of fear dripped down his face as he stomped from the room. Carol came on the run. "You are not going to believe this! Do you know what that kid said to me? What in hell did Harriet do to her?"

Chapter Three

Carol Mitchell sniffed the air as she made her way through the house, her arms piled high with folded linens. Christmas was a wonderful time of year, but not this Christmas, she thought, her shoulders slumping. This Christmas was already a nightmare, and the holiday was still a week away. Donovan had been working sixteen hours a day and was ready to drop when he walked in the door. In the six months they had been married, they had hardly had a moment alone together.

She hadn't thought it would be like this. She'd figured on Donovan needing her to help with the girls, but she hadn't counted on assuming the whole responsibility.

This wasn't what she'd planned, wasn't what she'd wanted. It was all becoming too much for her. Once the New Year arrived, she would make some hard decisions. What to do about Mallory would be first.

She cringed when she heard Mallory's strident tones coming from the bedroom. Should she check it out or let the girls solve it on their own? Donovan said she should step in only if things got out of hand, but things *always* got out of hand. Why couldn't she have just one day of peace and harmony?

The psychiatrist said Mallory suffered from separation anxiety because of the loss of her parents and that she was reacting normally. What a crock! Carol didn't buy it for a minute. Mallory was a miniature Jekyll and Hyde. She knew how to play the game, when to turn on the tears, when to make nice, when to be polite and sincere. Donovan seemed to think things were getting better, but then Donovan arrived home when the girls were asleep and left in the morning before they got up. He had no idea what was *really* going on.

All he seemed to care about was that people got into their new houses for the holidays. Carol was beginning to wonder if he'd make it home to share the holidays with his own family.

There was always someone or something coming between them, and she was sick of it.

She'd put the tree up on her own, decorated the house, baked cookies, bought the girls' Christmas outfits, and cleaned the house from top to bottom. "Looks good," was all Donovan had been able to say.

Some life.

Certainly not the kind of married life she'd envisioned.

This time it was Abby's voice she heard. "I'm gonna tell Aunt Carol. You stop that, Mallory!"

Carol opened the bedroom door. "Okay, what is it this time?"

"You're supposed to knock before you come in," Mallory charged.

"In my house I don't have to knock. Now, I'll ask again. What's going on in here? I heard you two all the way down the hall. What's going on?"

"You can't hear in the hall. You were sneaking around listening at the door," Mallory shouted. "You're always sneaking. I watch you. Mama used to watch you, too. She called you a slut."

Carol flinched. It was hard to ignore Mallory's tirade, but because she'd heard it all before, she let it go. She could see she was going nowhere with Mallory, so she focused on Abby. "Will you please tell me what's been going on in here, Abby?"

A tear slid down Abby's cheek. "Mallory said that Santa Claus isn't real. She lied, huh, Aunt Carol?"

Here it was, one of the most important questions in a child's life. *You're supposed to be here, Donovan. I can't do this all myself.* "I think Mallory just said that because you two were arguing." Then to Mallory, she said, "Now, explain what you really meant to your sister."

Mallory whirled around, her eyes full of hate. "You're such a crybaby, Abby. I meant the Santa at the store. Everyone knows *he's* not real because you can pull off his beard."

Carol crossed her arms and breathed a sigh of relief. "That's a good girl, Mallory. Thank you for clearing that up."

Abby's tears dried, and she was all smiles again. "When is Uncle Donovan coming home, Aunt Carol? I want to tell him what we did in school."

"Long after your bedtime, honey. Why don't you write him a note and put it on his pillow? I'll make sure he gets it."

"Okay." Eagerly, she reached for her crayons.

Mallory glared up at Carol. "Abby can't write. She doesn't know her letters yet."

"I *do* so know my letters," Abby argued. "My teacher said that I print my letters neater than anyone else in her class. I bet your teacher never told you that, Mallory."

"She did, too," Mallory snarled. She leaned over and pulled her sister's hair.

"Ow!"

Carol grabbed Mallory's arm and yanked her to her feet. "Ten minutes in the corner facing the wall." She walked Mallory to the back of the room. "I'll stay right here and play checkers with Abby until your time is up."

"I hate you!" Mallory squawked.

"Right now, I'm not very fond of you either."

Carol rubbed the back of her neck, then sat down on the child-size chair across from Abby. "I get the red ones, Aunt Carol," Abby said as she set her checkers down on their squares.

They played quietly, concentrating on each move. In the end Abby won fair and square, then hooted and laughed. "You just need to practice more, Aunt Carol."

"I can see that." Carol checked her watch and saw that Mallory still had two minutes to go. "Did you have a nice Christmas last year?" she asked Abby. "What kind of tree did you have?"

"It was pink with red balls and red lights."

Carol burst out laughing. "A pink tree! With red balls! Are you making that up, Abby?"

Abby shook her head. "No. It was in the living-room window."

"My mother said it was . . . fashionable," Mallory added, her voice buffeted by the wall in front of her. "She copied it out of a magazine. It was very pretty."

"Pretty ugly," Abby chirped, her eyes sparkling.

"Oh," was all Carol could think to say.

Abby picked up the checkers and put them in the box. "I like the one we have this year way better. It smells just like the one at school. When I told my teacher about Mama's pink tree, she said pink trees are silly. Are pink Christmas trees silly, Aunt Carol?"

One eye on the back of Mallory's head, Carol chose her words carefully. "What might seem silly to one person might not be silly to someone else. Traditionally, Christmas trees are green. Sometimes decorators use . . . other colors for . . . for effect like in a magazine. That doesn't mean it's wrong or right. It's a matter of choice." *Where the hell are you, Donovan?*

Like a whirlwind, Mallory flew out of the corner onto her sister, kicking and gouging at her arms. "You aren't supposed to tell our business," she cried hysterically. "Mama said our business is *our* business. Pink trees aren't silly. They're . . . fashionable. Mama said it was the prettiest tree in all Edison. Mama didn't lie. I hate your guts, Abby. I hate you, too, Carol, and I'm not calling you Aunt Carol anymore. You aren't my aunt. I don't care if you make me stand in the corner all night. I'm telling my teacher you're mean to me and that you do bad things to me."

Carol felt like she was going to pass out. She grappled to take a deep breath. What was that supposed to mean—that she did *bad things* to her? "I need some help downstairs with the dishes, Abby. Mallory, go back to the corner and stay there until I say you can leave it. You'll be there all night if you disobey me."

Mallory's response was to kick the wall. Carol knew there would be a hole in the drywall when she returned, but just then she didn't care. All she wanted was to get out of the house and never come back.

Carol sat on the sofa staring at the Christmas tree. It smelled heavenly and reminded her of when she was a little girl. Although it wasn't that cold out, she'd built a fire and was now on her third glass of white wine. Wine made the pain in her soul a little more bearable and maybe it would give her the courage to tell Donovan she was leaving him. If Donovan didn't come home soon, she would drink the whole bottle. Courage in a bottle. Such a stupid phrase.

Every once in a while she saw Mallory peek around the corner from the hallway and look at her, but she pretended not to see her. If she acknowledged her, she would have to do something, and, at the moment, she was afraid what that something might be.

She sipped her wine and leaned her head back on the sofa. The wonderful marriage she'd envisioned was falling apart right in front of her. Tears rolled down the side of her face. She was blowing her nose with gusto when Donovan walked through the door.

"Hi," she managed in a choked voice.

Donovan tossed his denim jacket over the back of a chair. "I swear to God, Carol, I tried to get out of there early. It was one damn problem after another. Today was a day from hell." He sat down on the sofa next to her and put his arms around her. It seemed he was always apologizing these days, for not making it home on time, for not helping her deal with the girls, for not paying her enough attention. He was doing the best he could do, but it just wasn't enough. She needed more, always more. He tipped her chin up to gaze into her tear-filled eyes. "Do you know how much I appreciate everything you're doing around here, taking care of the house, the girls, me? I honestly don't know what I'd do without you. I love you, Carol. I guess I don't say that often enough. I'm sorry, baby."

He was right. He didn't say it often enough. He could never say it enough as far as she was concerned. She knew she loved him more than he would ever love her, but she accepted it, made the best of it. Her mood rallied when he kissed her. *This* was how she'd envisioned being married to him. *This* was the way it was supposed to be, just the two of them, here, together, with nothing and no one between them. If only there was something she could do to make it stay that way. "Go take your shower, and I'll lock up and get you a beer."

"Sounds good to me." He got up off the sofa. "Other than the fact that I'm home late, is there anything else wrong?" Donovan called over his shoulder.

Carol hesitated before answering. Maybe now was not the

time to tell him how hateful Mallory had been today or to chastise him for not being there when she needed him. All that could wait. After all, she didn't want to spoil what was promising to be an eventful evening. "I was just feeling a little melancholy, that's all. It's the season, you know."

He stopped at the door and turned around. "Guess the kids are excited about Christmas, huh?"

"Abby is. I'm not sure about Mallory. She's remembering the pink Christmas tree with red balls they had last year."

Donovan threw his head back and laughed. "That godawful thing they had in the window? That had to be the ugliest tree I ever saw in my life. John was so embarrassed he wanted to close the drapes, but Harriet wouldn't let him. She said it was chic. It even had red lights." He laughed so hard he doubled over. "When Harriet finally let John throw it out, even the scavengers wouldn't take it. That should tell you something."

Mallory listened to Donovan talking about her mother's pink Christmas tree. Her eyes narrowed to mean little slits when he laughed. Through the crack in the door she watched Carol get a beer from the kitchen and take it into the bedroom. Then she scurried down the hall and took up her usual position outside Donovan and Carol's door. She sat down, crossed her legs Indian-style, and pressed her ear to the door.

Unaware of the one-person audience outside the door, Donovan walked out of the shower and playfully flicked his towel at Carol. "Let's see, what should we do first? Swing from the chandelier or roll on the floor? How come you're still wearing all those clothes, woman?"

Carol giggled. "We don't have a chandelier, and the floor is drafty. How's about we just get into bed?" she asked as she began removing her clothes. "You up for an all-nighter?"

Donovan groaned. "Frankly, my dear," he said in his Clark Gable voice, "I think it would kill me."

Carol unhooked her bra, tossed it aside, and motioned him toward her. "Make love to me, Donovan," she said in a low, seductive voice. "Slow and easy. With all the magic words. Let's put everything out of our minds except you and me." She felt her throat constrict and her eyes mist. "God, I love you. I loved you the moment I laid eyes on you. There was never anyone else for me but you."

He pulled her tight against him. "I must be the luckiest guy in the world. John said you were the best thing that ever happened to me and warned me not to let you get away. I'm glad I listened to him."

Carol stared at him, speechless.

"What's the matter? What did I say?"

"Oh, nothing—It's—" she stammered. "It's just that I never knew he felt that way. I'm flattered."

Donovan smiled. "John pretty much kept his feelings to himself, except around me."

"You must miss him terribly."

"Yeah, he was the best buddy a guy could ask for. And you're the best wife a guy could ask for," he said, moving his lips downward.

In the aftermath of their lovemaking, with Donovan asleep in her arms and wine softening her heart, all thoughts of leaving disappeared. Things would be better tomorrow. She would see to it.

"Uncle Donovan, how come you're late this morning?" Abby asked as she attacked the pile of pancakes on her plate.

"Because I wanted to see my girls before I left for work. Have you been behaving for Carol? Christmas is only a few days away, and Santa is watching," he reminded them.

"I know, I know," Abby squealed, bouncing up and down in her chair. "I'm being really good. Ask Aunt Carol. Are you sure Santa will bring me that pink bike?"

"I can almost guarantee it, Abby. How about you, Mallory? What did you put on your list for Santa to bring you?"

"A whole closet full of pretty dresses like my mama used to buy me. My own telephone and my own television, and a purse with real money in it."

"That's a pretty tall order. There are a lot of children in the world for Santa to remember. Sometimes he doesn't bring *everything* on a little boy's or girl's list."

"My mama said he would bring everything I ask for. Last year, he even brought stuff I didn't ask for. Mama said Santa likes me because I'm so pretty."

"Mama did say that to Mallory. I heard her, Uncle Donovan," Abby said as she poured more syrup on her pancakes.

Carol turned back to the stove. Donovan stared at the stiff set of her shoulders. Something was wrong. He could feel it.

"You two better hurry or you'll miss the bus," Carol said, holding out two lunch boxes. "I'll see you this afternoon. Have a good day."

Mallory stomped from the room without looking back. Abby hugged both Donovan and Carol. "See ya," she called.

The moment the door closed, Donovan said, "Okay, let's hear it. The whole enchilada. I knew the minute I walked in the door last night that something was bothering you, but you didn't seem to want to talk about it so I didn't ask. Tell me. Maybe I can help."

She slumped down in Mallory's chair. "You're right. I was going to tell you last night. I drank almost a whole bottle of wine to screw up my courage. There's no other way to say this except to say it. It's Mallory." She pushed Mallory's unfinished pancakes aside. "I detest that little girl. I never in my wildest dreams thought I would be saying this to you. Before you came home last night she threatened me the way she did you that day back in Edison. She said she would tell her teacher that I'm mean to her and that I do *bad things* to her. School officials don't take stuff like that lightly, Donovan, and neither do I. Do you have any idea what could happen if she did say those things to her teacher? She could destroy our lives, everything you've been working so hard for." She steepled her hands in front of her face. "I don't care what that shrink thinks, and I don't care what you think. She's not normal."

Carol grabbed an unused paper napkin and blew her nose. "There's a problem here neither you nor I are qualified to handle. I'm going to lose it, Donovan. This morning before you came down, I had to hold myself in check or I would have throttled her. I don't know if I'll be able to stop myself next time."

"Jesus. Why didn't you say something before this, Carol?"

"I thought I could handle it. I was wrong. I should have told you, but you've been working so many hours and then when you do come home you're exhausted. I didn't want to burden you. I love you, and I love Abby. I do not love Mallory. Hell, I don't even like her. She's sneaky, she's nasty, she's obnoxious, and she's cruel. I will never love her."

"What . . . what do you want me to do?"

"I don't know. This is one time I don't have the answer." Carol burst into tears. "And don't even suggest that *I* go for therapy. There's nothing wrong with me. It's her. All I know is that I can't live like this any longer. I *won't* live like this. I'm on the edge. I'll crack if you don't get her out of here."

"You should have told me how bad it was. I would have punished her. When I don't know something, I can't act on it."

"Don't you see, Donovan? Punishing her isn't the answer. She's beyond punishment. It has absolutely no effect on her. Last night I made her stand in the corner with her face to the wall. Then, the first chance she got, she attacked Abby."

"So, what's the answer?"

"You have to make a decision," she said with surprising calm. "Her or me."

"Carol, listen to me. I'll take some time off, and we'll find help. Maybe we can send her to one of those schools that deal with troubled kids."

Carol shook her head. "No, Donovan. She needs to be institutionalized."

Donovan's face fell. "Institutionalized? Don't you think that's a little drastic?" The look in his wife's eyes told him she wouldn't settle for anything less. "Okay, I'll make some inquiries."

"Today," she pushed.

"Yes, today. I'll call in and tell Steve I'm taking the day off." He raked his fingers through his hair. "I wish you'd alerted me to the problems earlier."

She took his hand and squeezed it. "I wanted to, but I kept thinking that with a little love and discipline, she'd be fine."

Donovan shook his head. "I asked too much of you, Carol, when I asked you to marry me and take on John's children."

"My heart was with you. I wanted to help you, and I truly, truly wanted to help the girls." She pulled her hand away and stared out the kitchen window. She shook herself. "Listen, you'd better go call Steve."

"Carol, are you sure you're all right? I mean—You look sort of frazzled."

"No, Donovan, I'm not all right, and I won't be all right until something is done about Mallory."

It was eleven o'clock when Carol gathered up her coat and purse to head for downtown Charleston. The phone rang just as she was about to lock the front door. She debated a moment before she returned to the kitchen to answer it, but when you have children, you have to answer the phone. As she listened to the principal's voice on the other end of the phone, her face registered horror. "I'll be right there."

An hour later, Carol left the school principal's office and

walked toward her car, where she immediately paged Donovan. Her breathing was ragged as she waited for him to call
her. She was bordering on hysteria when the car phone finally rang. "Don't ask questions, Donovan. Whatever you're
doing, stop and go home. You won't believe what I have to
tell you."

Forty-five minutes later, Donovan careened into the driveway and parked his pickup truck next to Carol's Ford Mus-
tang. "What the hell happened? Did one of the girls get
hurt?" he bellowed.

"I'll tell you what happened, Donovan," Carol said between clenched teeth. "Our little Miss Mallory sits outside
our bedroom door at night and listens to us. She told her
teacher—Oh, God. What she said was . . . that last night I
drank a whole bottle of wine and that when you came home
we took off our clothes, rolled on the floor, and swung from
the chandelier. She also told the teacher I was mean to her
and that you and I did *bad things* to her."

"Good God, no!"

Carol buried her face in her hands. "The principal warned
me that such implications could be dangerous if the wrong
people heard them."

"Calm down, Carol. You're going to have a coronary."

"You're goddamn right I'm going to have a coronary." She
flopped down on the sofa. "That's it, Donovan. I can't take
another day of Mallory. Not another day. Do you hear me?"

"If you'll just be patient, I'll take care of it. But I'm not a
magician. I can't pull a rabbit out of my hat or make Mallory
disappear." He knelt in front of her. "I got the name of a special school in Atlanta. I was on my way home to give them a
call when you paged me. Now, get your wits together and get
that awful look off your face. We didn't do anything wrong.
It's okay for you to drink wine, and it's okay for us to take
our clothes off and roll on the floor. For that matter, it's okay

if we want to swing from the chandelier—if we had one. We're married for Christ's sake."

"Call that school right now, Donovan, and make an appointment to see whomever you need to see."

Donovan reached across the coffee table for the phone.

Carol leaned back and closed her eyes. She was so physically drained she didn't hear the conversation or realize he'd hung up until Donovan took her hand in his.

"We can take Mallory to Atlanta the day after New Year's. They have one opening. We'll get the tour, check things out and . . . and . . ."

"Walk away," Carol said flatly.

"Why do I feel like we're doing something evil and wrong?" Donovan asked, his eyes searching hers.

"Because we're decent human beings. Things like this only happen to other people, not people like us."

"I'll take the next two weeks off so I can stay home with you and the girls. So I'll be here, Carol, day and night. You won't have to deal with Mallory alone."

PART TWO

Part Two

Chapter Four

1993

Abby raced up the stairs to her room, bellowing at the top of her lungs. "Carol! I'm home!"

Carol came out of her room and looked at the exuberant girl in front of her. "Do you have a date for the prom? I can hardly wait to pick out a dress for you."

"Yes, I have a date, but that's not the only reason I'm so excited. I got a letter today from Mallory. She sent it to the school. Do you believe that?"

Carol's happiness faded, and she leaned against the wall for support. "No, I don't believe it," she said in a grudging voice. The nerve that girl had. The absolute nerve! "Has she sent you other letters at your school?"

"No. This is the first. She said she didn't want to dredge up any old hard feelings." Abby looked down at the letter in her hand. "It was a nice letter, Carol. Sorta newsy and up-beat. I admit I was surprised. That's not how I remember her." She paused to gather her thoughts. "She graduates from her school this month. She wanted to know if you would let me go to her graduation."

Carol shook her head. "Oh, Abby—I don't think—" She put her arm around Abby's shoulders. "I want to say no, but you're an adult now; it's your decision, not mine. I guess the big question is, do you want to go?"

Abby sat down on the top step and hugged her knees. "I'm not sure. I'd like to, but this is a busy time for me. I have exams coming up. I'm working on our school yearbook, and I'm on the prom committee. And if that's not enough, I have to get ready for my own graduation." She rested her chin on her knees and wondered how she was going to manage it all as it was. "God, I haven't seen Mallory in five years." She turned her head and glanced up at Carol. "It seems like *somebody* should be there to see her graduate. I know this is going to hurt your feelings, but she doesn't want you or Donovan there."

Carol made a sound of disgust. "We're good enough to pay forty thousand dollars a year for her education, but we're not good enough to be invited to her graduation. I think that's pure Mallory." She shook her head in exasperation. "Don't let her letter manipulate you into doing something you don't want to do."

"Manipulate me? You told me her counselor said she's well adjusted now, that she could have left there a couple of years ago if she'd wanted."

"That's true. She could have left, but I'm glad she didn't. I hate to admit this, but I didn't want her coming back here, and neither did Donovan. We offered to continue to pay for her schooling if she stayed where she was." Carol saw Abby staring at Mallory's letter. "You surprise me, Abby, that you would even consider going to her graduation after all the hurt she caused you." She ruffled her ponytail. "Maybe I'm not so surprised. You always did have a big heart. I think it's wonderful that you can forgive her. I wish I could, but I can't." Carol crossed her arms and rubbed herself as if she'd felt a chill.

Abby stood up. "Hey, where's that brother of mine?"

"Bobby went to one of those roller-skating birthday parties. I have to pick him up at four."

Abby was on her way up to her room when Carol stopped her. "Oh, wait a minute! I almost forgot," she said, reaching into her pocket. She handed Abby an envelope. "Isn't that from that teen magazine you sent your short story to?"

Abby gasped, then froze, her eyes fixed on the imprint on the return address. "The envelope is too small for them to have sent back my manuscript with a rejection," she said as she slid her index finger under the back flap. "Maybe I forgot to put in an SASE or . . . Look at this!" She pulled out a contract and scanned what appeared to be an acceptance letter. "*American Teenager* is going to publish my short story! For two hundred dollars! And they want to know what else I have. Here, read their letter!"

Carol reached for the letter and quickly read it. "Abby, this is so wonderful. If I remember correctly, you sent that story out at least a year ago. I all but forgot about it." She threw her arms around the girl and hugged her. "We have to celebrate. I'm going to call Donovan right now! Where do you want to go for dinner?"

"Magnolias. I want those fried chicken livers!"

Carol laughed. "Magnolias it is. You're probably the only kid in the world who likes chicken livers. I'm so proud of you, honey."

Abby's voice turned shy. "Someday when Bobby is older, I want him to read my story so he'll know what you and Donovan went through to adopt him, and how excited I was to get a baby brother."

"I'm sure he'd love to read it but give him a few more years. Ten-year-olds are kinda . . . well, you know."

"I know," Abby said as she rolled her eyes.

"Bobby adores you, Abby. He'll be as proud of you as I am. And Donovan is just going to bust wide open."

Abby hugged Carol, her eyes full of tears. "You have been so good to me, Aunt Carol. I couldn't love you more if you were my real mother. Sometimes I think I should have called you mom. Why didn't I?"

Carol hugged Abby back. "Because that title is reserved for your real mother. No one else. I know how you feel about me. That's all that is important."

"My mother, she—She didn't even like me," Abby said, remembering the hurtful things her mother had said to her—things Mallory had taken delight in repeating. "I know it was because of my face. She used to call me a freak."

"She was a shallow, selfish woman, Abby. And she didn't deserve to have a daughter like you. But that's all in the past now. Don't go dredging it all up unless you're sure it's a place you want to visit emotionally."

"I suppose you're right . . ."

"I'm troubled about Mallory," Carol said, changing the subject. She stood back and stared at the wall.

Abby wished now she hadn't mentioned Mallory's letter, at least not until she'd decided what she wanted to do. For almost as long as she could remember, the mere mention of Mallory's name had sent Carol into a tailspin. She wasn't sure what Mallory had done that made Carol and Donovan send her away, but it must have been bad. Neither of them ever did anything without a good reason. "You know what? Now that I've thought about it. I think I'll just send Mallory a card and a graduation gift. She'll understand."

A look of relief washed over Carol's face. "I want you to

do whatever feels right to you. Mallory is your sister, your only living blood relative. Maybe she's changed. For her sake, I hope so."

"Me too," Abby said, nodding.

The two stood in thoughtful silence for a few moments, before Carol said, "Let's do something wonderful with our hair and makeup tonight."

"I say we pile it on top of our heads and use those new little butterfly clips that I got. Hair jewelry, it's called. Then we'll do our eyes—liner pencil, mascara, eye shadow—the works. And I'll wear my pancake makeup. With that on, and at night, no one will even notice my birthmark." Abby twirled around, giggling, "Look out Charleston, here we come!"

"I'll call Donovan and pick up Bobby. I have to stop at the grocery store for cold cuts. I should be back in about an hour or so. Take some time to reread Mallory's letter and to bask in your good fortune." She gave Abby a quick hug. "I'm so happy for you, honey. This is just a wild guess on my part, but I bet someday you are going to be a famous writer. Donovan and I will be able to say we knew her when."

Abby flushed, the port-wine stain turning a deep, purplish color.

Carol fought off the tears at the sight of the ugly birthmark.

"You're right as usual," Abby replied, her mind already someplace else. "That's exactly what I want to do. When you see me next, I'll be one-half of the ravishing Mitchell team."

Abby headed for her bedroom and closed the door behind her. The sudden silence was so startling, she looked around to see why. Normally Bobby was in the next room, whooping and hollering or had his television blaring. The silence unnerved her. Or was it Mallory's letter? *Why did it have to*

come today of all days? Why not tomorrow or the day after?
"You always had a knack for spoiling everything for me,
Mallory," Abby muttered as she sat down at her desk.

If only Mallory hadn't been so mean-spirited and difficult,
Abby thought. She would have liked growing up with her,
would have loved sharing this room with her. They could
have had pillow fights, fought over the shower and the blow-
dryer, worn each other's clothes, whispered about boys in the
dark, shared secrets, and been friends.

It was a perfect room for two sisters. Extra large—Donovan had seen to that when he had the house built five years
ago. There were twin beds with deep rose quilted spreads
that matched the drapes and thick, pale pink carpeting. The
furniture was a girlish pristine white; even the extra-long
desk to hold her computer and printer were white. She had
her own television and VCR and her own private phone.
Special heavy-duty bookshelves were full of bright-jacketed
books. Books that she'd read, not books for looks or show.
There was a walk-in closet full of skis, roller skates, a
hockey stick, ice skates, and her Flexible Flyer, whose run-
ners she waxed every year when they went to the mountains
in North Carolina. A comfortable room. Her own private
sanctuary.

The house had been under construction during Mallory's
last visit. Donovan had given them all a tour, pointing out
whose room was whose. When he'd come to the extra room,
he'd called it the "spare bedroom." Until this moment, Abby
had forgotten that day. She wondered if Mallory had.

Abby squared her shoulders as she marched her way to the
closet to take down a box Bobby had made for her in his
kindergarten class, five years ago. She smiled as she looked at
the shoe box covered with faded red construction paper.
Gold-sprayed macaroni dotted the top to spell out her name.

She carried it to the desk and set it down next to the two letters.

The letter from Mallory was exquisite, her penmanship beautiful, the stationery expensive and regal-looking. Abby turned the letter over, half-expecting to see a royal seal on the back. At the very least, a glob of red wax on the envelope.

Dear Abby,

I imagine this letter is going to be a bit of a shock. I apologize for that. I also apologize for sending it to you in care of the school. I thought it best so that Carol and Donovan don't have to deal with old memories. Of course, it's up to you if you share this letter with them or not.

I'm writing to invite you to my graduation. I know you must be up to your chin in activities of your own, as you are graduating, too. Yes, Donovan wrote and told me that you would be graduating a year ahead of schedule and that you're valedictorian of your class. I am, too. I think it's weird—you and me class valedictorians! He also said you were admitted to the University of Wisconsin. Congratulations! I got accepted at Georgia Tech. I'm not going, though. College doesn't interest me in the least. I want to see the world, and I want to live. I can do that with my inheritance. I'm tired of locked doors, curfews, rules, regulations, doctors, shrinks, and war dens. I know I could have left a couple of years ago, but I was afraid. Of what, I'm not sure. I believe these last years have given me the confidence I need to face the world.

You probably won't understand this, but I don't want Donovan and Carol to come to my graduation. It's just better for all of us. This way none of us will

*have to pretend things are normal. Most of the gradu-
ates here are in the same position I'm in. We talk about
it in counseling sessions. If you don't want to come or
if you're too busy, I understand. I'll be in touch.*

Your sister,
Mallory

*P.S. I'm taking back our old name of Evans as soon as I
can.*

Abby folded the letter and slid it into its envelope. She
lifted the top off the shoe box to stare down at the contents.
Souvenirs, mementos, snapshots, movie stubs, a tarnished silver bracelet Mallory had left behind, and *the picture.* She
wished she knew how many times she'd stared at *the picture.*
It was a cruel picture, a caricature of her with half her face
colored in purple and the word *UGLY* printed in big block
letters and underneath in even bigger letters, the words, *I
HATE YOU.*

Abby pinched herself so she wouldn't cry. It would never
do to have red eyes when she was going to a celebration dinner. She carried the box back to the shelf in her closet.

Did she want to go to Mallory's graduation? Did she want
to see her sister? No and no. Should she turn the other cheek,
be more forgiving? To what end? Donovan and Carol would
probably consider it a personal betrayal.

Abby reached for her pen and tore a sheet of paper from
her marble notebook. She scribbled furiously.

Dear Mallory,
*I'm sorry, but I won't be able to come to your grad-
uation. As it is, I don't know where I'm going to get
the time to do all that I have to do before I leave for
college. I wish you would change your mind about*

Georgia Tech. Education is critical these days.
Whatever you decide to do I know you will be success-
ful. I wish you well.
    I have some exciting news! I just sold a short story
to American Teenager *magazine. I might turn out to be*
a writer after all!
    One other thing, Mallory. I don't know too much
about financial matters, but it would seem to me that
you should invest your inheritance. Please don't fritter
it away on a good time. I'm not jealous, Mallory.
Mama wanted you to have her insurance money, and
that's okay with me. I just urge you to spend it wisely.
    Enjoy your graduation.

                                            Abby

Abby addressed the envelope and slid it to the side of her
desk. A wide grin split her features when she reopened the
second letter she'd received that day. She rolled her eyes as
she hugged her chest. "This is so wonderful! So very wonderful! Thank You, God! Thank You very much."

"I can't believe that you're actually going off to college,"
Carol said tearfully as she sat down between the boxes she'd
been helping Abby pack. "I'm going to miss you so much,
honey. I swore I wasn't going to cry and what am I doing? I
just want someone to tell me where these last three months
went."

"You're crying," Abby said, leaning over and wrapping
her arms around Carol. "Christmas isn't that far off. I'll be
home then for three whole weeks. By the time I'm ready to
leave, you'll be sick of me because I'll be a know-it-all with
all this higher education that's going to be jammed down my
throat. I'll call and write. I promise."

Carol mindlessly folded Abby's sweaters. "You'd better,

young lady. Are you still up for your first surgery? You aren't going to change your mind, are you?"

"No, I am not going to change my mind. I'm going to go through with it, but I think we both know it isn't going to work. I read all the latest articles on port-wine stains, and I can tell you, mine is too large and too deep." She touched the side of her face. "God gave me this birthmark for a reason, and I don't think He's going to allow some doctor to take it away. I'll do it this time on the off chance that it might help, but I can't promise any future surgeries."

"I understand, and I don't blame you one bit. Donovan has himself convinced it's going to work."

"I know. I hope he won't be too disappointed when it doesn't. I saw the date circled on the calendar. It's scheduled for the day after I get home." Abby took the stack of sweaters from Carol, put them in the box, and taped it shut. "I think that's the last of it."

Carol pulled her list from her pocket. "Sheets, pillows, blankets, down comforter, towels, toiletries, winter clothes, fancy clothes, writing materials, mittens, mufflers, shearling jacket, your little television, radio, tape recorder, computer, printer, pencils, family pictures. Oh, my God, where's Bailey?"

"In my carry bag. He goes with me in case they lose my luggage. Do you think I'm silly for taking him, Aunt Carol?"

"No, of course not," Carol said, smiling. "He's been your best friend for as long as I can remember. He's been washed, stuffed, and sewn so many times I've lost count. I wish he could talk."

Abby's face sobered. "No, you don't, Aunt Carol. Believe me, you don't."

"C'mon, ladies, let's shake it, or we're going to miss the plane. Don't tell me you're bawling! You are," Donovan groaned. "That's great. Now you both have red, puffy eyes. How's that going to look?"

Carol latched her arm through Donovan's. "It's going to look like Abby has a family who's going to miss her, and may I ask why your eyes are all bloodshot, Donovan Mitchell?"

"Because I was cleaning out the fireplace and soot got in my eyes."

Abby wedged herself between them. "You two have given me such a good life. I want to say something special, something meaningful, but I don't know what the words are." She looked from one to the other. "You never let this thing on my face bother you. You were always there for me. I hope I haven't disappointed you. I'll do my best to make you proud of me."

Carol burst into tears.

Donovan cleared his throat. "Get in the car, both of you. Bobby's waiting. He's liable to start up the car. That kid is so inquisitive. He's worse than you ever were, Abby."

Abby linked her arms through Carol's and Donovan's. "I love you both so much."

Donovan's shoulders started to shake.

"Easy, big guy," Carol hissed in his ear. "She'll be home for Christmas."

"Yeah, probably with a boyfriend in tow. That's how it usually works," he said matter-of-factly as he went around the front of the car.

Carol held back, stunned by his comment. She'd never given a single thought to Abby having a boyfriend. She'd had a date from time to time, but usually the boy had been a friend or one of Donovan's employee's sons. She'd never had a *boyfriend*, not in the true sense of the word.

All these years Carol had had Abby to herself. She'd dried her tears, bandaged her knees and elbows, patched her dolls, and given her a shoulder to cry on. She'd made her into the little girl she'd never been able to have because of a botched abortion as a teenager. The thought of Abby having a real boyfriend, then maybe a fiancé, and eventually a husband . . . The thought of her not needing her anymore, leaving . . .

A suffocating sensation tightened her throat.

"I swear, Abby Mitchell, you must have been out of your mind to come out here to college when you could have stayed in South Carolina where it's *warm*. It's five degrees below zero with a windchill of twenty below. Look at you, you're freezing. Here, borrow these long johns of mine," Bunny Webster said, tossing a bundle of clothing toward Abby.

"You want me to go on a date wearing long underwear? A first date, *and* a blind date as well? No thank you. I'd rather freeze."

"It's part of the wardrobe. Everyone here wears long johns. You're wearing slacks and boots. You aren't planning on showing off what you have, are you? On top of that, Connor Bradford isn't exactly a blind date. You already met him, he met you, we all ate lunch together. He wears long underwear and will tell you so. He is not put off by your birthmark, so what's our problem here?"

Abby headed for the bathroom. "You're just like my Aunt Carol. I never won an argument with her either. Tell me more about Connor."

"He's a what-you-see-is-what-you-get kind of person. Kind of in-your-face, like me. He's incredibly brainy, like you, but not a nerd, again, kinda like you. You two will have a lot in common. He wants to be a reporter for the *New York Times*. The investigative kind. He's majoring in journalism just the way you want to. Third-year man and belongs to the best frat house on campus."

"If he's that wonderful, what could he possibly see in me?"

"He said," Bunny said airily, "you tweaked his interest."

"These things itch," Abby said as she tugged and pulled at the long johns.

"That's because they're new. After a few washes they soften up. The makeup looks good, Abby."

"You can still see it, though, can't you?"

"A little."

"Most times it doesn't bother me. Sometimes I don't even think about it until I catch someone staring at me. It's bothering me today."

"Get over it. It doesn't bother me, and obviously it doesn't bother Connor. The others are okay with it, too. You know something, Abby, no one has ever mentioned it to me. You'd think they would, us being roommates and all. I think that says a lot for our friends. It's what's inside that counts. So, are you ready? Why in the hell did we ever say we wanted to go sledding anyway?"

Abby shrugged. "It's something you're supposed to do when it snows. We used to go to the mountains in North Carolina to ski and stuff. I love snow. I think I love sunshine more, though." She sat down on the edge of the bed to put her socks on. "You want to come home with me for Christmas, Bunny?"

"Are you kidding! I'd love to. My parents are going to my sister's ranch in Oklahoma because she just had twins. With all those kids and animals they won't miss me a bit. Are you sure it's okay?"

"I'm positive."

Bunny smiled, showing even white teeth. "Then I accept."

"Great. You'll be the first guest in my bedroom. Donovan got me twin beds in case I ever wanted to invite someone to spend the night. Someone of the female gender," she qualified.

"I'm honored," Bunny quipped.

"And well you should be." Abby was pulling on her gloves

by the window when she saw a red truck pull up in front of the dorm. "No one said we had to ride in the back of a pickup truck."

"Just out of curiosity, Abby, how did you think we were going to get the sleds to the hill?" Bunny asked smugly.

"Pull them."

"Five miles? We'd die in our tracks."

"Oh."

They ran out the front door, down the steps, to the street.

"Pile in," someone yelled.

"Hi, Abby, how's it going?" Connor asked as he helped her into the truck bed.

"Good, except this long underwear Bunny insisted I wear is so scratchy it's driving me crazy."

"Yeah, I know what you mean. It'll freeze up around the same time you do. Let's roll, guys."

Abby almost swooned. She was actually on a date with a guy. A guy who wasn't put off by her birthmark, a guy she'd just told that she wore long underwear. Carol was so right. College life was absolutely wonderful. Better than wonderful. In a word, spectacular.

"God, this is heavenly," Bunny said, cupping her hands around a huge mug of hot mulled cider. "The snow was perfect for sledding. I only fell off once."

"I wish I could say that," Abby said, laughing. "I was in the snow more than I was on the sled. This guy is one crazy driver," she said, pointing to Connor. "Ooh. This awful underwear is driving me crazy." My God, did she just say that? Obviously she did since everyone was laughing.

She felt good, better than good. Fantastic! It was fun to be a part of a group and even more fun to flirt.

"Hey, guys, guess what?" Bunny shouted, getting everyone's attention. "Abby invited me to go to Charleston with her for Christmas. I'm going. What do you think of that?"

"I think you should invite all of us. We all," Connor said, waving his arms, "live in places where we won't see warm temperatures until spring."

Abby held up her hands to stop him from going any further. "I don't think my family would know what to do if you all showed up on their doorstep. You have to start out small and work up to a group. How about next year?"

"It's a date, my dear." Connor leered. Abby's face flamed. She turned to the side, knowing her birthmark was going to stand out like a neon sign. Suddenly she felt her chin being cupped in one very large hand. "Don't do that," Connor said softly, for her ears alone.

Abby wanted to cry, to blurt out all her pain and misery. From somewhere deep inside her she dredged up some courage, and said, "It's just that when I get embarrassed or excited, it gets really dark. People stare."

"Nobody here is staring, Abby. You are who you are, and we accept it."

"I'll remember that." Abby looked around and smiled. For the first time in her life she had real friends. Friends who accepted her for who she was, not what she looked like.

Bunny nudged her and hissed in her ear when Connor went to the bar for refills. "He likes you. I can tell."

"How?" Abby hissed back.

"The way he looks at you, the way he cupped your chin in his hand. Boy, does he have big hands. I wonder if the rest of him is that big?"

Abby choked on the remaining cider in her cup. "Do you mean what I think you mean?"

Bunny's face wore a wicked look. "Yeah," she drawled.

"Okay, ladies and gentlemen, drink up. It's time to head

home. Tomorrow we do the impossible, we score perfect grades on our finals."

"Hear! Hear!" the group chorused.

Bunny and Abby were the first to be dropped off. Connor and a young man named Taylor walked them to the dorm door.

"I had a really good time, Connor. Thanks for inviting me and thanks for . . . that . . . you know, what you said in the Rathskeller."

"No problem. Want to go to a movie on Saturday?"

"Sure."

"Good. I'll call you."

Chapter Five

These were the times Abby liked best, all curled up and snug in her bed talking to Bunny about everything and nothing. Tonight, though, it wouldn't be a nothing discussion; it was going to be a *something* discussion with her best friend.

A Connor Bradford discussion.

For the first time in her seventeen years, she felt that she belonged, felt she had true friends, friends who saw beyond the ugly mark on her face. Life was good, wonderful! She would have to remember to say an extra prayer before she went to sleep.

Bunny leaped into her narrow bed and pulled the covers up to her chin. "I had a great time tonight. But I don't know if I'll ever be warm again. Brrrr." She reached up and turned out the light . . . "You know, we're really lucky that Helen Foster took notice of us and invited us into her little circle. We're the envy of the whole freshman class. We have to remember to do the same thing for some lowly freshmen when we become seniors." She turned on her side and propped herself up on her elbow. "Listen, Abby, were you serious about me going home with you?"

"I wouldn't have asked you if I wasn't. But I won't be coming back with you. I'm staying an extra week because of the surgery." Abby plumped her pillow. "I gotta warn you, we won't be doing much but hanging out with Aunt Carol and Uncle Donovan. They take some getting used to, but I think you'll like them. Bobby, too. He's a great little kid. If you can handle all the boring stuff, I'd love to have you come with me."

Bunny chuckled. "Listen, my idea of a good time is reading a book and watching TV. So what does that tell you? Hey, I might even be able to help you after your surgery. Are you nervous?"

"Nervous?" Abby looked up at the ceiling and pulled a face. "I'm petrified. I'm not as hopeful as Donovan that it's going to help."

"Are you *sure* you want to go through with it?"

Abby hesitated. She'd been asking herself the same question. "Yes and no," she said at length. "If you had a mark like this on your face, wouldn't you try just about anything to make it go away, even if only a little bit? When I was younger, I used to pray for it to be gone when I woke up in the morning. It's ugly. I hate it. On the other hand, the laser could scar me and make it even worse."

"It sounds too risky to me."

"It is risky," Abby said. "But I want to be normal, Bunny. Like you. Do you have any idea how hard it is to pretend people aren't staring at you? Little kids point at me. Guys look the other way when they see me. Girls snicker and whisper that they're thankful it's me and not them," she said with a bite of resentment. "This is supposed to be the best time of my life. I'd like to blend in, fit in, but this . . . this birthmark of mine makes me an outcast."

Bunny sat up and swung her legs over the side of the bed.

"That's not true," she protested. "Take tonight for example. Nobody made you feel like an outcast, and you know it. Nobody paid the least bit of attention to your birthmark. The medical makeup you wear makes it so it's barely noticeable."

"It wears off after a while."

"So then you put some more on. Maybe you need to re-think the surgery, Abby. What if it does scar you and make it worse?"

"Then I have to live with it," Abby said between her teeth. Her mind was made up, and she didn't want to have second thoughts. "Listen, let's talk about something else. What should I wear on Saturday?"

Bunny took the hint and jumped into the next subject. "Those spiffy boots with the stacked heels you bought, the glen plaid skirt, and navy blue sweater set. You can borrow my chunky earrings and the matching necklace."

"I'm not wearing long underwear," Abby said vehemently.

"Fine. Freeze then," Bunny said, kicking out her foot and hitting Abby's bed. "I like the idea that we're double-dating. I still can't believe that we got asked out by juniors." Bunny's face puckered up. "You know what they say about freshmen meat? We're new, untried, unknown, and we want to fit in."

Abby jerked upright. "You said Connor and Kyle weren't like that. You said they liked us for who we were. Right?"

"They aren't. And they do," Bunny said, answering Abby's questions in order. "We just have to be careful not to do anything to give them the impression we're . . . you know . . . easy."

Abby laughed out loud. "You don't have to worry about me. I've never even been kissed by a guy."

Bunny crawled back in bed and slid under the covers. "You're seventeen and never been kissed? Now that's one for the record book." She hooted.

Abby felt like crawling off someplace to hide. Instead, she flopped down and drew the sheet up to her chin.

"Seriously, Abby," Bunny continued, ignoring her embarrassment, "college life is so different from high school. High school was, you know . . . a place that prepared us. kind of, for what we're doing now. We don't want to be part of that date-rape thing that happens on campuses all over the country. If and when a guy does kiss you, you need to be aware and keep your emotions under control."

"You sound more and more like Aunt Carol, Bunny. I'm not going to hop into bed with the first guy who shows some interest in me. When I do that, it will be at the right time with the right guy. Do you think I'm going to be a pushover?"

"No, but I told you, most guys only think about one thing. Wouldn't it be nice if we really hooked up?"

"Aren't we getting a little ahead of ourselves, Bunny? Sledding and a movie isn't exactly going steady. First we need to have a really solid friendship and go on from there. We need to know what makes these guys tick. I do like Connor, though."

"And I like Kyle. By the third year everyone is pretty much spoken for. In Kyle's and Connor's cases, I want to think it's because they're taking this education business seriously and don't want to clutter up their lives with emotional baggage. Helen told me they both have goals and only allow so much time for R&R. I guess that's a good thing. I'm not one of those needy females. Are you, Abby?"

"No. I've had to survive alone. Aside from family that is. Guess we were meant to find each other, huh, Bunny?"

"I think so. Let's say good night, Abby. I have an eight o'clock final. I think I can ace it, but you never know. Put your laundry out, and I'll do it with mine." Bunny flopped over on her side and yawned loudly.

"I don't want to think about dirty laundry," Abby said as she snuggled down. "I want to think about walking through snow all bundled up with some guy holding my hand and telling me he can't wait for the Christmas holidays to be over so he can see me again."

"The guy—Is his name Connor Bradford?" Bunny asked.

"Uh-huh."

The kiss, when it came, was delicious and left Abby wanting more. She wanted to say something profound, but the words wouldn't come. Connor wrapped his arms around her and held her close to him. Shock flew through her when his cheek nuzzled hers. She wondered if he realized what he was doing, but after a moment, when he didn't pull away, she figured he did and that he didn't care about her birthmark.

Suddenly, the moon and stars seemed brighter, the air, crisper. Everything was right with the world, and she wished this moment would last forever.

"Still cold?" Connor asked. His warm breath frosted as it left his mouth.

"A little," Abby managed, even as a shiver ran through her. "It's sixty-five degrees in South Carolina," she blurted inanely. Carol had told her that when she'd called to confirm travel arrangements.

"You need to bottle some of that warmth and bring it back with you. It's cold in Oregon, too. Have you ever been there?"

"No, but I hear it rains a lot and that it's very green. Are you going to go back there to work after you graduate?"

"Just to visit, not to live. My future is in New York City. As soon as I get a job, I'm going to go for my master's. Kyle, too. We've got it all planned out. How about you? Are you going to go home to live and work?" Keeping his arm around her, he walked them toward her dorm.

"I'm not sure. Probably. My career goals aren't quite as set as yours. I want to write, too. Mystery/suspense novels. I know it isn't going to be easy to break into the business, so I thought I'd get two part-time jobs to support myself while I'm writing."

"Two jobs? What kinds of jobs?" he asked.

"One in a library and one on a newspaper. Libraries have always been magical places for me. Growing up, I always had my nose in a book. I thought if I could get a night job in a library, it would help me get a handle on what people are reading and why. I could also research to my heart's content. Then, as a freelance writer for a newspaper, I could hone my writing and editing skills. See? I've got it all planned out." She laughed at herself, knowing how naive she must sound. "Thanks for the movie, Connor. I really enjoyed myself."

He stopped and turned her around to face him. "Abby, is it true that you aren't coming back with Bunny after the holiday break?"

"I'm coming back, but it won't be till later. I'm having laser surgery on my face and . . . I'll need the healing time. It's not the kind of thing where you can go around with a Band-Aid."

His brows knitted together in a frown of worry. "I'm not going to pretend I don't know about it. Bunny talked to Kyle, and Kyle talked to me. We're friends, so don't be alarmed that we're talking about you. I guess I want to know if you're comfortable with the whole thing. Bunny said the laser could do more harm than good. I'm concerned."

"I appreciate that, Connor. I'm concerned, too, but it's a risk I have to take."

Connor leaned toward her and cupped her face between his hands. "You've read up on it, and you know what you're up against?"

Abby nodded. "I think I do." She lowered her gaze and stared at his Adam's apple. "Unless you've lived with something like this, it's hard to understand. If this surgery will help even in a small way, it'll be worth it. If it doesn't work, if it makes it worse, I'll have to learn to live with it. I want the chance to be like everyone else, Connor."

"I guess I belong to the mentality of, if it ain't broke, don't fix it." He grabbed the edges of her coat collar and pulled her toward him. "I like you a lot, Abby. It bothers me that things might not work out for you."

"I like you a lot, too." She gazed into his eyes, a question nagging at her. "If the surgery makes my face worse, will you feel differently about me?"

He hesitated before answering. "I don't know, Abby. I honest to God don't know."

A chill ran down Abby's spine. For a moment she didn't know what to say. "I appreciate your honesty, Connor. The surgery has been scheduled for months now. I have myself psyched for it. Even if it scars me, I'm not going to run and hide. One way or another, I'm coming back to school." She swung around, grabbed his hand, and started walking. "What time are you leaving tomorrow?"

"My plane leaves at seven in the morning. How about you?"

"Ten-thirty. I guess I won't see you till the first of February." They reached the steps of Abby's dorm. "Have a wonderful Christmas, Connor." She leaned into him and gave him a quick kiss on the cheek.

"You too, Abby," he said with feeling. "Oh, I almost forgot. I bought you a present. It isn't much, just a little something to make you remember how cold it is here so you can appreciate your Southern weather."

Abby sucked in her breath. A present. How funny! She

had one for him, too, in her pocket. "Oh, Connor," she said, laughter bubbling in her throat as she turned the small globe upside down to see the snowflakes flutter to the top. "I love it! I have something for you, too. I shellacked it myself and printed the date on the back. It's a sand dollar I found on Folly Beach. You hang it on your Christmas tree."

"This is neat," Connor said as he held the fragile ornament up to the light to see it better.

"Merry Christmas, Connor."

"Merry Christmas, Abby."

He pulled her into his arms and kissed her until the world rocked beneath her feet. When he released her, they could only stare at each other. Breathless with what she was feeling, Abby managed to gasp, "Would you mind doing that again, please?"

"Not on your life," Connor said hoarsely. "Once wouldn't be enough, at least not for me, and I like you too much to let things get out of hand." He gently pushed her away. "Give me ten minutes to get back to the frat house and call me with your phone number in Charleston. If you give it to me now, I won't remember it. Hell, I'm not sure what my name is right now. Have a safe flight," he called over his shoulder as he raced off in the crunchy snow.

Abby stared after him, her eyes wide, her body trembling, until his long, lanky form was out of sight. Then she raced into the dorm and ran up the flight of stairs to the room she shared with Bunny. She barreled through the door, her eyes on her watch. Ten minutes. Ten minutes until she heard his voice again. Taking off her hat and coat, she eyed the phone her parents had insisted upon because they hated the constant busy signals from the hallway pay phones. On the eighth minute, pure panic set in when she realized she didn't know the name of Connor's fraternity house, let alone the phone number. "Oh, God," she whispered, panic rising in her voice. She snapped up her coat, hat, and muffler and ran out of her room.

Abby took the steps two at a time and then broke the cardinal rule of going out late at night without a partner. She ran, wings on her snow boots, as she raced around corners over crunchy snow, her breathing ragged gasps. When she finally reached the frat house, she had a stitch in her side and her head was so light she thought she would pass out. She jabbed at the doorbell. "Could you please call Connor Bradford," she said between breaths to the student who opened the door.

Connor must have been close by because she barely got the words out of her mouth and he was there at the door. "Abby! What the hell! Are you all right? What are you doing here?"

"I—I didn't know the phone number of the frat house, and I couldn't remember the name to ask information. And since Bunny wasn't back yet . . . There was—I couldn't . . . think."

A smile lit his face. "Yeah, I know what you mean. That was some kiss, wasn't it?" He didn't wait for an answer. "Stay right there while I get my coat, then I'll walk you back to the dorm." He put his hand on her shoulder. "Relax. Take deep breaths."

Abby nodded, then closed her eyes and concentrated on catching her breath.

Connor returned momentarily. "I would have called you if you didn't call me, you know." He took her arm and guided her through the snow to the sidewalk.

"No, I didn't know." As soon as she glanced up, she felt her feet begin to slide. "Help!" she cried.

Connor caught her and steadied her. "Just in case you've got any ideas, I'm not kissing you again tonight," he said firmly.

She felt her face flame. Surely he didn't think she'd purposely lost her footing to trick him into kissing her again. He did. She could tell by the way he was smirking at her. "Okay," she said, remembering what Bunny had said about being careful not to come off like she was easy.

"Okay?" he asked, sounding hurt.

"Uh-huh, okay," she repeated, waving a hand. "Thanks for walking me back."

"Yeah, sure. No problem. I'll just wait here till you get inside." She took a step forward, then glanced back at him over her shoulder. "Go on now," he urged, "before I change my mind."

"Connor?"

"Yeah?"

She turned around. "Close your eyes."

The moment he closed them, Abby leaned closer and kissed him. "That's so you don't forget me," she said, pulling away and holding him at arm's length.

"Jesus, Abby," Connor said, then turned and staggered down the walkway.

Minutes later, Abby was sitting on the second-floor landing, still wearing her coat and hat, when Bunny bounded up the steps. "Whoa. What have we here?"

"What we have here, Bunny Webster, is a young woman who has just been kissed and who is in love. My toenails caught on fire, I grew hair in my ears, and my eyeballs stood at attention. What do you think of that?"

"Wow!"

"He said he's going to call me at home. Do you think he will, Bunny?"

"If he said he will, then he will. One kiss, and you're in love?"

"Uh-huh. What about you and Kyle?"

"He's a great kisser, but I'm not in love. The word *sex* hasn't come up yet. How about you?"

"No. Connor wouldn't even kiss me a second time. So, I

kissed him," she said with a giggle. "I'm pretty sure I left him wanting more. Isn't that the way it's supposed to go?"

Bunny laughed as she helped Abby to her feet. "Shift into neutral, girl. It's too early in the game to fall in love. Let's see if we can't tempt Steve Logan to part with a few of his beers. I saw him sneaking some in earlier today. Who's hall monitor this week?"

"Steve is." Abby laughed. "Let's go."

Bunny Webster sat down in the hospital waiting area with Carol Mitchell and shuffled the medical research papers Abby's uncle had given her. "From what it says here," she said, looking down at the most recent article, "I have to wonder if Abby has made the right decision. This whole thing is pretty scary if you ask me. *Nevus Flammeus* or as Abby calls it, port wine stains, are small marks," she said, reading from the article. "Abby's covers the whole side of her face. Surely, they aren't going to laser the whole thing today, are they?"

Carol Mitchell puffed furiously on a cigarette she neither wanted nor needed. It was something to do with her hands. "They're going to do as much of it as they can, which is just another way of saying as much as Abby can take. It's going to be very painful. They'll be burning her face. God, I want to cry. I feel so bad for that girl. Donovan, Mr. Mitchell, is up on all of this. He wouldn't . . . he wouldn't let Abby do this unless he thought it was the best thing for her. He loves her, as I do, just as though she were our daughter. The doctor doing the surgery is the best of the best in his field," Carol said as she sat down on the bench with a thump. She lit a new cigarette from the stub of the old one and continued to puff.

"How bad will the scarring be if it doesn't work?" Bunny asked in a tremulous voice.

Carol shrugged. "Young children react better and have a

lower percentage of scarring. Most port-wine stains are not as large or deep as Abby's. Donovan was against doing anything when she was little. Everything was still so experimental, and he didn't want Abby treated like a guinea pig. One of the doctors in there is simply an observer. He's going to be writing some kind of paper on Abby. It's all for the advancement of medical science, so Abby okayed it. From what I read, there are a lot of different kinds of lasers, but Abby's doctor thinks the argon laser is the best."

Bunny consulted her papers again. "It says here that in 1980, these two doctors reported on a decade of work using that particular laser on three hundred twenty patients. Fifty percent were good, twelve percent were poor, and seven percent had scarring."

"I read that, too," Carol said. "The follow-up period is only four months, but I don't think that's long enough. I tried to explain to Abby and Donovan that more data is needed. They didn't listen. Abby just wants to be normal, and Donovan wants whatever Abby wants. I . . . I went to the library and did some research on my own. I found a test group that was followed for a year after the treatment. Mild to moderate scarring occurred. Depending on the density of the stain it was still visible plus the scarring. Knowing that, would you opt for this, Bunny?"

Bunny squirmed in her seat. "I don't know. None of us has walked in Abby's shoes. I'm sure it hasn't been easy for her. She really doesn't talk about it."

"She never complains but I know when she was younger, she used to cry herself to sleep after I tucked her in." Carol sighed deeply. "I guess I'm just a worrywart. There's nothing I wouldn't do for that girl. Nothing."

"Is Mr. Mitchell going to stay with Abby through the procedure?"

"No. He just wants to make sure everything is okay, that Abby is wearing the protective goggles." Carol put out her cigarette. "This can't be much of a holiday for you, Bunny. Since there's nothing either of us can do, why don't we talk about something else? Tell me about college life, and if it isn't a secret, who is Connor Bradford? He called after Donovan left with Abby for the hospital."

"He's a friend of Abby's. A real nice guy. He . . . he doesn't care about the mark. Once he caught Abby trying to turn away because she was embarrassed over something and it got darker. He made her turn around and gave her a little pep talk. She was okay with it after that. You and Mr. Mitchell would like him a lot."

Carol resented Bunny's assumption, but she kept a conversational tone. "Abby likes him, too, I take it?"

"A lot," Bunny said with emphasis.

Carol's eyes darkened. "What's his major?"

"Journalism, just like Abby. After he graduates, he wants to go to work for one of the big newspapers in New York City."

"New York City! Good grief. I don't know why anyone would want to live and work in New York City."

"Just in case you're worried, let me assure you, he's not a jock in any sense of the word. He's a real regular kind of guy."

"Worried?" Carol looked up in surprise. She didn't think it showed. "I'm not worried," she lied. "I just like to keep abreast of things, especially things that concern Abby." She jammed her half-smoked cigarette into the ashtray.

Feeling a little uncomfortable talking about Abby and her love life, Bunny changed the subject. "I just love your Christmas tree, Mrs. Mitchell."

"Around here, we always make a big deal out of Christmas. It was so much fun when Abby was little. Donovan used to make Santa tracks from the fireplace to the tree by pouring salt around his shoes. We told Abby it was snow. Then the year came when she asked why the snow didn't melt. Bobby stopped believing in Santa several years back. He's growing up, too. He's been making presents like crazy all week. He's kind of like Donovan and waits till the last minute. Did Abby say anything to you about what she might want for Christmas?"

"Not a word, but knowing her, if all you gave her was a card, she'd be happy. She isn't a material person as I'm sure you know."

"She never was. Now, her sister—Unbelievably so. And as for Bobby—He always liked the box better than the gift. The bigger the box, the better he liked it. We bought him a ten-speed bike. Donovan put it together last night. If I tell you what we got Abby, will you keep it a secret?"

"Absolutely," Bunny said solemnly.

"A car. Well, it isn't a car, it's a four-by-four. One of those all-terrain vehicles. Donovan had such a good time picking it out. He's even hired someone to drive it to Wisconsin so it will be there when Abby gets back."

"Oh, she's going to love it. It's such a pain hitching rides."

"I know. I'm not so old that I've forgotten. Oh, here comes Donovan."

Donovan looked hopeful as he walked toward them. "Let's get ourselves a soft drink and go outside, ladies. It's stifling in here, and there's nothing we can do." He checked his watch. "We're looking at three hours for the procedure and another hour until Abby is ready to leave. We could go into town and have lunch. What do you think?"

Carol looked at Bunny and Bunny looked at Donovan. "Whatever you two want to do is okay with me. You could drop me off at the house, and I can stay with Bobby."

"Bobby doesn't get out of school until three, and then he's going home with a friend who is having a sleepover. This has all been planned for months. Yes, Donovan, lunch in town will do nicely. Abby was okay?"

"Abby's fine. Perhaps fine isn't exactly the right word. Jittery."

"Is she scared, Donovan?"

"I don't think so. If she asked once, she asked ten times how long before she healed. She didn't like the doctor's answer of 'depends on the individual.' She's in a hell of a hurry to get back to school, that's for sure. You'd think there was some guy waiting for her."

Carol reached into her purse for her cigarettes. "There is, Donovan. He called this morning after you left."

"You mean Abby has a boyfriend? I'll be damned! That's great. We need to check him out, Carol."

"Mr. Mitchell," Bunny said, "Connor Bradford is sterling. They don't come any better than him. He likes Abby and isn't put off by her birthmark. He's a dedicated student and takes life seriously. He's the kind of guy you and Mrs. Mitchell would pick for Abby."

Carol bristled. There it was again—the assumption.

"Okay," Donovan said, "we'll go with your testimonial. Abby with a boyfriend. Are we happy with this, Carol?"

Carol proffered a big smile. "Of course we're happy. Why wouldn't we be?" Before he could answer, she said, "How about picking me up in front? I want to use the pay phone and check my messages at home."

"Okay, meet you at the car. Come on, Bunny. All this worry is giving me a huge appetite."

As soon as Donovan and Bunny were out of sight, Carol let out a long sigh. She'd known the day would come when Abby would get herself a boyfriend. She'd known it and dreaded it because of the changes that would inevitably follow.

All these years, Abby had come to her with her problems, and she had solved them, or at least made them better. In the beginning, the biggest problem had been Mallory. How many times, Carol wondered, had she punished Mallory on Abby's behalf? Then there were the problems Abby encountered at school. Name-calling. Finger-pointing. Abby was never included in the children's games or activities. There had been only so much Carol could do, but she'd done everything within her power to make it easier on Abby. Because she loved her—loved her as she would have loved her own child if she'd had one.

Now Abby would start turning to her boyfriend for help in solving the small problems and to be comforted. Eventually, if things got serious, she would turn to him for everything, leaving Carol out altogether, making her no longer needed.

There was no doubt about it, her days of having Abby all to herself were numbered unless . . . the procedure made things even worse . . . and . . . the boyfriend couldn't take it and . . . She squeezed her eyes shut, not even wanting to think such a thing. She *wanted* the procedure to turn out well. She wanted Abby to look like the beautiful person she was inside. She wanted all that for her and more. Much more.

Her stomach clenched tight as she dialed the code to her home phone. She listened, making mental notes until she heard the last message. "Hi, Carol, this is Mallory. I'll be in town over Christmas. I was wondering if I might invite myself for Christmas dinner. I promise to arrive late and leave early. I have presents for all of you. If you think a visit will make you uncomfortable and you'd rather I didn't come, I'll understand. You can leave a message for me at the school at any time. Happy holidays."

"Happy holidays, my ass!" she shouted into the receiver. "I'll leave you a message all right. I'll leave you one you won't forget!" She slammed the phone back into its cradle. "I will not allow you to spoil our Christmas, not this year. Not ever," she muttered, then turned around.

The startled look on the face of the woman across from her reminded Carol where she was. With a calm she didn't feel, she smiled at the woman and walked away.

Chapter Six

Bunny looked up from the magazine she'd been thumbing through when she heard Donovan's voice. She jumped up and ran to the trio walking down the hallway toward her. She flinched as a lump formed in her throat at the sight of Abby's face. "Oh, Abby, are you okay?" Abby looked at her through pain-filled eyes but didn't speak.

"She's in a lot of pain, right now, Bunny," Donovan explained. "She'll feel better when we get her home."

Fifteen minutes later, Donovan pushed the automatic door opener and pulled into the garage.

Bunny popped out of the backseat before Carol or Donovan could get their seat belts undone and opened the right-front passenger door for Abby. "Give me your hand and I'll help you out," she said, ducking down and reaching in toward Abby. She couldn't even imagine the kind of pain Abby must be suffering. Her face looked like raw meat.

"Relax, Bunny. I'm okay," Abby said between her teeth, her lips barely moving. "I'm just a little shaky right now." She held out her shaking hand to Bunny.

In spite of Abby's brave words, Bunny knew her friend was anything but okay, but there was nothing anybody could do now except wait it out and hope for the best. Putting an arm around Abby's waist, they walked through the garage to the kitchen door, her grip on Abby's shaking body firm and tight.

Donovan bolted around to the front of the car and held Carol back until the girls were out of earshot. "It doesn't look good, does it?"

"No, it doesn't," Carol said, glaring at him angrily.

Donovan hated it when Carol's anger erupted. "This is one time I wish you disagreed with me," he mumbled.

"Me too," she said. She turned to follow Abby and Bunny into the house, shaking Donovan's hand off her arm.

More often than not, Carol was an open book where her thoughts and feelings were concerned. Right then, she was madder than hell. Mad at him for encouraging Abby to go ahead with the procedure. But there were the other times— the times when she was a closed book, never giving him a hint of what she was thinking or feeling. Those were the times that made him think he didn't know her quite as well as he thought he did. Thankfully, those times were few and far between.

He turned his thoughts to Abby. Was she angry at him, too? He'd read her all the case studies, told her what the doctors had said, given her a list of pros and cons. He'd convinced her that this was her only chance to get what she wanted—normalcy—just as he'd convinced . . .

Just as I convinced John that leaving Harriet was the best thing for all concerned. "Jesus Christ!" he said aloud as he raised his chin and tilted his head backward. He felt as if a bolt of lightning had ricocheted down his spine.

Inside, in the kitchen, Carol assumed control of her domain. "Bunny, why don't you fix all of us some of that herbal tea. I'll settle Abby in, then we'll have tea upstairs in her room."

Bunny recognized the hint. Or was it an order? She wasn't sure, so she reached for an exquisite teapot. Moments later, Donovan came in from the garage. Bunny was about to ask him which flavor of tea he preferred but decided against it when she saw his bleak expression.

Fifteen minutes later she had everything together on a tray that matched the teapot. She balanced it perfectly as she headed for Abby's bedroom. Her guts churned when she saw her friend propped up in a nest of pillows. Abby's soft whimpers brought tears to her eyes. She set the tea tray down on the nightstand, spread a napkin on top of the covers. She handed Abby a flowered cup that matched the tray and the teapot. *It must be a set,* she thought inanely. "Drink this. It's chamomile. My mother always used to fix it for us when we got wired up," she said, trying to sound confident. She stared at Abby a moment longer, before she served Carol and Donovan.

Abby sipped the tea. A moment later she looked at Donovan, her eyes full of pain and tears. "I need a pain pill, Uncle Donovan."

Donovan moved around to the side of the bed next to Abby. "I'm sorry, Princess. I can't give you one. The doctor gave you a shot for pain before we left and told me not to give you anything else for a couple of hours. Drink a little more tea. It'll help you to relax."

The tears spilled over. She howled in pain as her salty tears rolled down her burned face. "My face is on fire. Can't we put some ice on it?"

Donovan shook his head regretfully. "The doctor gave me explicit instructions, and ice isn't an option. The pain shot should be starting to take effect. Trust me."

Abby had always trusted Donovan, but this time he was as helpless as she. She gave in to the pain and moaned. "God, it hurts so bad. I didn't know it was going to be like this. I didn't know. You have to do something. Aspirin, something, *anything*," she pleaded.

Donovan sat down on the edge of the bed and reached for Abby's hand. "Shh, it's going to be okay." He took the cup and saucer from her hands and gave them to Bunny. "Close your eyes, honey. Try to sleep."

Abby squeezed Donovan's hand. "Sleep? It hurts too bad to sleep. It hurts all the way inside my head. They didn't say this would happen," she said sharply. "I don't ever want to do this again. I don't care if I'm ugly or not. I don't care. Do you hear me, Uncle Donovan, I *don't care*."

"Hush. You aren't ugly. You're the prettiest girl in the world. Isn't she, Carol?"

Carol stood behind Donovan, clutching his shoulders. "You're beautiful, Abby, inside and out," she said.

"No!" Abby said. "Mallory was right. I'm ugly."

"Mallory!" Carol spit contemptuously. "She's a hateful, spiteful—"

Donovan put his index finger to his lips. "Shh. She's asleep, Carol," he said wearily. "I could kill that goddamn doctor!" he said between his teeth. "He said it would sting. He didn't say she was going to be in this kind of pain. I feel like going over to the hospital and putting my fist into his face."

"I told you it would be like this. But no, you wouldn't listen." Carol's angry retort hardened her features. "Look at her, Donovan. Look at her face. It's *burned raw*. I never should have allowed her to do this. There was nothing wrong with her using that professional makeup. She was so skilled at putting it on that you could hardly even see—"

"She wanted to look normal, Carol," Donovan argued. "And I wanted whatever she wanted."

Carol wrung her hands in agitation. "This is your fault, Donovan. Your fault! You shouldn't have encouraged her."

She started for the hall, her anger building. It wasn't her intention to tell Donovan about Mallory's message, but she was so angry with him that she needed to strike out. "Guess who called today?" she blurted. "Mallory! She wants to come for Christmas dinner, and she has presents for everyone." She waited for her husband's reaction, but there wasn't one. "I'm going to call her and tell her to stay away."

"Whatever you think is best, Carol, is okay with me," Donovan said, reaching down and brushing Abby's damp hair away from her forehead. His insides roiled at the red, raw stain on her face. He turned to leave the room and spotted Bunny. He'd all but forgotten she was there.

"I'll stay here and sit with Abby if you don't mind," Bunny said.

"No, not at all. With luck she'll sleep for hours and wake up feeling better. We'll be in the den," Donovan said, motioning Carol to go ahead of him.

The moment the door closed, Abby opened one eye. "Are they gone?"

Bunny gasped. "You faker. Even I thought you were asleep. God, Abby, I wish there was something I could do."

"I feel a little better than I did a few minutes ago. I think the shot is starting to take the edge off the pain. I guess you're thinking what they're thinking, which is that I shouldn't have done it. Right now, I wish I hadn't done it either. How bad is it?"

Bunny grappled for her words. "It looks"—she shook her head—"incredibly painful."

"That's not what I asked you. Get me a mirror."

"Why don't you wait until tomorrow, when some of the redness and the swelling go down? Right now it probably looks much worse than it is."

"I want to see it now, Bunny," Abby said firmly. "Get me the mirror. Please."

THE GUEST LIST   95

Bunny retrieved the mirror from the dresser top and reluctantly handed it over. Abby's expression was one of total horror.

"My God! It looks like raw meat! Oh, Bunny, I had no idea. What if it stays like this?" Abby burst into tears.

Bunny reached for a tissue. "Listen to me, Abby. Don't cry. Please don't cry. Tears are salty, and your face is raw. Do you hear me? Don't cry."

"I'm not going back to school. I'm never going out in public again as long as I live."

"Oh, yes, you are going back to school even if I have to drag you by the hair. You will pick up your life and go on because that's what you have to do to survive. You're not a quitter, Abby Mitchell. You'll pull up your socks and go on and that's that," Bunny said, brooking no argument. "As soon as you stop feeling sorry for yourself I'll tell you who called this morning."

Abby put down the mirror. "Who?"

"Are you going to go back to school willingly, or am I going to have to—"

"Willingly," Abby said. "Come on, Bunny, was it Connor? Did he say he'd call back?"

"Carol talked to him, and, yes, he did say he would call back. Tonight. So you'd better get to sleep so you can dream about what you're going to say to him."

Abby handed the mirror to Bunny. "You know, before I left, I asked him how he'd feel if my face ended up worse, and he said he didn't know. How's that for honesty?"

"At least he told you the truth. That has to mean something. You're the same person inside you always were. That hasn't changed."

"Don't pep talk me anymore, Bunny. You know as well as I do that guys want girls who are pretty and popular. They don't want scary-looking girls with—" She cut herself off, tears welling in her eyes. She'd had such high hopes that the procedure would at least lighten the stain.

Bunny sat down on the side of the bed, her expression solemn. "Connor Bradford isn't the only guy in the world, Abby. My mother always said for every old shoe there's an old sock. If you take out the word *old,* it makes sense. Don't go getting desperate on me now. That just isn't your style, Abby."

Abby stared at the ceiling, ashamed of herself for being such a whiner. "Some vacation for you, huh?"

"Listen, except for worrying about you, the time I've spent here has been wonderful. It's peaceful and quiet. My house is always jumping. Noise, kids, animals, everyone screaming and yelling to be heard over someone else screaming and yelling. The kitchen is never cleaned up, and you need to stand in line for the bathrooms. I've enjoyed myself. Now stop worrying about me and go to sleep."

Dutifully, Abby closed her eyes, then opened them again. "I can't. I'm not sleepy."

Bunny groaned. "Then maybe I should leave the room. If either your aunt or uncle happens to peek in and see you talking to me, they'll blame me for keeping you awake."

"Believe me, they won't be peeking in. They have to decide what to do about Mallory. And that could be a very *long* discussion."

"What is it about that sister of yours? You've never talked about her. How come? I thought we shared everything."

"Trust me when I tell you that you don't want to know about Mallory. It hurts to talk, Bunny, and I'm finally getting sleepy. Will you wake me if Connor calls again?"

"You bet. I'll stay here until you fall asleep."

"I'm glad you're here, Bunny. You're my best friend in the whole world."

"Shh, we can talk later. Go to sleep now. I promise to wake you if Connor calls."

"You'd better."

Bunny sat in the daffodil yellow chair wondering why everyone hated Mallory. Of course, it was absolutely none of her business, but that didn't stop her from wanting to know. Bobby probably knew. She could ask him. Then again, what kind of friend would she be if she pried?

"Connor Bradford," she mumbled beneath her breath, "no matter what the outcome of all this is, you'd better not dump Abby, because if you do, I'll lay you out cold!"

"How dare she call and invite herself for Christmas? How dare she?" Carol raged as she paced the length of the book-lined den. "What are we going to do? I need your help on this, Donovan."

"I thought you'd already decided to call her."

"I can't call her. You know that." Carol flopped down on the leather sofa next to him. "I *hate* her, Donovan. She tried to ruin our lives. I can never forgive her. Look at what just getting her message has done to me. Can you imagine what would happen if I tried to talk to her, the things I might say? There's no sense stirring things up more than they are."

"So I take that to mean you want me to call her, right?"

Carol seemed surprised at Donovan's offer, as if she hadn't even considered the idea. "Yes, I think that would be best. You call her and tell her we won't be home because we're going to the mountains over Christmas."

"*Are* we going to the mountains over Christmas, Carol?"

"We could," she said, shrugging. "Bobby would love it. I think Bunny and Abby would like it, too."

"What if Mallory says she'll come over before we leave? Then what should I say?"

"Improvise, Donovan," she said, leaning toward him, her eyes hard as marbles. "Understand me on this. I *do not* want that girl in our house." Carol reared back and took a breath. "She's trouble. God only knows what she'll do or say when she sees Abby's face. We can't risk it. Abby isn't emotionally up to dealing with Mallory right now." Again, she leaned toward him, exhaling with agitation. "You need to call her, make it clear to her that she isn't welcome here. I don't care how you do it, Donovan, just do it!" The instant Donovan opened his mouth to reply, Carol pounced on him again. "Don't even think about making any of your lame excuses for her. I won't tolerate it."

"All right. I'll call her," Donovan agreed. In fact, he was relieved to be the one to do it. Carol was right. There was no telling what *she* might say. "Do you want me to do it now or wait until tonight?"

"Now will be just fine."

"Do you know the number?"

"It's there on the pad by the phone. If she isn't in, leave a message. And right after that, call the telephone company and get an unlisted number. I want it by tomorrow, Donovan. Don't look at me like that. I mean it."

Carol had always been controlling, sometimes a little too controlling, but her ordering him around like he was some lackey topped it. "I'll call Mallory," he said, refusing to let his temper get the best of him, "but the phone company will have to wait. In case you haven't noticed, it's almost five thirty." He stood up and walked across the room. "Even if they weren't closed, I wouldn't call them. Getting an unlisted number would be a slap in the face to Mallory. You know that, don't you? God only knows what she would do."

"*Do!*" Carol all but screamed. "You said she was *cured*. You said that, Donovan. Are you saying you lied to me? We paid a fortune to that place to make her well. But I think she's still screwed up. I don't care what those medical reports say."

"Maybe she's looking for a family, Carol." Donovan ran his hand through his hair. "Maybe she needs us."

"Maybe she needs money. Maybe she spent her inheritance. Did you see her offer Abby even ten dollars of it? No, you did not. That tells me she hasn't changed one little bit. She's greedy, she's selfish, she's arrogant, and she's goddamn *evil!*" Carol shrilled.

Donovan knew Carol wouldn't let up until he'd made the call. He picked up the slip of paper by the phone and pressed the numbers. When it started to ring, he forced himself to calm down. "Mallory Evans, please." Carol's short, blunt nails tapped the table beside the sofa. The sound was eerie to Donovan's ears. "Mallory, it's Uncle Donovan. Carol said you called earlier." He waited patiently while she presented her plans. "It would be wonderful to visit with you, but we have a houseguest, one of Abby's college friends, and we're probably going to go to the mountains for Christmas. Bobby wants to ski, and there's some new powder expected." He paused, his eyes on Carol. "Yes, maybe Valentine's Day. You have a wonderful holiday, too," he finished, before he hung up the phone.

He stared at the receiver. There had been such joyful expectation in Mallory's voice when she'd told him her plans and then . . . disappointment. She'd tried to hide it, but he'd heard it. He was sure Mallory knew that he and Carol didn't want her to come home—that they never wanted her to come home.

Jesus! What kind of man would swear on his best friend's grave to take care of his children and then throw one away like so much garbage? What kind of man would allow his wife to dictate the terms of his relationship with his adopted daughter?

He hesitated to answer himself, unsure as to whether or not he really wanted to know.

"Tell me what she said," Carol demanded.

Donovan took a deep breath. "She said she understood.

She was very upbeat, very cheerful, and pretended not to be the least bit upset; but she was, Carol. She asked me to wish everyone a Merry Christmas." He sat down heavily in the chair. "I feel like shit."

"Then why don't you go see her? Take her to dinner. Enjoy her evil company. But don't bring her anywhere near Abby or Bobby, or I won't be responsible for what I do. This is the end of it, Donovan. I don't want her name mentioned in this house again. Ever. Do we understand each other?"

Donovan sucked in his breath and glared at her. "Perfectly," he said, and was rewarded to see the color drain from her face. "I'm going to check on Abby."

Carol quickly regained her composure. "Take her mail in and leave it on the night table. There's a really impressive looking letter from a publisher. It's addressed to Bailey James in care of Abby Mitchell. I wonder what that means."

Donovan picked up the mail. "Make plans to go to the mountains, Carol. I've done enough damage for one day. I don't want to be a liar on top of everything else."

"I can't believe Mallory sounded upbeat and cheerful. She must be up to something. God, you have no idea just how much I hate that girl. Can you just imagine the glee on her face if she saw Abby now?"

"I thought we weren't going to mention her name in this house again. Let it be, Carol. I took care of it. That's the end of it. I know you don't want to hear this, but I feel guilty as hell. Yes, we paid a fortune to the Argone School, but that's *all* we did. We *dumped* her, and walked away. It doesn't matter that the doctors said it was best that way. She was a sick kid. We just threw her away. And in spite of it all, she made it. All she wanted was to come to dinner and drop off some Christmas presents."

"You know how I look at it, Donovan?" Carol said icily. "We saved one and we lost one. I don't care what that makes me in your eyes. I know what I saw in that girl and I know what I felt and it hasn't changed one bit. This *is* the end of it."

Carol sat up in bed when she heard a noise. "What's that?" she said, shaking Donovan's shoulder.

"What? What's wrong?" Donovan asked, groggily.

Carol listened intently. "I think—It's Abby. She's crying. She probably needs her pain medication. If I need you, I'll call you."

Donovan flung the cover off and stood up. "Like hell you will. I'm going with you."

Abby was huddled under the covers when Carol and Donovan came in.

"Abby, honey, what's wrong?" Carol said, taking the trembling girl in her arms.

"I can't stand it," she cried. "I feel like I'm on fire. It's not just my face either. I think I have a fever, and I can't get warm. I turned on the electric blanket, but I'm still cold. Can I have some more of the medicine and maybe some aspirin?"

Carol touched her lips to Abby's forehead. "Donovan, she's burning up. You need to call the doctor, and you need to call him *now!*"

Donovan turned the small bedside lamp to the third notch illuminating the room to a brightness that highlighted Abby's fire red, swollen face. He gasped. Carol blinked, her eyes filling with tears.

"Donovan, I think you should ask the doctor to make a house call."

"I think you're right," Donovan said, stomping from the room, his shoulders rigid. He loped down the steps two at a time to the alcove where a phone sat on a small table. He flipped through the list of pages of Carol's frequently called phone numbers and dialed. At three in the morning he wasn't surprised to hear the doctor's service pick up. "This is Donovan Mitchell. I need to speak to Dr. McGuire right away. This is an emergency. It's about my daughter, Abby Mitchell. He did some laser work on her face yesterday and she's running a sky high fever and the medication he gave us isn't working." The woman on the other end of the line said she'd try to get in touch with the doctor. "You won't *try*," Donovan lashed back at her. "You *will* get in touch with him. Right now, not two hours from now!"

Donovan slammed down the phone and raced upstairs. "I'm not sure, Carol, but I think the doctor is on his way."

"That's good, Donovan. Real good."

"Don't cry, Carol, I'll be okay," Abby said, her teeth chattering as she huddled beneath the electric blanket. "Is it bad?"

"It doesn't look . . . you know . . . pretty, it's kind of raw looking. Puffy actually."

"Did Connor call?"

"No, honey, he didn't call back. He'll probably try again in the morning. Or you can call him. Is the pain easing even a little?"

Abby closed her eyes and whimpered.

"I'll kill that son of a bitch doctor when he gets here. This wasn't supposed to happen," Donovan seethed. "It's going to be okay, Abby. Just hang on."

"What if he doesn't come, Donovan?"

"Then I'll go and get him!"

Carol's eyebrows shot upward. She nodded, knowing full well Donovan would do exactly what he said he would do. She felt pity for the unseen doctor as she watched Donovan stare at his watch. Abby continued to shiver beneath the electric blanket.

Thirty-seven minutes later the doorbell rang. Donovan's feet barely touched the steps as he headed for the ground floor. He yanked open the door, and barked, "Follow me."

Donovan and Carol huddled together while Bunny Webster, wiping sleep from her eyes, stood fearfully in the doorway.

"You said 'sting,' Dr. McGuire," Donovan said. "Meaning it was going to sting when you applied the laser. You didn't say anything about pain afterward. You used the word 'discomfort.' I think this is beyond discomfort. I don't need a medical degree to know Abby has a massive infection. Abby is not a complainer. If she says her face and head are on fire, that's exactly what she means. She has a fever and chills. Well?"

"You were right to call me, Mr. Mitchell. We need to get Abby to the hospital. I lasered too deeply. I'll call for an ambulance."

"Is she going to be all right?" Carol whispered.

The doctor stared at Carol for a long moment before he turned to leave the room without answering her.

Chapter Seven

Abby sat on the sofa, doing her best to wrap a radio-controlled car for Bobby in shimmering gold-foil paper. Earlier in the week, she'd made a detailed list for Bunny, who'd done her Christmas shopping for her.

She felt as if she'd been to hell and back this last week. The doctor had prescribed massive doses of antibiotics and a private duty nurse watching her round the clock. Her fever was gone, and the facial swelling was minimal. At times the pain had been unbearable, but her face was on the mend, and the pain was fast becoming a bad memory.

"Are you sure you're okay, Abby?" Bunny asked.

"I'm fine." Abby raised her head and smiled. "The worst is over. I can tell I'm starting to heal because my face itches." She wrapped a length of ribbon around the awkwardly shaped box and held it tight until Bunny put her index finger in the middle of it. "This has got to be awfully boring for you. I really can manage myself, you know. Carol could probably use your help in the kitchen. Christmas Eve is the one day of the year she allows helpers into her lair. She fusses and frets all day long as she cooks. I would think she would be behind with all her preparations because of the time she spent going back and forth to the hospital to visit me. Go on, Bunny. I know you're dying to help her. I'm okay. I'm just going to sit here on the sofa and wrap the last of these gifts. Then I'm going to sit back and admire this magnificent Christmas tree until it's time to eat."

Bunny clasped Abby's hand. "I'm so glad you're home. We were all so worried. I thought your family would go out of their minds. Donovan . . . I'm never sure what I should call him. Anyway, he really went to town on that doctor and the medical center. They listened to him, and man, did they hop around when he was in sight. I heard the words malpractice and lawsuits so many times I lost count."

Abby smiled. "Most of the time Donovan is more bark than bite. I'm not saying he wouldn't have followed through, but luckily things worked out. I sure would have hated to spend Christmas in the hospital."

Bunny grinned. "I hope you're up to talking to Connor when he calls tonight. I have to hand it to that guy, he's called twice a day, every day, for updates on your condition. Last night when he called, I told him you'd be coming home this morning, and he sounded very relieved."

"I begged the doctor to let me come home a few days ago, but he wanted to be absolutely sure everything was okay before releasing me. I suspect he was overly cautious because of Uncle Donovan. I really wanted to go to the mountains, too, but I'm just not up to it. You aren't too disappointed we aren't going, are you, Bunny?"

"Nope. I'm going to stay here with you, and we're just going to hang out. I'm going to cook and bake and eat and sleep and watch television. When I'm not taking care of you, that is," Bunny added hastily.

"Carol doesn't want to go now because of me, but Donovan is making her because he doesn't want to be a liar. We would have *all* been going but for me having to go back to the hospital. And I don't need you to take care of me. I just want you to keep me company. This isn't much of a Christmas vacation for you, is it?"

"Will you stop with all that? Believe it or not, I'm enjoying myself. This is the best, Abby. I really like your family. Everyone has made me feel so welcome. Don't worry one little bit about me." She gazed at the tree. "I can hardly wait to see what's in all those presents. I never saw so many in my life."

Abby laughed. "Carol starts shopping the day after Christmas for the following year. Donovan says she's the queen of the shopping brigade. Sometimes I think she spends more time choosing the bows and wrapping paper than the presents." Abby finished up the bow she'd been making and set the box aside. "There's something about a red bow on a gold-wrapped box," she said thoughtfully. "When my parents were alive, my mother just stuck the presents under the tree any which way. Mallory always got the most. On Christmas morning, she would get up before me and open my presents. Mama would say she could play with them until she got tired of them, then they would be mine." She shook her head at the hurtful memory.

"That's terrible!" Bunny said in outrage.

Abby picked up a rectangular box and laid it down on top of the Christmas paper. "I suppose it was. I cried a lot back then. I wasn't much of a scrapper."

Bunny glanced toward the kitchen, then whispered, "I probably shouldn't ask this, but is your family rich?"

"I think so," Abby said, looking sideways at Bunny. "The newspapers say Donovan's a millionaire ten times over. Sometimes I hear Carol and Donovan talking about their investments, where to put what, that sort of thing. Why?"

Bunny shrugged. "I'm just nosy, I guess. This is an enormous house. Carol doesn't work. School is expensive, and you aren't going on student loans like I am. You said Donovan paid a fortune for your sister to go to a private school. I've never known anyone rich."

Abby's forehead wrinkled. "Does my family being rich bother you?"

"No, of course not. But I have to admit I'm a little envious. I've always wondered what it would be like to live in the lap of luxury."

"This is all just *stuff*, Bunny," Abby said, waving her arm expansively. "In the scheme of things, it isn't important. At least to me it isn't. You know I'm not materialistic."

"Damn. Abby Mitchell, you are so well adjusted it makes me crazy." Bunny hugged her knees and gazed at the Christmas tree. "Don't you get melancholy at this time of year? Do you ever think about your parents and wonder what it would have been like if they hadn't died?"

"Sure. I miss my father most of all. He was very good to me, and I know he loved me." She paused a moment before speaking about her mother. "I don't think I ever really knew my mother. I don't have one good memory of her other than she was pretty."

Bunny looked down at her hands. "You never talk about them. How come?"

Abby shrugged. "Because I can't remember all that much."

"How'd they die, if I might ask?"

"Carol told me my mother had some kind of rare heart problem. Her sister, Donovan's first wife, had the same condition and died giving birth. Carol said when my father found my mother dead, he was so grief-stricken that he shot himself. Right after that we all left New Jersey and moved here. Donovan has never mentioned their deaths to me. Carol said she saved all the newspaper clippings if I ever wanted to read about it, but I've never wanted to. What's the point? Every year Donovan gives me a new picture of my father, one I've never seen before. They were really good friends, more like brothers."

"Oh, I just remembered," Bunny said suddenly. "Donovan put your mail in your room, and said there's a very impressive looking letter addressed to your pseudonym. Aren't you dying to know what it is? I mean—it could be another sale. That article you did on campus life or one of your short stories. There are also two letters from Oregon!"

"Two!" Abby squealed.

"Yep. Two. What are you going to open first?"

"Certainly not the one from the publisher. It could just as easily be a rejection letter, and you know it. You've seen me get enough of them. Besides, I don't feel like getting depressed on Christmas Eve. Where are Connor's letters?"

"In your room," Bunny said, obvious disappointment in her voice. "I'll get them, then I'll see about helping Carol in the kitchen. Where are Donovan and Bobby? I haven't seen them in a long time."

"I think they said they'd be in the garage. Hurry, Bunny. I want to read Connor's letters."

Bunny stood up. "You don't want the one from the publisher then?"

"No," Abby said, shaking her head. "I'll look at it after New Year's. I'll be stronger by then and better able to deal with rejection."

"All right." Bunny sighed before rushing off. She was grinning from ear to ear when she came back. "They feel kind of mushy," she said, handing them over. At Abby's long-suffering look, Bunny headed for the kitchen. "Guess I'll go help Carol."

Bunny was still grinning when she entered the kitchen. "I think Abby is going to be okay, Mrs. Mitchell. She's reading her mail. What can I do to help you?"

"Sit here and talk to me."

Bunny looked at the kitchen clock. "Do you want me to drive Abby to the cemetery tomorrow or the day after?" Carol looked up from the pie crust she was rolling out, her face blank. "Did . . . did I say something wrong?"

"No. It's just . . . why would you think Abby would want to go to the cemetery?"

Bunny flushed a bright red. "I'm sorry. My family always goes to the cemetery on Christmas to put flowers on my grandparents' graves. I just assumed . . . I'm sorry."

Carol slammed the rolling pin down on the piecrust. "It's not a problem, Bunny. You just caught me off guard. Abby's parents were cremated. Abby has her father's urn in her closet. Donovan gave it to her when she was sixteen. Don't fret, Bunny. You didn't know."

Bunny squirmed in her seat. "Abby never talks about her parents or her sister."

"She was only five when they died," Carol said as she carefully laid the piecrust in the glass dish. "I think it has all pretty much faded from her memory. She talks about her father from time to time, but the older she gets the less she speaks of him. She hardly ever talks about her mother. Basically, all she knows is Donovan and me when it comes to family. And then, of course, there's Mallory. Do you like ambrosia?" she asked, adroitly changing the subject.

"I love ambrosia!" Bunny closed her eyes and licked her lips.

"That's wonderful. You and Bobby can eat the whole thing. I always end up making four desserts because everyone likes something different. Donovan likes mince pie. I like strawberry rhubarb and Abby likes key lime. The same thing goes for dinner. Christmas is the one time of year when I make everyone's favorite dish. Since you're a guest, you get to sample everything."

"Well, I can handle that. I'm not sure about my hips, though," Bunny said, glancing around at the food-laden countertops. She'd never seen so much food in her entire life.

"That's why you make a New Year's resolution. You can diet then. By the way, we'll be back from the mountains New Year's Eve. We always like to spend it at home. I feel bad about leaving, but Donovan is insistent, and now that Abby is on the road to recovery . . . I'm glad you're going to be with her, Bunny. I'll feel much better knowing she isn't alone."

"Hey, Mom, come look," Bobby said, poking his head in the door that led from the garage to the kitchen.

"Oh, my!" Carol said, peeking in at the new Jeep Bobby and Donovan had spent the last half hour trying to wrap.

Bunny walked up behind Carol and looked in. "Wow! How many rolls of paper did that take?"

"Nine!" Bobby said proudly.

"Don't forget the six rolls of Scotch tape." Donovan guffawed behind Bobby. "And the miles of ribbon that we curled ourselves. Do you think Abby will be surprised?"

"She won't guess, will she, Mom?" Bobby asked.

Carol and Bunny burst out laughing.

"I think the wheels might give it away," Bunny said as soon as she could catch her breath.

Donovan threw his hands up in the air. "We ran out of paper."

"Mom," Bobby pleaded. "Do you have a little more that you could give us? Just enough to cover the wheels on this side. Two wheels, Mom. That's all."

Carol groaned. "Oh, all right. It's in the hall closet upstairs, but be quick about it. It's almost dinnertime."

As soon as Bobby was gone, Donovan inched toward

Carol. "If we ever do this again, let's just put a bow on it, okay? I don't know about you two, but I'm ready for my first cup of holiday cheer. What do we have?"

Carol linked her arm around his. The past week had been trying, to say the least, but now, finally, things were getting back to normal. As to their argument over Mallory—neither one of them had mentioned it or her again, which was fine with Carol. "How about a beer?"

"Ah, a woman after my own heart." He turned to close the door. "I never gift-wrapped a vehicle before. It got a little dicey when we got to the top."

"Abby is going to love it. Her first car," Carol said, sighing. "She's going to want to drive back to school. You know that, Donovan."

"I know, but she'll understand why she can't once I explain it to her. She's a sensible girl. Are we packed?"

Carol opened the fridge. "We are," she said, taking out a Corona and handing it to him. "How about you, Bunny?"

"Eggnog for me, please."

Donovan reached for the bottle opener. "I'd like to get an early start. I'm glad we're doing the Christmas Eve thing. Getting up at four in the morning and pretending I'm having a good time is not something I enjoy. We always look like bleary-eyed owls in the pictures you take, Carol. Where's Abby?"

Carol opened a wine cooler for herself. "She's in the living room, waiting for the phone to ring, no doubt," she said.

In spite of her teasing tone, Bunny noticed the grim set to Carol's jaw.

Bobby bounded into the kitchen, a roll of Christmas paper in his hand.

"Hurry up, sport," Donovan said sternly. "Wrap those wheels, then get cleaned up. Shirt and tie."

"Okay, okay, okay," Bobby grumbled as he peeled off a strip of tape. "She's never going to guess it's a car. She's going to think we wrapped up that old refrigerator box. I just know she's going to think this is a big joke. The joke's going to be on her, right, Dad?" Bobby smacked his hands together the way he'd seen his father do.

"What a great Christmas Eve!" Donovan shouted after the last present had been opened.

"I second that," Carol said.

"I got everything I wanted," Bobby said, scooping up a pile of discarded wrapping paper, tissue, and ribbon and tossing it into the air over Abby and Bunny.

Abby got up and waded through the sea of presents to kiss each member of her family. "I hope we can do this every year. I love you all so very much."

"Oh, jeez, my Corona's empty," Donovan said. "Abby, you're up. Would you mind getting me another one from the fridge in the garage?"

At the door to the kitchen, she stopped and looked back. "Anyone else want anything while I'm up?" Receiving no other requests, she made her way to the garage.

The moment Abby was out of sight everyone scurried to the kitchen. When Abby squealed, they all shouted, "Merry Christmas, Abby!"

Abby stood staring at her new Jeep, too excited to speak. After all the lectures Carol and Donovan had given her on why she shouldn't have a car of her own . . . and now this! Totally out of the blue. One of these days she'd have to ask them what changed their minds. It was probably Carol, she thought. Carol was the one who made the decisions.

"Phone!" Bobby shouted at the top of his lungs. When nobody made a move to answer it, he picked it up. "Hello," he said, then, "Hold on." He held the phone up in the air. "Abby, it's your sweetie, that Connor guy."

Bunny saw Carol grin when Abby said, "Tell him I'll call him back in a few minutes."

"Do you like it, Abby?" Donovan asked, watching Abby rip away a huge section of wrapping paper to get to the car.

"Are you kidding? I hardly know what to say. Thank you doesn't seem anywhere near adequate," Abby said, throwing her arms around Donovan, then Carol. "Can I drive it back to school?"

"We'll talk about that later on," Donovan said firmly. "I don't know about the rest of you, but I'm ready for bed."

Carol stood in the doorway, barring the path. "Hold it, everybody. We have a huge mess to clean up."

"Bunny and I will do it, Carol," Abby volunteered. "But later if you don,'t mind. I want to sit in my new Jeep for a little while, then I want to call Connor back."

"Okay, but if you start the engine, open the garage door," Donovan said.

"I won't start it up till tomorrow. I just want to sit in it," Abby said as she hugged Bobby. "And thanks for wrapping it up, squirt. I thought it was one of your gags. By the way, where is that old refrigerator box?"

"Trash. We wanted you to think that. Will you take me for a ride when we get back from the mountains, Abby?"

"You bet I will."

"Don't overdo while we're gone, Abby. You need lots of rest. We'll be back in the afternoon on New Year's Eve. I know we probably won't see you two in the morning before we leave, so let me say this now. Merry Christmas."

Bunny rolled over on her side. "Merry Christmas! I know you're awake, Abby. What are you thinking?"

"I'm just lying here thinking how very lucky I am. Maybe lucky isn't the right word. Maybe the word I'm looking for is blessed. I'm going to be able to return to school in a month. Scarring, according to the doctors, is going to be minimal. I have a boyfriend who really cares about me. My family loves me. And I have a brand-new Jeep!" Abby swung her legs over the side of the bed.

"That must have been some conversation you and Connor had last night. How long did you talk, anyway? It was midnight when I gave up and went to bed."

Abby hugged herself. "The last time I looked at the clock it was two o'clock. Let's get up and take a drive. We can shower and have breakfast when we get back. I want to give my new Jeep a road test if that's okay with you."

Bunny was already slipping into her sweats.

Abby wanted to get a feel for the Jeep before venturing out onto the main streets, so she drove through the neighborhood, going up and down the residential streets until she knew where everything was and felt confident. Ninety minutes later, she maneuvered the cherry red Jeep Wagoneer back into the driveway. "I love it. Love it," she shouted, her hands clenching the steering wheel. "It handles like a—" She stopped suddenly, seeing something out of the corner of her eye. "What's that on the front steps?"

Bunny looked out her window. "It looks like . . . like presents. Christmas presents. Who do you suppose—" her voice trailed off as she turned back to Abby.

"I think I might know," Abby said, pushing the remote for the garage door.

Bunny stared at her friend, her eyes wide. Something told her not to ask any questions. She waited expectantly.

Abby's mouth was set in a grim line as she made her way through the house to the front door. Bunny stood behind her as she bent down to read the name tag. "They're from Mallory," she said, staring at the boxes. There were eight of them, each one more beautifully wrapped than the last. "Oh, Bunny. I feel terrible that we missed her." Abby stood up. "I would have loved to have seen her."

Bunny's nose wrinkled in confusion. "I thought everybody, including you, hated her."

"No. Carol is the only one who hates her, and when Carol hates, she *really* hates. But that's Carol. She's all or nothing. Now Donovan—I think he feels guilty about Mallory. I think he'd like to let her back in the family but knows that as long as Carol feels the way she does, it's a lost cause."

"And you?"

"Mallory did some pretty awful things to me, but she's still my sister, my only living blood relative. I bought her a present thinking I might see her now that she's legally on her own. Actually, I've bought one for her every year. I've got them all safely stored away."

"Maybe she's in town. We could call around." Bunny clenched her hands into fists. "What's your big hotel here?"

"The Omni."

"Let's try it. Maybe we'll get lucky."

"Okay, but first let's bring the presents inside. We don't want them getting wet."

"Are you going to open yours?" Bunny asked.

"Not unless she can open hers at the same time. You're supposed to open gifts in front of the giver, especially at Christmas. It's part of the joy."

"Who said that?" Bunny wanted to know.

"I did," Abby replied, laughing. "Come on, help me carry them in. Do you think she wrapped these herself? They're so gorgeous. Bobby is certainly going to be happy. He loves belated presents."

"How about Carol and Donovan?"

"I don't know, Bunny. Carol won't, I know that. And Donovan—It's a mess. Let's not talk about it, okay?"

"Okay, we won't talk about it. Where's your phone book?"

"In the drawer under the phone."

Bunny yanked at the thick telephone directory and flipped to the Yellow Pages. "I'll read off the number and you dial it."

"Mallory Evans, please," Abby said, remembering that Mallory had gone back to using their real parents' name. She listened a moment, then said, "Thank you and Merry Christmas to you, too." She put the hand set back on the base unit.

"What's wrong?"

"Mallory checked out an hour ago. She must have come by here right afterward, while we were out driving around. Oh, Bunny, I want to cry."

"Then cry, Abby. Where is it written that you can't cry?"

"Poor Mallory. It's not right that she's all alone, and this is Christmas."

"Maybe your sister is one of those people who doesn't mind being alone on holidays," Bunny said, shoving the telephone book back into the drawer.

"If you truly believe that, then I know a bridge I'd like to sell you."

"There's nothing you can do, Abby. Maybe she'll call."

Abby stood staring at the Christmas tree. A few months back there had been Mallory's letter, and now she was sending presents. These were the first presents that Mallory had ever given her. It seemed to Abby she was trying to make a genuine effort to—To what? she wondered. To make amends for all the trouble she'd caused? "I'll clean up the living room, and you make breakfast," she said, leaving her thoughts behind. "Then, we're going to sit and do nothing. By the way, how's my face looking today? The truth now."

"Very red and scaly. It looks like it itches. There's a kind of white ring outlining the whole mark. Didn't you look at it, Abby?"

"No. I was afraid to. Will my makeup cover it?"

"Not the way it is now," Bunny said bluntly. She looked over her shoulder as she headed for the kitchen. She doubted if Abby even heard what she said. She was staring intently at the pile of presents in front of her, oblivious to Bunny and anything else around her.

"It's time to say good-bye. I'm going to miss you, Abby."

"No you won't. You'll be too busy studying and having a good time. I'll be back before you know it."

"Have a safe flight, Bunny," Carol said, hugging Abby's friend.

"Thank you so much for having me. I hope I get to see you again soon. Tell Bobby good-bye for me. I'll call you, Abby."

"Don't call, write. Long, newsy letters full of stuff."

"Okay. Bye, everyone."

"I wish I was going with her," Abby said, waving until her friend was out of sight.

"It's just a few weeks, Abby. It's important for you to do the follow-up on the surgery. You don't want all that suffering to have been for nothing. You went through hell. We all went through hell," Carol amended.

"No more surgery, Carol. I mean it. I don't care what Donovan wants. I will not put myself through that excruciating agony ever again. My God, I'm still not healed. The truth is, I think my face looks worse than it did before. Six months is a very long time to go around looking like this. It's awful, and we both know it. I wish I'd never done it. You don't know how bad I wish that."

"Oh, baby, I do know. I wish you hadn't done it either. The makeup was working fine. I also understand you wanting . . . Donovan wanting the best for you."

"It wasn't the best for me. They told me it was too deep, too large. Why didn't I listen, Carol? Why?"

Carol felt her throat start to close. "Because you believe in miracles, honey. We all do."

PART THREE

Chapter Eight

1997

The last four years had been the best years of Abby's life. She'd excelled academically, made lifelong friends, honed her writing skills, matured physically and mentally, and fallen deeply in love. Her world right side up, Abby sighed happily.

The rustle of the silky comforter was the only sound in the quiet room. Abby rolled over and propped her face in the palm of her hand. "I'm so happy that you could get the time off to come to my graduation. I've missed you, Connor. Getting together holidays and breaks—it's wonderful, but it just isn't enough. At least, not for me."

The lovers stared at one another. "I missed you, too. More than you know, but our time will come." He tweaked her nose. "You could move to New York, you know."

Abby sighed. They'd had this conversation before. "What would we live on? Your good looks?" She reached out and ruffled his hair. "It's too expensive to live in New York unless both of us are working full-time, and I don't want to work full time unless . . . unless I have to. I'm looking forward to my part-time job at the library and to writing on a regular schedule. I have to get together a new book proposal to give my publisher by the—"

"What did you say?" Connor interrupted, putting a hand on her bare leg.

Abby bit down on her lip to keep herself from smiling. She'd been waiting for the perfect moment to tell him her news, and this was the perfect moment. But rather than just come out with it, she wanted to tease him a little first. "I said I'm looking forward—"

"No. No. That's not the part I'm asking about. You said something about giving a new book proposal to your publisher. What publisher?"

Abby opened her mouth in feigned surprise. "Oh, *that* part," she teased. "I guess I forgot to tell you. Bryson Publishing made me an offer on my book, and I accepted it!"

"No kidding! That's great!" Connor grabbed her and kissed her.

Abby had dreamed of this moment for as long as she could remember. "It's going to come out in hardcover first, then in paperback," she explained. "They liked it so well that they want a second book. So I have to come up with an idea as soon as possible. If things go well, our finances may improve sooner than we expected."

Connor lovingly brushed a lock of hair back from her face. "One of these days you're going to be a rich and famous writer. I'm sure of it."

Abby laughed. It was Connor's encouragement over the last four years that had kept her writing in spite of the rejection letters. He respected her special needs. "I wish I was so sure. All I know is that between school and writing, I've worked my butt off these last four years."

"And now all the work is going to pay off." Connor grinned.

"I hope so. I'd sure like to show Carol a nice big advance

check. She used to encourage me to write, but these last few years she's done everything she could to discourage me. I'm glad I didn't listen to her. I suspect she thinks that my education will have been for nothing unless I go out and get a high-paying job." She rolled over onto her back and gazed up at the ceiling. "I'll tell you what. If I ever do become a famous writer, I want to have a big party—a blowout party with a guest list that will make *People* magazine sit up and take notice. All the important people who have helped me along the way and . . ." she flipped back over and took his hand, "all the people I love. You'll come, won't you?"

"Depends," Connor said with feigned indifference.

Abby sat up and did her best to look affronted even though she knew he was teasing her. "Depends on what?"

"Whether or not you dedicate the book to me."

"Well," she said in a huffy voice, "it just so happens that it *is* dedicated to you."

Connor's eyes lit up with excitement. He dropped his act. "Yeah? What did you say? Something mushy I bet, like: to Connor, the world's greatest lover."

Abby giggled. "I'm not going to tell you what I said, but I will tell you I didn't say *that*. I don't want the world to know what a wonderful lover you are. That's only for me to know. You'll just have to wait until the book's published." She expected him to try and wrest the information out of her, but instead his expression turned sober.

"Abby, does your family know about our plans for the future?" he asked, abruptly changing the subject. "I mean do they know—"

"That we're planning on getting married one of these days?" she finished for him. "I think they suspect, but I haven't come right out and told them."

"Don't you think you should?"

"Not yet. You have to understand, they are very over-protective. I have to tell them by degrees." The whole truth was that every time she brought Connor's name up in front of Donovan and Carol, Carol got preachy and warned her that life with a newspaper journalist would be difficult, that Connor would be gone at all hours, and that he would never be able to provide for her in the manner to which she had become accustomed.

"The other reason is," Abby added, because Connor didn't look completely satisfied, "that I don't want everyone in the world to know about us. And once Carol and Donovan know, then *everybody* knows. I've told Bunny, but she's different. She's like a sister, and we tell each other everything. She promised to keep an eye on you since she's going to be working in the city. I can't believe she landed a job at *Cosmo.*"

"A plum job, that's for sure," Connor said, following Abby from one topic to the next without a hitch.

"She's worked hard. She deserves it. If you save your vacation days for the winter months the way Bunny is planning on doing, the two of you can visit me at the same time."

Connor made a rude noise with his mouth. "Yeah, right. Like your aunt and uncle would let me stay at their house knowing we would be sleeping together."

"That brings up something else I want to tell you. My graduation present from Donovan and Carol . . . it's a house. Donovan had it built just for me. It's fifteen miles from their house. It has a pool, an office, and all kinds of good stuff. It was supposed to be a surprise, but Bobby spilled the beans. The kid is fourteen and starting to feel his oats or hormones or whatever the expression is. He said Carol has been busy decorating it so it would be ready for me to move into right after graduation."

"Well, shit! That clinches it," Connor said, jumping to his feet. He stood over her, his arms crossed, looking down at her.

Of all the reactions she'd expected from Connor, this wasn't one of them. "What does that mean, Connor?" she asked carefully as she sucked in her breath.

"What that means is, you won't ever want to come to New York to live with me."

"That's not true," Abby argued. "Once we're both making decent money, I'll be there in a heartbeat, house or no house."

"Yeah, sure. Why would you? Even if you wanted to, your family would never approve of a move like that."

Abby bristled. "What my family approves of or doesn't approve of is of no consequence, Connor. In case you've forgotten, I'm twenty-one years old and past the age of consent. I'll do whatever I want, and I *want* to live with you in New York, but when the time is right."

"All right. I admit the perfect time isn't right now, but it will be one of these days. And when that day comes, it's important that your family approves of the man you plan on marrying. As it stands right now, they don't like me. Even a moron can see through their facade."

"They barely know you, so how could they not like you?"

"I don't understand it either. What I do know is they don't like me. I pick up on their negative vibes. I don't know why you haven't seen it."

"I think you're reading them wrong. You're misinterpreting their protectiveness for dislike. All parents have trouble letting go. It's natural," Abby argued in Carol and Donovan's defense.

Connor groaned. "All right. Where Donovan is concerned, you might be right. But Carol—Carol hates my guts. And I don't like her. There's something about her . . ." His voice trailed off, but his eyes were intent on Abby's face.

Abby sat on the edge of the bed. "Other than being opinionated, controlling, possessive, obsessive, meddling, smothering, and domineering—what?"

Connor shook his head again. "I don't know," he said, his tone serious. "I wish I could put my finger on it, but I can't. It's just a feeling I have. A gut feeling that something about her isn't quite right."

Abby stared at him, wishing he could articulate his feelings. He'd always had the uncanny ability to read things in people that others couldn't, and she trusted his instincts. It was those same instincts that made him such a good reporter.

"Carol is . . . Carol," Abby said. "We haven't exactly been seeing eye to eye these last couple of years. I think she resents my newfound independence, and I *know* she resents my being in touch with Mallory. If I'd been smart, I wouldn't have said anything to her. It always riles her." Abby stood up and put her arms around him.

"Do Donovan and Carol know I'm here for your graduation?"

"No. But then I didn't tell them I invited Mallory either."

"Christ, Abby. Springing me on them and then Mallory—" He uncrossed his arms and threw them up in the air in frustration. "They were probably planning on having you all to themselves, and now they're going to have to share you."

Abby coiled her arms around his neck. "You're absolutely right. I should have told them. I don't know why I didn't. I guess I just wanted to keep you all to myself."

Connor's anger vanished as soon as he looked into her eyes. "You ought to be a writer. You have an incredible way with words."

Abby laughed lightly. "Really? Maybe I'll give it a try." She stood on tiptoe and planted a kiss on his mouth. "I'll tell you what. I promise to tell Donovan and Carol about us within the week. I'll sit down and have a heart-to-heart with them and lay it all out for them. Okay?"

"Okay, but in the meantime, I want you to pay close attention when they're around me. Watch their faces, especially Carol's."

"I will, but right now I want you to watch my face, especially my lips." She mouthed the words *make love to me*.

"I thought you'd never ask. I love you, Abby Mitchell."

"And I love you, Connor Bradford."

"How does it feel to be a college graduate, Princess?" Donovan said, sweeping Abby high into the air.

"I'm so proud of you, honey," Carol said gleefully.

"Way to go, Abby," Bobby said, hugging her. "I sure hope I do as well as you have," he whispered in her ear.

"You don't have to. All you have to do is your best. That's good enough for anyone," she whispered back.

"I really like Connor. Are you two going to get married?" Bobby continued to whisper.

"I'm glad you like him. Yes, one of these days."

Bobby's tone changed slightly. "Do Mom and Dad know?"

Abby tugged at Bobby's ear. "No. Not yet, sport."

The boy grinned. "I can keep a secret. You'd be surprised to know what I know and don't tell."

"I would, huh? We'll talk about *that* later."

Abby watched Connor and Donovan out of the corner of her eye even as she watched for Mallory. She smiled, then sighed with relief when she saw Donovan clap Connor on the back. Relief washed through her when Donovan burst into laughter at something Connor said. Maybe after today, Connor would have a better feeling about Donovan and Carol. What a wonderful day this was turning out to be. Everyone she cared about was there.

Everyone but Mallory. Apparently her sister had decided not to accept her invitation, which was to be expected since Abby hadn't accepted hers. A feeling of disappointment shadowed her happiness as she gave one last sweeping glance around the room.

And then she saw her, standing on the fringe of the crowd, looking so sophisticated, so beautiful, and so very vulnerable. Their eyes met, and Abby knew that Donovan had been right. Mallory was a changed person. Without another moment's hesitation, Abby ran to her. "Oh, Mallory, you came!" she cried, throwing her arms around her sister. "Thank you. Thank you. Thank you. You've made my day!"

Mallory clasped her arms around her sister and squeezed her. "No, Abby. You've made mine. Thank you for inviting me," she said, tearfully. They clung to each other, simultaneously laughing and crying.

At length, it was Abby who pulled back. "I prayed you'd come. I'd hoped but—" Her voice broke.

"I wouldn't have missed this for all the world, little sister." Mallory held Abby's hands and gave Abby a thorough once over. "You look fabulous. I've never seen you look so happy."

Abby gave a tremulous smile. "That's because everyone I love is here to celebrate with me." She saw Mallory's eyes well with fresh tears. "Don't you dare cry, or you'll get me crying, too," Abby warned.

Mallory stiffened. "Who's crying? I'm not crying."

"Yeah, right. Come with me. I want you to meet Bunny and Connor. And after that you can come to the graduation party Aunt Carol is throwing for me."

"I'd love to meet your friends, but I don't think going to the party would be such a good idea. Besides, I've got an evening flight to catch. How about if we go for some coffee someplace?"

Abby frowned, unable to hide her disappointment. "If you're sure that's what you want. I've got an hour or so before the party starts. I'd hoped we'd be able to spend more time together."

"There'll be other times. I promise," Mallory said, squeezing Abby's hand reassuringly.

"Wait here a minute. I have to tell my friends where to meet us." Abby sprinted off to find her group. She saw Bobby first and grabbed his arm and pulled him away from everyone else. "Listen, sport, I need a favor. I want you to tell Carol and Donovan that I had something I had to take care of but that I'll be there when the party starts. Okay?"

"What do you have to do?" He wanted to know.

"I'm going to meet someone I haven't seen for a long time."

"Mallory?"

Abby was tempted to lie, but instead she nodded. "She's standing over there in the red dress. Don't tell, okay?"

"Say hello for me."

"One other thing," she said quickly. "Will you tell Bunny and Connor to meet me at the Rathskeller?" At Bobby's nod, Abby threw her arms around his lanky form. "I love you, Bobby Mitchell."

"Yeah, yeah, yeah," the boy said, turning back to his parents, who were deep in conversation with Bunny's parents.

Abby made her way through the crowd to her sister. "I told Bobby to tell Bunny and Connor to meet us at the Rathskeller."

"Before you saw me, I saw you and a very handsome man looking at each other with cow eyes. Was that the guy you wrote me about? Connor?"

"It was. We're . . . you know." Abby shrugged.

"You're in love," Mallory said.

"Yes. And one of these days we're going to get married."

Mallory put her arm around her sister's shoulders. "That's

wonderful, Abby. I'm really happy for you. I can't wait to meet him."

Five minutes later they entered the Rathskeller, found a quiet table, sat down, and ordered coffee.

"How have you been, Mallory? I mean really."

"I've been fine. Why the serious concern? Don't I look all right?"

"You look better than all right. You look wonderful. And happy. You are happy, aren't you?"

"As happy as anyone can expect to be, I guess. I've got friends, a nice apartment, an old but dependable car, and a good job. I work for an insurance company in Atlanta, and I just got offered a promotion. If I take it, I'll be moving back to South Carolina."

"No kidding. Where will you be working?"

"In Columbia, a hundred or so miles from Donovan and Carol's. Maybe we'll get to see each other from time to time."

Abby reached across the table and put her hand on top of her sister's. "I'd like that, Mallory, I really would. I'd like that a lot. Do you know where you'll be staying yet?"

"No. The company is renting me a condo in town. If I'm lucky, it might be near a lake or some kind of water, but I don't think so."

"I'll give you my address," Abby said, reaching in her purse for a pen and paper. "For my graduation present, Donovan built me a house, and Carol decorated it."

"Wow! What a great present. I want to give you something, too, Abby. I know I should have given it to you a long time ago but I thought—I knew Carol and Donovan would take care of you, so I waited. Now that you're going out on your own, you're going to need a little nest egg." Mallory reached into her pocket and withdrew an envelope. "It's a check. It wasn't right what Mama did, leaving all her insurance money to me. I hope this makes up for some of what she did to you and maybe some of what I did to you, too. It comes from my heart, Abby."

Abby opened the envelope and stared at the check. "My God, Mallory. This is a fortune."

"I took your half, fifty thousand, and invested it for you. It did really well, as you can see."

"I—I can't take this." Abby put the check back in the envelope and handed it to Mallory.

"Yes, you can. I insist." Mallory pushed Abby's hand away. "I would appreciate it, though, if you didn't tell anyone about it. Can we just keep it to ourselves?"

Abby thought about her earlier conversation with Connor. With this money, they would be able to get married sooner than either of them had anticipated. "If that's what you want. I'm very grateful, Mallory. I mean that."

"It's what I want." Mallory wiped the serious expression from her face. "'If you feel like repaying me," she said with a catlike grin, "you can invite me to dinner at your new house once you're all settled in."

Abby hooted. "I'll invite you, but be warned, I am absolutely clueless in the kitchen. The only thing I know how to do is make a dynamite pot of tea. Tea brewing was a necessity living with Donovan. That man loves his tea. Constant Comment is his favorite."

"Carol didn't insist you learn to cook?"

Abby shrugged. "What can I say? She hates people messing in her kitchen except during the holidays."

"Well, believe it or not, I'm pretty good at cooking. Argone was a very well rounded institu . . . establishment. I can teach you if you want to learn."

The mention of Argone took Abby aback. She wasn't sure how she should respond. "I'd—I'd like that, Mallory," she said at length. "I really would and—Oh, here come Connor and Bunny," she said with relief. "Hey, this is my sister Mallory. Mallory, this is my best friend, Bunny, and this handsome guy is Connor Bradford."

"I'm glad to meet you, Mallory," Connor said, extending his hand.

"Me too," Bunny chimed in. "Abby's told me all about you."

Mallory laughed. "And I'll bet none of it was good!"

Bunny recoiled in horror. "Oh, no, that's not true. She—"

Mallory waved her hand. "I was only kidding, Bunny. Abby's far too nice to tell people how mean I was."

Abby was incredulous. "Mallory!"

Forty-five minutes later, Mallory stood up and smiled down at Abby. "I have a plane to catch, and all of you have a party to go to. No, no, Abby, don't get up. I'll call you, and we'll get together soon. I promise."

In spite of her sister's wishes, Abby leaped to her feet. "Not so fast," she said, coming around the table. "I know I said it before, but I really am glad you came. I hope you meant it when you said you would teach me to cook."

"I meant it, Abby. Congratulations. You have nice friends. Treasure them. True friendships are rare."

Abby hugged her sister. "I know," she whispered before she let her go.

Abby watched Mallory weave her way through the tables and prayed that this wouldn't be the last time she saw her. "I didn't think she'd come, but she did."

"She's beautiful," Bunny said. "I wonder if she has to work at it or she's just naturally beautiful."

"She's naturally beautiful. What did you think of her, Connor? A man's opinion."

"She's gorgeous, and she seemed nice. But I never met anyone who had such sad eyes. Did you notice them, Abby?"

"No, no, I didn't notice. I was too caught up with her just being here."

"Just remember I'm the one who told you she has sad eyes. And speaking of eyes, Donovan winked at me and thanked me for coming. Maybe I was wrong, and he does like me after all."

Bunny playfully punched Connor's arm. "What's not to like where you're concerned? You're good-looking, you dress like a hick, you need a haircut, and you're a starving reporter working in Sin City. After I get my feet wet at *Cosmo,* I might use you as a model for one of the ads. Do you wear Jockeys or boxers?"

"None of your damn business, Bunny Webster. Don't go thinking I'm going to be your guinea pig either. I'm a legitimate reporter."

Bunny rubbed her thumb and forefinger together. "Big bucks, baby." She giggled.

"Oh, well, in that case . . ."

"He's not modeling, Bunny!" Abby said.

"We'll see," Bunny said smugly.

Abby stood up. "Come on, both of you. It's time to party."

Abby looked around the apartment that had been home to her and Bunny for the last two years. Though small, it was cozy and comfortable. She frowned. It was now part of another life. It seemed like everything was part of another life. Her early-childhood years with her mother, father, and Mallory, then her adolescence and teenage years with Carol, Donovan, and Bobby, then her college years with Bunny and Connor. Now she was going to enter another phase in her life. Tears misted her eyes. She wiped them away and focused on the future. She had a lot to look forward to—a job, a house of her own, a soon-to-be-published book, and a lifetime with Connor.

Inside the bathroom, she could hear Connor gargling. She smiled. He sounded like a frog in distress. She decided she loved the sound as much as she loved the man himself.

"I don't want you to go back to New York," Abby said a moment later when she slipped into his arms.

"Guess what? I don't want to go either. However, work calls. I want you to call me as soon as you get to your new house. I still can't believe you're driving home. How did that get by Carol?"

"I put my foot down and told her that I had things I didn't want to leave behind or sell off and that I was going to pack them up and drive home myself."

"I'm proud of you," Connor said, lightly slapping her on the back. "You need to assert yourself more often. Okay, I'm ready. Let's go have breakfast with the dragon and the dragoness."

"Come on, Connor. Cut the teasing. They're good, kind people, and they mean well."

"Of course they are. It's just my own insecurities showing through," Connor said tightly. "I didn't say good-bye to Bunny."

"She's meeting us at the restaurant. You'll probably see more of her than you will me in the coming months."

"This will have to be a quick breakfast on my part, or I'll miss my plane. Toast and coffee. That's it. Listen, Abby, I want to ask you something. How would you feel if I was offered a six-month stint in say, someplace like Saudi Arabia? Sort of like an apprentice to one of the foreign correspondents? The experience would be invaluable. Not to mention the good pay. I'd also get to see another part of the world."

"What?" Abby squawked, stopping dead in her tracks. "If you're trying to tell me something, Connor, just tell me, don't beat around the bush."

"It's not certain, but I'm being considered along with two other guys and one woman. I have the most experience. There's a good chance I might get it."

"Is it what you want, Connor?"

"I think I would kill for it. I talked about it to my boss, and he said you need to strike while the iron is hot. Then he told me how he'd kicked around the world for ten years or so. He said he still gets attacks of wanderlust. He had the strangest damn look on his face when he was telling me about all the places he'd been. The only problem in all of this is that I don't want to leave you. Six months is a long time."

Abby's heart fluttered in her chest. "Each of us needs to follow our own dream, Connor. I would feel terrible if I thought you lost out on yours because of me." She took hold of his hand. "If the offer comes, take it. They must have computers over there. We can still e-mail each other every day, even with the time difference. Your boss is right. When the iron is hot, you need to strike. I'll still be here when you get back."

"Are you sure you'd be okay with it, Abby?"

"No, but I'd hate myself if I was the cause of your missing such an opportunity. Six months isn't forever. You better not find your way into any of those harems over there."

Connor threw back his head and laughed. "Fat chance."

"I love you so much, Connor, it hurts. I'm missing you already."

Connor squeezed Abby's hand. "I don't even know if I have the job yet."

Abby wished now that she had not promised to have a going away breakfast with everybody. She could have had another couple of hours with Connor.

She looked around the crowded restaurant. For one heart stopping moment she thought she saw Mallory. She blinked and saw that the person, whoever she was, was walking away. She shrugged it off as being her imagination and turned her attention back to the problem at hand—how she was going to say good-bye to Connor in front of her family. She could always count on Bunny to create a diversion. Were they going to shake hands, peck each other on the cheek, or was he going to kiss her until her teeth rattled? Knowing Connor, he'd probably wave and say something breezily like, "See you around."

Abby bounded out of her chair and whipped around the table. "Come on, I'll walk you to the door. Your cab should be here any minute." She would kiss him outside until his toes curled.

"Connor, wait," Donovan said, holding out a paper bag. "Here's a Danish and some coffee to take with you."

"Thanks. That was nice of you." Connor seemed perplexed. "Thanks again for everything," he said to the group around the table.

Abby suffered through the handshakes, eager to get Connor to herself. Seconds later she was outside in the warm spring sunshine. "Oh, Connor, I don't know how I'm going to get along without you for six whole months."

"It isn't for sure, you know," he reminded her.

"They'll choose you, and we both know it." She took out a tissue and dabbed at her eyes.

"Listen now. Remember to put a hammer in your car in case the electric windows lock up. Don't pick up any hitchhikers even if they look sweet and innocent. And do not drive over sixty miles an hour no matter what the speed limit is. Drink coffee if you feel sleepy, and stop when you're tired. Do you have scissors in the console in case the seat belts jam up?"

"Yes to everything. You're beginning to sound like Carol." Out of the corner of her eye, Abby saw a cab round the corner. "Your cab is here." Her eyes swimming in tears, she stared up at the man she loved with all her heart. He kissed her then, a sweet, gentle kiss that promised the best was yet to come. She blinked away the tears and smiled. "Have a safe trip. I'll call you as soon as I get home."

Connor climbed into the cab and stuck his head out the window. "Remember everything I said, Abby."

"I love you, Connor," she whispered.

"I love you, too, Abby."

Abby stood, her feet rooted to the concrete, until the yellow cab was swallowed up in traffic. A fat pigeon circled her feet, making it impossible to move. When the pigeon finally waddled off, Abby turned to go back inside the restaurant. A flash of red caught her eye. Mallory? She turned, but in the time it took to whirl around, the woman in red was gone.

"Damn," she muttered.

Bunny appeared and threw her arm around Abby's shoulder. "Hey, girl, what are you doing out here all by yourself? Your family awaits. Carol sent me out to get you. I dilly-dallied as long as I could to give you time with Connor. How'd it go?"

"Terrible. I think he's going to go to Saudi Arabia with some foreign correspondent to learn the ropes. I told him I thought he should follow his dream and go. God, I miss him already." She wiped the tears from her eyes and straightened. "Either it's my imagination, or I saw Mallory a moment ago. Did you see a girl in a red dress in the restaurant?"

"No, I didn't."

"I swear it was her. I saw her in the restaurant and then again out here. If it wasn't Mallory, then she has a double."

Bunny reacted to the concern on her friend's face. "If it had been your sister, Abby, every male in the restaurant would have stopped chowing down. Ditto for all these people milling about outside. She's a showstopper. It was probably just someone who resembled her, that's all. As for your family, I'd say they are more or less finished and just dawdling over their coffee. They both *acted* like they really like Connor. Maybe *acted* is the wrong word. I think they do like him."

"I hope so. Too bad if they don't," Abby said smartly.

"Hey, I gotta go. I still have some stuff to pack."

"We'll stay in touch, won't we, Bunny?" Abby asked, worry etching her features.

Bunny smiled reassuringly. "You can count on it. You're my best friend in the whole wide world. And listen, don't worry about Connor. He's a big boy, and he has a real good head on his shoulders. If he does go to Saudi—Well, you know what they say—absence makes the heart grow fonder and all that."

"I know, I know."

"Come on, your family is waiting for you, and I have to go. God, it's going to be weird without you. I want you to know I'm going to work very hard at keeping in touch with you, and you have to promise to do the same. I expect to be able to call you at three in the morning if I'm having problems or even if I just need to talk, okay?" At Abby's nod, she continued. "We were so lucky to find each other. Think about it, Abby, four years and we never had one serious disagreement."

Abby managed a tremulous smile. "I know. I think we're both blessed. As soon as you get settled and get a phone, call Carol and leave your number, or give it to Connor and he'll get to me. It's going to take a week or so for me to get all set up. Once we're all organized, we can e-mail."

"Will do."

"Bye, Bunny. I'll see you at Christmas." Abby waved her friend away.

"Ah, here you are," Donovan said as he pocketed his credit card. "Did Connor get off all right?"

"Yes. And now Bunny's gone, too." Abby heaved a sigh. "God, I'm going to miss everybody."

"You'll all be together in just a few months." Donovan checked his watch. "Hey, you'd better get going if you want to put some miles behind you today. Remember to call us on our cell phone when you stop for the night. Carol said we'd be home by seven. Are you sure you have enough money for gas and everything?"

Abby thought about the sizable check in her purse. If there was ever a time to mention it, this was it. But she'd promised not to. "I have enough, and I promise to call." Bobby and Carol came outside to join them. "Okay, sport, pucker up," Abby said to Bobby.

"I think I just saw Mallory," Bobby whispered. "She winked at me and put her finger to her lips."

Abby shivered in the bright sunshine. So she wasn't imagining things after all. She forced a smile that was more a grimace than anything else. "I thought I saw her, too," she whispered back.

She turned from Bobby and faced her adoptive parents. For the first time in her life, she couldn't wait to say good-bye to them.

Carol's voice turned suddenly shy. "I hope you like how I decorated your house, honey. I tried to picture you in each of the rooms and used all the colors you like. I even took some things from your room at home and placed them around. And I want you to know that you won't hurt my feelings one bit if you change things. It's your house to do with as you please. Donovan and I just want you to enjoy it."

"There's even a room for me," Bobby piped up. "Mom said I can visit you this summer if you want me."

"Of course I want you. Come and stay as long as you like." Abby dug into her purse for her car keys. "Well, this is it," she announced, her jaw tight. "The first day of my new adult life." She clutched her keys to her chest. "I don't know how to thank you both for everything you've done for me all these years. Just saying the words doesn't seem adequate."

"It'll do," Donovan said gruffly. "By the way, I like that young man of yours. He's got ambition. I like that." Abby felt her cheeks puff out at the compliment.

"Drive carefully, honey," Carol said, tears rolling down her cheeks.

"Don't pick up any hunks on the way," Bobby said.

"Bye," Abby said, climbing into the Jeep.

Two days later, Abby crossed the Tennessee state line just as it grew dark. The Holiday Inn looked new and clean. She lugged her overnight bag from the cargo area and headed for the office. She looked forward to washing her hair and taking a nice hot shower. If she went to bed early, got up around five, and drove all day, she might make her new home by tomorrow afternoon. First things first, though. She reached for the phone the moment she bolted the door.

"Hi, Carol. It's me. I'm in Tennessee. Did you have a good flight home?"

"Abby. I don't—Oh, Abby," Carol said, tearfully. "I don't know how to tell you this."

"Carol, what's wrong? Stop crying and tell me. What's happened?"

"It's Connor. He's dead, Abby."

"Dead!" Abby's legs gave out, and she sat down on the edge of the bed. "What do you mean, he's dead? What are you talking about? Please, Carol, what happened? Tell me what happened," she screamed.

Suddenly Donovan's voice replaced Carol's. "Abby, Princess—"

"What happened? What happened to Connor? Tell me, Donovan!"

"We're not exactly sure. Connor's brother called not fifteen minutes ago looking for you, and said Connor collapsed in a cab on his way to the airport in Wisconsin. By the time the cab driver got him to a hospital he was dead. It's all we know right now. Connor's brother left a number for you to call him. Do you have a pencil and paper?"

Abby grabbed for the hotel pad and pen. "Yes. Read it to me," she said hoarsely.

"Will you call us when you know something more?"

"This has got to be a mistake of some kind," Abby said. "I'll get back to you." She started to hang up, then put the receiver back to her mouth. "Pray it isn't true, Donovan. Okay?"

"We'll all pray, Princess."

Abby broke the connection and stared at the phone. Connor couldn't be dead. He just couldn't be. They were going to get married and have four children. Connor was going to write a Pulitzer Prize–winning article, and she was going to be his famous mystery-writing wife. Connor was supposed to go to Saudi Arabia.

It had to be a mistake. Or a prank.

Her shoulders stiff, her eyes dry, she carefully dialed the number in front of her. When a voice said hello, she said, "This is Abby Mitchell. Could I please speak to Dennis?"

Chapter Nine

Abby stood in the driveway, tears streaming down her cheeks. She waved good-bye to her family. She couldn't imagine what she would have done without them this last week. They'd taken care of all the arrangements, bought the plane tickets for all of them and Bunny, too, to fly to Oregon, arranged a hotel, and sent flowers to the funeral home. They'd showered her with love and understanding. Now they were gone, with only Bunny staying behind. She felt herself clench her teeth wondering if the old saying, grit your teeth until they crack, was something that could really happen. Like she cared one way or the other. Weary to the point of collapse, Abby leaned on Bunny. The path into the house seemed miles long. She wondered if she would make it.

"Abby, I know you don't want to hear this or even believe it, but in time everything will be all right," Bunny said.

"No, Bunny, time will not make everything all right. Connor's gone. Forever." Abby closed her eyes as a wave of pain washed over her. "He never told me he had a heart problem—that he'd had rheumatic fever when he was little. He never said one word. Why wouldn't he tell me something like that, Bunny? Why?"

Bunny shrugged helplessly. "I don't know, Abby. Maybe it's one of those guy things. They think they have to be physically fit, macho, that kind of thing. If you believe in God, and I know you do, then you have to understand it was Connor's time. It's that simple." She rested the side of her head against Abby's. "By the way, your eulogy was wonderful. Everyone said so. I don't know how you got through it."

She didn't either, but she'd done it because she didn't want anyone else doing it. She didn't want someone she didn't know saying generic things about the man she loved. She'd wanted the words to mean something, to let people know what a really wonderful man Connor Bradford was and how much she'd loved him.

"Oh, Bunny," she said, her voice breaking, "I don't know how I'm going to go on without him. I loved him so much. He was my world."

Bunny closed her eyes for a second. "One day at a time, Abby. One day at a time."

Hand in hand they went into the house and headed for the kitchen. Bunny sat down at the table, and Abby opened the fridge and looked inside. "I'll make you some lunch and then take you to the airport. Did I tell you how grateful I am to you for going with me? Starting a new job and then leaving the second day can't be good for your career."

"They were very understanding. I wish I could stay longer, but I'm afraid if I do, I'll be testing the limits of their understanding. I'm surprised Carol didn't insist on staying with you."

"She did, but I was more insistent that she leave. She would have smothered me, Bunny. You know how she is. She thinks she always knows what's best. I need to be alone now. I have to handle this in my own way, and I still have a lot of crying to do. The library is holding my job open. But to tell you the truth, I don't know if I want the job anymore. I've

been thinking about staying home and writing full-time."
Abby took packages of ham and cheese out of the deli
drawer and laid them on the counter.

"Don't make any rash decisions right now. Think things
through before you act. You're hurting. Work is probably the
best thing in the world for you."

Abby whirled around and leaned her hip against the cabinet. She felt so lost, so empty. "What am I going to do,
Bunny?"

"You're going to pull up your socks, stiffen your backbone, and say, 'I can get through this. I *will* get through this.'"
Lowering her voice, Bunny continued, "I'll always be there
for you, just a phone call away. You're my friend. This is
what friends do for each other. Come on, you said you were
going to make me lunch, and I'm hungry."

Abby composed herself. There would be time enough for
all her questions later. A lifetime of time. "I did say that,
didn't I?" she said, trying to sound brave.

Bunny glanced around the kitchen. "By the way, I didn't
get a chance to tell you before, but this is quite a house. Oh!
Before I forget, your housewarming present is coming later
this afternoon. I'll call you tonight to see how you like it.
Make sure you answer your phone."

"Give me a hint," Abby said, slapping three slices of ham
and two slices of Swiss cheese on top of a sourdough roll.
"Mayo or mustard?"

"Both."

"Come on, tell me what the present is," Abby cajoled.
"Do your wear it, eat it, use it, or just look at it?"

"No hints. It's a surprise," Bunny said, watching Abby
spread a huge glob of mayo on the other side of the roll. "But
I will tell you this," she teased. "It'll fit right in with this
house." Before Abby could pose another question, Bunny
changed the subject. "I can't believe Carol and Donovan fur-

nished this place for you. I hate to ask, but is it decorated to *your* taste?"

Abby put the sandwich on a plate and looked for some chips to go with it. "You know what, Bunny? I was only here overnight before we left for Oregon. I really didn't look at anything, so I don't know." She looked up at the pot rack over the island. It was loaded with copper-bottomed pans. "I haven't even been in all the rooms. I'll check it out later when I'm up to it. The truth is, I was kind of hoping for a little bungalow or a cottage kind of house. You know, something cozy with a real fireplace for those cold, wintry days? Instead, I get a monster house." She waved a hand in disdain. "It must be three or four thousand square feet. This should be Mallory's house, not mine. She likes things overblown, if you know what I mean." Abby carried the plate and a can of soda over to the table and set it in front of Bunny, then sat down across from her. "Speaking of Mallory, I wonder where she is and what she's doing. I keep seeing her everywhere I look. Remember last week at our breakfast good-bye? I really did catch a glimpse of her in the restaurant. Bobby confirmed it later when he said he saw her, too. And then I saw her, or thought I saw her, standing behind a tree at Connor's funeral. I don't get it. Maybe I was overwrought. No maybes about it; I was and still am."

"I don't get it either. If she was at the breakfast good-bye, then she lied to us the day before when she said she had an evening flight to catch. What do you suppose would be the point of her watching you?"

"I can't imagine unless . . ." Abby felt the color drain from her face as she stared at Bunny's untouched sandwich. She didn't like the first thought that came to mind—that Mallory might want to do her harm. She remembered Connor saying Mallory had the saddest eyes he'd ever seen. Sad because . . . because she'd grown up in an institution, unloved and unwanted? Because she hadn't had the advantages Abby had? Yes, she could be sad for both those reasons and probably a few more. But it wasn't Abby's fault, and Mallory knew it. *No,* she thought, dismissing the troublesome idea. *Mallory has changed. She isn't mean and hateful anymore.*

"Abby, what are you thinking?"

"Nothing. I was just letting my writer's imagination get away with me. Do you think I'm teetering on the edge of a mental breakdown, Bunny?" Abby asked fearfully.

"I don't think any such thing, and you need to stop talking like that. Plain and simple, you're dog-tired. You haven't slept more than a few hours in five whole days. You had just come off that long car trip home from school and then emotionally you got wiped out. What you need is a hot bath, a good stiff drink, and bed. But not until after you take me to the airport and your housewarming present gets here," she qualified.

Abby stared blankly at Bunny as she ate her sandwich. "You know, now that I think about it, I should have insisted on talking to the doctor who admitted Connor to the hospital."

"What?"

Abby shook her head in dismissal. "Oh, I was just thinking. I wish Dennis had authorized an autopsy. I just can't believe Connor had a heart attack. He was too young."

"It happens more often than you realize. Remember that ice skater? And the basketball player? You just have to accept it." Bunny looked at her watch. "Come on. I gotta go." She scooted her chair back. "Be sure to come right home after you drop me off. Don't go to the store or anything."

"The store? Are you kidding? Carol filled my refrigerator and freezer to the gills. She told me there's even an extra refrigerator in the garage that's full of soda, beer, juice, and all kinds of stuff. I could hole up here for months and never stick my nose outside the door. On top of that, she said I have a newspaper delivery, a real honest-to-God milkman, bottled water delivery, et cetera, et cetera, et cetera. Sometimes I feel like Carol has complete control over my life. Then I feel ashamed because I know how much she loves me. It's the excess that bothers me. I don't need all this."

Bunny took her plate and empty soda can over to the sink. "Throw it all out and start over. It will give you something to occupy your mind," she said cheerfully.

"I can't do that. It would be wasteful."

"Then stop bitching and moaning. Is there anything I can do for you before I leave?"

Abby nodded. "A hug would be nice. Bunny?"

"Yes."

"You didn't say anything before, but did you happen to see Mallory at the funeral?"

"No, but that doesn't mean you didn't." Bunny took Abby by the shoulders. "If you did see her, then she probably meant for you to see her. And in that case, I think she wanted you to know she was there for you."

Abby quirked an eyebrow. "But why not go with me, stand with me, be with me?"

Bunny rolled her eyes. "You're not thinking. Carol and Donovan are why. She didn't show herself to them at our graduation either. Remember?"

"Yeah, I remember." She was going to ask about the break fast good-bye, then thought better of it. Rather than all this speculation, she should just call Mallory and ask her point blank, except she didn't have a phone number for her sister as yet.

"The Abby Mitchell I know and love will sort it all out. That's something else you can do to keep your mind busy. C'mon, we need to get this show on the road."

Abby hugged her friend. "From the day I met you, you've

been my port in every storm I've gone through. I want to thank you for being my friend, Bunny."

"God, you're going all mushy on me. Move, girl. I need to get to the airport."

Abby pressed the remote for the automatic garage-door opener. She sat in the Jeep for a long time, wondering if she had the energy to get out and walk into the house. Keep your mind busy, Bunny had said. Rest and read a book, Carol said. Drink some hot tea and take a nap, Donovan said. As if any of their remedies would make the pain go away.

Abby turned the security bolt on the door that led to the kitchen. She sniffed at the new paint and carpet. Everything in her state-of-the-art kitchen gleamed and sparkled, thanks to Carol. Even the green plants nestled in the corners of the count ers had a waxy shine that came from a bottle. Nothing but the best, the top of the line, she thought, wondering why she felt so irritable. Did she really need double ovens when she couldn't even cook? Did she really need a forty-two-inch-wide Sub Zero refrigerator?

Everything was green and yellow. The ceramic bowl of short stemmed yellow roses drew her eye. They were just too damn perfect with their baby's breath and lacy green fern. In the blink of an eye, Abby whisked the bowl off the table and carried it to the garage, but when she looked at the glass-topped table it looked bare and naked. The whole look of the kitchen had suddenly changed. How could one bowl of roses do something like that? Abby walked back to the garage to bring the green bowl with the yellow roses back to the table.

Get on with it, Abby, she told herself. *Go through the rooms so when Carol calls you can goo and gush over her decorating.*

The great room was a work of art, its focal point being a monstrous fieldstone fireplace with raised hearth and wood-storage inset—complete with stacks of perfectly shaped birch logs. The mantel was old and intricately carved. On it were displayed family pictures, even one of Connor sitting next to Bobby on a bench outside a restaurant.

Move on, Abby, move on.

Deep comfortable chairs, the kind two people could curl up in, dotted the four corners of the room, with little tables full of mementos she'd had in her bedroom at Carol and Donovan's house. They didn't make the room better or worse. It was just a room with white walls and gay watercolor paintings on every inch of wall space. A sixty-inch television sat in a white cabinet with louvered doors. Next to it was an elaborate built-in surround-sound system. Misty green vertical blinds covered the French doors that led to the patio and pool area. She looked down to see that the blinds matched the ceramic tile on the floor, right down to the sea-green grout. The room was so put together—so controlled. It made Abby cringe.

The living room was formal and done in soft mint green with touches of brilliant yellow. Exquisite draperies that matched the stiff-looking furniture were pulled back from the bow window and allowed for a view of her immaculate manicured lawn and shrubs. Connor would have hated the room. In fact, Connor would have hated the whole house. His first question would be where was he going to prop his size thirteen sneakers for his daily beer. Once again she looked downward. Who in her right mind would install white carpeting?

Abby sighed as she meandered into the dining room to look at the long expanse of table with eight chairs. Who was going to sit at this long table and eat? She didn't have eight friends. And even if she did, she didn't know how to cook.

White carpeting there, too.

Abby continued down a short hallway, opening and closing doors. The linen closet was fully stocked with sheets, towels, bathroom essentials, and a new Water Pik still in its box. She counted twelve boxes of Crest toothpaste and six new toothbrushes still in their cardboard wrappers. The second and third doors led to walk-in closets with shelves for shoes, purses, luggage, and racks and racks for clothes. The only thing missing was a conveyor belt. The last door off the short hallway was an office with its own bathroom and minikitchen. Elaborate was hardly the right word. A state-of-the-art computer sat in the middle of a custom-built desk with yards and yards of space. Everything looked to be geometrically aligned. Did she dare move anything?

In a fit of something she couldn't describe, she swept her arm across the right-hand side of the desk, sending a China Doll houseplant, pencil holder, and a paper-clip box crashing to the floor.

Maybe she needed to go outside and sit in the sun for a little while even though sun was her face's enemy. Like she really cared anymore. If she did that, though, would she hear the deliveryman when he brought Bunny's housewarming gift? It seemed like a lot of trouble, but she wrote out a note and taped it to the front door.

Before she popped a Coca-Cola, Abby looked down the hallway that led to the atrium and the four bedrooms and baths that completed the house. She could always look at them some other day. Maybe she'd never look at them.

The pool was beautiful, the arranged patio furniture with the striped umbrellas looked just right for a party. Too bad she didn't know anyone to invite.

She burst into tears. Her feet picked up wings as she raced into the house, through the rooms, and down the hall that led to her room and the one thing that had given her comfort over the years, Bailey, her old stuffed dog. She crushed it to her breast, her fingers working at the frayed, worn, nubby ears, and cried as she'd never cried before.

It was a long time later, her eyes red and puffy, before she stirred and made her way back outside. She was blowing her nose when a man suddenly appeared from the side of the house.

"Yo!" he said by way of a greeting. "I'm looking for Abby Mitchell."

Abby sniffed. "I'm Abby Mitchell. And you are?"

"Steve Carpenter. I have a delivery for you from a Miss Bunny? The note on the door said you would be in the backyard. Nice place you got here," he said, looking around.

Abby stood in the shade of one of the umbrellas, not wanting him to see her tears. "Just leave it over there. I'll take it in later."

The man glanced back toward his vehicle. "It's not the kind of delivery you can just leave. It's the kind you need to take possession of."

Abby started toward him, her frustration mounting. "What does that mean? Oh!" she said with sudden dawning. "You want to hand it to me so I'll give you a tip. Okay, wait here," she told him, turning and starting back toward the house.

"Lady, I don't want a tip," he said, sounding insulted. "Stay put, and I'll bring it to you."

"Look, I'm not in a very good mood right now, so let's not play games."

"I'm not playing games. Just stay there, and I'll be right back."

Sometimes Bunny had a weird sense of humor, Abby thought. In spite of Mr. Carpenter's command, she followed him to his car.

"Eager to see what I've got, huh?" he said, when he turned to see her standing behind him. He opened the car's back door and reached inside. "Here you go," he said, handing her a leash, then a clipboard. "Sign here. No returns. Just so you understand that."

Abby blinked, then blinked again. At the end of the leash

was a huge dog. "Is this—Is this my present? Oh, my God. It's a dog!" Her face lit up with excitement. "Is it full-grown? Is it a boy or a girl? What's its name?"

The man standing in front of her with his baseball cap on backwards grinned. "Yep, it's a dog all right. I'd say he's a mix of shepherd and a little Lab. He weighs ninety-three pounds. He's full-grown and is three years old. He was a K-9 dog but got wounded in the line of duty so he can't work anymore. On rainy days he limps a bit, but otherwise he's fit as a fiddle. Your friend seemed to think he'd make a perfect pet for you. He really is a great dog. His name is Beemer."

"Beemer," Abby repeated with a laugh. "He's wonderful. Where do I sign?"

"On the only line on the paper, lady."

"I have a name. Why don't you call me by name? I hate the term *lady*," Abby muttered as she scrawled her name, one eye on the dog and the other on Steve Carpenter.

"Okay, lady, I mean, Miss Mitchell. He's all yours. Remember what I said, no returns. This is a live dog, not like that stuffed dog on your chair over there. You are going to take care of him, aren't you?" He gave her a critical look.

Abby narrowed her eyes. "Of course I'm going to take care of him," she flashed back. "Why would you think I wouldn't?"

"Because I'm a vet, and that makes me suspicious by nature. People are always dumping dogs and cats off on my doorstep, thinking because I'm a vet, I have unlimited resources for feeding them, taking care of them, and finding homes for them. Do you have any idea how many abandoned and unwanted dogs I have at the clinic as we speak?"

"I have no idea," Abby said, scratching Beemer behind the ears.

"Nineteen."

"Do you want me to take some of them for you?" She

waved her hand to encompass the fenced-in yard. "This is a big place as you can see, and I don't have any neighbors. If you'll take care of them—feed them and see to their health needs, they can have the run of the place. I'd hate to see you put any of them to sleep. You won't, will you?"

"Never in a million years. That's not why I went into veterinary medicine. Do you mean what you just said?"

"Of course I mean it. Do you have doghouses? I suppose they can sleep in the garage at night. It's air-conditioned."

"Air-conditioned. Wonderful. You're sure now? You know, they'll ruin your bushes and grass. You don't look the type to do pooper-scoop duty."

Abby didn't like what he was implying. "Exactly what type do I look like?"

Steve shrugged. "Rich. A little spoiled. This house looks like it costs more than I'll earn in a lifetime."

"For the record, Mr. Carpenter, you're wrong. I'm not rich. The house was a gift from my adoptive parents. All I wanted was a small house, you know, a cottage with some flower boxes. This," she said, waving her arms, "is what I got instead, and, like it or not, I'm stuck with it."

Steve looked anything but sympathetic to her problem. "Do you know anything about dogs? Feeding them? Caring for them? Training them?"

Abby shook her head. "No, but I can learn."

"Well, there's nothing like a ninety-three-pound ex-K-9 to teach you I guess." He handed her a piece of paper. "I've written up a few instructions, information about old Beemer here." He closed the car door and opened his trunk. "I brought you a bag of dry dog food and some pig ears. Beemer is a highly trained police dog, Miss Mitchell. He'll protect you and love you. I hope you'll do the same for him."

"I love him already," she said, bending to the dog's level and allowing him to bathe her face with dog kisses.

"Are you sure about this? Me bringing you all those dogs? The reason most people abandon a dog is because it digs or chews or barks or all of the above. If they'd just take the time to train their pets . . ." He broke off with a sigh. "It's sort of a vicious cycle, if you know what I mean."

"Yeah, I do. It'll be good for me, give me something to occupy my mind, and right now I really need to do that."

"Why?" he asked, scrutinizing her as if she had a screw loose.

Unable to help herself, Abby's eyes filled with tears. "I guess I want to do something good for someone. You look sort of frazzled, kind of the way I feel right now. Is that a good enough answer?" She hoped it was because she sure as hell couldn't tell him the whole truth.

"It'll do. Are you going to be home tomorrow?"

Was she? She was supposed to report to the library at nine o'clock. But she had pretty much decided to call them and tell them she wasn't ready to work yet. "Actually, I will be here. All day. I'm a writer. I work at home," she blurted.

The die was cast.

"A writer! That's pretty neat. I can't hang two words together. What do you write?"

Abby stared at the man across from her. Thirty at least. Wonderful dark, caring eyes, sandy hair, winsome smile. Rugged. Works out. "Mysteries. Well, actually one so far. I just sold my first book. I based it on a case that has never been solved, put my spin on it, and, well, you know." Uncomfortable with talking about herself, she asked, "How old did you say Beemer is?"

"A little over three years. Smart as a whip." He consulted his watch. "Listen, I gotta get going. I'll be by tomorrow with the crew. You're sure now that you want to do this? They aren't going to be easy to take care of, and they're going to make one hell of a mess out of that beautiful yard of yours."

"I'm sure. I could use the company. I don't want to be alone, especially now. The house is so big and . . ."

"Are you all right? You look . . . Well, you look like you've been doing a lot of crying," Steve said hesitantly.

"I have been crying," she admitted. "My boyfriend . . . he died . . . unexpectedly . . . last week. I just got back from Oregon, from his funeral, a few hours ago."

Steve flinched with embarrassment. "I'm sorry. I didn't know. Listen, if there's anything I can do—" She shook her head. "How many dogs should I bring, do you think?"

"All of them. Some of them. Whatever you think we can handle."

"We?" He looked perplexed.

Abby swiped the wetness of her cheeks. "Yeah, *we,*" she said firmly. "That was the agreement. I said I would provide the place if you would feed them and take care of their health needs, remember?"

Steve removed his baseball cap and scratched his head. "Yeah, right," he said.

"So what time is feeding time?"

"Seven o'clock in the morning."

Abby gasped. "That early?"

Steve smiled smugly. "I'm afraid so. I have to feed them early so I can do my rounds and open my clinic by nine."

"Oh, sure." Abby nodded. "That makes perfect sense. Who's going to pay for all the dog food?"

"I will, unless you'd care to split it," he said hopefully.

Abby thought about the check Mallory had given her that she had yet to deposit. "Okay," she said, knowing in her heart that Connor would approve. He'd loved animals. Carol and Donovan, on the other hand, would go ballistic. She felt light-headed at the thought.

"Then I guess I'll see you tomorrow," Steve said, heading toward his car.

Abby nodded. "What do I do if Beemer doesn't like me?"

"It won't happen. An animal loves the person who feeds him and is kind to him. The only thing a dog knows is loyalty. Beemer might take a few days to really warm up to you, but once he does he will never leave your side. Trust me on that."

Abby smiled a real smile. "Okay, see you tomorrow, Steve." She started back toward the house when she had a thought. "Hey, you want to come for supper?" she blurted. Bunny would view the invitation as getting on with her life.

Sam stopped in his tracks. "What are you having?"

"Well . . . ah . . ."

"You don't try out weird recipes on unsuspecting guests, do you? I'm a meat-and-potatoes kind of guy. I don't like anything with strings or that looks like a weed. I love sweets. I would kill for sweets. I'm also partial to caramel-coated popcorn. I've also been known to nibble on dog biscuits when money is tight, which is most of the time."

Abby laughed out loud. Steve Carpenter had a wonderful sense of humor. "It will probably be something frozen or something out of a can. I can't cook," she admitted, grimacing. "Except eggs," she qualified. "I can cook eggs, fried, scrambled, or hard boiled."

Steve grimaced back. "I like eggs. Sure. What time?"

"Seven," she said as she calculated how long it would take her to shower and set a table. "The dog won't fall in the pool, will he? Do I need to walk him on a leash or what?"

"A leash will be good for a while. Take him to the edge and see what he does. If he looks like he'll go in, swat his back end with a rolled-up newspaper. Do that a few times, and he'll get the idea. Dogs *can* swim. It's instinctive." He pulled his cap down low over his face. "You know, this is a really good thing you're doing."

"My friend Bunny, the one who had you deliver Beemer to me, said her grandmother always said when God is good to you, you have to give back."

Sam looked perplexed. "But you said . . ."

"That my boyfriend died," she finished for him. "Yes, and God gave him to me for four wonderful years. And now that I have all this," Abby said, waving her hand about, "I can give back." To hide her tears, she turned her head and looked over the expanse of green lawn. "Do you think I'm going to need a gardener?"

Steve laughed. "Hell, no! After the crew is here a few days, there won't be anything left to take care of. See ya."

Abby started back toward the house, Beemer at her side. Out of the corner of her eye she noticed a silver streak heading down the road. Was it Mallory driving the car? What would Mallory be doing all the way out here? It was probably a trick of the sunlight. She walked into the house and locked the door, her insides shaking.

Was it Mallory?

Chapter Ten

Abby woke slowly and snuggled against the comforting warmth of Connor's back. She smiled, rolled over and threw her arm across . . . a furry body? She opened her eyes and shrieked.

"Beemer!" The big dog was lying next to her, his head on the pillow beside hers.

She burst into tears as reality hit her: Connor would never sleep with her again. Then, moments later, Beemer's confused expression penetrated her tears, and she started to laugh.

"I bet your handler, whoever he was, didn't let you sleep in *his* bed," she said, wiping her tears away. "You took advantage of me, Beemer." The dog stretched and yawned, then rolled to his feet and jumped down off the high-rise bed. When Abby made no move to get up, he barked at her. She looked over the edge of the bed and saw him staring at her. "What? What do you want?"

He barked again.

"You want to go out, is that it?" He turned toward the door. "Okay, okay. I get the message." She climbed down out of the big bed and headed for the French doors that led to the patio. "Okay, you go do your thing, and we'll meet up in the kitchen for breakfast."

Ten minutes later Beemer found Abby in the kitchen grinding coffee beans. He sat down across from her and gazed up at her expectantly. "You want some breakfast?" she asked as if he might actually answer. She finished making her coffee, searched for and found the bag of dog food Steve had brought, and scooped some into a bowl. When she set it down in front of Beemer, he looked at it with disdain. "What? Didn't I fix it right?" She reread the list of instructions and realized she'd forgotten to add warm water. "Sorry, boy, I missed that part. You must think I'm a real jerk." She picked up the bowl, held it under the filtered hot-water dispenser, then stirred the kibble until it was swimming in a tasty-looking gravy. As soon as she set it down, Beemer started eating. Abby watched in delight as the big dog ate every last morsel.

She was about to sit down with a cup of coffee to ponder the day ahead of her when the kitchen door opened and chaos erupted. "What? Hey!" she sputtered as dogs of every size and color invaded her house. She watched in horror as a fat basset hound waddled over to the center of the floor and squatted. "Oh, my God. Stop! Not in the kitchen!"

"Olivia! Bad dog," Steve Carpenter yelled as he charged into the kitchen behind the dogs. "Why the hell did you let them in?" he shouted as he ran past her.

"I didn't," Abby shouted to be heard above the barking dogs. "The door must have been ajar."

"Woody! Gus! Mickey! Come here, you guys," Steve called, heading for the dining room. "Harry, no! That's not a tree!" And then a moment later, "Jesus Christ! White carpeting."

Abby followed Steve and the dogs. She stopped at the door and her whole body started to quake with laughter. Never in her life had she witnessed such a hilarious scene. Dogs were running every which way, panting, barking, and yipping. One of them jumped on the couch, then hopped over the back and ran down the hall, another one was digging into the chair cushion while a third was making its bed in one of the antique satin draperies pooled on the floor.

Steve was in the middle of it all, a dog under each arm, his expression horrified. "Call them toward you and maybe we can route them back outside."

"Come on, guys," Abby said, clapping her hands to get their attention. "Let's go outside." None of them moved or even looked her way. "They're not listening," she said. "What now?"

"See if you can catch a couple of them—that one—Harry. I'll take these two outside, then come back to get a couple more."

Abby ran after the one Steve had called Harry and scooped him up in her arms. She was about to go after a pug when Harry licked her chin. She looked down at him and he licked her again. "Ah, you're a cutie," she said, hugging the furry canine.

"Big help you are," Steve said, coming back through the dining room.

"Can I help it if I'm a sucker for animals?" she asked as she headed for the kitchen to put Harry outside. She hurried back in time to see Steve chasing a Lab around the table in the foyer, threatening to take the dog's toys away and to introduce him to the dogcatcher if he didn't obey. Steve was so entertaining Abby forgot what she was supposed to do, and by the time she remembered and went after the pug, it was too late. "Oh, no," she said, seeing the homely little dog kicking out his back legs in a useless attempt to cover up his mess. "There goes Carol's white carpet." Grimacing, she looked up to see Steve pulling the Lab by the collar toward the kitchen.

When it was all over and the dogs were outside, Abby and Steve sat down across from each other at the kitchen table.

"I'm sorry," Steve said. "As soon as I get a second wind, I'll clean up the mess in the living room."

"I'll do it a little later," she said. "I'm not mad if that's what you think. I haven't laughed like that in a long time, and to tell you the truth it felt good," she grinned at him.

"Who in the hell would put down white carpeting anyway?"

"Don't look at me," Abby said, getting up. "It was like that when I moved in." Slippers flapping, she made her way across the kitchen. "Uh-oh. We forgot one."

Steve turned around and saw Olivia sitting behind him. He got up and went over to her. "Bad dog," he said again, waving his finger under her nose. "Bad dog, Olivia." He pointed toward the puddle she'd made. "Where are your manners?" he asked the sad-eyed basset. "Come on, you're outta here."

As soon as he came back inside he found the paper towels, peeled off a few sheets, sopped up the mess, and disposed of it in a trash can outside the kitchen door.

"Want some coffee, breakfast?" Abby asked.

"Sure. Nothing heavy, okay?" He went over to the sink and thoroughly washed his hands. "Listen, I'm really sorry about canceling out on you last night. There was an emergency at closing time."

"Your assistant explained everything," Abby said. "Besides, I really wasn't up to it anyway. How do eggs and Pop-Tarts sound?"

"Pop-Tarts! You might as well have said dog poop on a cracker."

"Like them that much, do you? I'll have to remember that."

"Where's the bag of dog stuff I delivered to you yesterday along with Beemer?"

Abby turned and pointed to the counter next to the stove.

Steve retrieved the bag and found the box of Snausages. "Pay attention now. This is one way to get the dogs to come to you." He grabbed a handful, stepped outside, then whistled between his teeth. The dogs came running from every direction to get their treats.

"Wow! I'm impressed," she teased, when he came back inside. "Do you think I can learn that?"

"Possibly, with a few lessons," he kidded. "By the way, how did Beemer do last night? Any problems?"

"He did just fine but . . . I'm embarrassed to say he took advantage of me."

Steve sat down again. "Took advantage of you? How?"

"When I woke up this morning, I found him in my bed!"

Steve's forehead wrinkled in confusion, then smoothed out when he caught the drift of her joke. "Lucky dog," he said, watching her expectantly as if he was afraid she might not take his joke in the same vein.

Abby broke four eggs into the frying pan. "So what is it with all these dogs? What's wrong with them that nobody wanted them? I'm having trouble comprehending all this."

"Nothing's wrong with them. Olivia was given up because her family was moving out of state. It's beyond me why they couldn't take her with them. They didn't leave their children behind. Old Woody—Woodrow Wilson, I call him, the pug—his owner thought he was sick and didn't want to spring for the vet bill. All that was wrong was that he had an enlarged prostate and needed to be neutered. Of course, he never would have gotten an enlarged prostate if he'd been neutered when he was young. Gus and Harry were found by one of my clients wandering the streets, half-starved. The problem is that people treat dogs and cats like throwaways. They don't realize or care that animals have feelings—that they worry, get scared, and even go into depression. Believe me, I've seen and heard it all."

Abby's eyes filled with tears. "I know what it's like not to be wanted. My mother didn't want me, and the people who adopted my sister and me—they didn't want her." She shook her head.

Steve gave her a thoughtful look. She sensed he wanted to say something comforting but he didn't. "There's a book in this somewhere. I know it."

"You know what, you are absolutely right. A book about the dogs, not me or my sister. I could call it *Canine Capers* or something like that. I'll dedicate it to you . . . and the crew. What's that one's name?" she asked, pointing toward a terrier she hadn't seen before.

"Solomon. Their names are on their tags. They've had all their shots, by the way, and they've all been neutered or spayed. Be sure to put down plenty of water."

"Speaking of water, I think I'd better have a fence put up around the pool so I don't have to worry about them falling in."

"That would be nice, but I don't know if it's entirely necessary. You can probably teach them to stay away from it, except for the Lab. Labs love water. He could probably give you a few swimming lessons."

"I still think I'll fence in the pool. Meantime, I'll keep the dogs in the house with me and take them outside every couple of hours."

"I don't think that's such a good idea, what with that white carpet. Every accident is going to show. And considering how many of them there are . . ."

"I have an idea. How about if I close off all the rooms except the path from the kitchen to my office? That way if there's an accident, I'll see it right away. I know this will make me sound really ungrateful, but my adoptive parents gave me the house as a graduation gift. Carol, my adoptive mother, decorated it and—well—it's way too formal for me. The minute I saw those pooling draperies and all that white carpeting I knew they would have to go. And most of the furniture and accessories, too. So, you see, if the dogs have an occasional accident, it's no big deal."

"What you're saying, if I'm hearing you right, is that your adoptive mother is a little on the controlling side. My mother was like that, always thinking she knew what was best for me. You wouldn't believe some of the outrageous schemes she pulled to get me to do what she wanted." He took the mug of coffee she handed him.

Abby eyed him narrowly, his comments ringing in her ears. Controlling, yes. Carol was that, among other things. The last three years she'd been more controlling than ever, and Abby had found herself wanting to distance herself from Carol, which meant she had to distance herself from Donovan, too. As for schemes . . .

"What you said—it makes me wonder," she said as she put the Pop-Tarts into the toaster oven, "if this house wasn't sort of like bait."

"Bait?"

Abby turned around and looked at him. "Yeah. A year or so ago, I mentioned the possibility of moving to New York after graduation, and then what do I get for a graduation present?" She turned her hands, palms up. "This house."

"Well, I for one am glad you didn't move to New York. All these dogs were starting to take a toll on my practice. Taking care of them properly requires a lot of time—time I need for my patients." He stared at her intently until Abby looked away.

"So, when are you going to ask me about this?" she said, smoothing her hand over the port-wine stain.

"I wasn't planning to ask. I know what it is. I'm glad you

THE GUEST LIST   165

aren't one of those people who constantly keeps putting her hand to her face or wears one of those cockamamie hairdos to try to hide it. Obviously you're comfortable with it."

"You're never comfortable with something like this," Abby said coolly.

"You know what I mean. We all live with one cross or another. I suppose you've looked into laser surgery?"

"I *had* laser surgery a few years ago, and it actually made it slightly worse."

"I'm sorry. That must have been disappointing."

Abby divvied up the eggs from the frying pan onto plates, added the Pop-Tarts, then took the plates to the table and set them down. "Since you missed out last night, you want to come for supper tonight?"

"Sure, but since we're having eggs now, could we have something else for supper? I like eggs, but not for every meal. Can't you cook even a little bit?"

Abby bubbled with laughter. When she could talk again, she said, "To tell you the truth I've never really tried, but I noticed there were some cookbooks on the shelf, and I *can* read. Yesterday you said you were a meat-and-potatoes kind of guy, so how about I cook meat and potatoes?"

Steve's face turned dubious. "Okay."

They turned their attention to their food, finishing a few minutes later. Abby sat back and sipped her coffee, savoring the flavor and the aroma.

Steve looked up at the clock. "I'd better get going," he said, putting his silverware on his plate. "Thanks for breakfast. You cook some mean scrambled eggs."

Abby balled her napkin and threw it at him. "They weren't scrambled. They were fried!"

"Oops!" he said, looking suitably embarrassed. "I think it's time for me to go." He opened the door and was immediately surrounded by the dogs.

They love him, Abby thought, following him out. *No,* she amended, *they* adore *him.* "Be sure to latch the gate on your way out. And if you have a padlock lying around, bring it with you tonight. I don't want my dogs getting out."

"Your dogs?" he yelled back over his shoulder.

"Yes. I'm going to adopt each and every one of them, unless you can find them other homes." As if in agreement with her plan, Olivia threw her head back and howled. "Oh, my God!" Abby said, laughing. "She's wonderful. She's got such character."

Steve laughed, too. "With this many dogs you might need a kennel license. I'll look into it for you."

"Okay," Abby said agreeably.

"You're pretty unflappable, you know?"

Abby nodded. "I guess I'll see you this evening. Seven o'clock."

"Are you sure you can handle all this?" he asked, looking from dog to dog to dog.

"'I'm sure. What's the worst thing that could happen? Never mind. Dumb question."

"I hate leaving you here like this," he said once he was on the other side of the gate.

"I hope you aren't thinking about moving in. The dogs are one thing, but you—Now that's a different matter entirely. Go on. I'll be fine, and so will they."

The moment Steve left, Abby looked around at her new canine family, who were watching her with a great deal of curiosity. "Okay, you guys . . . and girls. It seems to me the best thing to do is to get you all some water. I assume you've already had breakfast, but from here on out, food will be served on the patio. I'll ring a bell or whistle or something. I'd appreciate it if you"—she turned her gaze on Olivia, then the pug—"would do your business outside in the bushes or on the grass." The pug stood up on his hind legs. "Very nice. Shall I take that as an okay?" She walked back to the sliding kitchen door, then turned around. "Beemer, you take charge while I go find water bowls."

Beemer offered up a sharp bark. It was almost as good as a salute. Olivia, obviously smitten with the big, handsome former police dog, waddled to his side and gazed at him adoringly.

Abby went back inside. Bunny would be proud of her, she thought. If this didn't qualify as getting on with her life, she didn't know what did.

She liked Steve. He was fun to be around, and she loved his camaraderie with the dogs. But what she liked best was that he had no expectations of how she should be acting or feeling. She hadn't told him much about herself, other than that her boyfriend had died. Around him, she could pretend everything was normal.

Abby opened the freezer to see rows and rows of neatly wrapped packages of meat, all clearly labeled. Steaks, chops, chicken, ground beef—just what she was looking for. She set a package of ground beef in the sink to thaw.

The first thing on the day's agenda was to call the library and tell them that she would have to pass on their job offer. She wasn't going anywhere until she got the pool fenced in.

Abby went to her office and phoned the library, and after that several fencing companies. She set up three appointments for bids that same afternoon.

She took a long shower, then spent the next two hours getting acquainted with her office and its equipment, all the while keeping her eye on the dogs through the sliding door that opened to the patio. She needed to think about getting a proposal together for a second book. The check Mallory had given her was more than enough to see her comfortably through the next two years if she didn't earn a dime doing anything else, but it was also the only money she had for emergencies or a nest egg.

Before Connor's death, she'd toyed with an idea about a murder involving two female corporate icons, but now her thoughts turned to what she and Steve had talked about. She jotted some notes down on a piece of paper and did her usual clustering technique to get her brain working. Three hours later she had a succinct working outline for a new mystery titled *Canine Capers*. For research, she figured all she had to do was talk to Steve. His years of experience as a vet would provide her with more than enough detailed information.

She spent the rest of the afternoon tidying things up and familiarizing herself with her new home. By the time she was finished, one thing was clear: The white carpet would have to go . . . quickly. She couldn't bear looking at it. With all these dogs, she could think of only two kinds of flooring that would hold up to the kind of accidents that were bound to happen: ceramic tile or vinyl.

She spent an hour outside with the dogs, getting to know their names, petting them, and brushing them. Then it was into the kitchen with Beemer and Olivia, to look for a meatloaf recipe. When she was finished putting everything together, carrots and potatoes lined the sides of the baking pan just the way the cookbook said to do it. Strips of bacon as well as a fine dusting of sesame seeds covered the top. It was a half hour before Steve was due to arrive, and suddenly she realized she was short on time and that the kitchen was an unholy mess. Pots and pans, potato and carrot peelings seemed to be everywhere. "Who knows. I might turn into a gourmet chef one of these days."

Olivia snorted, and Beemer cuffed her on the hip with his paw, at which point Olivia nipped his leg. Beemer howled his outrage. Abby grinned. "We need to get along here, kids. Be nice."

A sudden urge to call Connor and tell him she'd just made her first meat loaf brought tears to Abby's eyes. She was never going to be able to tell him anything ever again. Not about her first attempts at cooking, about the dogs she'd adopted, or about the idea for her new book. She wiped her tears on the sleeve of her shirt.

Beemer must have sensed her unhappiness and nudged her hand. She turned around, sat down on the floor beside him, and pulled him into her lap. Olivia struggled up from under the table, barking jealously.

Her tears vanished. How could she feel sad when she was surrounded by so much love?

"Treat time," she said, blowing her nose with gusto. She grabbed the bag of Snausages and headed outside. She'd no sooner finished passing out the last Snausage when the telephone rang. Abby found an extension on the patio table.

"Hello, Abby, this is Mallory. I accepted that promotion I was telling you about, and I've moved back to South Carolina. I was hoping we could get together soon. That is, if the invitation is still open and you want me to teach you how to cook."

"I—" She hesitated, not sure what to say. So much had happened these last ten days. Nothing was the same. Now she even had to wonder if Mallory had been sincere in her intentions to be sisters again, or if there was some other reason—some dark, sinister reason why Mallory wanted to be back in her life.

"Abby, are you okay? Do you want me to call back later?"

"No," she said, thinking quickly. "I'm fine, and yes, the invitation is still open. How about tomorrow, say . . . early *afternoonish?*"

"Sounds good to me. I'll bring you my favorite recipe book."

"Okay, see you then." As she lowered the handset, she heard Mallory's voice calling her name.

"What? What is it?"

"I need directions to your house."

"Oh, of course you do. You take highway . . ."

Chapter Eleven

Abby sat alone, savoring the warm November sunshine. Today was going to be a wonderful day. She could feel it in her bones and wasn't sure why. Was it because Mallory was coming for lunch as well as bringing the lunch with her? In spite of Mallory's valiant efforts, Abby couldn't cook any better now than she could five months earlier. "I'm a writer," she told the dogs sitting around her. "Not a cook!"

She laughed out loud as she thought back to the day Mallory first called and invited herself over. She really had let her imagination run away with her, thinking Mallory was planning to do her harm. Abby's suspicions were put to rest when Mallory explained why she'd been in the restaurant the day Connor died. Her flight had been canceled, and she couldn't get another one until the next afternoon. She'd found a hotel room near the airport and was just finishing breakfast in the hotel cafe when the whole Mitchell family came in and sat down. As for the other two times Abby thought she'd seen Mallory—Mallory indicated she was as perplexed as Abby.

Abby shuddered to think what her life would be like today without her sister. In just five short months, she'd become the kind of older sister Abby had always dreamed of. A sister to share the good times and the bad. A sister whose shoulder she could cry on. A sister with whom she could share her most intimate secrets. A sister she could love.

She realized now there was truth in what Bunny had said—that one day everything would be all right again. Time was indeed healing her pain.

Her life was full, and she had a lot to look forward to. The holidays were coming soon, and her agent had called just that morning to tell her that her first book had been picked up by a book club and was being optioned for a movie of the week. And then there was Steve. They'd started out as friends but after last night—That kiss! She didn't think she would ever look at him quite the same way again. Who would have thought a veterinarian could kiss like that?

Was Connor fading from her memory—something she promised herself would never happen? No, she told herself. He would always be there. Always.

Beemer barked, as Olivia scurried to his side. Abby laughed. The unlikely duo were inseparable. Abby laughed again when she looked across what had once been a well-manicured back yard. It looked straggly with winter approaching. What little grass was left had turned brown, and as far as the eye could see there were holes—dug by the dogs to bury their precious bones and chews. There were just seven dogs left, including Beemer and Olivia. Steve had found good homes for the others. The animals pretty much had the run of the place now that they were housebroken. A doggie door had helped speed things along. For the most part, they liked hanging out in the kitchen or her office, and that was all right with her. She considered them her family. Even Mallory was taken with Olivia and brought toys and chews when she came to visit.

Beemer tensed suddenly before running to the gate, Olivia on his trail. He barked again when Mallory reached over the fence to unhook the latch. "Yoohoo! You out here, Abby?"

"On the patio. Beautiful day, isn't it?"

"Gorgeous."

"What's for lunch?"

"I was going to make something last night, but I had to work late so it's pastrami on rye for me, liverwurst and onion on rye for you. Deli pickles, chips, and two Cokes. Do you want to eat out here or in the house? I brought the dogs some pig ears so they won't pester us while we eat."

"You finally got the hang of it, huh?"

"So tell me, how did the big date go?"

"Steve kissed me and it was . . . nice. Really nice. I like him but—"

"Yeah, I know, he isn't Connor. That's why his name is Steve. Give him and yourself a chance. A kiss isn't a commitment, you know. Just be open and enjoy his company."

"I turned in *Canine Capers* last week. My editor read it over the weekend and said this book moves me out of the bush leagues. There's only one problem."

"What kind of problem?" Mallory said, biting into a crunchy pickle.

"They want a picture for the back of the book jacket."

"Oh. Wait a minute. What's wrong with a profile or a silhouette?"

"They don't do that. They always want full face," she said with a sigh. "How would you like to be Bailey James?" Abby blurted.

"What?"

Abby put her sandwich down and sat forward. The offhanded thought suddenly seemed like a damn good idea. "You could, you know, Mallory," she said with all sincerity. "Neither my agent nor my editor has ever seen me. So far all my business dealings have been done by phone, e-mail or fax. They have no clue what I look like." An indulgent smile told Abby that Mallory wasn't taking her seriously. "They want me to go to a photographer in New York, but first they want to send me to one of the expensive salons where they do your hair and you know, a makeover." She saw Mallory's eyebrows arch. "I won't do it. I just can't open myself up to that. They'll have to forget the picture unless . . . unless I can talk you into pretending to be me."

"Abby, I thought you said you had a handle on all that. The makeup covers the mark."

"I do have a handle on it. It's not the picture so much that bothers me. It's—I'm a private person, Mallory. Sort of an introvert, where you, you're an extrovert. You would like all that glamour stuff. Come on, admit it, you would, wouldn't you?"

"Sure, but—"

"My agent thinks that if the first book does as well as they expect, the publisher will want to send me on tour with *Canine Capers*. TV appearances and stuff. I would absolutely hate it, every minute of it, flying from city to city, dinners with people I don't know . . . It would be worth it to me to pay you to do it. That way I could stay here and write more books."

Mallory stared at her sister as if trying to read her mind. "But—But this is what you've been waiting for," she stammered. "You're a successful writer now, and you deserve all that's going to come your way. If I pretended to be you, I'd be stealing your thunder."

Abby made a rude noise with her mouth. "I don't give a damn about thunder. All I want is the money and the satisfaction of knowing that people are enjoying my books. Look, Mallory, you'd be doing me a huge favor. Think about it, it's really no different from me hiring an assistant to help me with fan mail, the research, and all the other stuff—As a matter of fact that's exactly what you could do. Between book promotions you could work as my assistant."

"I have a job, remember?"

"But I bet it isn't as much fun and doesn't pay as well as the one I'm offering."

"Even if I agreed, it wouldn't work," Mallory said, upending her Coke can as if to say that was the end of the subject.

Abby wasn't about to let Mallory dismiss her idea so easily. "I think it would. I think it would work wonderfully. Once you read the books and discuss them with me, you'll be able to answer any question they throw at you. As to discussing money and contracts, all you have to do is listen and tell them you need time to think about whatever it is they want. We can make this work, Mallory."

"Oh, Abby, I don't know. . . ."

"You could move in here with me. God knows the house is big enough. You'd have to cook, though, and help out with the dogs. Will you at least think about it?"

Mallory's expression stilled and grew serious. "I guess I just don't understand why you want me of all people to do this. What about your friend Bunny?"

"Bunny isn't right for the job. You are."

"If I did it, does that mean you'd hide from the world forever?"

"It's not hiding. It's protecting my privacy. I'd like your answer as soon as possible. I need to get to work on the next book, and I've got a lot of research to do. They want the completed manuscript in six months."

"Hold on here. If I'm pretending to be you and doing all this promotional stuff, when am I supposed to find the time to write? It doesn't pencil out, Abby."

"They'll believe whatever we want them to believe. You just take a laptop with you and let them think you're writing between interviews."

"What about Donovan and Carol? You know they'd resent my living here with you. I don't want to start a family feud. You've always been so close. Think what my living here would do to your relationship."

"You're my sister, my only living flesh-and-blood relative. If they can't understand that I love you and want you in my life, then . . . that's their problem."

"If only they'd give me a chance to prove to them I've changed, that I'm not the hateful little girl I used to be. People *can* and *do* change. Surely they realize that."

"I know. If you want to know the truth, I think Donovan would love to make nice. It's Carol who refuses even to discuss the possibility. It's weird."

Mallory stared blankly at one of the dogs. "Look, Abby, Donovan and Carol aside, I don't know anything about the book-publishing business, but I do work with people on a daily basis. What happens if somehow it gets out that I impersonated you? Don't you think your readers will feel you betrayed them, cheated them? If you're moving into the big time, as you say, maybe you need to give this some more thought. What's wrong with a profile shot? Insist on it."

Abby's face turned glum. "I guess that means you don't want to do it, huh?"

"That's not it, Abby. I don't want you to have regrets later on. We're just starting to be comfortable with one another. We were separated for a lot of years. We can't get those years back, and I don't want to ruin what we have now. It took me a long time to get to this point. But if it's what you really want . . . I'll do it. I also want to go on record as saying it's not a good idea. When do you want me to start?"

"As soon as they call me and tell me they want me to come to New York."

"Okay, it's a deal."

"That's great, Mallory. You won't be sorry. We need to discuss money."

"Later. Right now, I have to get back on the road." She

gathered up hers and Abby's trash and tossed it into the trash can. "I enjoyed lunch as always. By the way, Abby, I'm awfully glad that you, at least, were willing to let me prove . . . to show you . . . you know what I'm trying to say."

"That's because I have an open mind. Like you said, people can and do change. You're nothing like the big sister I used to know."

"So, what's your new book going to be about? Murder and mayhem, body bags and grisly accidents? One of these days I'll have to tell you about this plot I have for a surefire bestseller, or is it blockbuster?"

"Both. What kind of story?" Abby asked, her interest piqued.

"A real-life story. A case I discovered when I was researching insurance files. I suppose, in a way, you could say I found it by accident and then again, maybe I was meant to find it just so I could share it with you. It's a case that has never been resolved and is still on the books. Big payouts always stay on the books. When you're dry and can't come up with a plot, we'll talk about it." She looked down at her watch. "Whoa, I'm going to be late. See you next week. Call me if you need me to do anything. I won't give my notice till we're certain this is a sure thing, okay?"

"Mallory! That's a dirty trick, leaving me in suspense like that. Drive carefully."

At the gate, Mallory turned, and shouted, "You didn't tell me what kind of kisser Steve is."

Abby laughed. "It's none of your business."

"Wow! That great, huh?" Mallory laughed.

Abby smiled as she finished cleaning up. She was on her way inside when the phone rang. Friend or foe, she wondered as she raced to get it before the answering machine picked up. She was breathless when she said hello.

"Hi, honey, it's Carol. How are you? I've been thinking of

you for days now. Donovan wants to know if we can plan on you for Thanksgiving dinner."

"Oh, Aunt Carol, hi!" Abby paused a moment to gather her thoughts and decide what to say. "I can't. I'm trying to put together a new book proposal," she said, knowing Carol had no idea what the statement entailed. "And after that, I have to go to New York," she added, hoping to forestall Carol from volunteering to bring Thanksgiving to her. She'd already promised Mallory that the two of them would have Thanksgiving together.

"How wonderful for you. I'm so disappointed, though. It won't be the same without you. We can plan on you for Christmas, surely?"

"Umm. I don't know yet. I promised Bunny I'd spend Christmas with her this year since she spent the last four Christmases with us." The truth of it was that she and Bunny had only discussed the idea, but Abby needed the excuse. "I thought you'd be going to the mountains this year."

It wasn't Abby's imagination—the chill she heard in Carol's voice when she said, "We were hoping you'd come with us. Donovan is going to be so disappointed."

On one hand Abby felt bad for making up excuses to avoid seeing Carol and Donovan, but on the other hand she couldn't forgive them for not giving Mallory a chance to show them that she'd changed. It wasn't fair.

"I'm sorry, Carol. I really am. I hope you understand." All of a sudden the dogs started barking. Abby looked out the window and saw them streaking toward the back fence. It was probably the neighbor's cat.

"My God, Abby, how do you stand it?"

"Stand what? The dogs? I love them, Aunt Carol. I can't tell you how much company they are."

"You don't let them in the house, do you?"

She'd never gotten up the courage to tell her aunt she allowed the dogs in the house. It would only upset her, and things were bad enough as they were. They had become more estranged since Carol found out Mallory was back in Abby's life.

"Actually, I do, but they're very well trained, and I had a doggie door installed so they can go in and out whenever they want." She heard Carol gasp and knew it was time to hang up. "Listen, Aunt Carol, I've got a lot of work to do yet today so I've got to get off the phone. But I'll get back to you in a few days with an answer on the Christmas thing, okay? Thanks for calling."

Long after she'd hung up, Abby sat by the phone and questioned her feelings toward Carol. It wasn't the first time she'd made up excuses to get off the phone or to avoid seeing her. When she thought back, she realized she'd been doing it since before Connor's death. Resentment concerning Mallory was part of it, but there was more to it than that.

She remembered a conversation she'd had with Connor, just before her graduation. He'd been adamant when he insisted that Donovan and Carol didn't like him, especially Carol. And he'd asked her to watch them throughout the day.

She had, and he'd been half-right. Donovan's actions had seemed typical of every father who thought he might be losing his daughter to another man. But Carol—Carol had treated Connor with a sort of veiled contempt and shown a possessiveness toward Abby that had made her wary. After Connor died, Abby had found herself resenting Carol's phony sympathy. Later, of course, she'd begun to wonder if Carol hadn't used the house to lure her away from Connor.

Controlling—that was the word Steve had used to define Carol furnishing, accessorizing, and stocking the house. Carol had always been a take-charge person, arranging things, seeing to this and that. It was just her way. But was it controlling? Was Carol trying to run her life?

Maybe she should talk to Donovan. No. If she did that,

Donovan might think she was ungrateful, and if not ungrateful, he was sure to think she was exaggerating. In his eyes, Carol was the perfect wife and mother, a wife and mother who could do no wrong.

Maybe what she needed to do was just exactly what she'd been doing—make herself less available, less agreeable to Carol's plans. She could put some added distance between herself and Carol simply by leaving her answering machine on all the time and monitoring the calls. That way she could talk to her when she wanted to, not when Carol wanted to.

"It's okay, Beemer, I'm not going to cry. Don't look so sad, Olivia. Everything is going to be okay. I promise."

Chapter Twelve

"Are you ever going to relax, Abby? For God's sake, in two days it'll be Christmas. Why are you so uptight?" Mallory asked as she emptied the dishwasher.

"I'm remembering . . . other Christmases . . . with you and Mama . . . with Connor," Abby responded with a sad smile. "When I think about Connor, I think about Carol and Donovan. I told them I was spending Christmas with Bunny." Feeling a chill, Abby rubbed her arms. "You know what, Mallory? My feelings for them have changed. I used to . . . adore them, especially Donovan. But these last three years . . . I don't know. I feel like a Judas."

Mallory closed the dishwasher, looked around the kitchen to see that it was tidy before she sat down across the table from Abby. "You know, Abby, we really never talked about why you decided to put some distance between yourself and them. I hope to God I'm not the cause of it."

"It didn't start with you. It started quite a while ago, while I was in my second year of college. As I became more and more independent, Carol became more and more controlling, and Donovan supported her. I got to the point where I stopped telling her what I was doing so she couldn't add her nickel's worth." She gazed at the china Carol had bought for her and stacked in the glass-fronted cupboards, and wondered what anyone could have given her for a wedding gift that she didn't already have. "As far as you're concerned, Mallory, I'd be a liar if I said you weren't one of the reasons why things have gotten worse between us. They threw you away, just like Mama threw me away. Like people who throw dogs and cats away. Carol and Donovan allow all their friends and business associates to think they are these compassionate, charitable people, and yet they won't even give you a chance to show them you've changed." She stared down at the tabletop, her heart heavy. "Another reason is . . . Did I tell you that I think Carol might have used this house as bait to lure me away from living in New York with Connor?"

"No, but that wouldn't surprise me. She's very manipulative."

Abby groaned and slumped over the table. "I'm just starting to put two and two together. Carol has dominated and manipulated me all my life. This house and the things in it are testimony to her achievement. I use the shampoo she bought because she said it was good for my hair. I take the vitamins she filled my medicine cabinet with because she said they were what I needed. The way the house is laid out and decorated—She always wanted me to socialize more, to entertain. I'd say that this is definitely a party house, wouldn't you? There are other things, too, but I think you get the idea." She sat back, out of steam. "The day before Connor died, he told me there was something about Carol that wasn't quite right. He tried to define what it was, but in the end he couldn't. He finally said it was just a bad feeling he had. Ever since then, I've been more aware of her behavior, and I have to agree with him. But like him, I can't put my finger on what it is." She sighed with frustration.

Mallory frowned. "You know, it's funny that you feel Carol manipulated you, because that's exactly what Mama did to me. She told me what to say, when to say it, whom to like, and whom to hate." She leaned forward and looked at Abby straight on. "All those years I spent hating you—I never knew the reason why until a few years ago. It was because of Mama. She didn't like you because you weren't perfect, so she didn't want *me* to like you. It wasn't until I was around fourteen, when a new shrink came on board at the school, that I really got the help I needed. She worked with me daily instead of weekly. She cared about me, and I guess I sensed that, so I started to cooperate, where before I just sort of skated. Constance was her name. She cried with me, laughed with me, held me. She even hypnotized me a few times. I'd like you to meet her someday. I thought about inviting her for the holidays but she has her own family. Maybe Easter or the Fourth of July."

"Sure," Abby said, meaning it. "This is your house now, too."

"No. This is not my house, Abby. This is your house, given to you by Donovan and Carol, and," she said, exaggerating a shiver, "I do not look forward to the day when they find out I'm living here." She rolled her eyes. "By the way, what did you think about the newspaper's write-up on Donovan? They said he's the biggest contractor in the Carolinas. In the entire South for that matter."

Abby shrugged. "I pretty much already knew that. I've always known he was wealthy. He works very hard, Mallory. I just wish he didn't work so hard to please Carol. I think he would have been there for you throughout your schooling if it hadn't been for her. I remember more than one occasion when he tried to talk to Carol about you, to reason with her. I remember, too, that Carol always refused to listen. I'm thankful to Connor for making me more aware of their behavior. It's been enlightening to say the least."

"I could use a drink. We have wine, don't we?"

"Are you kidding? Didn't you see that climate-controlled wine cellar Donovan built? Go down there and bring some up. I don't know anything about wine other than it relaxes me. Connor knew all about wine. God, I miss him."

Mallory stared at Abby as if she wanted to say something. Instead, she got up and opened the door to the basement.

Abby stood at the top of the stairs and talked to Mallory's back as she went down the steps. "I'm still wondering why Connor didn't tell me about his heart condition. We were together four years. You would think he would have mentioned it . . . unless there wasn't anything to mention."

Connor had been on her mind a lot recently, but she'd only recently tried to make sense of the details of his death. She'd told him everything there was to tell about herself and thought he'd done the same. And then there was the fact that just prior to starting his new job, he'd had a physical and every single test had come back A-OK.

Mallory bounded up the stairs, a wine bottle in her hand. "Maybe he didn't want to worry you," she offered. "Or maybe he just didn't think it was worth mentioning." She closed the door behind her. "Not to change the subject but— What's going on between you and Steve?"

"We're just friends right now." Abby thought about their first and only date and their good-night kiss. Having just talked about Connor, thinking about Steve and what he was beginning to mean to her came hard. "He's nice, don't you think?"

Mallory searched the drawers until she found a corkscrew. "He's *very* nice. And handsome. And intelligent. And best of all, he really likes you." She struggled with the cork, then poured the wine into exquisite wineglasses. "Baccarat. Nothing but the best," she said with a grimace. "A hundred bucks a pop."

"For one glass!" Abby was outraged. "How do you know all this stuff?"

Mallory held the glass up to her nose and inhaled the bouquet. "I started out as an insurance investigator. I was in all kinds of homes, rich, poor, middle-class. I had to be observant. I also had to catalog stuff. Sometimes it was interesting, and sometimes it was incredibly boring. Constance had me on a work program with the same insurance company the last two years of school. They liked me and asked me to go full-time when I was finished at Argone. You'd be surprised what you can learn from insurance files. Here's to us. Sisters," Mallory said, holding her glass high.

A chill ran up Abby's arms when the phone in the kitchen rang. The sisters looked at one another. Abby shook her head.

The answering machine clicked on. Mallory turned to add more wine to her glass when Donovan's brisk, cool voice knifed through the kitchen. "Merry Christmas, Princess. I just wanted to call and say Carol and I will be stopping by in a few hours. Bobby talked us into it. If you're not home, as I suspect, we'll leave your Christmas presents on the doorstep. We're going to spend Christmas in Orlando this year. Carol thought it would be something different to do. We're taking a few of Bobby's friends with us. We love you."

Abby set down her wineglass. "Get your stuff, we're taking the dogs to Steve's house. Donovan's full of hot air. He was on his cell phone. They're probably already on the way here. We have to turn everything off to make it look like I'm gone."

"Abby, stop it! Listen to yourself. You're running away. This is *your* house. They gave it to you. Whatever's wrong, you have to confront them with it. You can't keep avoiding them."

Abby crumpled. "I don't know why, but I can't confront them. Not until I sort things out in my head. In the meantime, I don't want to see them. I told them I was spending Christmas with Bunny. I let them think I was going to her house when the truth is she's coming here. So explain to me why they're coming here when they think I'm away. Huh?"

"They must have known you were lying. You aren't a very good liar, Abby. If you want to leave, we'll leave. I just don't think it's a good idea. And there's the matter of Bunny. What time is she supposed to be here?"

"Oh, my God. I'll call her on her cell phone to tell her to meet me at Steve's house."

"I'll follow you over to Steve's. If Donovan sees my car outside, I'm sure he'll recognize it since he's the one who gave it to me," Mallory said, sticking the cork back into the wine bottle.

Abby slammed the door to the dishwasher, wondering if the exquisite wineglasses broke. "What? You never mentioned that to me."

"It never came up before now."

"But I thought they all but abandoned you."

"Donovan visited me a few times, but they were always short visits—just minutes really—and very impersonal. I'd like to think that he did it because he cares for me, but probably he did it out of a sense of responsibility." Mallory put the wine bottle on the countertop next to an unopened liter of Coke. "You realize, don't you, Abby, that you're making a choice here. You're choosing me over Carol and Donovan. It's not too late to change your mind."

"Why would I want to do that?" Abby glanced around the kitchen to make sure everything was tidy and in place so as not to give her away. "Come on, Olivia," she said, opening the garage door. "You, too, Beemer, round up the others. Let's go for a ride."

As soon as Abby had both dogs in the garage, Mallory put a hand on her sister's shoulder. "Think about this, Abby. Think about what you're doing. I don't want you regretting your decision later."

Abby whirled around. "You're my sister. The only thing I regret is that it took us so long to get back together." She threw her arms around Mallory and hugged her. "Donovan and Carol have each other and Bobby. I never really belonged to them. I wanted to call Donovan Dad a million times, but I could never get the word past my lips. You and I are just now finding our way. Maybe it was supposed to happen like this. You're all I have, Mallory, and I love you. I've always loved you."

Tears rolled down Mallory's cheeks. "I swear before God, that is the nicest thing anyone has ever said to me in my entire life. I love you, too, Abby, I really do. Okay, you call Steve and Bunny, and I'll go around the house and make sure all my stuff is out of sight." She started toward the dining room, then stopped and turned around. "Wait a minute! What are we worried about? They won't be coming in the house."

"I wouldn't be so sure about that. I'll bet Carol still has a key." She locked the back door and jiggled the handle to make sure the door was secure. "You know what I think we should do? I think we should drop the dogs off at Steve's house, come back here, and wait outside in the dark and watch to see what they do."

Mallory giggled. "You sound like a detective out of one of your own books."

"I do, don't I?" Abby grinned.

In less than ten minutes all the dogs were secure in the cargo area of the Jeep.

"You go out the front door and set the alarm," Abby instructed Mallory. "I'll go through the garage and get the rest of the dogs. Boy, this is going to rile them. They aren't used to going in the car. They're going to be scared. Steve will calm them down once we get there. He's got this magical, I don't know, call it presence, when it comes to animals. He's just great."

"He's great, huh? That's a step up from a little earlier when you said he was *nice*," Mallory drawled, winking at her sister.

Twenty minutes later, Steve drove them back and parked his car in a grove of trees next to Abby's house. "I think you two are crazy," he grumbled, switching off his headlights. "We're going to freeze our asses off. This is what guys do in a duck blind. Long underwear would go a long way right now." He blew his breath into his hands and rubbed them together. "Maybe your adoptive father wasn't calling from a cell phone after all."

"He was. Trust me." Abby moved up close to him and wrapped her arm around his. "I told you to dress warm. You're a *wuss*, Steve. You don't hear me or Mallory complaining, do you?" Abby grumbled.

"That's because both of you are crazy and don't know any better. Uh-oh, I see headlights coming. We better get out of the car now, or we risk them seeing the interior lights when we open the doors."

To a casual observer it would have looked like a Chinese fire drill as the three of them jumped out of the car and ran around it to the clump of evergreens.

"This way," Abby said, pointing to a tall hedge that flanked her house. "Two cars," she whispered. "Carol's probably driving one and Donovan the other." They ducked behind the hedge just in time.

Three pairs of eyes strained in the darkness.

The two cars pulled into the driveway. Carol got out of one, and Donovan climbed out of the other. "The house is dark, Carol. I told you she wouldn't be here," Donovan said. "The dogs aren't barking, so that has to mean she boarded them and went away like she said she was going to do. It's getting late, and I'm tired."

"Open the front door, Donovan," Carol ordered.

"Are you crazy? This is Abby's house. I'm not committing a B&E on Abby's house. Abby is of age, and she's on her own. That's the end of it."

Behind the hedge, Mallory and Abby clasped hands.

"Maybe I was wrong about him," Abby whispered, only to have Steve shush her.

"C'mon, Mom," Bobby's young voice piped up from inside the car Donovan had been driving.

Carol stood on the steps, her arms crossed. She looked every inch a commanding general. "I spent a lot of time to say nothing of money on this house. I'm not leaving until I see what she's done to it. Or should I say what those dogs of hers have done to it? Not only that, I suspect she's hiding something from us, and that's why she's been avoiding us. Once I see the inside, I'll know if my suspicions are right or not."

Abby and Mallory gave each other questioning looks in the darkness.

Donovan put his hands on his hips. "All right, Carol. I can't stop you, but I'll be damned if I'll go in there with you."

"Fine."

"To tell you the truth, I hope the alarm goes off and the police come. I'd like to see you explain yourself to them," Donovan snapped.

Abby's eyes widened. She'd been so sure Carol knew the code she hadn't even considered the consequences if she didn't.

Steve shook her hand and gave her a look that said he was wondering the same thing. With a confidence she didn't feel, Abby whispered, "Wait," and hoped she was right.

"The alarm won't go off, Donovan, unless Abby has had the code changed."

"She could have changed it, Carol. She could have changed the locks on the doors, too. Come on, we don't belong here."

Steve looked at Abby. "Did you?" he whispered.

"No, but now I wish I had," she whispered back, making a fist and pounding the air.

"Give me the master keys, Donovan," Carol demanded coldly. Her voice indicated to Abby that she was very sure of herself . . . and of Donovan.

Abby's mouth gaped when she saw Donovan hand over the keys. So much for the kind thoughts she'd had about him a moment ago.

Mallory whispered in Abby's ear. "You know what I said earlier about not looking forward to the day they find out I'm living here?" At Abby's nod, she went on. "Well, I think that day has come. If she goes into my room and starts snooping around, she's going to know I've moved in. My name is on a lot of my stuff." She gritted her teeth. "Boy, is the fur going to fly! Uh-oh, there she goes."

Donovan walked back to his car and stood leaning against the passenger door.

"Excuse me for my ignorance," Steve said, turning Abby toward him. "But I'm a little in the dark here. Would you two mind telling me what the hell is going on? Why all this subterfuge?"

"I'll explain it all later," Abby muttered, putting him off when she saw the rooms light up one by one. "God, wait till she sees what the dogs did to her white carpeting." Abby pulled her lips back from her teeth. "And the dining-room table," she said, seeing the chewed table legs in her mind's eye.

"And the yard!" Steve added with a grimace.

"I hate it that she's probably going to go in my office," Abby said, thinking about the personal and financial things she had lying around. *There's a lesson to be learned here,* she thought. "This is giving me a real creepy feeling. There go the living-room lights. Aah!" she gasped. "She's checking the presents. Where are the presents Donovan said they were bringing me?"

Mallory sniffled. "This reminds me of the year I left the presents on your front doorstep. I sat in my car and cried for a whole hour. I wanted you to be home so bad so I could come in. I wanted to belong, to be a part of your Christmas."

Abby shrugged her sister's arm from around her shoulder and put her arm around her. "You belong now. That was a long time ago. Shhh, she's coming out."

"Well, are you satisfied?" Donovan called out. "I want to tell you I think that's about the lowest thing you've ever pulled, and you've pulled some good ones."

"Shut up, Donovan. At least now I know why Abby's been avoiding us," she snarled. "It's Mallory. Mallory is living with her. How could Abby betray me like this? I think you've known all along, Donovan. You betrayed me, too. I've always had the feeling that if it came to a choice between those two girls and me, they'd win."

Abby couldn't believe what she was hearing. Carol was jealous of her and Mallory. Jealous!

Donovan shook his head as if he, too, was incredulous. "It's Abby's home," he said in a reasonable tone. "If she wants Mallory to live with her, that's her business and only her business. Mallory *is* her sister for God's sake."

"All the money I spent on that house— The dogs have ruined everything! It looks like a pigpen!" she said, completely ignoring what Donovan had said. "I never thought I'd live to see the day when I'd say Abby's just like her deranged sister. It just goes to prove blood is thicker than water. Abby was never the least bit grateful when it came to this house and everything I did for her. She's changed."

"Yes, I imagine she has changed in more ways than one. She's suffered the loss of a loved one, and she's grown up. Did you really think you could keep her *your* little girl forever? I know you'll deny it, but you thought that damn birthmark of hers would tie her to you for the rest of her life, didn't you?"

"I don't know what you're talking about," Carol flashed back, wrapping her coat tightly around her shaking body.

"The hell you don't. I remember how surprised you were when you first learned about Connor. You didn't think any man would ever bother to look beyond that birthmark to find out what kind of person our Abby was. Then, when things looked like they were getting serious between them and that Abby might move to New York, you started pressuring me to build this house. I never should have gone along with you, Carol. But you make life so damn miserable when you don't get your way. I should have been a man and—"

Carol waved a hand to interrupt him. "You never liked Connor any more than I did, so don't pretend you did now that he's dead."

"I didn't have anything against Connor other than the fact that he was taking my place in Abby's life. I was jealous. I admit it. I never in my life thought I would have those kinds of feelings—I felt like I was her *real* father, and I was losing her."

Abby's hand flew to her mouth to stop herself from crying out.

"Well, obviously she doesn't share your feelings," Carol said viciously, flinging her words back at him. "When someone dies, you grieve and you get on with your life. You don't turn against your family. It's Mallory's influence that has done all this. I bet Mallory planned all along to find a way to get even with us for sending her away."

Abby reached for Mallory's hand and squeezed it. "They're just words, don't pay any attention," Abby whispered reassuringly.

"You're sick, Carol. Really sick. Mallory is a well-adjusted girl and is living a good, productive life, no thanks to us."

Carol's face registered surprise. "How the hell do you know that, Donovan?"

"I've managed to keep my eye on her in spite of you," he barked in return.

"Mom. Dad. Stop it," Bobby pleaded, yelling out the car window.

Carol swung around. "Close the window and be quiet, Bobby. This is between your father and me."

"But what about the presents?" the boy asked, holding one up for her to see. "Do you want me to take them inside?"

"You can dump them on the ground for all I care," Carol said through clenched teeth.

"But, Mom . . ."

"What a bitch!" Steve seethed from his position behind the hedge.

Bobby opened the car door and carried the presents into the house. A moment later he came back out and got into the car.

As soon as Bobby had closed the door, Donovan said, "You've done your damage, Carol. Let's go. This is the end of it."

"You bet it is. I loved Abby as if she were my own daughter. Maybe more. I don't ever want you to mention her name or her wacko sister's name to me again." She stormed down the steps toward her car.

Donovan watched her, disbelief written across his face. "Aren't you going to turn the lights off and lock the door?"

"No, I'm not. I didn't see even one small gift under that tacky-looking Christmas tree that had any of our names on it. I saw a pile for Mallory, Bunny, and someone named Steve. There wasn't even one for Bobby."

"Oooh," Abby bristled. "Obviously she didn't look in the back bedroom, or she would have seen them."

Donovan intercepted Carol at her car and reached for his keys, dangling from his wife's hand. "You can go to Orlando by yourself, Carol. I'm going home, and I'm taking Bobby and his friends with me." He turned around and started up the steps to the house.

"The guy has some spit to him," Steve said as he shifted his weight to a more comfortable position.

Carol started her car, then peeled around the circular drive, her headlights shining briefly on the hedge.

With a hint of laughter in his voice, Steve asked, "Are you the deranged wacko Carol was talking about, Mallory?"

"I'm afraid so," Mallory whispered, watching the lights go off one by one.

Minutes later, Donovan exited the house, locked the door, and drove away. When his taillights disappeared into the night, the three of them walked out from behind the hedge.

"I'm going to sell this house. Do you have any idea of how I feel right now? I feel violated. In a million years I would never have believed Carol would . . . could . . . do what she just did."

"No, you're not," Steve said, putting his arm around her to calm her down. "But you do need to change the code on your alarm system and get new locks on your doors."

Abby took one look at Mallory's tear-filled eyes and stopped her before she could go inside. "Listen to me, Mallory. The things Carol said, they were just words. Hateful words from a hateful person. They can only hurt you if you allow them to hurt you."

"I know," Mallory said, smiling through her tears. "It's just that it upsets me to think that I used to be just like her. Look how I hurt you with words when we were little. You still remember all the hateful things I did to you. There's nothing I can do to repair those memories. You'll have to live with them for the rest of your life, and so will I. I'm sorry, Abby. I'm sorry I hurt you."

"I know," Abby said, putting her arms around her sister. "I know."

Later, after they'd brought the dogs home, they plugged in the Christmas-tree lights and made a cozy fire. While Mallory was in the kitchen opening and pouring wine, Steve caught hold of Abby and took her in his arms.

"You can drop the act now," Steve said, smiling down at her. "I know you're hurting because of what your adoptive father said."

Abby leaned into him and laid her cheek against his shoulder. "It never occurred to me that Carol thought my birthmark would tie me to her or that no man would . . ." Her voice cracked. It was too painful to repeat Donovan's words. "Donovan's right," she said a moment later, her voice strained. "I can see it clearly now. Everything was fine between me and Carol until I started dating Connor. Am I really that ugly she . . ."

"No, dammit," Steve cut her off, then squeezed her close to him. "Don't even think such a thing. Your birthmark didn't stop Connor from loving you, and it sure as hell won't stop me. You're a beautiful woman, inside and out, Abby Mitchell, and I feel damn lucky just to know you." To prove his feelings, he kissed her, tenderly and sweetly.

Abby kissed him back with an intensity that made her pulse leap with excitement, an excitement she'd thought she would never feel again. When they broke apart, both of them were shaken from the experience. "I think I like you, Dr. Carpenter. I think I like you a lot."

"Funny you should say that, because I think I like you, too. A lot," he said, ruffling her hair.

Mallory entered the room carrying a tray. She looked calm, composed, and dewy. Abby wondered if she'd washed her face.

"If you two will excuse me, I need to check out my office. I want to see what I left out that Carol might have seen. Steve, don't forget to open the damper," she called out as she hurried down the hallway.

"I was a Boy Scout. I know all about these things."

Abby turned on the light in her office and winced at the mess she'd left. Neat, tidy, fastidious Carol must not have appreciated the orange peels, the Twinkie wrappers on the desk, the paper plates, wadded-up napkins, and empty coffee cups. Stacks of books and magazines were everywhere, some open, some chewed on the corners, while others sat in stacks ready to be used. The wastebasket was filled to overflowing, days of mail piled high on the chair. A real mess, she thought, feeling a funny sort of satisfaction as she turned off the light. She sobered immediately when she remembered how Mallory's body had trembled at Carol's ugly words.

Abby joined Mallory and Steve in the living room. "You know what? I think after I have the alarm code and locks changed, I'll install some high, wrought-iron fencing and one of those electronic gates like the celebrities use. Anyone can climb over the fence I have now. I'll have a keypad and be able to open the gates from the house or from the keypad. Then, *no one* can get in here unless I want them to come in."

"That would work," Steve said. "Not to change the subject or anything, but I have some good news I'd like to share with you two."

"Yeah? What is it?" Abby asked, sipping her wine and inadvertently thinking it didn't taste all that much better than any other wine she'd had at Steve's house, wine he'd purchased at the grocery store. So much for Carol's expertise.

"The humane society wants to build an animal shelter on the property next to the clinic, and they want me to be their nonresident vet."

"That's wonderful news, Steve. When are they going to start?"

"Next month!"

The front doorbell chimed to life. Everyone looked at each other, fearing another invasion.

"Hellllloooo! Anybody here?" Bunny's voice rang out.

Abby ran to the door and flung it open. "Bunny! Boy, am I glad to see you!"

"I followed your directions, Abby, and went to Steve's house first but nobody was there so I came on over here. What's going on?"

Abby doubled over in laughter. "You don't want to know," she managed.

"Merry Christmas, everyone!" Mallory said, holding her glass high.

Abby took that particular moment to stare into her sister's eyes—overly bright eyes, sad eyes. "Merry Christmas!"

PART FOUR

PART FOUR

Chapter Thirteen

Abby jerked to awareness, tearing her eyes from the computer screen when Olivia and Beemer let loose with simultaneous ear-piercing barks. Beemer, his ears flat against his head, his teeth bared, leaped out from under the desk, over a stack of reference books, and over Olivia, who was waddling to the window. He slammed against the glass door, then deflated the moment he saw who was standing on the other side.

"Hey, Abby, it's me," Steve said, banging on the sliding glass door to her office.

"How'd you get in here?" Abby laughed as she opened it for him.

"I climbed that damn spiky fence of yours. I'm lucky to still have my balls. I forgot the remote gizmo. I have something I want to tell you. Let's go on a picnic."

"I can't. I have to finish this chapter if I'm going to stay on schedule."

"Then why are you watching TV?"

"Because Mallory is going to be on the *Regis and Kathie Lee* show. Come on in and watch her with me. Oh, here she comes. I hope she remembers everything we discussed."

The interview questions were standard stuff: How did you get started writing? Where do you get your ideas? Is your life as exciting as your lady sleuths'? How much money do you make? Mallory answered each one with confidence and poise, saying just enough to whet the viewer's curiosity without giving anything confidential away.

"Bailey's new book, *Canine Capers,*" Kathie Lee said, holding the book up to the audience and the camera, "is in bookstores now." She turned back to Mallory. "I want to tell you if I wasn't already an animal lover, this book would have made a convert out of me. The dogs—Olivia and Beemer, right?" At Mallory's nod, she continued. "They made the book as far as I was concerned." She smiled and shook her head. "I noticed you dedicated the book to a veterinarian by the name of Dr. Steve Carpenter. Is he someone special in your life?"

"Yes, he's very special. I couldn't have written *Canine Capers* without him. He opened my eyes to the problem of pet overpopulation and the plight of homeless animals, which is, of course, the backbone of the story."

Abby looked askance at Steve and saw tears in his eyes. He reached across the space between them and took her hand in his.

"Backstage you told me a little about the book you're working on now," Kathie Lee said. "It sounded fascinating. Do you mind giving our audience a hint on the story line?"

Abby leaned forward, teeth clenched. She had no idea how Mallory was going to answer; that was one topic they hadn't discussed.

"The next book is called *Proof Positive,*" Mallory said, without blinking an eye. "It's loosely based on a real-life double murder that happened almost twenty years ago. At the time, there was no evidence of foul play, so the police didn't pursue or investigate. Consequently, the murderer, whoever he or she was, got away with it." Mallory looked out at the audience. "If I say any more, I'll give away the plot," she said, laughing.

Abby breathed a sigh of relief. She would have to give Mallory credit; she was a quick thinker.

"Do you think there's a chance your book will cause the police to do a belated investigation?" Kathie Lee asked.

Mallory shrugged. "There's always that possibility."

Watching her sister play to the audience, Abby knew she'd made the right decision in having Mallory pretend to be Bailey James. Kathie Lee wound up the interview with another plug for *Canine Capers*, then broke for a commercial. "I couldn't have done better myself," Abby said, swiveling her desk chair around to face Steve.

"I didn't know your next book was based on a real murder case," Steve said, obviously feeling left out. "Why didn't you tell me?"

Abby laughed out loud. "I don't know. I didn't think you'd be interested."

"Well, hell yes, I'm interested. And now that I know, I'm also concerned. This is heavy stuff, Abby. What if the book really does get an investigation going? And what if the killer gets worried he'll be found out and comes after you?"

"He?"

Steve waved a hand. "Or she," he qualified.

"That's very unlikely," Abby said, trying to calm him down. "The case is twenty years old. Mallory ran across it when she was still working for that insurance company. She thought it would make a great murder mystery, and I agreed. Authors do it all the time. I'll just put my own spin on it. That's why we call it fiction."

"Well, I don't like it. I don't like it at all."

Abby stood, placed her hands on Steve's shoulders, and gazed into his eyes. "Next time I want to do something wild and crazy I'll be sure to tell you first, okay?" The right side of his mouth lifted in a half smile. "Now, what's so important that you climbed over my fence, risking your life and your . . . you know, to tell me?"

"I don't know if I should tell you now," he said, pretending to be angry.

Abby clucked her tongue. "C'mon, Steve. Tell me."

"Okay, you talked me into it." He took a deep breath, then let it out in a whoosh. "I came over here to tell you that . . . I love you."

Abby let loose with an audible gasp. "You what?"

"You heard me. I love you. And you damn well know it, so don't pretend you don't."

Abby's eyes widened with disbelief. "I'm not pretending, Steve. You never said anything. You—I mean—" At a loss for words, she shrugged helplessly.

"Abby!" He stood up and pulled her up with him. "You are without a doubt the most infuriating woman I've ever had the misfortune to fall in love with."

"Really?" Her eyes flashed. "And just *how many* women have you had the misfortune of falling in love with, Dr. Carpenter?"

"Enough," he countered, with a teasing grin.

"Infuriating, huh? I like that," she said, teasing him back. She had always loved the way they teased each other. Her relationship with Connor had been totally different, more serious in nature.

He wrapped his arms around her. "I hope I'm right in thinking you love me, too."

She smiled and nodded, her heart swelling with love. It was time to let the past go. Time to let her heart dictate what she'd been feeling for a long time.

"Look, Abby. I don't want to push you or anything, but I'm sick and tired of waiting for you to invite me into your bed. We've known each other for a long time now, and I've respected your mourning period for Connor, but I love you, and I want to *make* love to you. Here. Now." He bent his head and nuzzled her neck.

"Steve," she said, pulling away. "It's ten-thirty in the morning. I look like who done it and ran. I haven't even had my shower yet." She looked at him and grinned. "I want you as much as you want me, but I want it to be the right time and place and this isn't it. Maybe it's a girl thing. Maybe it's anticipation. I just know I want it to be right, and this isn't right for me."

"You look just fine to me, and we can take a shower together afterward."

"But—But—No!" she said, shaking her head. "I want our first time to—you know—be something to remember, to cherish. I'm not saying this wouldn't be completely right. It's just . . . I wasn't expecting this . . . At least not right now. I don't want a wham-barn-thank-you-ma'am kind of thing." The words were no sooner out of her mouth than she wished she hadn't said them.

Steve's brows pulled together in a deep frown. "Thanks, Abby, but I—"

"Steve, I didn't mean to insult you. What I meant was, I want our first time to be romantic. Come on now. Look at us. Here I am in my sweats and here you are in your lab coat, or whatever you call it. And it's not even noon yet."

"Okay," he said, holding up his hand in surrender. "I get the message. You want me to romance you with flowers and wine and candlelight, right?"

"I'll do the wine and candlelight," she offered.

"Okay, then—"

"Now wait a minute," she said, stalling him. "There's something you should know first. I'm thinking of going for this new surgery," she said. "It's kind of experimental."

"Yeah, and?"

Abby remembered the day she'd had a similar conversation with Connor. "There's a possibility it could make the birthmark worse. If it does, will you still love me?"

"That's a dumb-ass question if I ever heard one. I love you, your heart, your soul—all of you. That mark is not something I pay any special attention to. It's just a part of you. I love the whole of you. Why are you making me say all this, dammit? Do you want me to list my sterling attributes?"

"It wouldn't hurt," Abby sniffed. Olivia nipped at her bare toes. She yelped as she jerked her foot away.

"Okay then. I'm not hard to look at. I like to cook. I'm well educated. I have a successful business. I pay my bills. I like kids. I have a *kazillion* dogs and cats. I like your sister and Bunny. I read your books and say nice things about them. Hell, I buy tons of your books and give them as gifts. And I'm willing to let you keep Connor's picture on our mantel. That's it. My big pitch. I'll never get the guts to say all this again."

"You'd really let me keep Connor's picture on our mantel?" Abby asked.

"Sure. He was part of your life, Abby. I don't have any claim to that time or to anyone in your life back then."

Abby felt a warm glow spread through her. Suddenly her whole being seemed to be filled with wanting him, but still she resisted. "Tell you what," she said, trying not to sound overly eager. "Go back to work and come back this evening about eight. I'll light some candles, chill a bottle of really good wine, put on some romantic music, and heat up the Jacuzzi. What do you think?"

Steve closed his eyes and sighed. "All right," he said. "I'll wait until tonight."

"Good. I'll have everything ready and we'll—You know."

"Eight o'clock?"

Abby nodded, almost afraid to speak. As soon as he left, she let out a long breath and sat back down in front of her computer. If she worked at the speed of light, she should be able to finish what she was doing by midafternoon. Then she could spend the rest of the day preparing for tonight. What to wear? she wondered. More to the point, what *not* to wear? There was wine to chill. Snacks to make. A bedroom to clean up and sheets to change. She groaned at the thought of all she had to do and wondered if she wouldn't have been better off just to let him take her right there on the desk. At least that way, she wouldn't have to think about *it* all day long.

Hours later, just as she was about to step into the bathtub, the phone rang. She debated a moment before picking it up. She didn't want to take a chance that anything or anyone would intrude on her happiness. "Hello," she said brightly, her thoughts on Steve and the romantic evening they would share.

"Hello, Princess, how are you?"

Her spirits plummeted. "Uncle Donovan!" she gasped.

"Hi. I'm good. How about you?" Abby made a face at Olivia, who was sitting on the floor staring at her intently. She could count on one hand the times she'd talked to Donovan since the night Carol had entered her house uninvited. She hadn't spoken to Carol once, which was the way Carol had said she'd wanted it.

"Working round the clock," he replied. "There aren't enough hours in the day."

"You need to slow down and smell the roses, Donovan. You aren't forty anymore, you know. How is Carol? How does Bobby like his school?"

"Bobby loves that private school in New Jersey. He really wants to play hockey in college, and that school has one of the best programs in the East. I think it will be good for him.

Carol was smothering him of late. As you know, Carol is busy as always. Sometimes I wonder how she does it all. You should call her once in a while, Abby."

Abby leaned her hip against the counter. There was so much she wanted to say to him, but they were all tied to *that* night, so she couldn't say anything at all. "Carol and I—we don't see things the same way anymore, Uncle Donovan. You know that. She hasn't exactly said so, but she's made it clear that she's upset that I brought dogs into *her* house. And I *know* she doesn't approve of Mallory moving in with me. God, that's a given! So you see—there's really no point in calling her."

She heard Donovan sigh. "You're right. I'm sorry. It's just that I want everything to be the way it used to be. I want us to be a family again. I don't even know for sure what happened, why we became estranged." There was a short pause, then, "Listen, Abby, Carol called me here at work this morning and told me to turn on the TV. I couldn't believe my eyes. Why is Mallory pretending to be you?"

"It's about the way I look, my face," she said. "My publisher wanted me to do a book tour, but I couldn't bring myself to do it, so I hired Mallory to be me." Abby stiffened, a thought suddenly coming to her. What if Carol called the show to tell them they'd been duped? Neither she nor Mallory had considered that possibility.

"Oh," he said. "I should have realized it was something like that."

"In spite of our differences, I hope you and Carol will keep our little deception to yourselves. If my publisher found out—"

"Of course we will, honey. Don't give it another thought."

"I appreciate that, Donovan. Thank you."

"About your new book," he said, changing the subject. "*Proof Positive*. I know you, Abby, so I know you wouldn't go snooping around in other people's business. This book, it has to be Mallory's idea. Right?"

"More or less, but . . ."

"I knew it!" he said. "I just knew it."

"Okay, so it was originally her idea. I agreed and went along with it. Why do you care?" she asked, glancing down at Olivia.

"I care because you could be opening a huge can of worms. Have you considered the possible ramifications, Abby? What if . . ." She heard him mutter under his breath. "I know I'm going to regret saying this, but there are some things you can't forget, some things you can't put behind you. The things Mallory used to do . . . They were mean, hateful things, Abby. Once, when she didn't get her way, she threatened to tell her teachers that I'd done bad things to her. Then another time when she got angry, she really did go to her teacher and told her that Carol drank a whole bottle of wine and we were rolling around on the floor naked and that we'd been swinging from the chandelier. We didn't even have a goddamn chandelier."

"Donovan, please, I don't want . . ."

"No, let me finish," he said, cutting her off. "I haven't been around Mallory enough to know if she's really changed, so I don't know if I'm right or not. The doctors told me she had changed and was well adjusted. And she told me herself that she had changed. She apologized profusely. I wanted desperately to believe her. That young lady has the saddest eyes of anyone I've ever met. I think that's what convinced me she had changed. But what if she fooled everyone? *Or* what if she reverted to the way she used to be? What I'm trying to say here, and not doing it very well, is that she could be setting you up for something. Don't ask me what because I don't know. But as to why . . . My guess would be revenge. Look at her life compared to yours. You had everything under the sun. She had nothing, not even our love. Maybe I'm way off base, and for your sake I hope to hell I am. All I ask is that you think about what I've said and be on guard. Just in case, okay?"

"I'm ashamed of you, Donovan," Abby shrilled. "You sound just as mean and vindictive as Carol, and I'm sorry for you. I can't tell you how much it means to me to have Mallory back in my life. She's been nothing but a help to me. I don't know why you and Carol want to tear us apart."

A pregnant pause, then a heavy sigh hummed over the wire. "I'm happy for you, Princess. And believe it or not, I understand how you feel." Abby heard him clear his throat. "Any nice young men in your life?" he asked, changing the subject.

"Nope." She was so angry she didn't want him to know about Steve. "I'm much too busy building my career to worry about men. Besides, I think I was meant to have just one love," she added, hoping she sounded convincing.

"Don't say that, Abby. The right man is out there. He just hasn't found you yet."

Abby forced a laugh. "I'm not all that hard to find."

"Can we look forward to a visit from you anytime in the near future?"

There was a long silence. At length Abby said, "I'm really busy right now. But you know how that is, I'm sure. I'll have to get back to you in a week or two." She knew she sounded cold and heartless, but she was hurt. "Excuse me, Donovan. I've got to run. Take care of yourself." She slammed the phone down on the base unit and walked into the bathroom. She wasn't going to let his phone call ruin her happiness. Those days were long gone.

Abby lowered herself into the bathtub. She wished now that she hadn't answered. Why hadn't she let the answering machine pick it up? Donovan's call had put a pall on the whole day.

How could he even think such awful things about Mallory? Because he didn't know her, she told herself. He didn't know her because he hadn't taken the time to know her. Like Carol, he refused to let go of the past. It wasn't right, and it wasn't fair. Poor Mallory.

So much for not letting Donovan spoil her happiness. She leaned back and tried to think about the evening ahead. She smiled when she thought about Steve. She'd accused him of not being romantic, but he was. Coming to her in the middle of the morning, declaring his love and his need . . . that was so sweet and romantic. Cute, too.

In the beginning, she'd compared Steve to Connor and found Steve lacking. She couldn't remember when Steve's light started to outshine Connor's. She only knew that the realization had frightened her. To admit that she'd fallen in love with Steve was to put her love for Connor behind her. A huge step. A final step. A step she hadn't been sure she could make until that morning.

She climbed out of the tub, dried herself, and smoothed fragrant lotion all over her body. The mirror told her that where her body was concerned, she could be proud. Her measurements were model-perfect. She had high breasts, a flat stomach, and shapely legs.

The swishy, electric blue dress shot through with silver threads and gossamer straps just begged for a naked body underneath. One touch to the straps and it would slither to the floor. Sandalwood-scented candles of every size had been strategically placed around her bedroom. Their fragrance filled the air, and their flickering light-cast shadows against the walls. She'd made up the bed with brand-new sheets made from Egyptian cotton with a four-hundred-thread count that made them feel like satin and down all at once. A bottle of fine wine sat in a silver bucket, and the Jacuzzi had been turned up and a fragrant scent poured in. By the time Steve arrived it would be just right.

"Be careful what you wish for, Steve," she said, smiling at herself in the mirror. Olivia and Beemer stared up at her with keen interest. "Okay, guys, you're consigned to the kitchen tonight. *All* night. I've put blankets down and water, so don't try to tell me you're being deprived." As if in protest, Olivia threw her head back and howled. Beemer started barking, the noise obviously hurting his ears. Seconds later, Mickey, Harry, and the others came into the bedroom and joined in. Abby put her hands over her ears.

"One hour and counting," Abby shouted above the din.

Olivia scurried out of the room, returning moments later dragging Abby's old stuffed dog, Bailey.

Abby gasped at the sight of her old friend in Olivia's mouth. Then she softened. "All right, you can play with him in the kitchen. But please don't tear out the stuffing. I don't think I could bear it." Seeming to understand, Olivia turned and waddled out of the bedroom, her tail swishing proudly.

When the doorbell rang at quarter to eight, Abby almost jumped out of her skin. She hoped it wasn't Mallory coming home from the book tour early. That was silly, Abby thought. Mallory wouldn't bother to knock on the door. She had a key.

"Calm down," she told herself. It had to be Steve. He was the only other person with a remote control for the front gate. She opened the door and stood back. "Steve! You're early! Oh and, you're all dressed up," she said, gazing at him in awe. "You look . . . wonderful. I don't think I've ever seen you in a sport coat before."

Steve gave a low whistle. "And I don't think I've ever seen you in a . . . What do you call that thing you're wearing?"

"A dress!" Abby said brilliantly.

"Oh. Sure. Well, it's beautiful and I especially like the way . . ." Steve tilted his head to the side. "You can see right through it! Yes sir, right through it."

"Um-hmm. C'mon, Steve," she said, grabbing his arm. "We're acting like two teenagers here. We both need to relax and loosen up."

"I'm loose, I'm loose," he said tightly.

"Sure you are, and so am I. That's why I feel like I'm going to jump out of my skin. Let's have some wine and sit out on the patio. We both need to . . . you know . . . get it together."

"Wine's good. Together is good. The whole thing sounds good," he agreed.

Abby led him through the living room. "You don't think that having sex will spoil our friendship, do you?"

"Look, we don't have to do this if you don't want to, but I'm sure as hell going to be disappointed. I've been thinking about making love to you all day. I could hardly get any work done."

"I don't want to disappoint you, and I'd be a liar if I said I wasn't looking forward to it, too. It's just that it seems so . . . *calculated*. Almost businesslike. It should be natural, don't you think?"

"A bottle of wine should do it. I don't know about you, but I lose all my inhibitions after a couple of glasses."

Candles lit the patio as well. Abby had even put a few floating candles in the pool.

"Let's make a toast," Steve said, filling two wineglasses. "To a future full of love and happiness and . . ." Simultaneously, he touched his glass to hers and kissed her.

"And what?" she murmured against his lips.

"I love you, Abby."

"I love you, too, Steve. I don't know why I waited so long to tell you or to show you. Because of Connor, I think."

"I knew what you were going through, and I understood. Why do you think I've been so patient?"

Abby smiled, thinking about what she'd put him through. "Thank you for being so patient."

"You're worth waiting for. But don't press your luck, lady. After tonight, I'm through with cold showers, understand?"

Abby sipped her wine. She didn't know how long it would take Steve to lose his inhibitions, but she hoped it would be soon because she didn't think she could wait very long. In fact, she didn't think she could wait one more second.

She set her wineglass down on the table. "Will you excuse me a moment?" Before he could answer, she hurried into the house, checked the ice bucket and the candles. Everything was ready.

Taking a deep breath, she went back outside. "Steve?" He turned around to see her standing in the doorway to the bedroom. "I umm . . . I . . ." It was no use. She couldn't think of any way of telling him she was ready other than to show him. Gulping down her fears, she flicked first one strap then the other off her shoulders. The dress floated to the floor and pooled around her feet.

"Christ, Abby!" Steve upended his glass and swallowed the contents in one gulp. He looked at her as if he were taking pictures of her, from head to toe, one inch at a time.

"Do you approve?" she finally managed to whisper.

His Adam's apple bobbed. "I had no idea you looked like . . . that. No idea," he said again, staring at her breasts. "You're beautiful, Abby. More beautiful than I ever imagined." He set his glass down and walked toward her, his eyes never leaving her breasts.

Abby twined her arms around his neck. His cologne was subtle and sexy. The nearness of him sent her senses spinning. "As much as I like that you got all dressed up for me, I think you're wearing entirely too many clothes." She lowered her arms and worked the knot of his tie loose, then sent it sailing over his shoulder. The buttons of his shirt were next. She had run out of patience by the time she reached the last one and practically ripped the shirt off him.

"Steve," she said, "if you don't help me, I'm going to ruin your clothes."

It was all the encouragement he needed. He scooped her into his arms and carried her into the bedroom. "We should have done this a long time ago," he said, laying her down on the bed.

She watched as he removed the rest of his clothes and was more than a little surprised at what had been hidden underneath. Compared to Connor . . . there was no comparison to Connor, she thought. Connor had been twenty-three when he'd died . . . still a boy, not quite a seasoned man. Whereas Steve . . . Steve was over thirty, a mature man. His arms, shoulders, and stomach muscles were testimony to his lifting and carrying heavy animals.

When he lowered himself over her, she sensed an immediate change in him and allowed herself to be carried with it. One moment his arms cradled her, soothing her, the next they became her prison, hard, strong, inescapable. She sensed a wildness flooding his veins, and she could feel it beating through him. It brought her a sense of power to know that she could arouse those instincts in him. She yielded to his need for her, welcoming his weight upon her, tightening her legs to bring him closer.

His hands were in her hair, on her breasts, on the soft flesh of her inner thighs. He stirred her, demanded of her, rewarded her with the adoring attention of his lips to those territories his hands had already claimed. And when he possessed her, it was with a joyful abandon that evoked a like response in her, hard, fast, then becoming slower and sweeter.

She murmured her pleasure and gave him those caresses he seemed to want. Release was there, within their grasp, but like two moths romancing a flame, they played in the heat and postponed that exquisite instant when they would plunge into the inferno.

* * *

Mallory cut the engine of the powerful Corvette and sat for a moment. She was almost at the bottom of the long driveway, the high iron gates and small guardhouse in her full line of vision. All kinds of emotions rivered through her body. She'd sworn never to come back here and yet, here she was.

It was a beautiful estate, with rolling emerald lawns and beautiful old oaks with lacy Spanish moss dripping from the branches. In the spring and summer, all manner of flowers bloomed in profusion. With autumn in the air, she could smell the scent of burning leaves.

The building known as Argone sat high on a sloping hill. Once it had been a thriving Southern plantation. Now it was a medical facility and school all rolled into one. An *institution,* no matter what you called it. The doors all had locks and dead bolts. The windows carried invisible security lasers that set off sirens throughout the building if tampered with. She should know. In the early years, she'd set off those alarms more times than she cared to remember.

A vise of fear gripped Mallory as she turned on the engine. She took three deep breaths and exhaled slowly. She was a visitor, not a guest, as the doctors liked to refer to the patients. The word *inmate* was more appropriate. Visitors could leave anytime they felt like it. Now, no one could keep her there, not even her adoptive parents. She was of age now, her own person. Still, she hesitated, perspiration dotting her forehead.

"Just do it, Mallory. Drive up to the guardhouse, salute if you want to, announce your name, and drive up to the building. Park the car in Visitors Parking, go into the lobby, sign in, ask for Constance Oldmeyer, and wait for her to come out to greet you. You can do it! You have to do it!"

Mallory pressed her foot on the accelerator and shifted

gears. She stopped precisely on the yellow line. Leaning her head out the window, she said in a clear voice, "April Jones to see Constance Oldmeyer. I called earlier, she's expecting me." Mallory had decided to use an alias to cover her tracks. She'd given Constance the alias when she'd called ahead.

"Yes, your name is on the list. Drive through the gates and up to the main building. I'll call Dr. Oldmeyer and tell her you're on your way."

Mallory's heart thundered in her chest as she drove up the long driveway. A driveway she had never thought to see again.

She was waiting, a plump apple-cheeked woman with wire rim glasses and a coronet of silver braids piled high on her head. She held out her arms, and Mallory flew into them.

"Thank you for seeing me, Constance. Am I taking you away from anything?"

"Not a thing. I finished my dinner and made my rounds earlier. The only things waiting for me are some very dry periodicals I've been postponing reading. Let's walk down one of the bicycle paths. It's a lovely evening. I do love the scent of burning leaves, don't you? Makes me think of all the wonderful times I had as a child carving pumpkins and making scarecrows for Halloween."

"I never did anything like that. It must have been fun."

"I saw you on television this morning in the rec room. I think half the staff saw you. They were very impressed. I thought you carried it off very well. Do you think Mr. Mitchell saw it?"

"If he didn't, he would have heard about it from Carol. I found out from Bobby that Carol watches that particular show religiously. Knowing her, she probably took notes on everything I said." Mallory's expression tensed. "Do you think I said too much? I didn't want to give anything away. You know what I mean."

"Yes, I know. But I think what you said was just right; however, I still wish I could talk you out of this plan of yours. It's so risky. Won't you at least consider talking to the police?"

"It wouldn't do any good at this point. I don't have solid proof, and I don't know that I ever will. It's all just speculation, putting two and two together. The police need facts."

Constance took a deep breath. "What does your sister think of your plans?"

Mallory bent her head. "I haven't told her yet."

"My God, Mallory. You have to tell her. If you don't, you could be putting her life in jeopardy."

"I know. And I will." She glanced around. "Aside from the guard at the gate, do you think anyone knows I'm here?"

"I certainly didn't tell anyone. The guard is new since you left. No one looks at the guest sheets unless something goes awry. I'm glad you used another name, though. It pays to be cautious. Let's sit over here under the tree and talk." Before sitting down, she pulled a piece of paper out of her pocket. "This is a copy of the bookkeeping entry you asked for. I don't know if you can call it a bribe, but you can certainly see how it would influence the board of directors."

Mallory looked at the paper. There was barely enough moonlight to make out the numbers. "Is this right? Two million dollars?"

"That's right. They used it to build a new wing onto Argone."

"You know what concerns me, Constance? Sometimes I get scared that I haven't changed, that I'm still that horrible little girl who derived pleasure from hurting others. Tell me I'm doing the right thing in exposing Donovan for the murderer he is, and that I'm not doing this to get even with him and Carol for putting me here."

"Mallory, my dear. Being mean and hateful isn't a disease.

It's a learned behavior, and you learned to be that way from your mother, who probably learned it from her mother. I taught you a new behavior. Kindness. Generosity. Compassion. Love. If I had any doubts about you, I would have recommended further treatment." Constance squeezed her hand. "You mustn't let your fears consume you, or you won't be able to do what you need to do."

Mallory nodded.

"Aside from all this, are you happy?"

"You always ask me that, and I never have the answer you're looking for. I'm contented. Perhaps one day that euphoric feeling will hit me. I'll call you right away if it happens."

"Open up, dear child. I think you're afraid to be happy for fear someone will rip that happiness away from you."

"Perhaps you're right, Constance. Now, enough about me. Tell me how you are and what you've been doing. In your private life. I don't want to know anything about this place."

"Well . . . I bought a new dress last week and I . . ."

Mallory smiled in the darkness as she snuggled against the old doctor.

Chapter Fourteen

"You look tired, Mallory. Are you taking your vitamins?" Abby said, concern ringing in her voice.

"Yes, I'm taking vitamins *and* herbs, but five days of eating and sleeping on the road has taken its toll." She sat down at the kitchen table and reached for the cup of coffee Abby offered her. "I'm really glad to be home. Don't take that the wrong way. I love doing the interviews and book signings. It's the *pretending* to be you part that wears me out. It's stressful. I'm always afraid I'll say something I shouldn't and blow your cover."

"You're beginning to sound like a real-life sleuth." Abby grinned.

Mallory's face broke into a tired smile. "I am a real-life sleuth. I bet I know exactly what you did while I was gone. You and Steve got it together, finally." She leaned forward. "And it's about time! I was beginning to think you two were never going to make it."

Abby stared at her sister in awe. "What was your first clue?"

"Ahhh . . . ? Are you asking me to give my supersleuthing secrets away?" When Abby rolled her eyes, she said, "Okay.

There were candles all over the patio for one. They weren't there when I left. And I saw empty wine bottles in the trash can. I've never known you to drink alone. And there's this fragrance . . . sandalwood, I think . . . coming from your bedroom. Nice but a little strong," she said, looking down her nose until her eyes crossed.

Abby felt a warm flush work its way through her body. "You're right, and I'm in love," she admitted. "Totally, completely, wonderfully in love. I never thought it would happen again." She smiled, knowing how lucky she was. "Steve is the most patient and understanding man I've ever known. You should have seen him. He was so funny," she said, reaching across to touch Mallory's hand. "He recited a whole list of his qualities and one of them was that he's willing to let me keep Connor's picture on the mantel." Abby pulled her hand back and picked up her toast.

"Sounds like true love to me." Mallory grinned.

"I've been thinking, though, that I need to put the picture away. Connor will always have a special place in my heart, but he's part of the past and the past is gone."

Mallory's eyes grew intent as she stared at Abby. "Do you really believe the past is gone? Don't you ever think about Mama and Daddy?"

Abby stared at her sister. There was something in Mallory's weary expression that alerted Abby that something was bothering her sister. "Occasionally, but it's all so painful that I don't like to dwell on it. How about you? Do you think about them?"

Mallory swallowed her coffee. "Lately, every day of my life," she said, emphasizing each word. "Do you have any pictures of our parents?"

"One of Mama, but it isn't very good. Uncle Donovan always gives me a picture of Daddy at Christmas. I have them all in an album. Do you want to see them?"

"Maybe later."

Abby drew a steadying breath. "I wish—I wish that they'd been buried instead of cremated. It would give me comfort to know there's a place I could go with flowers. Donovan gave me Daddy's ashes. What did you do with Mama's?"

Mallory tilted her head inquiringly. "I don't have Mama's ashes. I didn't even know they were cremated until I was around thirteen, and then I assumed the ashes had been scattered somewhere. Don't look at me like that. I would remember getting an urn full of Mama's ashes, believe me."

Abby forced herself to think logically. "I don't understand why Donovan would tell me he gave you the urn if he didn't. He gave me Daddy's when I was . . . I don't know . . . fifteen or sixteen. The urn used to give me the creeps when I would see it sitting up there on the shelf in my closet."

"I'd like to see it if you don't mind," Mallory said, searching Abby's face with troubled eyes.

Abby led Mallory to her bedroom. She took the plain white urn down from the closet shelf and handed it to her. "It doesn't weigh much."

Mallory examined the urn, then handed it back to Abby, who slid it as far back on the shelf as it would go. She turned out the closet light and closed the door. "If *you* don't have Mama's urn, then who do you suppose does?" She sensed a sudden tension develop between them and wished she'd never brought the subject up.

"Why don't you call Donovan and ask him?" Mallory suggested tightly. "If you don't want to, I will. This isn't right."

Abby could see the agitation building on her sister's face. "Relax, we'll get to the bottom of this. Let's go back to the kitchen and think about it." The moment Abby refilled their coffee cups, she sat down across from Mallory. "Try to remember if Carol and Donovan ever brought a package or a box to you at Argone that might have gotten misplaced. Or maybe they gave it to a member of the staff and it just never found its way to you."

Mallory burst into hysterical laughter, then sobered when she saw Abby's look of hurt confusion. "I'm sorry. It's just that . . . well . . . in all the years I was there, Carol *never* once came to see me. As for Donovan—I already told you, he visited me a few times, but he never brought me anything. If either of them told you otherwise, they're lying."

"But last Christmas when Carol broke into the house . . ." She cut herself off, her thoughts swirling. She remembered Donovan saying the reason he knew Mallory was well adjusted and living a good, productive life was because he'd kept his eye on her in spite of Carol. Then, just the other day when he called, he said he hadn't been around Mallory enough to know if she'd really changed. She wondered why he would contradict himself.

"What? What were you going to say?"

Abby waved a hand. "It isn't important. I was just thinking."

Mallory eyed her uncertainly. "I can tell you have doubts. I don't blame you. I would, too. But I can prove what I told you. We can drive to Argone and talk to Constance. She has documented records of every one of Donovan's visits since the day I arrived there." She handed Abby the portable phone. "We can talk about this later. Call him. I can't wait to hear what he says about Mama's urn."

Abby's stomach rumbled sickeningly as she placed the call. "Yes, this is Abby Mitchell," she said to Donovan's secretary. "I'd like to speak to Donovan please."

A moment later, Donovan's voice boomed over the wire. "Princess, it's so good to hear from you. Are you calling with good news or bad?"

"Neither. I just have a question."

"Fire away."

"I've been thinking about buying a plot and burying Daddy's ashes," she said, saying the first thing that came to mind—a lie, the second one she'd told him within the space of a few days. But what else could she say that wouldn't sound as if she was interrogating him? "I thought it would be nice if I put Mama's and Daddy's urns in the same plot. Does Mallory have Mama's ashes? I vaguely recall you saying she did. I forgot to ask her, and she's away right now and I can't get in touch with her." *Lie number three,* she thought, turning her gaze on Mallory while awaiting his answer. "That's what I thought. Darn it. Oh, well. I guess I'll just have to wait until she gets back. Thanks. Give my love to everyone. Bye." She set the phone down and took a deep breath. "He said he turned the urns over to both of us the same weekend."

"That's a goddamn lie, Abby." Mallory pushed her chair back and sprang to her feet. "You have to believe me. I have no reason to lie about something like that. Why would I, for God's sake?"

By the same token, Abby thought, what reason would Donovan have to lie about it? What was there for either of them to gain? Or lose? Her mind reeled with confusion.

Mallory stood by the stove, drumming her nails against the tile countertop. "Listen, Abby, this probably isn't the best time, but there's something I've been meaning to tell you. You aren't going to like it. You probably aren't going to believe it either. But promise me you'll keep an open mind and withhold judgment until I've said what I have to say."

Abby saw her sister's jaw tense and felt a wave of apprehension flow through her. "Okay, but you're being awfully dramatic."

"I'm just going to come right out and say it—I don't think

our parents died the way the police say they did. I think they were murdered. And I think Donovan Mitchell murdered them."

Abby's face went white, the port-wine stain standing out like a huge glob of grape jam on her face. "Mallory! How could you possibly say such a terrible thing? I know you hate Donovan and Carol for putting you in Argone, but accusing Donovan of murder . . . That's taking your revenge too far." Abby broke the promise she'd made to Mallory about passing judgment.

Ironically, the conversation she'd had with Donovan popped into her head at the same moment. He'd warned her that Mallory might be setting her up, looking for revenge. He'd cautioned her to be on guard.

She was now.

Mallory remained cool in spite of her sister's anger. "I've had a long time to think about this, Abby. I wouldn't be telling you if I didn't think you needed to know." She turned toward the window and gazed outside. "Right now you're thinking I'm crazy. That I belong back in Argone. That's okay. It's what I expected. After I've told you everything, I think you'll feel differently."

Abby wasn't about to argue. She knew next to nothing about Mallory's mental problems, and she didn't want to give her any reason to reveal them. The best thing she could do was to sit still, stay calm, and humor her sister while she continued to play her game or until she was so tired of it she would be forced to call someone. Who? She didn't know. But someone.

"Why would Donovan want to kill our parents?" Abby asked, continuing the discussion with the most important question that was front and center in her mind. "Give me one good reason. Just one. In case you haven't noticed, I'm having a real hard time with this." She crossed her arms in challenge.

Mallory turned back. "Donovan and Mama were lovers. He came over to our house on the nights Daddy went bowling. I told Constance that I used to see him walking across the lawn. The minute he and Mama went into the bedroom, I would sit outside the door and listen, just like I used to sit outside Donovan and Carol's bedroom door. One night, Mama caught me and told me if I promised not to tell Daddy about Donovan's visit, she would get me a new toy and a Barbie outfit. After that, I watched for Donovan to come over so I could blackmail Mama. That's why I had so many toys."

Was it true? Abby wondered. Or had Mallory imagined Donovan's visits? "Okay, so they had an affair," she said, pre tending to accept her story. "That's still not a motive . . ."

"All these years," Mallory talked over her, "you thought Mama hated you because of your birthmark. That was probably part of it, but I think there was more. I think she hated you because you were Daddy's child, and she *hated* Daddy."

"Of course I was Daddy's . . ."

"Wait!" Mallory wagged her finger. "She *loved* me because she loved Donovan, and I was Donovan's child."

"No! That's not true." Outraged, Abby bolted to her feet, her chair flying out behind her. "You're making all this up." Too late she remembered her concerns about Mallory's mental state and knew a moment's fear when her sister walked toward her.

"No, I'm not, Abby," Mallory said, sounding tired. "Donovan doesn't know I know. Hell, I didn't know until Constance started hypnotizing me. That's when it came out. Constance has it all on tape . . . all the things I heard and saw when I was little. I have the proof right here," she said, reaching behind her and grabbing her purse off the counter. She took out a large manila envelope and sat down. "When I was working for that insurance company, Steve Franklin applied for a key-man insurance policy for Donovan. When you apply for a policy like that you have to give a blood sample. I was good friends with the guys in the lab and I conned them into running a DNA test to compare Donovan's blood with mine." She searched through the envelope and extracted a single white sheet of paper. "They match, Abby."

Abby took the lab report out of Mallory's hand. She'd acquired a similar report a few months ago, for research purposes, so she was familiar with the process. There was no doubt. Donovan and Mallory were father and daughter.

She looked up from the report and saw tears swimming in Mallory's eyes. She felt her guard slip several notches. "There's more, isn't there?" she asked, the challenge, the fight gone out of her.

"You asked what motive he would have to kill them. I don't know for certain. I can only speculate. Maybe Daddy found out Donovan was having an affair with Mama, they got into an argument about it, and Donovan killed Daddy and . . ."

"Wait a minute. None of this is making sense. I remember that Donovan hated Mama."

"Maybe he said one thing and felt another." Mallory paused to rub her neck. "Here's what I think happened. I think he loved her so much he couldn't stand the thought of her and Daddy having sex, so he made her promise to abstain." Before Abby could comment, Mallory added, "Under hypnosis, I remembered that Donovan had accused Mama of lying about something. She screamed back that she hadn't lied, that she'd been *true* to him. *True* to him, Abby. I'm sure I didn't know what that meant way back then, but I do now." She paused to take a breath. "Just for the sake of argument, let's say that Donovan did ask her to abstain and she gave him her word. Now let's say that somehow he found out you were Daddy's child and not his. How angry would he be that Mama had lied to him? Who would he take his anger out on? Isn't it conceivable he might lose it . . . as in commit a murder?"

"Yes, I suppose so, but he doesn't seem the type." *Stupid comment,* Abby thought. *Really stupid.* She'd researched enough murders to know that there was no "type."

"They never do."

Abby remembered bits and pieces of her early childhood. "Mama died of natural causes, didn't she? And Daddy . . ."

"Supposedly committed suicide," Mallory finished for her as she withdrew more papers from the envelope. "Here's a copy of the newspaper article that carried the information about their deaths, and here are their death certificates. There was no major investigation and no autopsy done on Mama."

Abby read the article, then the "cause of death" information on the death certificates. "It says that Mama died of heart failure and that Daddy died of a bullet wound."

"That's right," Mallory agreed. "And I don't dispute that, but I don't think Daddy killed himself or that Mama died of natural causes. I think Donovan shot Daddy and made it look like suicide and that he gave Mama some kind of poison . . . something that would simulate heart failure. There are a lot of poisons that would do that." She handed Abby another piece of paper. "Here's a copy of the police investigation, which is, by the way, the worst I've ever seen. And here's a copy of Daddy's suicide note."

Memories of that day, so long suppressed, flooded Abby's mind. She remembered coming home from playing at her friend's house. It was around lunchtime, and she and Mallory were both hungry. Mama wasn't in the kitchen, so they went in different directions to find her. She found Daddy sitting at his desk, sound asleep. She tried to wake him up, but he wouldn't open his eyes. Then Mallory came down and said Mama was sleeping, too, and that she couldn't wake her up. The next thing she knew there were a bunch of people in her house and they were taking Mama and Daddy away.

Putting her memories back where they belonged, Abby read the paperwork from start to finish and had to agree with Mallory that the police report left something to be desired. Donovan was quoted as having said that he and John had a long conversation the night before, that he talked John into leaving Harriet and going with him to his new job. The suicide note backed that up and went on to say what had happened—that Harriet had been so upset by his news that she'd had a heart attack and died. He blamed himself for her death, he said, and that was the reason he was taking his own life. Donovan was again quoted as saying that he didn't know that John owned a gun. Also, that it was entirely possible Harriet died of the same heart condition that had killed his own wife.

Abby could see why the police wouldn't feel the need for a big investigation or an autopsy. They had a suicide note, a gun, probably with her father's and only her father's fingerprints on it, and the testimony of a brother-in-law who knew the couple, their problems, and even had a likely answer for the wife's cause of death. Why make mountains out of molehills? Why do pounds of paperwork?

As much as it looked as if Mallory might be on to something, it wasn't concrete enough to make Abby switch over to Mallory's way of thinking. She loved Donovan, always had, always would. She felt sick to her very soul. *"If . . . if Donovan did murder our parents . . . I mean my father and our* mother. Without an autopsy on Mama . . ." She trailed off, leaving Mallory to fill in the blanks.

"We could tell him we know what he did and can prove it and see if he confesses," Mallory said jokingly. "Or we could try to pin him to another murder, one that it's not too late to get some facts on."

"*Another* murder!" Abby's brain spun out of control as she mentally tried to glean Mallory's thoughts. "Who?" she asked, almost afraid she knew the answer.

"Connor."

"No." Abby shook her head. "No way, Mallory. No!" She thought she screamed her response, but she'd barely whispered it. It was unthinkable.

"Think about it," Mallory said reasonably. "Let's start with the motivation. That's where you start when you plot your novels, isn't it?" She pressed her lips together. "Think back to last Christmas . . . that night we hid behind the hedge and watched Carol break into your house. Carol argued with Donovan about all kinds of things, but two things Donovan said really hit me. First, that he was jealous of Connor. Second, that he never thought he would feel like he was your *real* father."

Abby remembered Donovan saying those things. At the time she'd felt warmed by them, thought of them as expressions of love. "You're taking everything and twisting it to suit your needs, Mallory. I didn't think that at all."

Mallory nodded. "Remember wondering why Connor never told you about his heart condition? I heard you say you couldn't imagine why he wouldn't mention it unless there wasn't anything to mention."

"His new job required him to have a physical, and everything checked out fine," Abby said by way of an explanation.

"Fine, as in no heart condition or any other condition,

which is why he never said anything to you. There was nothing to say. Yes, he had rheumatic fever as a child, but it might have been a very mild case and didn't cause any damage to his heart."

"That may be. I don't know. All I know is that Connor was perfectly fine when I said good-bye to him outside the hotel café that morning. And the next thing I knew he was dead."

"I know. And the question is: What caused it? He *appeared* to die of heart failure . . . just like Mama *appeared* to die of heart failure." Mallory raked her fingers through her hair. "Could he have been poisoned, too? Think about it. You were there. Could Donovan have slipped something into his breakfast?" When Abby didn't answer, she let out a long sigh. "You wouldn't be normal if you didn't have doubts about the things I just told you. But Dr. Oldmeyer can back most of this up . . . the number of Donovan's visits, the urn I never got, the audiotapes of my hypnosis sessions. She has the patient records. She has other things, too, though I'm not sure how they figure in or even if they do. She gave me this copy of the bookkeeping record showing Donovan's two-million-dollar donation to Argone."

"'Donovan made a two-million-dollar donation to Argone? Why?" Abby asked in stunned surprise as she wondered where this latest bit of information would lead.

"Your guess is as good as mine," Mallory said, handing over the copy of the journal entry. "Guilt maybe? They'll probably name a school holiday after him. Donovan Day. They do that, you know. But getting back to Constance, she was the one who told me about Connor's death. She called Donovan and Carol on some matter and got hold of Bobby, who filled her in on all the details. When she told me, I went off the deep end because I already had suspicions. I got it in my head that you were going to be next. So I followed you, thinking I could protect you somehow. I know you caught a glimpse of me at Connor's funeral."

"Then I didn't imagine it. You were there! I thought my eyes were playing tricks on me. You came around once here, too, right after I moved in, didn't you?"

Mallory snorted. "Uh-huh." She gathered up all her papers, carefully refolded them, and put them back in the manila envelope. "I think you should call Connor's family and ask them just how serious his rheumatic fever was."

"What?" The single word exploded from Abby's mouth like a bullet.

Hours later, Abby was sitting in her office with four of the dogs at her feet. She was still reeling from everything Mallory had told her and needed time to absorb it all. The thought of Donovan killing her parents . . . and Connor . . . Sure Donovan had his faults but . . . a murderer?

Mallory had brought up something else that seemed odd. Neither she nor Mallory had ever been given any of their parents' personal effects. There must have been something worth keeping—jewelry, old letters, photos, mementos of some kind. What had become of them?

Abby turned off her computer. She'd tried to use her emotional state to write a critical, emotional scene, but it had ended up reading like a Saturday morning cartoon.

Mallory passed by the office and peeked in. "Having writer's block?"

Abby nodded. "I can't stop thinking about everything you told me."

"Then you believe me?" she asked, looking hopeful.

Abby thought a moment before answering. "I don't doubt that you believe the things you told me. And I don't doubt the DNA test or the other documents you showed me. But . . ."

"But you don't believe Donovan murdered our parents and Connor."

"I don't *want* to believe it, Mallory. I'm not real happy with Donovan at the moment, but I still love him."

"I understand," Mallory said with a sad smile. "I guess I don't blame you. I don't have any hard proof or anything, only speculation." She stepped into the room. "Listen, you're on schedule with the new book, and I don't have any more public appearances, so I thought we could go to Atlanta, to Argone. We'll talk to Dr. Oldmeyer, and I'll ask her to show you my records. Either on the way there or coming back, we could stop by Carol and Donovan's and ask them for our parents' stuff. It's probably packed away somewhere in boxes. Are you with me or not, Abby?"

Was she? Abby stared at her sister. She wanted to believe Mallory, but her accusations were just too wild. Maybe things would change once she talked to Mallory's doctor. "Yes, I'm with you."

"Good. How soon can you be ready to leave?"

"First thing tomorrow morning. I have to clean up this mess and arrange for all the dogs to go over to Steve's. I hope he can take them. He's been awfully busy lately with the added workload from the humane society."

Mallory turned to leave, then came back. "I almost forgot," she said. "How did you like my interview with Kathie Lee?"

"I thought you were great. Really great. You looked so poised, so professional. Steve was here, and he got teary-eyed when you answered her question about the book's dedication. I have to admit, though, I got a little nervous when she asked you about *Proof Positive*. I had no idea what you would say. But you said just enough to titillate without giving anything away. Like I said, you did great."

"How long after the interview was it before Donovan called?"

Abby nearly dropped the research book she'd been about to place on the bookshelf. She swung around, her eyes wide-open, her jaw dropping. "How did you know . . . ?"

"It was a given. I knew Carol would be watching the show, that she would tell Donovan everything I said and did, and that he would call you to find out what I was doing impersonating you. Isn't that what happened?"

It took Abby a few moments to digest Mallory's explanation, but once she did, she had more questions. "Excuse me for not catching on here, but how did you know Carol would be watching the show?"

"That was easy," Mallory said, waving her hand in dismissal. "When I knew I was going to be on, I called and talked to Bobby. I disguised my voice and told him I was conducting a daytime TV survey. I asked him what his mother's favorite talk shows were and how often she watched them. He told me she loved the *Regis and Kathie Lee* show and that she watched it every day. He even told me she taped it when she was going out."

Abby's nose wrinkled. "Did you learn all this stuff working for that insurance company?" Mallory nodded. "That's incredible, you know? To go to all that trouble to . . ." She tilted her head. "Why *did* you go to all that trouble if you don't mind me asking?"

"I wanted them to see me, to see how I turned out . . . in spite of them. I deserved that, Abby. I really did."

Mallory was on her way down the hall when the phone in the kitchen rang. Since Abby was putting the dogs into the Jeep, she let the machine pick it up and went about getting the last of her things together.

The phone rang again as Abby came back from the garage.

"Boy, you're popular today. It just rang a few minutes ago," Mallory said.

"I'd better answer it," Abby said, picking it up.

"Princess, it's Donovan. You sound a little out of breath. Are you all right?"

"I'm fine. I was just out with the dogs."

"Listen, honey, Bobby's appendix ruptured. He collapsed at a football rally. Carol and I are on our way to Jersey. She wants to be there when he comes out of surgery. I thought you might want to call him later or send some flowers."

Abby looked at Mallory. "Is he going to be all right?"

"Yes, he's going to be fine. I talked to the doctor myself before he took him into the operating room."

"I'm glad you called and, yes, I will call or send flowers."

"Abby? Don't hang up. There's something I want to say." He paused. "I've been thinking about that conversation we had. You know, the one about your sister? I want to apologize. I realize now that it did sound like I was trying to tear you and Mallory apart. That honestly wasn't my intention, honey. I just wanted to caution you, but it came out all wrong. And for the record, you were right. We did throw Mallory away. But as God is my witness, Abby, we didn't know what to do with her. She was out of control. She hated us and was out to destroy us. That said, I want you to know that I love Mallory in spite of the things she did. I love her in spite of Carol, too. And I love you, Abby. I miss having you in my life."

Abby swallowed hard and bit back tears. "You and Carol have a safe trip and give Bobby my love," she said, wishing with all her heart that she could tell him she loved and missed him, too. But she couldn't. Not now. "Bye."

Mallory tapped her foot impatiently, her face dark and

brooding. "What he said about loving me . . . It was a crock!" she snarled. "You need to wake up, Abby, before it's too late."

Abby flinched at the ominous-sounding words. She tried to shake off the feeling that was rivering through her. "Guess you heard everything, huh?" Abby asked needlessly.

Chapter Fifteen

A bby preferred to do the driving whenever she and Mallory traveled because of her sister's heavy foot. She hated careening around corners and hanging on to the Jesus Christ strap overhead. Like many Corvette owners, Mallory drove too fast and wove in and out of traffic, causing Abby to clutch at her chest as she prayed for safe travel mercies. Whether because of the family-style rental car they'd decided to get at the last minute or because Mallory was dead-tired, she didn't kick up her usual fuss. She'd fallen asleep within a few minutes of getting on the interstate.

With no one to talk to, it was almost impossible for Abby to think about anything other than Mallory's and Donovan's charges against each other. *Is he a murderer? Is she mentally unstable? Are his warnings about Mallory justified? Is she looking for revenge?*

Who is telling the truth?

Who is lying?

Whom should I trust? My sister with her troubled past or the man who raised and loved me?

She'd promised herself she would keep an open mind until she had more information. Maybe there would be something among her parents' effects that would shed some light on the truth. And there were Mallory's school records and Constance Oldmeyer herself.

Resolutely, she turned her thoughts to something more positive, something productive: her new book *Proof Positive.* Mallory's instincts had been right; the case was a natural for a murder mystery. She could see why the insurance company hadn't closed the files. There were too many unanswered questions. And so many red herrings that the reader would be leaping to all sorts of conclusions about the identity of the murderer . . . all of them wrong.

She was only five chapters into the book but she sensed a degree of difficulty with writing it that she hadn't experienced before. It was probably because the killer's motives weren't clear-cut. He had all kinds of issues and agendas. Funny, she thought, how in many ways the book paralleled . . .

"Oh, my God!" She slammed on the brake.

"What? What's wrong?" Mallory bolted upright, eyes wide. "Did you hit something?"

The tires screeched as Abby guided the car toward the shoulder. "Not yet, but give me a moment." She put the car into neutral and twisted the key in the ignition. "You lied to me, damn you! You led me to believe *Proof Positive* was loosely based on an insurance case. But it's our parents' deaths and Connor's that I'm writing about, isn't it?"

Mallory turned in her seat to face her sister. "Yes."

Abby felt her body shake with anger. "How could you do this to me? How could you betray me like this? How could you, Mallory?" she demanded.

"Because if you'd known the truth, you wouldn't have gone along with me."

"You're damn right I wouldn't have gone along with it," Abby said, grabbing the steering wheel with both hands, wishing it was Mallory's neck. "Tell me, sister mine, just *when* you were planning on telling me? After the book came out?"

"I almost did tell you yesterday morning, when I asked you how you liked my interview with Kathie Lee. But I chickened out. I figured you already had enough to digest, so I decided to wait until after we talked to Constance."

Abby stared through the windshield at the oncoming cars and had another revelation as she thought back to their discussion about the show, specifically the part where Mallory had revealed the book's basic plot. "You *used* me," she said, disgust ringing in her voice. "You used me, my career, to . . ."

"Wait a minute, Abby," Mallory said, holding up her hand to stop her sister. "Before you draw all kinds of wrong conclusions let me explain. First of all, I did not lie to you, I simply didn't tell you everything. What I said to Kathie Lee about *Proof Positive* . . . Yes, I did it intentionally. In fact, I manipulated her into asking me about it, knowing that everything I said would get back to Donovan. I will probably never have enough proof to convict him, so I thought . . ."

Eyes squinting, Abby interrupted her sister to venture a guess at how she would have finished her sentence. "You thought you would frighten him?" Before Mallory could agree or disagree, Abby contradicted herself. "No, you thought you would put him on alert that you were on to him. You think he'll tip his hand somehow . . . and you'll have your proof. Right?"

"I know it sounds far-fetched, but he *did* call you after the show, which says something . . ."

"Yeah, it says he was confused about why you were impersonating me, Mallory." Abby stared at her sister without seeing her as Donovan's words flashed through her mind. *You could be opening up a huge can of worms.*

"What? What are you thinking?"

"Nothing," Abby denied, the heat of her anger cooling

slightly. "No, that's not true. If your suspicions about Donovan are right . . . and I'm not saying they are . . . we could be in real danger. Did you ever think about that? Anyone who has killed three people isn't going to hesitate to kill again, especially if he thinks he's going to be exposed."

Mallory rubbed the sleep from her eyes to draw a steadying breath. "I know that. If there was another way, I would take it, but I can't think of one."

Abby shook her head, refusing to let herself believe what was going on around her. "You can deny it all you want, but I know you're doing this for revenge. You want to get back at Donovan and Carol for institutionalizing you. But listen to me, Mallory, in spite of what you think, they saved you from yourself."

"I am not doing this for revenge," Mallory protested. "I know what kind of kid I was. I couldn't stand myself! Putting me in Argone was the best thing for me. It scares me to think what would have happened to me if I hadn't been sent there. I'm doing this because he murdered our parents and your boyfriend. Do you want his crimes to go unpunished?"

Abby found herself at a loss for words. She sat staring at her sister, remembering even more of her conversation with Donovan. Was this the *something* he'd predicted she was being set up for? No, she thought. It would be the book's ending, when the murderer was revealed. Though everything would be fictionalized, Donovan wouldn't have any problem recognizing himself unless . . . she broke the contract. Of course that would be committing author suicide. But the way things were going, she was going to die anyway.

Donovan Mitchell swung the full-sized rental car onto Route 1 and headed north.

"Can't you drive any faster, Donovan?"

"No, Carol, I cannot drive any faster. I'd like to get there in one piece if you don't mind. You need to relax because this is out of our hands, and there's nothing either one of us can do at this precise moment. Bobby is going to be fine. You do not die from appendicitis."

Carol turned her head to glare at him. "Do you live on some other planet, Donovan? People *do* die from a ruptured appendix. Do not tell me not to worry," she said, giving him a withering look. "I'm a mother. I also have to wonder why you aren't worrying more. You sure as hell worry about Abby and that fruitcake Mallory. Why is that, Donovan? And while you're explaining that, I'd like to know why you felt compelled to call Abby and tell her about Bobby. She doesn't give a damn about him or us, and you know it." She looked at him from beneath lowered eyelids.

"Will you listen to yourself, Carol. I don't know you anymore. What the hell happened to us? We're constantly at each other's throats. Even Bobby has picked up on it. He asked me what your problem was and wanted to know if you were going through menopause. I don't know what's the matter with you. It can't be money. Do you feel overworked? If you don't want to do the interior design on the model homes anymore, just say so. Personally, I think you're bitter about your failed relationship with Abby. If you hadn't tried to control her life, everything would have been fine. But no, you couldn't stop. And now what you did has even rubbed off on me. So now that's two daughters I've lost. Against my better judgment, I hardly ever went to see Mallory because you wanted it that way. And I mistakenly thought I should respect your wishes. I'm not proud of that decision. I just wish to hell I could make it up to her somehow. God, I'd give anything . . ."

"Shut up, Donovan," Carol grumbled. "I'm sick and tired of you talking about how I'm this way and that way. And I'm sick of you talking about Mallory and Abby. For that matter,

I'm sick of you, too. Sometimes I wonder why we stay married."

"I've been wondering the same thing myself," Donovan flashed back. "Do you know how long it's been since we made love? My God, we don't even share the same bed anymore. Maybe we should think about a divorce."

"What? So you can latch on to some bimbo? Not likely," Carol snarled.

"We can't even talk to each other anymore without fighting. What kind of life is this?"

"That's almost funny, Donovan. How can we talk or have a life when you leave at five in the morning and get home at midnight? Maybe you need to explain all that to me when you finally get around to explaining all those other things."

"You always did have a problem with my schedule. Yes, the hours are long, but Jesus Christ look at the vacations we take—three to four weeks at a crack. I thought I was making up for all those late nights."

"I really wish you'd drive a little faster," she said, ignoring him.

"I don't even know where the hell I'm going. What hospital is Bobby in? You didn't say."

"Jersey General, and I did tell you. As usual, you weren't listening."

"Why not St. Peter's? I think Abby thinks it's St. Peter's."

"Abby, Abby, Abby. If it isn't Abby, it's Mallory. Ask me if I care what she thinks. On second thought, don't ask me. I don't care."

"Abby cares, Carol. She was very concerned when I told her about Bobby. She adores that boy, and you know it. I think you're jealous of their friendship."

"We'll see how upset she is if she shows up, which we both know she won't do. Saying I'm jealous of my own son doesn't even bear discussing."

"You don't give up, do you, Carol?" Donovan clamped his lips shut and concentrated on the road and the traffic ahead of him. Carol slouched in the corner, her eyes closed. Donovan risked a glance at his wife out of the corner of his eye. He sighed when he saw a single tear roll down her cheek.

Abby pulled around the back of the house and parked between the patio and the guest house, out of sight of the neighbors. She was glad now that Mallory had suggested renting a car. Her Jeep and Mallory's Corvette would have been much too easy to describe.

Her nerves strung tight, Abby stared at the house where she'd spent her teenage years and remembered the good times. *Stay alert and shift your mental gears into neutral,* she told herself. She needed to remember why she was here.

"If they left in a hurry, maybe Carol didn't set the alarm," Mallory said, heading toward the kitchen door.

"Carol sets the alarm if she goes outside to bring in firewood. She believes in security. It's one of the high-tech selling points in the stuff Donovan builds. It doesn't matter if it's a private house or a shopping mall." God, was this flat-sounding voice really hers?

"It's a pretty house," Mallory observed. "It kind of reminds me of Argone with those huge white pillars in the front." Abby watched as her sister crossed her arms over her chest and shrank into herself. "Do you remember the security code?" Abby nodded. "Do you have your key?" Abby nodded a second time.

Abby slipped the key into the lock. "Carol has a phenomenal memory for detail. What that means is, if we move something, she'll know. We need to be very careful. I don't feel right doing this, Mallory. I feel . . . God, I don't know what I feel. We shouldn't be doing this."

"Not that it makes it all right, but don't forget what they

did at your house last Christmas. We may never get another chance like this. Someone is watching over us. In a million years we couldn't be this lucky again. I'm just sorry it took Bobby's appendix to rupture, though. Quick, key in the code."

Abby stared at the square white panel until she saw the disarm button turn green. When she saw the way her hand was trembling, she shoved it into her sweat suit pocket.

"If Carol is as paranoid as you say, you have to wonder why she never changed the code," Mallory said, looking around at the pristine kitchen.

"It's Bobby's birthday. Maybe it's easy for her to remember. Maybe she felt safer with something she holds dear to her heart."

Mallory shrugged. "Whatever. How do you want to do this?"

"You're the brains of this outfit, Mallory. Tell me what to do, and I'll do it."

"All right. Mama's urn probably looks the same as Daddy's, and we need to look for our parents' personal stuff. Let's start with the house and work our way to the garage. What do you say?"

"There's a storage area off every bedroom, and a really big one on the landing where Carol keeps all the Christmas decorations. She marks the contents of all the boxes, so that should make it easier."

"It must have been nice growing up here," Mallory said wistfully.

Abby's shoulders stiffened. "It was a little too stiff for my tastes. We never sat in the living room. That was for show. We only ate in the dining room on holidays. The family room isn't particularly comfortable. It looks like it is, but it isn't. I spent most of my time in my bedroom. Bobby did, too."

"My room at Argone had a lock on it, one I couldn't open."

"I'm sorry about that, Mallory."

"I know you are. Most of the time, it seems like a very long time ago. But occasionally, it seems like only yesterday. This is a wonderful view of the grounds from this window. Who does all the gardening?"

"Carol. She uses scissors," Abby said tightly.

"What are all those bushes?"

"Camellias. They bloom when it gets cold, usually around Christmas. The ones on the left are azaleas. The borders around the fence are oleanders. They're planted all along the battery to buffet the wind coming in from the ocean. The flowers are pretty. My God, why are we having this stupid conversation?" Abby dithered. "Let's just do what we came to do and get the hell out of here."

"Then let's get to it. I'll take the storage area off the landing, then meet you upstairs."

Abby thought her skin would crawl right off her body as she went from room to room, looking in cupboards, drawers, closets, and storage areas. When she came up dry, she walked down to the landing and called out to Mallory. "I hope you're having better luck than I'm having. I didn't find a thing. How about you?"

Mallory walked out of the storage area dusting her hands. "I didn't find anything either. You looked in all the bedrooms?"

"All but Bobby's. But you'd have to be a ghoul to put a dead person's ashes in a kid's bedroom."

"Check it anyway. You never know. I'll go downstairs and start checking all those rooms. They must have kept something that belonged to our parents. Their wedding rings, for instance, or a watch. *Something* for God's sake. Constance said I need closure. I thought I already had it, but I was wrong."

"Right now, Mallory, I don't care about closure. I just want to get out of here. What if the neighbors were looking out the window and recognized me as the driver of the car?"

"No one saw us, and even if they did, chances are they couldn't give a description. People mind their own business and don't want to get involved. That's the bottom line."

Abby walked back up the steps to Bobby's room. It was so spick-and-span, she blinked. Not a wrinkle in the NFL bedspread. The dressers and night tables were clutter- and dust-free. It didn't look like the room had ever been occupied by a teenage boy. How long had he been gone now? Just a few months wasn't it? She wondered if he'd liked this room. Maybe, if he'd been allowed to toss his clothes around, to blast his stereo and play his television after nine at night. Where was all his sports equipment, or had he taken it with him?

Abby looked at everything, moving things just to see if there was anything wedged or nudged behind something else. Then she saw it . . . sitting behind a papier-mache castle and a box of Pick-up Sticks. She was so excited she felt a head rush. "Mallory. Come here!" she shouted.

Mallory bounded up the stairs. "Did you find it?"

Abby pointed to it. "We can't take it, Mallory. If we do, they'll know we were here. As long as we know it's here, it's okay."

Mallory's lips pressed into a thin tight line. "If we don't take it, he could destroy it. I don't want Mama getting thrown out as junk. Do you?"

"No, but . . ."

"There are no buts. We're taking it, Abby. Let him blame Carol or even Bobby. Trust me, he's not going to mention it to either one of them. How would he explain it? You already asked him about it. He knows we're curious. The natural thing for him to do would be to get rid of it. If you don't want to carry it, I will." She took the urn off the shelf. "Come on, let's go downstairs. You're finished up here, right?"

"I didn't find anything I recognized as being Mama's or Daddy's, but I'm not sure I would know even if I did find something. I was so young, and my memory . . ."

"Maybe we should just go and after they get back you can call him and ask him if he saved anything. It's a long drive to Atlanta. I'll call Constance from my cell phone and ask when she can see us."

Back on the road, Mallory said, "Let's talk about the future. Your future, Abby. Let's plan your wedding."

"What wedding?"

"Yours and Steve's. What kind of dress do you want?"

"I'm not planning on getting married for a very long time," Abby responded, looking askance at her sister, wondering if she'd finally snapped. "Maybe never."

"Steve's the marrying kind. He's going to want lots of kids to play with all those animals. It's a wonderful thing. Abby, so don't close your mind to it. I'd like to be your maid of honor unless that spot is reserved for Bunny."

"The spot is yours, Mallory. You're my sister. You better plan on hanging around for a long time, though. Marriage is way down the road."

"Can I be your first child's godmother?"

"That's even further down the road."

Mallory leaned her head back against the headrest, her hold on the urn secure. She smiled in the darkness. "I can wait."

Abby's thoughts buzzed inside her head. She had to admit that she'd thought this whole venture was going to be one big

wild-goose chase, but the very first stop had proved Donovan to be a liar. *Does it follow, then, that he's lied about
everything else, too? Mother of God, how did it come to
this?*

"Hello, baby, how are you?" Carol asked, stroking her
son's hair. "You gave us a bit of a scare."

Bobby looked as white as the pillow behind his head.
"Sorry," Bobby mumbled.

Donovan gently ruffled his son's hair. "They say you'll be
out of here in no time and back to the old study grind. Your
mom wasn't kidding. You did give us a scare."

"You can recover at home," Carol said reaching for
Bobby's hand. "That way I'll know how you're doing."

"No, Mom. I'm not going home. Finals are coming up. I
can recover here as well as anyplace. Besides, I don't want
you to fuss over me. I hate it when you fuss. I'm not a little
kid anymore."

"Bobby, this wasn't a walk-in-the-park surgery. What happened to you was serious. You're going to need to take it easy
and be monitored. I can do that."

"I'm staying here," he said firmly. "The guys will watch
out for me. Stop treating me like a baby. Did you tell Abby?"

"I called her, son," Donovan said, nudging Carol out of
the way. "She was very concerned. I expect you'll be hearing
from her soon."

"Did you read her book, Dad? *Canine Capers?* I read it,
and I couldn't believe my own sister wrote it. All the girls,
even some of the guys in the dorm, are taking turns reading
it. She's going to be famous, Dad. Right up there with
Stephen King and Tony Hillerman."

"I know, and it couldn't happen to a nicer person. She deserves it. Did you see Mallory impersonating Abby on the
Regis and Kathie Lee show?"

"Yeah, I taped it and watched it afterward. But I knew before what the plot of the new book is going to be. Abby told me it was based on an insurance case Mallory found. I think it's really great that they're collaborating, don't you?" When he reached for his water glass, Carol intercepted it before he could touch it. He pushed the glass away and continued talking to his father. "Abby promised to come up to see me after the holidays. She wants to do some research here in New Jersey since that's where the crime took place. I'm kind of sleepy, Dad, do you mind if I doze off?"

"Sure. No problem. Sleep is the best thing for you right now. Your mom and I will go for some coffee and be back later. Don't let those bedbugs bite now, you hear?"

"Dad, that's what you say to little kids. Don't make me laugh, okay? It hurts."

"See you in a little while." Donovan put his arm behind Carol's back and moved her toward the door.

"He doesn't look good," Carol said in the hallway.

"Jesus Christ, Carol, the kid just had surgery. He's groggy, he's in pain, and the last thing he wants is to be cheerful for his parents. Give it a rest already."

They walked down a long, bustling hall. At the nurses' station, Donovan asked for directions to the cafeteria. Carol went on ahead. He watched her walk. She looked like the same woman he'd married, but she wasn't. Or maybe she was. Hell, he didn't know anything anymore. Briefly, he wondered if Carol had any idea how manipulative and controlling she was. The thing with not letting Bobby get his own glass . . . it was the way she was with everything and everyone. He likened it to a sickness.

"I had no idea Bobby and Abby were in close communication," Carol said over her shoulder as they entered the crowded cafeteria. "Did you know that, Donovan?"

"No. It doesn't surprise me, though. They were always very close."

"I don't like it. He knows how I feel. It's almost as though he's flaunting their relationship. Imagine Abby sharing her plots with him. He's just a youngster."

"Yeah, imagine," Donovan said, tongue in cheek. "How long are you planning on us staying here, Carol?"

"Until Bobby's out of the hospital, of course. That was a stupid question, Donovan."

"I can't stay here that long."

"Then go home to your job, Donovan. This is only your son who was at death's door. Go back to your shopping malls and twenty-thousand-square-foot houses. See if I care. Bobby won't care either."

"I'm not going to argue with you, Carol. You do what you want to do, and I'll do what I want to do. But take some advice from me. Stop doing to Bobby what you did to Abby. Stop now before it's too late. There's still some wiggle room where the boy is concerned. You're on the edge of blowing it."

"Ah, the eight-hundred-pound gorilla has spoken," Carol said.

Donovan's shoulders slumped. He wished he was on a plane heading home. The moment he was certain Bobby was in the safe zone he would leave.

Outside in the crisp November air, Donovan fired up a cigarette as he hunkered down inside his heavy jacket. With nothing to do for an hour or so, he could get in the rental car and drive to Edison and check out his old house. Abby might want to know who was living there now. He didn't stop to think or to tell Carol where he was going. She wouldn't care anyway. Carol didn't care about anything lately, except herself.

Thirty minutes later, Donovan was on Nevsky Street, where he made a right turn on Fleet Avenue and then another right onto Alexander Street. He drove slowly up to the dead end and crawled around the circle. It wasn't the kind of street that had mailboxes at the curb, so he had no way of telling if the neighbors were the same or not.

There were cedar shakes on his house now. John and Harriet's house was painted a warm beige with dark brown shutters. The old landscaping was gone on both houses. He thought it strange that there were no cars in any of the driveways. Maybe the neighborhood had turned over and everybody worked. So the Valentinos put in a pool. Or, if it wasn't the Valentinos, then someone else. A cloak of depression settled over him as he drove away and headed to the Friendly Shop for coffee.

It was time to do some heavy-duty thinking that could possibly result in some heavy-duty decision making.

Three hours into the five-hour drive to Atlanta, Mallory broke the silence. "Why don't we switch up, Abby? I catnapped."

"I am kind of tired. I'll pull over as soon as I see a shoulder that's wide enough. I'm tired but not sleepy. Figure that one out."

Within minutes, Abby slowed the rental car and pulled over to a wide shoulder on the side of the road.

"I feel like I'm brain-dead," Mallory said as she handed the urn to her sister. "If it spooks you to hold Mama, we can put her on the backseat."

Abby leaned over the backseat and wedged the urn between their two overnight bags. She didn't want to have anything to do with her mother's ashes.

Mallory steered the car into the moving traffic. "Do you want to talk about any of this, Abby?"

"What's the point?"

"The point is, you're confused. You don't know who to believe, Donovan or me. I know he told you something that is making you uncomfortable. If we talk about it, maybe we can clear the air."

"There's nothing to talk about, really. I just can't believe that Donovan murdered anyone, especially Daddy. He loved Daddy like a brother. And me. He was like a second father to me even before Daddy died."

"Of course he loved you, and I'm sure he still does. And you were always sweet and loving in return. I, on the other hand, was a mean and vicious little girl. I hated you because Mama said I was supposed to hate you. I remember crying once because I didn't want to be mean. Mama punished me and took my toys away. I wanted her to love me, and if being mean to you was what I had to do to get that love, I did it. It was wrong. Even as a child I knew it was wrong. But I did it anyway. Make Abby's life miserable. That was the name of the game. A sick, ugly, hateful game. I could try to make it up to you for the rest of my life, but it wouldn't be enough time."

"I don't hold any resentment toward you. I never did."

"That really says something about you, you know? I could never understand why you continued to love me after all the hateful things I did and said to you. Do you remember the nights you used to crawl into bed with me?"

Abby had forgotten those times, but Mallory's words brought it all back. "I remember. I remember how you shooed me out before it got light out in the morning so Mama wouldn't see that I slept with you. You were never mean to me then." She blinked back tears. "I remember one night when you were falling asleep, you rubbed my cheek and said you wished you had a magic finger to make my mark go away."

Mallory took her right hand off the steering wheel and reached for Abby's. "In spite of the way things look now, everything is going to turn out all right. You'll see."

Abby smiled. She wished she had the confidence Mallory had. "Are you still up to flying to New Jersey after we see Constance? I'd like to see Bobby . . . and I need to check out the lay of the land for the book. I don't want to make any mistakes."

"Sounds good," Mallory replied.

Chapter Sixteen

Donovan Mitchell sat in the parking lot of the small strip mall drinking his coffee and smoking as he watched the busy shoppers entering and exiting the A&P and the CVS drugstore. It had been years since he'd been in either a supermarket or a drugstore. Anything he wanted or needed, Carol took care of. Carol took care of everything. She always had, even before they were married. He'd always thought she was making his life—everybody's life—easier, but now he knew just the opposite to be true. She'd complicated all their lives by trying to control them.

He adjusted his sunglasses to ward off the late-November sunshine. Was that his old neighbor, Mrs. Lascaris, standing by the long row of grocery carts? He stretched his neck out the window to get a better look. "I'll be damned. It is," he said, bolting from the car and racing up to the entrance of the A&P. "Mrs. Lascaris?"

She looked disgruntled. "My goodness, it took you a long time to get here, young man. I called the cab company a half hour ago."

Donovan laughed. She was just as he remembered her; a curmudgeon. "I'm not from the cab company. Don't you remember me, Mrs. Lascaris? Donovan Mitchell. I used to live next door to you."

The spry little lady looked at him over the top of her wire-rim glasses. "Lord have mercy, it is you, Donovan. How are you? What in the world are you doing here?"

"I'm fine, and you?"

"A lot older than when you saw me last. Are you thinking of moving back here? Oh, I do hope so. I don't much care for the people who bought your house. They have two teenage boys with earrings in their ears and tattoos all over their arms and neck. I've never seen the likes! I thought teenagers liked to do odd jobs to earn a little money. But not these boys. I remember how you used to rake my leaves for me every fall. And shovel my snow in the winter. I miss you, young man."

Young man. Donovan grinned from ear to ear. It had been a long time since anyone called him a young man. "How about if you forget the cab and let me take you home?"

"I'd like that. Those cabbies take forever to show up and then they don't want to carry the groceries inside unless you give them a ten-dollar tip. I can't afford that kind of money on my pension. Everything costs so much these days," Estelle Lascaris fretted.

Donovan touched her arm. "Wait here and I'll fetch the car." He started to leave, then turned back. "Do you still bake those raisin-filled cookies that are so good for dunking?"

She smiled brightly. "Yes. I made some yesterday as a matter of fact. Would you like some, and maybe some coffee to dunk them in?" she asked, her voice filled with hope.

"You bet I would," Donovan called over his shoulder as he hurried across the parking lot to get his car. He pulled the car up in front of the store, helped her into the passenger seat, then put her two bags of groceries in the trunk.

"I think it's going to snow," Estelle said as she settled herself in the front seat of the car. "I wonder if I should have bought more food. When the weather turns bad, it's hard for me to get out."

Donovan turned his head to look at her. "Isn't there anyone to help you?"

"Not anymore. My son lives in California now. Dentists are too busy these days to . . . to interrupt their lives by . . . visiting their aging parents. He calls once a month or so. Julie, my daughter, is in Costa Rica. She's been there now for four years. She's a journalist. My brother and sister-in-law passed away a few years ago."

Donovan's thoughts filtered back twenty-plus years. Mrs. Lascaris had been such a comfort to him after Emma and the baby died. She'd been like a mother, watching over him, seeing that he ate properly. She'd even tidied up his house a couple of times. He'd tried to pay her, but she'd stubbornly refused, saying that was what friends and neighbors were for.

Now, when she needed help, there was no one to help her. Or was there?

"Have you ever considered living in one of those self-contained retirement communities?"

She shook her head. "I had my son check into it for me, and he said I couldn't afford it. I was hoping he might offer to help, but he has his own family to worry about."

"If you could afford it, would you consider relocating to say . . . someplace in the South?"

"Warm air and sunshine all the time?" She lifted her heavily padded shoulders. "That's the stuff dreams are made of." She turned her head to look out the side window.

"Not necessarily. I'm a rich man now, Mrs. Lascaris. If you're willing, I just might be able to make your dream come true. Would you have trouble leaving here?"

She turned back, her eyes full of excitement. "Lord, no. All my friends are gone now. The only friends I have are books and soap operas, and my television set is starting to go. The TV repair shop wants sixty-five dollars just to come and look at it."

Inexplicably angry, Donovan asked himself what kind of world was this when caring old ladies had to pinch every penny. He stopped the car in front of her house. "We're here," he announced. "You go on in, I'll bring in your groceries."

Estelle Lascaris stepped out of the car and started up the walk. She'd only taken a few steps when she stopped and turned to look at him. "I am just so happy you came by, Donovan. This is the most excitement I've had in years."

Donovan stared at her, unable to comprehend how a visit from him could bring her so much joy. "Hurry up and get inside before you freeze to death," he said, waving her away. He popped the trunk and started to pick up one of the bags when something caught his eye. "Spam?" he said aloud, not quite believing what his eyes were telling him. He counted two cans of it, several boxes of grocery-store-brand macaroni and cheese, canned soup, tuna, and scrapple. Jesus.

"Come in. Come in," she said, motioning him toward her. "Take the chill off."

The house was too cold to take the chill off, he thought as he followed her to the kitchen. She turned on the stove and rubbed her blue-veined hands over the gas burner.

"You shouldn't do that," he warned, setting the bags down on the yellow Formica-top table. "Isn't your furnace working?"

"Yes, it's working, but the heating bills are so high that I have to conserve."

Donovan blinked as his good life flashed before his eyes. He started to unload the groceries.

"I'll put all that away later. Sit down and talk to me while

I make a pot of coffee." She bustled around the kitchen, her movements slower than he remembered. "Here are the cookies," she said, setting a plate down in front of him. Knowing she expected it, he immediately popped one into his mouth. "Do they taste the same as you remember?"

Donovan smiled as he chewed. "Better than I remember," he said, smacking his lips in appreciation. He longed for a cup of good strong coffee but when she finally filled his cup, it was little more than colored water.

"Do you miss the old neighborhood, Donovan?" She eased herself into the chair across from him.

"Sometimes, but that's not why I'm here. My son is in the hospital. His appendix ruptured. He's doing fine though. I expect he'll be back in school in no time."

"Mercy, time certainly does fly, doesn't it? Before we know it, it will be Christmas." She looked sad, Donovan thought.

"I have an idea, Mrs. Lascaris. Since there's nothing holding you here, why not sell this place and come to South Carolina? I build retirement communities and shopping malls. I can fix you up with a two-bedroom, two-bath condo in my newest retirement village. The model condo is vacant. I'll give you a big break on the price, and I'll arrange for a small down payment. It's completely furnished right down to the pots and pans and silverware. There are all kinds of activities for seniors. You'll make friends. There's a chapel, a grocery store that delivers, a heated pool, a movie house with first-run movies, bowling alley, pizza parlor, everything and anything you could possibly want. When you sell this house, you can put the extra money into treasury bills and have income from the interest. I'll take care of it for you if you're willing."

"Why would you do that for me? You haven't seen me in almost twenty years."

"I might not have seen you, but I've thought of you. You were very kind to me when Emma died, and you always put a Christmas card in my mailbox. All you have to do is pack your clothes. Are you interested?"

"No more cold winters and no more snow," she said, longing in her voice.

"Well, we do have a cold snap now and then," Donovan said. "But there's a fireplace in the condo. You can turn the heat as high as you want and you can turn the air conditioning as low as you want."

"I'd like that," Estelle said smartly. "If you're serious, I'll call the real-estate lady tomorrow morning and list the house."

"I'm very serious. Do you think your son will mind you making the move?"

She shrugged. "No, but he will want to know what I'm going to do with the extra money. Treasury bills, you said? I like to be independent. God willing, I hope to live another twenty years. That will make me a hundred and two!"

"Each and every one of those days will be filled with sunshine and new friends. Listen, I have to head back now." Donovan reached into his inside jacket pocket, pulled out his wallet, and took out a business card. "Put this someplace where you won't forget it and give me your phone number. I'll call you in a few days to see how things are going. As soon as I get home I'll send you a brochure so you can see what the village looks like and what your condo looks like. I think you'll be pleasantly surprised. With any luck, this house will sell quickly and you can be in your new home before Christmas."

Estelle giggled like a schoolgirl as she carefully wrote her number down with the stub of a pencil. "What happened to the two little Evans girls? I heard talk in the neighborhood that you took them in. The little one with the terrible birthmark, is she okay? She was such a dear little thing. I sometimes have to ask myself what God was thinking when He did that to her. And the other little one, too pretty for her own good. It didn't seem fair to me. Then there was that really weird woman who was so nosy and always skulking about."

"Yes, I did take the girl in. And after I got married, I adopted them." He shook his head in confusion. "But I don't know the weird woman you're talking about unless you mean Harriet."

"No, not Harriet. I remember her. Oh, well. It doesn't matter. Sometimes my memory is good and sometimes it isn't. You really adopted those two little girls? That's wonderful, Donovan. That's why God blessed you with such good fortune. John was a good man. A nice neighbor. He always took my Christmas-tree lights down for me. He said if you put them on, he'd take them off. It was such a shame. I'm no hypocrite, but I didn't much care for Harriet. She had, in my opinion, a high snoot factor. I could never figure that out. The girls, are they okay?"

"They're well and happy," Donovan said, hoping it was true. "Perhaps you'll see them one of these days, but I don't know if they'll remember you. They were awfully young."

"So unfortunate," she said, her thoughts obviously still on John's untimely death. "We were all in shock. I remember you flying back from somewhere. You were in a daze for weeks. So sad."

It was worse than sad, he thought. It was devastating. Once he'd gotten the initial decision making over, he'd gone into a long funk. "Yes, it was sad," he agreed. "Well, I have to be on my way." At the door he hugged the little woman, marveling at how she smelled the same after all these years. Lavender and lemon, she told him eons ago. Better than any perfume. "Will you promise to bake cookies for me when you're in your new condo?"

"Every Friday is baking day. You stop by on any Friday afternoon, and they'll be waiting for you. Bless you, Donovan. I'll say a prayer for your boy."

It was dark when Donovan climbed into his rental car. He headed back to the Friendly Shop for coffee to drink on the way to the hospital. He decided he should probably call Carol and tell her where he was and that he was on the way back. Thirty minutes later, Donovan dialed the number he'd taken from Bobby's bedside phone. "How are you, son?"

"Okay, Dad. Where are you?"

"In Edison. I'm on the way back to the hospital. I took a drive around the old neighborhood and stopped for coffee. I saw one of my old neighbors, an elderly lady, waiting for a taxi with her groceries, so I gave her a ride home. She invited me in for the best cookies in the world. She was lonely, so I visited with her for a while. Where's your mother?"

"Seeing if she can get a room here at the hospital. Dad, will you make her go home? All she does is fuss and fret over me. I'm gonna be okay. Hey, Abby called. I talked to her for about fifteen minutes. She said she and Mallory are coming up this way and will stop to visit. Don't tell Mom, okay?"

"Don't tell Mom what?" Donovan heard Carol ask in the background.

"That a girl just came to see me," Bobby said sourly.

"Is that your father on the phone? I want to talk to him." Donovan heard Bobby grumble. "Where have you been, Donovan?" Carol asked, her voice throbbing with anger.

"Here and there. I went by the old neighborhood. Then I went to Friendly's for coffee and met Mrs. Lascaris and gave her a ride home."

"Lookie-loo Lascaris! I bet she had a ton of gossip for you. That woman never missed a trick. She knew everyone's business, and what she didn't know she made up."

"That's not fair, Carol. She's a kind, gentle old lady no one cares about. I made her a deal on the model condo in the new complex, and she's going to sell her place and move in."

"You didn't! Good God, tell me you didn't."

"I did and that's that. She's eighty-two years old and she barely squeaks by on her pension. She keeps her heat turned low because of the high gas bills. She wears two sweaters and heavy wool socks and she eats Spam and macaroni and cheese. That's no way to live, Carol. It's in my power to help her, and that's exactly what I'm going to do. If you don't like it, screw it." He'd never talked to Carol like that before, and he wasn't sure how she would react.

"Do what you want. I don't care. Are you talking about the model in Camellia Haven, the one I decorated?"

"That's the one!"

There was such outrage in Carol's voice. Donovan winced when she said, "All that work for an eighty-two-year-old lady who probably wears Depends."

"For crying out loud, Mom," Donovan heard Bobby say. "Don't you two ever stop? Go on, Mom. Go back to the hotel. My coach and a couple of the guys are coming by in a little while. Dad?"

This time it was Bobby who had the phone. "I heard you, son. I'll be at the Hyatt in New Brunswick if you need me. Do you want me to get you anything?"

"I'm good. Jell-O, cookies, Mars bars, and a banana. What more could I want? The guys will probably bring some pizza."

"I'll see you in the morning before I leave, Bobby," Donovan said.

"I'll be staying," Carol said in the background.

Carol arrived at the hotel just as Donovan was checking in. As soon as they were in their room, she tossed her coat and purse onto the king-size bed with its muted orange bedspread. After the way he'd talked back to her on the phone, he'd expected his wife to be in a red-hot rage. Instead, she was acting like Miss Congeniality.

"Let's do room service for dinner, okay?"

"Fine with me," he said, tossing his jacket over the closest chair. It was going to be a long night. He could tell. She was waiting for him to get settled in before hauling out the big guns. But this time he was prepared. *This* time he was going to stand up to her, regardless of the outcome

Donovan gathered his things from his overnight bag, waiting for what he thought was the inevitable: a rip-roaring tirade. He watched as Carol sat down on the edge of the bed and kicked off her shoes.

"I want to apologize to you, Donovan, for . . . everything," she said.

It was the ring of truth in her voice that stopped him on his way to the bathroom. Eyes narrowing, he turned around and stared at her, waiting for the proverbial other shoe to drop.

"I know now that I have been out of line. I've been trying to ride this midlife thing out on my own, but it isn't working. When we go home, I'm going to get a GYN checkup and get some hormones. Everything you said on the ride here is true. It's me, not you. The business with Abby just rocked my world out from under me. I loved that girl. I still love her just the way I love Bobby. I consider both of them mine even though I didn't give birth to them. I can't tell you how many times I picked up the phone to call Abby, but then I'd either set it down or dial the number and break the connection before the machine picked up. I don't know why it's so hard for me to admit I was wrong. And you were right about me trying to control Bobby the way I did Abby. I hate myself for it, Donovan. I really do. And I hate it that we say ugly, hurtful things to each other. I love you. I always will. I think part of my problem is that I've never been one hundred percent sure in my own mind that you loved me as much as I loved you. Sometimes I think you just married me to be a mother to Abby and Mallory," Carol said tearfully.

He didn't know what to say, what to do. She acted sincere, but she'd acted sincere before when she wasn't. Could it be that her behavior really was due to menopause? He'd heard enough TV and radio doctors talk about it to know that some women went through sheer hell. But was Carol one of them, or was this just an excuse for being a full-time bitch? He felt a twinge of something as he did his best to swallow his anger. Everybody deserved a second chance, and who was he to deny Carol hers?

"C'mere," he said, holding out his arms to her.

Carol snuggled into her husband's arms. "I'm going to the hospital tomorrow and apologize to Bobby, then I'm going to call Abby and apologize. If she doesn't answer the phone, I'll write her a letter."

"And as soon as we get home, you'll make that doctor's appointment, right?"

"I promise. Pretty soon everything will be just the way it used to be."

"Good. Now what should we order for dinner. I'm starving."

They'd made good time. They left Charleston around ten in the morning, stopped for lunch and a couple of bathroom breaks, and were on the outskirts of Atlanta. Mallory had called Dr. Oldmeyer only to find out that she wouldn't be able to see her until the following morning.

"There's a Holiday Inn," Abby said, pointing off to the left. "Let's stop there, relax, and have a nice dinner. What time is our appointment?"

"Ten." Mallory started to hum a tune, then stopped suddenly. "Do you know any lullabies, Abby?"

Abby looked askance at her sister. "I know that hush little baby one. Why?"

"Will you sing it to me when we go to sleep?"

The fine hairs on the back of Abby's neck stood at attention. "Ah . . . sure," she said hesitantly. She started to shake. "You aren't going to take . . . Mama to bed with you, are you?"

"I was just thinking about that. Maybe just this one night unless you think it will spook you?"

"It will spook me. Please don't. Leave the urn in the car."

"Okay but . . . It doesn't seem right somehow," Mallory said, her voice sounding childlike.

A scream started to build in Abby's throat. "Why the hell not? God only knows how long she was wedged between that papier-mache castle and that can of Pick-up Sticks. Closet, car, what difference does it make?"

Mallory sat up straight. "Hey, hey, easy does it here. Okay. I'm not arguing with you. She . . . I mean, the urn stays in the car. No problem."

"Thank you very much, Mallory."

They checked in, inspected the room before they carried their bags in from the car. Mallory unpacked her cosmetic bag and blow-dryer and announced that she was going to take a long, hot shower.

Abby reached for her cell phone and dialed Steve's office number. The second he picked up she could hear dogs barking in the background. "Hi, it's me," she said in a tired voice. "Everything okay?"

"Everything is fine here. How about you? I was beginning to worry when I didn't hear from you."

Abby smiled into the receiver. It was comforting to know he worried about her. "We found Mama's urn," she said. "But we couldn't find anything else. We've decided to ask Donovan if he saved anything."

"Hang on a minute, Abby, I have to write out a prescription and give it to my assistant." He was back a moment later. "So what's next on the agenda?" he asked.

"We have a ten o'clock appointment to see Constance Oldmeyer, Mallory's doctor. After I hang up from you, I'm going to call the airlines and schedule an afternoon flight into New Jersey to see Bobby. I guess we might be home late tomorrow night or early the next morning. Do the dogs miss me?"

When he didn't immediately answer, Abby got nervous. "Steve . . ."

"I don't think they miss you as much as you'd like them to," he said.

"What's that supposed to mean?" Again, he delayed answering her. She pressed her ear to the phone and heard sounds . . . whimpers and whines.

"They're all here on the visiting couch with me," he admitted with a reluctance that came through loud and clear.

Abby started to laugh. The visiting couch was a battered old sofa he kept in the back for customers to sit on while they visited their ailing pets. She could just see him sitting there with all seven dogs trying to cuddle up next to him.

"Thanks for taking care of them," she said. "I love you."

It was nine o'clock in the morning when Mallory pulled alongside the Argone security guard for the second time in three days and offered up her alias. "They have to call Dr. Oldmeyer to clear us through," she explained when the guard turned away.

"You can drive up to the building, miss, but Dr. Oldmeyer wanted me to tell you she's been delayed and can't see you till eleven o'clock. She suggested a stroll around the grounds. She'll meet you on the bench under the magnolia tree."

"This is beautiful," Abby said stretching her neck to view the rolling emerald lawns.

"Yes it is. All the rooms have a great view of the lawns and gardens. When I first got here, I used to cry because I wanted to run barefoot through the grass. You had to be really, really special to be able to do that." Mallory steered into the parking lot and cut the engine. For long minutes, she sat staring at the building.

"Mallory, are you all right?" Abby asked with concern. She wasn't sure how to interpret the peculiar expression on her sister's face.

Mallory climbed out and stood by the car door. "Yeah, I'm fine. You know, if it wasn't for Constance, I'd still be in there." She gestured toward the pink-brick building. "The other doctors gave up on me. That's the part that really hurts. Not Constance, though. The day she told me I could call her by her first name was the day I knew it was all going to work out. Isn't that strange? Just a little thing like that. She let me go outside and run barefoot through the grass as much as I wanted. Sometimes we'd both take off our shoes and play tag. We did a lot of kid stuff that I had missed. Don't say anything, Abby. I'm okay with it now. I guess I'm just trying to make conversation. I saw where you lived all those years. I want you to see where I lived."

"Mallory, I know I've said this before, but I do so wish things had been different."

"So do I, Abby. We grow and we learn. It's called life. Neither one of us can unring the bell."

Side by side they strolled through the gardens. "That's a beautiful pool and tennis court. Are you a good tennis player?"

"I have no idea. I never played. In all the years I was here, I never saw anyone on the court. Actually, I never saw anyone in the pool either. Yet, both are maintained. There's a heated pool indoors, too. I never saw anyone in it either."

"Maybe that was because you were locked up all the time."

"That's true, but I talked to some of the other kids and they'd never seen them being used either. Schools like this . . . they're big-money operations. I think the pools and the tennis court are just for show. The clients . . . the parents . . . are led to believe their kid is going to have access to *all* the amenities. It's soothing to their consciences to think their juvenile delinquent won't be totally deprived. They have no idea what the truth is. No idea at all. Get it through your head, Abby, every single one of us here was a throwaway."

"Why didn't you tell Donovan? You could have called or written."

Mallory waved her hand in front of Abby's face. "Earth to Abby. Phones? Surely you jest! Now, letters . . . Letters were okay. Of course, they went through a thorough examination first to make sure they didn't contain anything they shouldn't. You know, like complaints? By the time the letter was acceptable, it was pretty generic. You could have almost written a form letter and just filled in the blanks every time you sent it out."

"So why didn't you tell him when he came to visit?"

"Our visits . . . how many were there? Three? Four? I don't recall. Anyway, our visits were supervised. I couldn't say anything. But even if I could have told him, I don't know if he would have cared or that he would have believed me. Why did he adopt us anyway?"

Abby shrugged. "Because our father was Donovan's best friend, and he felt responsible."

"Look!" Mallory pointed to the caretaker's cottage. "Doesn't it remind you of our old house in New Jersey, the way the roof slants over the front door? I remember everything about that house, even what the wallpaper in my bedroom looked like, all those little roses on that blue background. How about you? Do you remember it?"

"Not the house so much, but I remember running across the yard to Donovan's. I think I remember his house better than ours. Ours was brown and his was a kind of earthy green." Abby checked her watch. "It's almost time to meet Constance. We should be heading back."

"There she is," Mallory said, pointing toward Argone's front steps. "Uh-oh, something's wrong. I can tell by the look on her face."

Abby felt a bolt of fear run up her spine.

Chapter Seventeen

"Dr. Oldmeyer, this is my sister Abby. Abby, my dear friend, Dr. Constance Oldmeyer."

The psychiatrist held out her hand. "Mallory has told me so much about you. I feel I already know you," the psychiatrist said looking Abby squarely in the eye. The sincerity and concern in the woman's eyes eased the tension between Abby's shoulders.

Dr. Oldmeyer didn't look anything like Abby had expected, which was a tall, stylish, coiffed, and manicured professional. Instead, she looked like a gentle, elderly woman. The motherly type. Not a psychiatrist. "She's told me a great deal about you, too," Abby replied.

"Let's sit down," Constance suggested. She glanced down at her watch. "I've so looked forward to seeing you two together and spending time with you, but it doesn't look like today is the day. There's a very important meeting I must attend in fifteen minutes. It has something to do with one of the school's major contributors canceling a sizable contribution the board was counting on."

Abby glanced at Mallory and knew by her sister's expression that they were both wondering the same thing. But it was Mallory who asked the question.

"Is it Donovan?"

Constance reached for Mallory's hand and covered it with her own. "I won't know until I go to the meeting. But all things considered, I think it's entirely possible."

Abby paled as she remembered the after-TV-interview conversation with Donovan. Had he been trying to tell her something when he'd asked her if she'd considered the possible ramifications of writing *Proof Positive?* Was he withdrawing his financial support from Argone to get even with Mallory for appearing on national TV? But how could taking away his contribution affect Mallory, now that she no longer needed the school's services? Like everything else in the ongoing puzzle, it didn't make sense.

A pulse started to throb behind Abby's right eye. She didn't know if she should share her thoughts with Mallory and Constance or not. What purpose would it serve? None she could think of, though she was certain it would arouse even more suspicion against Donovan. And it seemed to her there was already enough suspicion without her adding to it.

"It *is* Donovan," Mallory stated unequivocally. "I know it as sure as I'm sitting here. The timing is too coincidental for it not to be him."

Dr. Oldmeyer's gaze turned speculative. "I wonder—" She tilted her head and looked at Mallory. "No," she said, evidently dismissing the idea, whatever it was.

"What?" Mallory persisted.

"Well . . ." she said. "Something else very strange has happened, and I was wondering if there was a connection. But I'm sure it's nothing."

Mallory looked at Abby, who was sitting on the opposite bench. "Tell us anyway."

"It's just that when I went into my office to get the things you asked me for, I learned that the file boxes containing all our 'case closed' files had been removed and put in a more secure location in the school. I'm sure I'll get them back, but at

the moment I don't know where they are so I don't have anything to show your sister."

"Didn't you put everything on the hard drive of your computer?"

"Yes, but when I got my new computer last month, I trans-
ferred your files to disc and put them in with the hard copies
so everything would be together in one place. You don't
think . . ."

"I don't know what to think," Mallory interrupted. "It
could be nothing, or it could be something. Was there anything in my files that would have caused Donovan concern? I
mean, did I tell you anything under hypnosis that would im-
plicate him? Something we didn't discuss or something I
might have forgotten."

"Not that I can remember, but your files went back to the
day you were admitted. After I came on the scene there was . . .
Let me think. Visitation records, of course, and the letters
Donovan sent you and copies of the ones you sent him along
with the audiotapes of your hypnosis sessions. I wish you
had told me you wanted those things the other day when you
were here." She consulted her watch again. "Oh, dear, I really
do have to be going. These money meetings take precedence
over everything in this place. In addition to everything else
going on, Dr. Malfore told me that he was going to hand
in his resignation following the meeting, but wouldn't tell
me why."

"Who is Dr. Malfore?" Abby asked.

"He was my first psychiatrist here at Argone. Now he's
chief of staff," Mallory answered. When Constance stood,
Mallory took her hand. "Please, Constance, just one more
minute. I need you to tell my sister I'm not crazy. Tell her I'm
mentally healthy and that my suspicions about Donovan are
well-founded."

Constance Oldmeyer placed both her hands on Abby's shoulders. "She's telling you the truth, my dear. My files contain Mallory's childhood memories of Donovan having an affair with your mother, which may or may not be a motive for murder. If you need added reassurance, I'll be happy to fax you copies of my findings. I'll need a signed release from you, of course, Mallory. It was such a pleasure meeting you, Abby." She turned to Mallory and gave her a hug. "I'll call you as soon as all this gets straightened out. A few days at the most. Take care of each other. Love each other." And then she was gone, her shoulders slumping as she trundled down the brick path that led to the main part of the building.

Mallory turned to look at her sister, her face miserable. She dropped down to the apple green grass and crossed her legs Indian fashion. "What do you make of all this, Abby?"

"I'm not sure, but like you I have to wonder if Donovan is the one who canceled his contribution. Obviously you and Constance have discussed him at length. This whole thing is so unrealistic I wouldn't be able to get this stuff past my editor even if I was planning on using it in the book."

Mallory stared off into the distance. "Don't say that, Abby, because you have to use this stuff. It's all part of the plot, don't you see? Some of it will turn out to be nothing at all—red herrings, so to speak, and the rest—Somehow in the end it will all fit. I know it." She plucked a blade of grass. "Tell me if this makes any sense. Donovan knows I know something. But he's not sure exactly what I know. He knows Dr. Oldmeyer would have kept records of everything I told her. It's those records that worry him, so he has to get rid of them. But he can't just barge into Argone and get them himself now, can he? No. He has to get someone to get them for him, someone who has the authority to move the records. As chief of staff, Dr. Malfore is the only one who has that authority. But, of course, he would never get rid of patient files, closed or not . . . unless he was pressured into doing it by someone threatening to take away Argone's main line of financial support. I *know* Dr. Malfore, and if in fact he did take those files for that reason, in my opinion, he would feel he'd betrayed his own high principles. Leaving Argone would be a likely step for him to take, especially if after his taking the files, the gift to Argone was canceled anyway."

Abby's mind was reeling. Mallory should have been the mystery writer. She could put two and two together and come up with five and sometimes six if she thought about it long enough. "Everything you've said could be true. But it could just as easily be a series of coincidences."

"Time will tell," Mallory said, getting to her feet. "It all depends on who the 'big' contributor is." She took a deep breath and let it out in a resigned sigh. "Well, I guess we might as well head for the airport. God, this makes me crazy."

"Bad word choice, Mallory," Abby said, jokingly.

Mallory didn't appear the least bit amused. "Abby, wait a minute. I know all this sounds fishy. I drag you here and suddenly everything goes haywire. It seems like everything I tell you or try to prove comes back to bite me on the ass. I'm afraid if I lose my grip, I'll slip right back into that dark place I inhabited for so long. I need you to believe in me. There was a time when I thought as long as Constance believed in me, that was enough. You've now jumped ahead of Constance. I wouldn't lie to you, Abby. That's not who I am anymore. Please. Look at me. Tell me you believe me."

Right then Abby had to make what was probably the most important decision of her life, but all she wanted to do was close her eyes, go to sleep, and wake up with Olivia and Beemer licking her feet. She held out her arms. "I believe everything you said to me, Mallory. I'd trust you with my life. I'd even trust you with Olivia and Beemer. From now on it's *us* against him or them or whoever."

An instant later she realized everything she'd just said was true.

"Are you sure you want to do one more drive-by, Mallory? We've been up and down this street at least fifty times. We took pictures of our old house, Donovan's old house, and we even took pictures of the house where the raisin-cookie lady lived. She used to bring them to Donovan's house and he'd share them with me. We have pictures of the malls, the police station, and the town hall. We have street maps, gas-station locations, bank locations. I think we have more than enough background material to finish *Proof Positive* and a couple more books besides. I don't want to overload the reader with details. They'll get bored, and if they get bored— bye-bye book. Hello, trash can!"

Mallory sat forward in her seat and peered out the windshield. "I don't think I'd want to live here again, would you, Abby?"

"I barely remember it, so I can't answer that. The only memory that's alive for me is of all the times I ran across the lawn to Donovan's house," Abby said in a choked voice. "To think that he killed our parents . . . and Connor . . . I can't bear thinking about it, Mallory. I know everything looks really bad for him but . . . Oh, I don't know. To tell you the truth, I pray to God it isn't true, that you're wrong. I'm sorry, but that's how I feel."

Mallory's fine chiseled features took on a pinched look. "I understand. I really do."

"I don't want to think about this any more today," Abby said firmly. "I want to visit Bobby, make sure he's doing all right, then go home." She pulled a slip of paper out of her purse. "Here, you be the navigator."

Abby made a right-hand turn on Calvert Avenue and headed out to Grove and then to James where she picked up Route 27. "I think we just did the long way around," Abby grumbled as she drove through the small town of Metuchen. Thirty minutes later, Abby turned the car into the hospital parking lot.

"Hey, little brother," Abby said, peeking around the door into Bobby's private room. "What's up?"

"Abby! Boy am I glad to see you." Cautiously, Bobby inched himself up into a sitting position.

"I have a surprise for you. Come on in, Mallory. It's time you and your little brother got better acquainted."

Bobby's jaw dropped. "Wow! Mallory."

Mallory walked over to the side of the bed, leaned down, and gave the boy a big hug. "Once they let you out of this joint, you and I are going to have to get really acquainted. I've always wanted a little brother to torment, and you look really tormentable," she teased, putting her fist against his chin.

"Yeah, well don't think I can't put up a good fight. Ask Abby. She'll tell you."

"Oh, boy, can I ever," Abby agreed. "Be careful what you wish for, Mallory."

"Hey, this is great. Really great," Bobby said. His smile reached to both of his big ears.

"How long ago did Carol and Donovan leave?" Abby asked.

Bobby rolled his eyes. "I'm trying to forget they were here. Mom's wacko. Big-time. First she insisted that I go home to recuperate so she could take care of me. Then, she was going to try to get a room here in the hospital to be near me . . . She wouldn't lay off. It's like she's obsessed or something."

Abby squeezed his arm. "She was that way with me, too, Bobby. Finally, I just couldn't take it anymore. That's why we've become so estranged. I feel real bad about it, but like you said, it's as if she's obsessed. What am I saying? She *is* obsessed. Obsessed with controlling people's lives. And when they refuse to let her take over their lives, she freaks."

"Tell me about it," Bobby agreed.

"Listen, we can't stay but a few minutes," Abby said. "We have a plane to catch. We just came to make sure you're feeling okay. Are you?"

"Not bad, considering. I get tired easy, but they tell me I'll be back to my old self in no time."

"Hey, Bobby," Mallory said, wiggling his foot. "Maybe you can help us, you being a guy and all. This book Abby's writing, *Proof Positive* . . . it has this teenage boy who needs to hide stuff from his parents. Private stuff. You know, junk that only means something to him." Abby gave her a disgusted look, but Mallory ignored her. "If you wanted to hide something, where would you hide it?"

Bobby's brow furrowed. "Well, if I was old enough and had a car, I suppose I'd probably hide something under the spare tire in the trunk."

"Will you listen to that, Abby! In a million years we never could have come up with that!"

Abby grimaced. She hated the way her sister was duping Bobby. On the other hand, she wasn't eager to call Carol or Donovan and ask them where their parents' stuff was, so she let it go.

"What about boxes of stuff, like old papers and pictures and stuff?" Mallory asked. "Think about home. Picture the house and all the storage areas. Where would a kid hide something so bulky?"

"How many boxes of stuff?" Bobby asked.

Mallory shrugged. "Two to four maybe. Probably two."

Bobby narrowed his eyes and twisted his lips. "In our garage, there's a pull-down ladder that leads up to a big storage space. You wouldn't know the ladder was there unless you were looking for it. If I was going to hide something, I'd probably hide it up there."

"How come I never knew about it?" Abby asked.

"I don't know," Bobby said. "Probably because Dad keeps his guns up there. The only reason I know about it is because I caught him coming down the ladder one day. He asked me to keep it between the two of us. He said it was the only place where he could hide Mom's Christmas presents so she wouldn't find them."

Guns? Abby had never known Donovan to own guns. Did he use them to hunt? Or did he collect them? She had a million questions, but at the moment she couldn't find it in her heart to ask even one. "I'd love to stay longer, little brother, but we really have to get going if we're going to catch that plane. If you're going home over Christmas break, come over. I want to introduce you to my canine family."

"The ones you wrote about in *Canine Capers?* Sounds great. You'll be there, too, right, Mallory?" he asked hopefully.

"Sure will."

Both Abby and Mallory kissed Bobby good-bye, then hurried away, neither of them speaking until they reached the car.

"I feel awful tricking him like that," Mallory spoke first. "You aren't mad at me, are you?"

"I was a little miffed at first, then I realized it was better than my calling Donovan or Carol and asking them where the stuff was." She turned on the ignition key and sat a moment while the car idled. "What's going to happen to Bobby if . . ." She choked up, the words never quite reaching her lips. "I wish none of this had ever happened. Sometimes it's better not to know things so you don't get hurt."

Abby couldn't believe her eyes. Steve's dining-room table, a garage-sale find, looked like an interior designer had come in and set it. He'd dressed it up with colorful Fiesta dishes, heavy silverware, pewter serving dishes, and multicolored cloth napkins.

"I can't believe you did this all by yourself," she said, her expression full of awe.

"Yeah, well, as they say, I am a man of many talents, but I wanted to get in practice for turkey day. I just wish I were a faster chef. I was up half the night cooking." His tone and expression begged for sympathy.

She put her arms around his neck. "I know I wasn't gone very long, but I really missed you."

"Really? It didn't sound like it when you called. It sounded like you only missed the dogs."

She knew he was kidding by his little-boy tone. "Well, I did miss them . . . but I missed you more. And tonight, after dinner, I'm going to show you just how much."

He wrapped his arms around her and pulled her close. "So, when are you going to tell me what happened?"

"Later. I don't want to deal with it right now. I'm staying the night by the way," Abby said boldly.

"You are, huh?"

"Yep, and I didn't bring a stitch of clothing with me other than what I'm wearing."

"Uh-huh," Steve said, his face brick red. He released her

and went back to his cooking. "Things are about ready here. I think we should feed the dogs now. That way they'll be occupied while we're eating and leave us alone so we can moon over each other."

Abby stared at her dogs in disbelief while Steve prepared their dinner. "How did you get them to sit still like that and not bark?"

"Discipline."

"Discipline as in you beat them or what?"

"Hell, no, I didn't beat them. Haven't you ever heard the word *no?*"

Abby looked perplexed. "They don't understand that word."

"That's because you don't use it. But you can take it from me . . . it works."

The feeding was accomplished in a quiet, organized manner, nothing like the noisy chaos she was used to. Steve was amazing, she thought. No wonder he was such a good vet. He really did understand the animals and knew how to make them behave. She reached for the wooden spoon to stir the white sauce bubbling on the stove. She realized she wasn't the least bit hungry. At least not for food.

"Steve? I know how hard you worked cooking all this, but the truth is there's only one thing I'm really hungry for, and that's you. Do you think we could put dinner on hold a while and satisfy our other appetite?"

Wordlessly Steve started to race around the kitchen like a short-circuited robot, turning off the stove, the oven, wrapping and securing the food in the refrigerator.

"Sex is a great emotional release, isn't it?" Abby said, sighing heavily with exhaustion.

Steve's heart was still racing. "Yeah! No kidding. What emotion was that exactly?"

Abby chuckled and playfully squeezed his upper thigh. "I think it was a combination of emotions. Too much for you, huh?"

"No, no! Never too much. Me Tarzan," he said, beating himself on the chest. He pulled her closer. Neither of them spoke for several minutes. When their ragged breathing calmed, he asked, "Are you ready to tell me what you two were up to? Needless to say, I'm just a little curious."

Abby wished she could twitch her nose so he would instantly know everything there was to know, but she didn't possess any magical powers. If she did, she would make this whole awful situation just go away. She decided to start right from the beginning, with Mallory's television interview, Donovan's phone call, his accusations against Mallory . . . everything. "We thought if we could find the urn and our parents' personal effects, they might shed some light on the truth, so we broke into Donovan and Carol's house. Well, we didn't actually break in, since I have a key. We went through their things, though, and we found the urn shoved into the back of Bobby's closet, which proves Donovan lied about it and makes me wonder how many other lies he's told."

"My God, Abby, this is serious. Deadly serious."

Abby's eyebrows shot upward. "I know, Steve. I don't want it to be true. I love Donovan. I find it hard to believe that he could do anything so . . . so terrible but . . . finding the urn and talking to Dr. Oldmeyer—"

"Who's Dr. Oldmeyer?" Steve cut in.

"Mallory's psychiatrist. After leaving Carol and Donovan's house, we drove to Atlanta, to Argone, the school, slash, institution where Mallory lived all those years. She wanted me to meet Dr. Oldmeyer so I'd hear from the horse's mouth so to speak that she was sane. On top of that Mallory was hoping to see her case files and records, specifically the

ones dealing with her hypnosis sessions and the records prov-
ing Donovan had an affair with Mama and the frequency . . .
or rather infrequency . . . of his visits and letters during Mallory's incarceration. You see, I'd been under the impression
that Donovan had been checking on her regularly, but it
seems not."

"That's terrible!" Steve said, his face registering horror.

"When we got there, everything was in a state of upheaval,
so Dr. Oldmeyer didn't have much time to spend with us."
Bit by bit she filled him in on the details of their visit to Argone and told him what she and Mallory thought it all meant.

"Obviously, you're feeling better about Mallory now. You
believe her."

"Yes. I do now. Just before we left, Dr. Oldmeyer assured
me Mallory is perfectly sane and that I could put my trust in
her. When she told me that, I felt a ton of bricks slide off my
shoulders. There were times I had my doubts. Lots of times."

"Okay, so in essence all this trip accomplished was to
make you more suspicious. But you can't convict a man on
suspicions. Especially a man like your adoptive father. Donovan Mitchell is . . . hell, Abby, he's practically an icon. They
don't call him Mr. Land Developer for nothing. His creden-
tials are so impressive they make you gasp for breath. I saw
something in the paper about a retirement village he's building. It's ready now, but the owners won't be moving in till the
week before Christmas or maybe the New Year. It's one of
those one-of a-kind places that is a community in itself with
a twenty-four-hour-a-day tram service that virtually does
away with the need for a car. Donovan's quote was, 'This is
the wave of the future!' He said he was committed to building four more communities just like it. The guy is so rich he
could burn his money if he wanted to. *If* he is a murderer and
if he thinks Mallory is on to him, he might—" He abruptly

stopped. "You girls need to be careful. Maybe you and Mallory should move in here for a while so I can keep an eye on you."

"No to moving in here. Steve, you can't be serious. Donovan would never hurt me. He loves me."

"I love you, too, honey. And I'd hate like hell to lose you."

Chapter Eighteen

Abby sat at the kitchen table playing with the two letters that had come from Carol in the morning mail. One was for Mallory and one was for her.

Mallory watched her sister over the rim of her coffee cup. She reached out to touch the beige envelope. "Do you think it's a letter bomb? It could be, you know. You open yours first."

"No, I don't think it's a letter bomb. You open yours first," Abby countered as she moved Mallory's letter closer to her coffee cup.

"Let's compromise," Mallory suggested. "You shuffle them around. I'll close my eyes and pick one. Whichever one I pick gets opened first. This is really silly, you know. It's probably nothing at all."

"Maybe," Abby said, holding the letters up to the light. "But it could just as easily be *something*." She set the letters down on the table. "Okay, close your eyes." She flipped the envelopes over, address side down, and switched them back and forth a few times like a sideshow shell man until she didn't know which was which. "Go for it," she said, holding her breath.

Mallory studied the envelopes. "This one," she said, slowly turning one of them over.

Abby gasped when she saw her name. "I think you cheated," she said, picking up her butter knife to slit it open.

"Read it out loud," Mallory ordered, smiling like a Cheshire cat.

"Dear Abby,

"I made a promise to Donovan and to myself that as soon as we got home from visiting Bobby, I would call or write you. For the last two days, I have sat here by the phone trying to get up the nerve to dial your number but couldn't for fear you might hang up on me.

"If only I could turn back the clock and do things differently. There is so much I would change. For one, I would have listened to you when you tried to tell me that I was smothering you and trying to control your life. I didn't believe you. I thought you were exaggerating. I know now you weren't. I was every bit as smothering and controlling as you said. If you hadn't alienated yourself from me, I probably would have totally taken over your life. I am so very sorry, Abby.

"Abby, there are no words to tell you how much I regret my behavior. I want to blame it all on menopause but I know that's only part of it. As I look back, I see I have always been the kind of person who needed to be in control. I don't exactly know why, but I promise you it's ended. I'm getting help.

"I beg you to give me another chance. I know I'm asking a lot but you mean a great deal to me and I can't live knowing that my own daughter (I have always thought of you as my own) hates me.

"On the chance that you can't forgive me, please reconsider your relationship with Donovan. He knows very little

about what's gone on between you and me, and he is entirely blameless. He's so proud of you, Abby. You have always been his little princess.

"*The grand opening for Donovan's first retirement village will be December 15. It is such a momentous milestone in his life. He's going to be honored by many civic groups as well as his peers. People will be coming from all over the country to view this village. It would mean a great deal to him if you and Mallory could be there. Yes, I said Mallory.*

"*Please let me know your decision by phone or letter. And again, I'm sorry for all the trouble I've caused you and hope you'll give me an opportunity to make it up to you.*

"*Love,*

"*Carol.*"

Abby took a deep breath, refolded the letter, and set it down. "Your turn."

Mallory used her fingernail to open her letter.

"*Dear Mallory,*" she began, then looked up at Abby.

"*After all these years of refusing to communicate with you, I imagine this letter will come as a bolt out of the blue. I'm sorry about that. I wish I could turn the clock back and change things. I have wronged you terribly. I gave up on you and never gave you a second chance. I'll have to pay for that one of these days, and I'll deserve whatever punishment I get. I am the one responsible for keeping Donovan away from you. He wanted to visit you more often, but I vowed to make his life hell if he did. I'm afraid I made it hell anyway.*

"*I won't even bother to ask you to forgive me or to give me a second chance, as I don't deserve it. I don't think the damage I've done can ever be repaired. But I am asking that you give Donovan a second chance and come to the dedication of his first retirement village. Whatever ill feelings you hold toward me, and they are justified, I hope you can set*

*them aside and do this for Donovan's sake. Please, Mallory,
think about it and make plans to attend.*

"*Best wishes,*

"*Carol.*"

The two sisters stared at one another. "You doing eggs or
what?" Abby asked as she struggled to clear her throat.

"Yeah, I'm doing the eggs," Mallory said, setting the letter
down and getting up. "You do the toast. Make the butter
soft, okay?"

"Wait a minute," Abby said, shoving her chair back. "I'm
really not very hungry. Are you?"

Mallory stopped midway to the sink and turned. "I think
I'd choke on the food if I had to eat it. I think we're just talking to hear ourselves talk."

Abby stared at Mallory, seeing her but not seeing her. She
had never known Carol to apologize for anything. Why, all
of a sudden, would she do it? Was it really because of Donovan? Was she so devoted to him and his wants that she would
compromise herself for his sake? Her brain clicked and
whirled. It simply didn't compute.

"What should we do?" Abby asked. "About the invitation, I mean."

"I can't believe you're asking me that," Mallory said,
looking genuinely astonished. "We're going to accept . . . of
course."

"Of course? Why of course? Why is it a given that we're
going? I can't think of a single reason why *you* would want
to go. Do you know how tense it will be, especially around
Carol? You can't just put years of bitterness aside and act like
nothing has happened."

"I don't intend to put anything aside, but it won't be me
who is feeling the tension, it'll be Carol and Donovan. As to

why it's a given that we're going . . . to see what Donovan will do, if he'll slip up and tip his hand. Remember he *knows* I know something, but he's not sure exactly what it is I know. He's bound to be nervous. This would be a perfect time for him to make a mistake."

Fear and frustration rose in Abby's throat. She swallowed. hard. "This is all way over my head, Mallory. Way over both our heads, if you ask me." She ran her hand through her hair. "You forget, I'm just a mystery writer, not a detective."

"You're afraid. I understand. So am I. But we have to do this. He has to pay for what he did."

"*If* he . . . did anything," Abby reminded her. "We don't have proof, and until we have proof . . ."

"We'll never get the proof," Mallory interrupted, "unless he accidentally does something to reveal himself. All we've got to go on is motivation and speculation. None of this would be happening, by the way, if the police had done their job properly and investigated our parents' deaths. I mean really investigated. They should have done an autopsy on Mama to determine if she died of natural causes or something else. That would have told the story right there."

Abby crossed her arms behind her neck and laid her head down on the table. "This is going to spoil Christmas." Her voice was mumbled. "You know that, don't you? You think about this, Mallory. We go there, we tour the retirement village, we suffer through all the ceremonies, and we probably have dinner with them. Then what?"

"I don't know. All this is like a chess game. It'll be Donovan's move. He'll either play his pawn or . . ."

"Checkmate!" Abby broke in, making a pistol out of her hand and pointing it at Mallory.

"If it'll make you feel better, I'll take my gun, and don't even think about asking me if I know how to use it. I came in first in the sharpshooters' class. I always hit my target even if it's moving. The insurance company loved me."

"You have a gun. Donovan has guns. I don't like guns, Mallory. Guns kill people."

"Wrong. People kill people. Guns are just a tool that people use to achieve that end. I don't like guns either. Sometimes they are a necessary evil."

"I want to talk to Steve about this before I decide. Maybe we should take him with us. Now that he's got another vet working with him, he can take off now and then. I'd feel better if he went with us."

"If that's what it takes to get you to go, then fine, but you'll be giving away the fact that you're in love with him. And considering what happened to Connor . . . It's time to make that call to Connor's parents, Abby. Time to find out if he died of natural causes or if he was murdered."

"I can't. His parents are elderly. It would upset them."

Mallory sighed. "Okay. It's up to you. But I need to call Dr. Oldmeyer back and find out who the big contributor was and ask if she got her files back."

Steve was just finishing up checking a cat for ear mites when Abby came in the back door. Steel cages lined one long wall, all of them filled with animals. The majority were dogs and cats, but today there was also a box turtle in one of the cages.

"Hey!" he said. "Did you come for your rabies shot? We're running a blue-light special on them today."

She couldn't help but laugh. "What's with the turtle?" she asked.

"He's sick."

Abby walked over to the cage and looked in. The turtle's head was buried inside its shell. "How can you tell?"

Steve walked up behind her and put his arm around her shoulder. "Well, he's a little pale, and he's listless."

Abby wrinkled her nose as she studied the turtle more closely. His shell looked like any other turtle's shell. Maybe Steve meant his body was pale. But since his body was inside the shell . . . She felt Steve shaking and blinked up at him to see him trying to contain his laughter. The second their eyes met, he burst out laughing.

"Oh, you're good," she said, shaking her finger at him. "Very good. I bought it, hook, line, and sinker."

"I'm sorry, but I couldn't resist."

"Okay, what's wrong with the turtle?"

"Nothing. I'm boarding him while his owner is on vacation."

She turned on him, a lethal look in her eyes. Step by step she moved him backwards until they were both inside his private office, where she put her arms around him and kissed him with all the passion she could muster.

"Hmm," he said, coming up for air. "That was some serious kissing. I like this stalking business, especially in the middle of the afternoon. Is this a preview of what I can expect tonight?"

"I think you can count on it." She kissed him again, more passionately than the first time.

Steve reached behind him to lock the door. "Just to make sure we aren't disturbed." He grinned.

Thirty minutes later, Abby rolled off the sofa onto the floor. She reached for her jeans. "Thank you, Dr. Carpenter. Your diagnosis was, as usual, right on target. I feel better already. Do you have any idea how much I love you?" she said, looking up at him, a smile of contentment on her face.

"I'm hoping it's just as much as I love you. Sure you don't want a rabies shot?"

"What I really need is to have my head examined," Abby responded. She proceeded to tell him about Carol's letters. "I don't want to go, but Mallory says we have to attend. She's hoping Donovan will do something that will give him away."

"I've said this before, and I'll say it again—this is a dangerous game she's playing, but I agree with her, you have to go. If there's even a remote chance Mallory's wrong and he's innocent, then you have to know so you have peace of mind. By the same token, if Donovan's guilty, you have to know that, too. But you don't have to go alone. I'll go with you."

"Oh, Steve," Abby said cupping his face in her hands to give him a smacking kiss. "I was going to ask you, but I'm so glad you offered instead. I would feel so much better with you along."

"Me too. I'd be worried sick the whole time you were gone."

"I love you, Dr. Carpenter. And I thank God that you love me, too." She kissed him one more time, a sweet, gentle kiss. "I'll see you later, big guy."

Mallory's car was gone. Good, Abby thought. This would be a perfect time to call Carol and tell her they were going to attend the dedication. She knew if she called when Mallory was around, she'd be listening to her every word, and it would make her even more nervous than she already was.

She eyed the telephone. Five minutes. That's all it would take to call Carol and accept the invitation. Then she could go into her office and work for the rest of the afternoon. Five little minutes. All she had to do was pick up the phone and dial the number.

"First, I need to shift into neutral," she said to all seven dogs, who were sitting in a semicircle around her feet, staring at her intently and listening to her with rapt attention. "I want to keep my voice brisk and professional-sounding and not veer from the subject. I hate this, I really do, but I can do it, I know I can. The truth is, guys, I have to do it."

Beemer barked when her hand snaked out to pick up the phone. "You're right. Maybe I should give this some more thought," she said, looking down at him for approval. Olivia yawned. "The truth is, there is nothing to think about. I have to do this."Resolved, she dialed the number. "Please let the answering machine pick up," Abby whispered to the wall.

"Hello?"

"Carol, it's Abby," she said briskly.

"Oh, Abby, it's so good to hear from you. I assume you got my letter. Don't torment me, Abby. Are you coming?"

"Yes, Carol, I'll be there."

"And Mallory?"

"Mallory will be coming also."

Carol breathed heavily. "This is wonderful. Donovan will be so excited to see you. I want to keep it as a surprise, so if he calls you, don't give it away. Okay?"

"Sure. What time is the ceremony?"

"It hasn't been carved in stone yet. At first it was set for ten o'clock, then someone wanted to make it a luncheon and someone else wanted it to be a dinner ceremony. The last I heard was yesterday and it was back to lunch. I'll let you know as soon as it's in granite. How's your new book coming?"

"Oh, it's coming," Abby said coolly. "The research is very time-consuming but fun. Now I just have to put everything in order."

"I've always wanted to write a book. Maybe one of these days I'll get around to it. It must be a little like having a child. First you conceive it, then you give birth to it, then you nurture it until it's grown and ready to go out on its own."

Abby thought a moment about Carol's analogy. "Yes, I suppose it is. For some strange reason I'm closer to this book than the other two. And you know what's funny? I don't even know how the book will end yet, if the killer gets caught or gets away with it." She knew she was babbling, but she couldn't help herself. *So much for brisk and professional,* she thought wryly.

"How are things going between you and Mallory?"

The inevitable question, Abby thought. It deserved a better than a "good" answer. "Mallory has been a fantastic help to me. I don't know what I'd do without her. She amazes me the way she thinks. She has one of those analytical minds and digs up the most interesting research tidbits. This book is set in Edison, you know, right in our old neighborhood. While Mallory was digging up stuff for background information, she found the newspaper article covering our parents' death. She says that the coroner should have done an autopsy on Mama and not just assumed that Mama died of the same thing Aunt Emma did."

"It's wonderful she's so helpful," Carol said with a noticeable bite to her voice. Then there was utter silence on her end of the wire. "What did you just say?"

"I said the coroner should have done an autopsy on Mama rather than assume she died of the same heart condition Aunt Emma died from."

More silence. "Really? I didn't know that. But then I don't know much about that type of thing. I would suggest, though, that you take everything Mallory says with a grain of salt. She used to take great pleasure in stirring up trouble and making mountains out of molehills. I don't wish to speak ill of her, but that *was* the reason we had to put her in Argone. She stirred up so much trouble we were afraid she would destroy us."

"Carol, in your letter to Mallory, you told her you had wronged her by not giving her a second chance. I hesitate to point this out, but you're still not giving her that second chance," Abby said boldly. She looked at her left hand to see she'd clenched it into a tight fist, the knuckles white.

Abby listened to Carol's quick intake of breath and knew that for the first time in her life she had the upper hand. She felt dizzy with the knowledge.

"I'm sorry, honey. You're right. It's just that . . . How can I begin to explain the awful things she did, the tales she carried to her teacher about Donovan and me? I can't put that behind me, and as much as I want to, I can't believe she's changed *that* much."

"She has, Carol. Do you think I'd let her continue to live here if I didn't know that to be a fact? You know, you and Donovan aren't the only ones she hurt. Don't you think I suffered from her abuse when I was little? Trust me, I did. But unlike you, I forgave her, and I've given her a second chance."

"You've always had a big heart, honey. Even when you were little. I wish to God I could be more like you, more forgiving. Maybe you could help me see what you see in Mallory. Maybe you could be the liaison between her and me. I love you so much. I'll do anything you want. Anything at all. Just ask."

Abby swallowed. "All right, Carol. Everybody deserves a second chance. All I ask is that you keep an open mind about Mallory and give her a chance to prove herself."

"You have my word, honey."

"A woman is only as good as her word, Carol."

"You're absolutely right. Thank you, Abby. See you soon."

Abby slammed the phone down. "Damn, damn, double

damn!" So much for not veering from the subject! What had gotten into her, blurting out all that stuff about the newspaper article and the coroner? It had been on her mind ever since Mallory had mentioned it. And she was right. None of this would be happening *if* a proper investigation had been done. Maybe Mallory was right. Maybe it wouldn't be such a bad idea after all to talk to Connor's parents—better yet, his brother. An autopsy would tell her the truth of how Connor died. Without it, she would always have doubts.

She told herself she would think about it and discuss it at length with Mallory. Mallory would know all the right questions to ask.

For the moment, she needed to sit and think about what she'd said to Carol. She might have added fuel to the fire because, of course, Carol would tell Donovan. The more worried he was, the more likely he would be to make a mistake and say something he shouldn't . . . something that would either tie him to three murders or absolve him.

What would Mallory say? That she'd blown it? Or would she think she'd done something pretty tricky?

Mallory rolled over and looked at the bedside clock: 2:47 A.M. She hadn't slept a wink even though she'd gone to bed an hour later than her usual 11:30 bedtime. She and Abby had talked and talked. Tired as she was, she had to laugh when she thought about what Abby had said to Carol. Damn Abby for not waiting until she got home.

The problem was, Mallory realized, she couldn't stop thinking. *Maybe I need some warm milk with a generous jigger of brandy in it. Maybe a sleeping pill is the answer. God knows I have enough of those,* she thought as she got out of bed and tiptoed down the hall to the kitchen. She stared out the kitchen window into the darkness while the milk warmed.

How easy would it be to scale an electrified fence? Her eye went to the alarm pad on the kitchen wall by the back door. Two red dots glowed. That meant the system was armed and woe to anyone who tried to enter without knowing the proper code. Abby had changed the code four times in the past few weeks. She'd even gone so far as to call a local security company to change the microchip so that Donovan's master key wouldn't work. It didn't matter. Abby still didn't feel safe, and neither did she. Even with her gun under her pillow.

Mallory gulped at the warm milk and brandy that was more brandy than milk. She all but jumped out of her skin when a hoot owl let loose with a loud hoot-hoot-hoot outside the window. She literally ran back to her bedroom, dived into bed, and pulled up the covers, her heart beating faster than a trip hammer until she realized she had neither closed nor locked her door. She barreled out of bed and ran to the door to lock it, her gaze swiveling to the long casement windows with their vertical blinds and heavy drapes. Closed tight. She even pinned them in the middle where they met before she got into bed. And she thought Abby was paranoid. Her hand went to the gun under her pillow. So cold. So hard. So deadly. So comforting.

Mallory plumped up the pillows before she pressed the remote control for the small television/alarm/radio that Abby had given her. *The Brady Bunch* sprang into view. Mallory snorted. That bunch wouldn't know a problem if it smacked them in the face. What else could one expect at this hour? It was either the Shopping Channel or *The Brady Bunch*. She lowered the volume and settled back into her nest of pillows to let the brandy calm her body.

Ten minutes later she drifted into a restless sleep.

Even in sleep Mallory knew she was dreaming when she was suddenly back in New Jersey and in the bedroom she'd shared with Abby when they were children. She knew she was dreaming because an eternity had passed since she was a six-year-old child. She hated the dream that had plagued her for years, a dream Constance Oldmeyer had tried to put into perspective for her.

Outside the wind and rain lashed against the house. She wanted to climb into bed with Abby but knew her mother would be in shortly so she didn't dare. She had to stay up to see what was going to happen. She'd seen *him* cross the yard when lightning ripped across the sky. He was coming. *Again*. He always came after Daddy went to the bowling alley. If she kept the secret, there would be a new Barbie outfit on her bed and a coloring book for Abby when she got home from school tomorrow. A secret Mama trusted her to keep. Abby couldn't know and Daddy couldn't know. She felt like crying, but then her mother wouldn't trust her anymore, and there would be no more Barbie outfits.

She counted on her fingers. Four times for both hands before her mother tiptoed into the room. How good she smelled. How pretty she was. "Time to go to sleep," she whispered over the rolling thunder outside the windows. "Give Mama a big kiss and hug. Remember now, stay in here and don't come out until tomorrow morning. I want your promise, Mallory."

"Is *he* here?"

"Shhhh, or you'll wake up Abby. Abby can't keep a secret. You're the only one who can keep a secret. You didn't promise."

"I promise. I'm afraid."

Harriet's voice took on an edge. "Thunder is just noise. It can't come into the room. If you don't obey me, Mallory, there will be no more presents on your bed after school. Now give me a kiss and get under the covers."

"Aren't you going to kiss Abby, Mama?"

"Abby is asleep. I don't want to wake her up."

"*He* likes Abby. *He* doesn't like me."

"He loves you. We'll talk about this another time, Mallory. I want you to go to sleep right now. Do you understand me?"

"Yes, Mama."

"That's my good girl."

The moment the door closed, she was out of bed. Her whole body shook with fear when a violent gust of wind slammed against the window. Thunder pounded the heavens as she slipped into her robe and slippers. She wanted to climb into bed with Abby so bad but she couldn't. Not tonight. She couldn't *ever* get into bed with Abby on the nights *he* came to the house.

Cautiously, she cracked the bedroom door and listened. The television was off. She looked down the hall. A small lamp by the front door was on. Otherwise, the house was dark. It continued to rain and thunder as she crept down the hall to her mother's bedroom door.

Quiet as a mouse, she dropped to the floor to sit Indian fashion, her ear pressed to the door. She listened intently, tears rolling down her cheeks.

A long time later, she heard the words that sent her running back to her bedroom. More time passed before her mother opened the door and peeped inside. Now it would be all right to climb into bed with Abby. But first, she ran to her little desk and rummaged until she found a new box of Crayolas with sharp points. Tomorrow when the coloring book appeared on Abby's bed she would add the Crayolas so Abby didn't have to use the old stubby ones she kept in a coffee can.

She curled next to Abby, her hand reaching out to touch her sister's ugly birthmark. "Mama makes me hate you, Abby. But I don't hate you. I hate *him*. That's *our* secret."

Mallory woke, her body drenched in sweat. If she had a fairy godmother who would grant her any wish in the world, it would be that she could crawl into bed with Abby right that minute.

So much for sleep.

Mallory headed for the shower.

Tomorrow—today really—will be better. At least she hoped it would.

Chapter Nineteen

Abby spent the morning in the backyard brushing and playing with the dogs. Beemer liked to play fetch. Harry loved chasing Beemer when he ran after the ball. Woody liked to referee. And Olivia liked to congratulate Beemer with licks when he brought the ball back to Abby. The remaining three dogs were in the house with Mallory. They were more the lapdog variety and preferred lounging around while Mallory cuddled and coddled them.

Playing with the dogs was therapeutic for Abby. Lately, she'd sought out their company more and more. It seemed to her when she was around them, she was able to shift into neutral, to relax and think more clearly. These last few weeks had been particularly stressful. It seemed like every time she turned around, Mallory was coming up with some new theory. But as with all her other theories, she still lacked the hard proof needed to make them conclusive.

Mallory didn't mind the endless waiting and the wondering, but Abby did. She minded a lot, and she wanted the whole thing over and done with so she could get on with her life. But nothing was happening. She had to wonder if anything would ever happen.

"What I need to do," she said to Olivia, whose big, brown eyes were full of understanding, "is to call Connor's brother." Olivia made a noise that was somewhere between a growl and a grumble. "I know just how you feel," Abby said as she struggled to her feet. "Let's go, guys. Time to go inside. Treats for everyone," she called out to the stragglers. The word *treat* spurred the dogs.

Thirty minutes later, with time on her hands, Abby walked in the back door of Steve's clinic. He was on the phone with a client as he motioned her to come closer. The minute he hung up the phone, he put an arm around her shoulders. "What's the matter? You look like you just lost your best friend."

"I am down. I'm tired of theories and speculation. I want answers, and I want them now!"

"Hey!" he said, taking her into his arms. "What happened to bring all this on?"

"Nothing," she mumbled, her cheek against his chest. "I'm just tired and frustrated and . . . Oh, hell. The problem is that I don't want to believe Donovan killed my parents and Connor." She put her arms around Steve's waist and clung to him. "It's important to Mallory that I believe in her one hundred percent, but I can't, Steve. I think she's going out of her way to make things seem worse than they are because . . . because I think she wants to get even with Donovan for sending her to Argone."

Steve squeezed her shoulders. "You could be right. Has Mallory heard from Dr. Oldmeyer yet?"

"No. And it's past the time when she said she would call, too."

"Hmm. It seems like everything depends on hearing from her and on the dedication ceremonies. I guess you'll just have to be patient. I know you don't want to hear that, but it's true. This is one of those times."

"No, there *is* something I can do," Abby said, tilting her head back so she could see his face more clearly. "First, I can tell Mallory to call Dr. Oldmeyer. Second, I can call Connor's brother, tell him the situation, and ask if he'll order an autopsy. If he agrees to it, then we're on our way to solving part of this mystery anyway."

"And if he doesn't agree?"

"We're right back where we started."

"Then I say call him. Get it over with."

Abby looked down at the floor. "Did I tell you that Connor was the first guy who looked beyond my birthmark? He gave me a confidence I never had before. He was kind and gentle, like you, Steve," she said, smiling up at him. "He had so many hopes and dreams. We all do, but his hopes and dreams seemed more passionate somehow." Steve squeezed her gently. "You know what's funny? Connor liked practically everyone, but he didn't like Carol and Donovan. Especially Carol. He said there was something not quite right about her, but he never could decide what it was."

"Very perceptive of him," Steve said. "If he'd seen her last Christmas, breaking into your house, he would have known."

Abby hugged him. "I knew I'd feel better if I talked to you. You always make me feel better." *In more ways than one,* she thought, loving the way he felt in her arms.

He kissed the tip of her nose. "Yeah, well, if you don't stop hugging me and making *me* feel better, it could prove embarrassing."

Abby looked around the empty clinic. "So who's going to know?" she teased. "Everybody's gone."

"That's what you think," Steve said, turning her around to face the cages full of curious dogs and cats.

"Oh! You're right. Okay, later," she said backing away.

Steve picked up a file from the Formica countertop and started thumbing through it.

"I talked to Carol yesterday," Abby said, knowing Steve wasn't so thoroughly absorbed he couldn't listen. "She called to say the dedication ceremonies would be at one o'clock but that we're all going to have lunch first in the Village Restaurant at eleven-thirty. I wish the conversation had ended there, but she wanted to talk, to tell me that she'd decorated all the models herself and how much fun she had doing it."

Steve looked up from his papers. "What was wrong with that?"

"Nothing. It's just that when she was talking, I realized I didn't really care that she'd decorated the models or was having fun. I didn't care about anything she had to say. I don't understand how that can be. She was like a mother to me. I loved her."

Steve tucked his file folder under his arm. "From what I've heard you say and from what I've seen, she drove you away with the way she smothered you. I imagine your feelings are just buried. Give yourself time. They may resurface one of these days."

"She's *still* smothering me," Abby said. "She just doesn't realize it. In one breath she says how lucky I am to have Mallory back in my life and in the next, she cautions me about her. If you want to know what I think, I think it eats at her that I've forgiven Mallory and that we're together. She probably never thought that would happen in a million years." Abby picked up a small glass jar from the countertop and peered inside. "What's this white thing in here?"

Steve took the jar out of her hands. "It's a tapeworm from Mrs. Clark's cat."

Abby made a sour face as she rushed to the sink to wash her hands.

"I've been thinking," she said as she dried her hands. "I'm tired of all this tension. I want to have a party! And not just a wine and beer and cheese and crackers party either. A big, posh party, with champagne and caviar and a guest list that will make your eyes pop out." She sat down on the stool in front of the counter. "I'd like for it to celebrate the release of *Proof Positive,* but it's not scheduled to come out until next fall. I *could* just have a party to celebrate finishing it. Or maybe I could have a theme party. A murder-mystery party. They have these games where everyone participates. It could be a lot of fun. What do you think?"

While she'd been talking, Steve took a beautiful long-haired white cat out of its cage and set him on the examination table. "I wouldn't tell Mallory you're thinking about having a murder mystery party, or she'll figure out a way to use it to expose Donovan."

Abby laughed. He was right. That was exactly what Mallory would do.

"What's the cat's name?"

"Snowball. He's been urinating all over his owner's house. She was thinking about making him an outside cat, but I asked her to let me do a test first. Oftentimes a urinary tract infection will cause a cat to forget to use its litter box."

"What's wrong with putting him outside?"

"Well, in Snowball's case, the problem is that he's solid white. That makes him vulnerable to things most other cats don't have to deal with. During the summer, those cute little pink ears and nose of his would get sunburned—that is if he survived through the summer and didn't get eaten by a predator on some moonlit night. With all that white fur, he'd be like a beacon."

"Ah. Poor kitty. I had no idea," Abby said. "Well, I guess I better get home. If you don't see much of me for the next few days, it's because I'm working on the book. It's almost finished."

"How can you have an ending until you decide who the murderer is?"

"I thought I told you. I had to go ahead and assume I knew who the killer was so I could finish plotting the book. The way things are going, it could be months before I know the truth, if indeed I ever know. Publishing waits for no man . . . or woman."

"So—Who is it?"

"Who's what?"

"The murderer?"

"Oh! Donovan, of course. Aka Joe Mooney. That's the character's name." She swiveled the seat around in a circle. "I'll be so glad to be done with it. It's bringing up old memories about Mallory and Mama that I would just as soon forget."

"Just out of curiosity, are you going to tell your editor about Mallory or are you going to continue the charade?"

"What she doesn't know won't hurt her is my philosophy. Don't look so skeptical, Steve. If it does come up, I'll just say we're a writing team, which on this book we are, sort of. Once she meets me, she'll know why I did what we did." She swiveled around again.

"Stop that. You're making me dizzy."

Abby jumped down off the stool and walked over to him. "Have I told you lately how much I love you?" Before he could answer, she planted a big kiss on his mouth. "Bye. Have a nice day. Oh, and . . . when this book is finished and everything that goes with it, let's go away for a little while, just you and me."

"I think I might be able to get a few days."

"By the way, what are you getting me for Christmas?"

"None of your business. Get out of here!"

On the ride back to her own house, Abby smiled all the way. Mallory was sitting at the kitchen table when she opened the door. "You look upset. Is something wrong?"

"This is the third time I've tried calling Constance at home and at Argone. No one answers at home, and the receptionist at Argone says she's out of the office and that she has no idea when she'll be back."

A flicker of apprehension ran down Abby's spine. "I didn't realize you'd tried before. You don't think she would avoid your call, do you?"

Mallory shook her head. "No. She would never do that. I'm starting to get a little worried because this isn't like her."

Abby sat down across from her sister. "I've been thinking," she said, hoping to get Mallory's mind off Constance. "I can't stand all this waiting and wondering, so I'm going to call Connor's brother. But first, you and I are going to make a list of things I should say. Okay?"

Mallory reached for a pen and pad. "Number one," she said, "make nice, talk about the weather, how he's doing, his parents, etc. Number two. Lead in gradually, apologetically, and . . ."

Abby listened to Mallory's suggestions, then added a few thoughts of her own. "What if he says no?"

"Then he says no. You'll be polite and ask him to please think about it. Believe me he *will* think about it. He won't be able to help himself. You said he was very close to Connor. He'll want to know the truth. Maybe he won't call back today, maybe not even tomorrow, but he will call back eventually. Trust me."

"You keep saying that. What if it's a flat-out no and it stays no?"

"It won't."

Abby thumbed through her address book until she came to the phone number. "Give me that list," she said, when the phone started to ring.

"Hello, Dennis. It's Abby. Abby Mitchell. Yes, I'm fine and you?" She asked about his parents and the weather and his plans for Christmas. The fact that he sounded just like Connor unnerved her a little, but she forged ahead, the list guiding her. "Listen, Dennis, I have something I need to talk to you about. I'm so sorry to have to burden you with this, especially at this time of year and all, but I have good reason to believe Connor didn't die a natural death but . . . was murdered. Please, before you say anything let me explain." She told him everything in great detail, starting with the death of her parents seventeen years earlier. He expressed disbelief, dismay, confusion, but he never said he thought she was crazy. "I have all kinds of evidence but no proof," she explained, "which is why I'm calling. Would your parents consider exhuming Connor's body so an autopsy could be performed?" Abby listened to the sputtering on the other end of the line. She waited until he finished. "I know how it sounds, and believe me this isn't something I want to do, but . . ." Mallory pointed to a sentence on the list. "But I can't get on with my life until I know the truth. Connor would want this, too, Dennis. I know he would." She took a deep breath and glanced up at Mallory. "Yes, I know it would upset your parents. Maybe since you have their power of attorney, you could do it without telling them. Of course, I understand. Will you at least think about it? You have my number, don't you? I could come to Oregon, Dennis, if that would help." Her face drained of color as she looked at Mallory. "I'll wait for your call, Dennis." She stared at the phone a long time after Dennis had hung up.

"That was tough, sis. I'm sorry. Was he the least little bit receptive?"

"Toward the end," she said, looking away, her face pained. "He said he'd call me back in a day or two, after he'd had time to think about it."

Mallory watched as her sister got up stiffly to fix herself a cup of coffee. Abby didn't say another word as she picked up the cup to take with her to her office, leaving Mallory alone in the kitchen, staring at her retreating back.

Abby felt like her head was going to blow off her shoulders when she finally turned off her computer at five o'clock. She squeezed her eyes shut and took a deep breath, hoping to ease the tension between her shoulder blades. She debated answering the phone when it rang, the first call she'd had all day. She grabbed for the phone. Maybe it was Dennis calling back. *Please, please, please let this be Dennis and please, please, please let him say yes,* she prayed.

"Hello?"

"Abby, this is Fran."

It was her editor. Abby sat up straighter in her chair. "Hi, Fran. How are you?" she asked, wondering why she was calling this late in the day. She never called just to chat. Their relationship was strictly business.

Fran gave the usual polite responses before she got to the point of the call. "I know *Proof Positive* isn't due until February, but I thought I'd check in with you to see if there's any chance you might be through with it sooner. We ran into some legal problems with one of our March books and have had to do some rescheduling."

Abby had never heard her editor sound so frazzled. "As a matter of fact, I'll be finished with it this week, Fran."

Abby heard a huge sigh on the other end of the line. "Wonderful. Absolutely wonderful. Can you put all the finished chapters in attachments and e-mail them to me? Then I can get started on them right away."

"I thought it took several months to get a book into print."

"We can do it overnight if we have to."

"Overnight? Are you serious?"

"That was an exaggeration, Abby. But being we're really

in a bind here, the entire staff has agreed to work together to make this happen in record time."

Abby had a million questions. "What about the book tour and all the publicity stuff we were talking about?"

"We'll reschedule everything. Don't worry. I'm on top of it. Everything I promised you will still happen, only sooner. Listen, send those chapters out as soon as we hang up, okay? I'm going to get started on them tonight. And thanks, Abby, for being such a good sport."

Abby hung up the phone and started to work. She didn't want to keep her editor waiting. Fran was depending on her. It took her a little over an hour to e-mail off twenty chapters. In the body of the e-mail, she explained that the last two chapters would be e-mailed by Friday afternoon. She was glad she wasn't one of those writers who saved their spell-checking and punctuation for last. When she finished a chapter, it was finished, right down to the last comma.

The smell of roasting meat reached Abby's nose. It obviously reached Olivia's nose, too, because she woke up and sniffed the air. Abby turned off the computer, turned out the lights, and followed Olivia to the kitchen.

"What *is* that delicious smell?" she asked, her mouth watering.

"Ribs. Are you hungry?"

"Starved," Abby replied as she poured each of them a glass of red wine. "I have news. My editor called a little while ago and wants the book as soon as I'm finished with it, which will be this Friday. There was some legal glitch with another book that was scheduled, and they're putting mine in its place." She repeated her editor's conversation to her sister.

"So much for all that talk about it taking months to produce a book. It's too bad things didn't work out so you could use the final chapters of our own little mystery. But it's probably better this way. By the way, I finished all that stuff you wanted about my dreams. It's right there by the phone."

"Good. Your input has been great. I just wish it wasn't so painful for you."

"It's just as painful for you," Mallory said. She opened the oven door and basted the ribs with a thick, reddish brown sauce. "I was thinking about calling Dr. Oldmeyer's daughter. She lives in Atlanta near Argone. What do you think?"

"If she gets mad, just tell her how worried you've been. That will calm her down."

Mallory adjusted the top burners on the stove. "Where's my purse?" She turned around in a circle. "There it is," she said, spying it on the counter where she kept her car keys. She rifled through her purse until she found her digital address book. She punched in the numbers. "Keep your fingers crossed," she said. "It's the damn machine," she whispered a second later, disappointed. "Hello, this is Mallory Evans. I'm a good friend of your mother's, and I'm worried because I haven't been able to reach her for several days. Could you ask her to please give me a call at area code 843-871-0909."

Dinner was basically a silent affair, each young woman busy with her own thoughts. They finished at the same time and stared across the table at one another. Mallory refilled their wineglasses.

"Do you suppose Carol has any inkling that Donovan had an affair with Mama?" Abby asked. "If your memories are one hundred percent right, Donovan dated Carol and had an affair with Mama at the same time. Boy, if that isn't a macho trick. Carol would have been livid *if* she knew about Mama." She peered over the rim of her glass at Mallory. "Mama *would* have known about Carol. There was nothing hush-hush about their relationship. You have to admit that was pretty shitty of him." She set her glass down and put her hands on either side of her face. "Oh, God, this is way too much for my peabrain."

Mallory resembled a melting candle as she leaned back against her chair. Her expression told Abby the thought hadn't occurred to her. "You're right," she said at length. "Jesus, you're right, Abby."

"Okay, I'm right. So exactly what does that mean? I'm so confused I don't even know what I said."

"I know what you said but I don't know what it all means. At least not yet. I have to think about it, mull it over, but I'll bet you it means *something*. And don't say it could just as easily mean nothing, please."

Abby bit back what she was about to say. "I wasn't going to," she said, the lie hot on her lips. She took a sip of wine and stared into the bottom of the glass where it was safe.

"Donovan has to be real nervous about now. I'm sure Carol told him we're coming to the dedication. I don't think she would want to surprise him. When you're forewarned you're forearmed. We have to remember that."

"But, Mallory, if Donovan killed our parents, why did he take us in?"

Mallory's voice was cold and hard when she said, "Guilt!"

Abby crossed her arms and tried to draw comfort from their warmth as she stared into her sister's glittering eyes. She didn't succeed. Instead she started to cry.

"Don't fall apart on me now, Abby. This is when you have to be strong and tough. I can't do this alone."

"I know, Mallory, I know. I'm okay. I'm just tired and stressed, and I think I've had too much wine."

"Okay, let's dump these dishes in the sink and go in and be couch potatoes. I think *Diagnosis Murder* is on."

"No thanks. No murder mysteries, if you don't mind. A comedy or a love story, anything but a murder mystery."

The phone rang as the sisters were heading into the great room. Mallory picked up the cordless and kept walking. "Hello? Oh, yes, thank you for returning my call. Constance was supposed to call me several days ago and when she didn't,

I tried calling her, but I haven't been able to reach her. I know I shouldn't worry but . . ." Her relieved smile faded. "She what?" Her eyelashes flew upward, her eyes round with horror. "Oh, God no. How?" Abby hurried to Mallory's side and steadied her. Mallory clutched her hand. "You did order an autopsy? I see. When is the funeral? Yes, I'll be there. Thank you and . . . I'm so sorry. She was a wonderful woman. I literally owe her my life. Good-bye."

Abby put her arms around her sister and held her while she cried. Hot tears stung her eyes as she tried to comprehend what this latest news could mean.

Chapter Twenty

Abby and Steve sat close to each other on the sofa in the great room, their hands entwined, Abby's head on his shoulder. Mallory sat across from them, slowly sipping her coffee. Only her eyes betrayed her misery. Sad eyes, Connor had called them a long time ago. Today they appeared even more sad if that was possible.

"You need to get some sleep. You look absolutely exhausted, Mallory," Abby said. She knew for a fact that Mallory hadn't had a full night's sleep since before Dr. Oldmeyer's funeral.

Woody jumped up onto Mallory's lap and curled up. "I'm too wired to go to sleep. My mind is like a buzzing beehive right now. I can't stop asking myself questions, like why didn't it occur to me that Constance would be a threat to Donovan? How in the name of God did I miss that?"

Abby's forehead furrowed with confusion. "A threat? What are you talking about, Mallory?"

"Constance was my confidante. She knew everything I knew. She knew about Donovan's affair with Mama, about the DNA test . . . Everything! It makes perfect sense that he would want her dead. I just wish I'd thought of it sooner. Maybe I could have stopped him."

Abby's jaw dropped. "How could you possibly think Donovan had anything to do with Dr. Oldmeyer's death. That's too far-fetched to my way of thinking." She closed her eyes a moment and reminded herself to be patient, to remember that Mallory wasn't herself right then, that she was upset. "You talked to Constance's daughter," she said in a soothing voice. "You heard her say her mother died in the hospital, that she was with her, and that the autopsy she insisted on confirmed a heart attack. Tell me how that could be anything other than what it is."

"I know it looks like natural causes on the surface," Mallory said calmly. "And I'll admit there's a fifty-fifty chance it is. But ask yourself if it isn't awfully coincidental, Constance dying of a 'heart attack' right after talking to us. As far as the autopsy goes . . . the doctor performing it would only have been looking to confirm a heart attack. If he found the evidence, he wouldn't have looked for anything else. So you see, the autopsy wasn't conclusive."

Abby turned to Steve. "Please tell me she's wrong."

"I can't," Steve said with obvious reluctance. "If the doctor had no reason to suspect anything other than a heart attack, he wouldn't waste his time looking further."

Abby thought a moment. "All right. There's a way we can resolve this. Call Argone, Mallory, and ask them if they have your records. You think Donovan's killed Constance because of what she knew, but what she knew was also in those files of hers. If they have them, case closed. Right?"

"Right," Mallory agreed as she stood up and stretched. "I'll call them first thing tomorrow morning. If you two will excuse me, and I know you will, I think I'll go to bed. We've got a big day tomorrow."

Abby struggled off the sofa to head toward her sister. "Please don't be upset with me for disagreeing with you, sis.

I feel for you. I really do. I know how hard it is to lose someone you love. But I think you're reaching where Dr. Oldmeyer's death is concerned."

"I'm not upset, and I understand how you feel, Abby.
Honest. We're each entitled to our own opinions, and I just
stated mine." Mallory hugged Abby. "See you in the morning."

Abby sat back down on the sofa next to Steve. He took her
in his arms and held her tight. "Considering how Mallory
feels right now, don't you think you should cancel your plans
to go to the dedication ceremony tomorrow?" he asked.

"If she wanted to cancel out, she would have said so, but I
am going to ask that you not go with us. I love you too much
to lose you. If by chance she's right, and Donovan did kill
Connor because of jealousy, then he would be just as jealous
of you. So far, he knows nothing about you, and I would like
it to stay that way until this is over."

Steve released her and turned sideways. "I don't want you
to go without me, Abby. I'd be worried sick and . . ." His
beeper chose that particular second to sound off. It was his
answering service. He picked up the cordless phone and dialed the number. "This is Dr. Carpenter," he said. Abby saw
his face undergo several expressions: disbelief, anger, concern. He reached for the pad and pen on the coffee table.
"It'll take me a half hour to get there," he said as he replaced
the cordless phone on the table.

"What's wrong?"

"The police raided a house outside of town and found a
puppy mill in the backyard. I'm not going to go into detail,
but it's pretty bad. They need my help, Abby. I know it's
going to take tonight and most of tomorrow to treat the
most critically ill animals. Unless I can get another vet to
come in . . ."

"No, Steve. You have to stay. It's your job, and those dogs need you. Mallory and I will be fine, trust me."

"Please reconsider."

Abby waved her hand in dismissal. "Nothing's going to happen, Steve. Donovan wouldn't be so foolish as to try anything in public. And besides, I'm still not convinced he killed anybody, especially not Dr. Oldmeyer. Go on now, you need to hurry. Call me on my cell phone if you get a break."

"What about your dogs?"

"We'll be back early tomorrow evening. They'll be fine. I've trained them well, thanks to you. Go now."

Mallory almost seemed like her old self the following morning. The minute she finished her first cup of coffee, she called Argone, only to be told the person in charge of records was out sick and wouldn't return until the following week. She slammed the phone down in disgust.

Over breakfast the girls made a list of questions and talked about how they might discreetly work them into the day's conversations, should the opportunity present itself. "We want to know if Donovan was the big contributor Constance was concerned about. And we want to know if he saved any of our parents' stuff. What else? Oh, I almost forgot. We want to find out where Donovan was when Constance died. Did I miss anything?"

Abby shook her head as she stared at her sister, whose eyes were too bright, her jaw too grim. "We're nothing like the heroines in my books, you know. They never have this much trouble solving their murder cases. We're like bumbling idiots in comparison. All we have are our suspicions, suppositions, and theories which translated means the same thing. In other words, we're duds."

"I have to admit it does seem like the more questions we

ask, the further away from the answer we get," Mallory responded.

During the twenty-five-minute drive to the retirement village, Abby brought up the possibility of having a party to celebrate the completion of *Proof Positive*.

"Hey! I have an idea," Mallory said.

Abby had heard those words before and was beginning to fear them. "What?" she asked.

"I'm going to wing this and think as I talk, so don't take everything I say for a book. I'm still in the formulating stage, okay?"

"Okay," Abby said, steeling herself.

"Donovan and Carol saw me on TV and heard me talk about *Proof Positive*. Just so you know, it was my intention to make Donovan suspect that I wasn't talking about any old double murder case, but about our parents' deaths. I think it might have gotten through to him, but I can't be certain. We need to make sure that he's suspicious of us and what's in the book."

Abby didn't like what she was hearing and feeling. She said so.

"What we need to do today is," Mallory continued, "talk a little about the book, drop a little innuendo here and there and make sure one of us mentions that the book is done and has been sent to the publisher. Then we invite Donovan and Carol to the party to celebrate its completion. If I'm right, he'll be very worried that we're going to announce the answer to 'whodunit.' "

"But we wouldn't do that under any circumstance, would we, Mallory?" Abby said more as a firm statement than a question. "Because if we did, we could buy ourselves some serious legal trouble."

"Of course we won't. However, we will let him give himself away," Mallory said airily.

Abby checked in at the guard gate and proceeded to maneuver Mallory's Corvette into the parking lot.

"Holy cow!" Mallory exclaimed as they pulled into a reserved spot. "What a place! It's beautiful."

"My sentiments exactly," Abby agreed, looking around at the gardens and ponds and waterfalls.

A tram came by, picked them up, and took them to the Village Restaurant. After giving their names to the hostess, they were escorted to a table near the back of the restaurant. Abby sucked in her breath when she saw Donovan stand up to greet them.

He looked handsome in his three-piece navy suit and two-hundred-dollar tie. And so normal. He didn't look like a murderer. How could he have killed four people and still look like Businessman of the Year? Or could he?

Carol turned around just as Donovan stood up. Despite her Donna Karan outfit and her professional grooming, she looked considerably older than the last time Abby had seen her. She looked careworn. This definitely wasn't the same Carol Abby had once loved and adored.

Bobby, not quite the gentleman his father was, remained seated and grinned.

"Now this is what I call Christmas, New Year's, and the Fourth of July all rolled into one!" Donovan said, opening his arms to both girls. "When Carol told me the two of you were coming, I could hardly believe my good fortune. This is some day, ladies." He hugged them each in turn, then pulled out chairs, and waited until they were comfortably seated before taking his own seat across the table from them, directly in their line of vision.

"My God, Mallory, it's been a long time since I've seen you," Donovan said, his eyes shining with love and regret. "You've grown up and turned into a beautiful young woman.

Tell me about yourself. What are you doing besides playing Abby on TV?"

"I'm working as Abby's assistant, helping with her research, answering fan mail, that sort of thing. A simple but rewarding life. After living in such a regimented environment for many years, one tends to be more grateful for the simple things in life, if you know what I mean," Mallory responded sweetly.

Donovan looked like he was about to ask for an explanation when Carol interjected, "I'm sure you're more than a capable assistant and a wonderful companion for Abby. I've always had the impression being a writer was a very lonely, solitary kind of life. Abby's lucky to have you." Carol picked up her napkin and spread it across her lap. "Speaking of your writing, Abby, I hope you don't mind that I put copies of your books in all the model homes."

Abby looked at Mallory, then back at Carol. "No, of course I don't mind. That was very thoughtful of you. Thank you. Any kind of promotion helps."

"I did it because I'm so proud of you. I want all of Donovan's clients to know what a talented daughter he has."

They spoke in generalities, staying on safe and familiar ground until the waitress came for their order. Outside the window an elderly lady was walking her dog. It all looked so normal, so peaceful.

"What a cute little sheltie," Carol said, observing the woman and her dog. "That reminds me, how is everything at your house, Abby, with the dogs, I mean? I never would have thought you'd turn out to be an animal lover. We didn't have any pets while you were growing up. How did that happen anyway?"

"After Connor's funeral, Bunny gave me a dog to keep me company. His name is Beemer. He's a retired K-9. The vet who delivered him has a clinic nearby and was overloaded with dogs he'd rescued. I volunteered to help him out by taking care of some of them. It's been quite an experience and it helped me through the roughest time of my life. One I would gladly experience again." The list she and Mallory had made came to the forefront of her mind. "You donate money to a lot of worthy causes, Donovan," she said, briefly glancing at Mallory. "Now that you're no longer contributing to Argone's coffers, I wish you'd consider contributing to a worthy animal cause."

"How did you know? . . . What makes you think I've stopped? . . ." He turned to his wife, his expression suddenly cold and hard. "Carol?"

Carol's face paled. "You've been giving them money for years, Donovan," she said. "I thought it was time to let someone else benefit from your generosity. I was going to talk to you about it this weekend as a matter of fact."

"Well, I'm glad to hear that," he said in a tone that left no doubt that he was angry. He turned to Abby and Mallory. "Carol takes care of the details," he said by way of explanation.

"Do you have a particular animal charity in mind, Abby?" Carol asked, her lips pursed tightly, obviously trying to redeem herself in her husband's eyes.

"Actually our local humane society is in serious need of funds. They need to expand the facility so they can house more animals for a longer period of time. They need money for educational materials as well. Their goal is to make people understand the need to have their pets spayed and neutered. If there wasn't such a pet overpopulation problem, you wouldn't see so many abused and abandoned animals. It's terrible. It really is. People treat their animals like so much garbage and throw them away."

"Sometimes people treat kids like that, too," Mallory slipped in, a wounded smile on her face.

As prepared as Abby was for anything Mallory might say, she wasn't prepared for the long silence that followed.

"I didn't know such a problem existed, Abby," Donovan said, breaking the silence. "I'll be glad to help." To prove his point, he pulled out his checkbook and quickly wrote out a check. "Here's twenty-five hundred to start with. Tell me if they need more, okay?"

Abby was momentarily at a loss for words. Her hand trembled as she accepted the check. Steve would be so excited.

"How's *Proof Positive* coming?" Bobby asked, innocent of all the subterfuge.

Abby had been dreading this topic. "It's all finished," she said with false cheer. "It went much faster than the other two because of Mallory doing all the research."

"Is it really based on a real murder, or are you just saying that to get publicity?" Bobby asked.

"Of course it's based on a real case. Loosely based," she qualified. "Mallory ran across the case files when she was working as an insurance investigator through the work program at Argone. She brought it to my attention and asked me if I thought it would make a good plot for a book, and I said it would." She turned and smiled at Mallory for effect. "I'll tell you, though, it sure makes you wonder about the intelligence of our police. The case could have been solved if they'd done a proper investigation," she said, improvising as she went. "Actually, it can still be solved. We have more than enough evidence to get them to reopen the case."

Bobby leaned close to Abby. "Aren't you worried that the real murderer will try to stop you?"

"The book is already with the publisher, Bobby. It's too late to stop us or the book now."

"I meant to try to kill you."

"Nah!" Abby said with false confidence. "How would he . . . or she . . . find me? I used my pseudonym."

"Wait a minute," Donovan said in a voice that gave him total complete silence. "Bobby's right, Abby. You could be putting yourself in danger. If you have proof, you need to go to the authorities with it so they can nab the guy." He looked from Abby to Mallory. "Are you sure you aren't just making this up? This sounds like a publicity stunt to sell books and maybe get a movie deal." Donovan's eyes glittered like polished sapphires.

Carol finally spoke. "This is serious, Abby. What kind of proof do you have? Can you tell us?"

Abby shook her head. "It's a long and complicated story, Carol. Just read the book when it comes out. Oh, and that reminds me of something I wanted to tell you. I'm going to have a publishing party in February, and I want all of you to come. I'm going to have it catered and everything. Flowers, balloons, band, fortune-teller, the whole nine yards."

"Will the book be out that soon?" Carol asked. "I thought you said you just turned it in."

"I did. It will be out in March, but I thought I'd have the party in February. I don't know the date yet, but I'll be sending out invitations. I expect you both to be there in tux and gown. It's black tie. You should see Mallory's gown. What there is of it." She grinned. She put her hand on Bobby's arm. "You too, sport."

"I have to wear a tux?"

"Yep. That's what black tie means. Time to grow up, kiddo. You can bring a date if you want."

Lunch arrived. Abby welcomed the break. Mallory discreetly tapped Abby's knee, a warning to get ready for more.

"Abby and I were talking the other day, and we wondered if you saved any of our parents' personal effects. I know they didn't have a lot, but we'd be grateful to have anything, their wedding rings, an old watch, letters, photographs. Anything at all."

"Good Lord, I forgot," Donovan said. "Of course I saved some of their things for you. I saved all of your mother's jewelry, pictures of them when they first met . . . oh, and, your mother's diaries. In fact, there are two boxes of stuff in the attic over the garage," Donovan said without hesitation. "You forgot about them, too, didn't you, Abby?"

"I don't recall you ever mentioning the boxes. All I remember is Carol saying she saved the newspaper article about my parents' death."

"Yes, that's in there, too," Donovan said, his voice taking on a hard edge. "I'll have Bobby get them down tomorrow. You can either come and get them, or he can bring them over. Whatever is easier for you."

"That would be great, wouldn't it, Mallory?"

"Mama kept diaries?" Mallory asked.

Donovan nodded.

"How far back do they go?"

"I have no idea. I never read them. But there are a number of them. Eight or ten, anyway. I don't remember."

"Oh, by the way," Abby said, remembering something that hadn't been on the list. "We found Mama's urn. Actually," she said laughing, "it was never lost. Mallory had it all along. I just didn't know it." Abby looked at Carol, whose face drained of color, then to Donovan, who was sipping the scalding coffee in his cup.

"I'm really looking forward to showing you girls around the village," Carol said, changing the subject. "You've never seen anything like this in your life. Donovan did himself . . . all of us . . . proud."

"What we've seen so far is very impressive." Abby's thoughts turned wild as she tried to think of a way to maneuver the conversation the way she wanted it to go. "I bet you haven't had a moment to yourself in months, have you, Donovan?"

Donovan guffawed. "I've had three work crews going twenty-four hours a day, seven days a week, for the last five weeks. I'm surprised I haven't worn ruts in the road going back and forth between here and home. I haven't been anywhere, not even into a convenience store in weeks. After today, I don't care if I never see this place again."

"That's not true, Donovan, and you know it," Carol said, shaking her finger at him.

So much for where Donovan was when Dr. Oldmeyer died, Abby thought, sliding a sideways glance at Mallory.

"Are either of you romantically involved?" Donovan asked, as the waitress refilled his coffee cup.

Abby stiffened. She wondered if she could answer the question without giving anything away. "I've been dating a guy pretty regularly for a few months," she said hoping to leave it at that.

"Oh?" Carol's interest was obviously piqued. "Tell us about him. Does he live near you? What does he do for a living?"

Something in Abby snapped. "Oh, no, Carol. What is it they say? Once burned, twice shy? I learned my lesson telling you about Connor. So if you don't mind, I think I'll keep my new romance to myself."

Carol's face registered shock. "Abby, how can you say such a thing to me?"

"Because it's true. You even admitted it to me. Don't you remember?"

Donovan scowled, his brows meeting in the middle of his forehead. "I'm sorry, Abby. I wish we could unring the bell. However, in our own defense, we were just looking out for you in our own misguided way." He whipped out his wallet and tossed bills on the table. "I assume everybody's finished." He didn't wait for an answer but walked around the table and out of the restaurant, wearing his anger like a badge.

Abby and Mallory didn't speak until they were inside the car with the doors closed.

"He was definitely pissed," Abby said. "Donovan is usually so in control, but he wasn't just now. I'd say he pretty much lost it there for a few minutes."

"I'd say so," Mallory agreed. "How do you think we did? We covered everything on our list."

"Yes, but we didn't solve anything. We found out that Donovan was the big contributor but Carol was the one who made the decision *not* to contribute. That caught him off guard. He told us where he was when Constance was killed, and I guarantee you he can prove it. He answered our question about our parents' stuff, and I think it's pretty clear he hasn't been hiding it. And you saw that he didn't even flinch when I mentioned finding Mama's urn. So what all of this says is . . . nothing. Absolutely nothing. Which is neither more nor less than what we had when we started. I'm starting to get a headache."

"Did you know Mama kept a diary?"

"No," Abby said as she followed Donovan out of the parking lot.

"I wonder if she wrote in her diary about her affair or about me and my real father." Mallory smiled when Abby glanced her way. "I'll bet he goes through the boxes and takes out anything he thinks might incriminate him before he gives them to us."

"Mallory," Abby said wearily, "you have to stop trying to make a quarter out of fifteen cents."

"Yeah, yeah, yeah. We're going to have to try to get Bobby alone," Mallory said, completely ignoring Abby's comment. "Remember that scenario we ran by him in the hospital? He's

probably thinking about the closet shelf, the castle, and maybe
the urn. He might have seen it and not realized what it was. He
knows now. He's going to think we betrayed him."

"You're right but what are we going to say? We think your
dad is a murderer? I-don't-think-so. We're here."

The whole scene was picture-perfect, right down to the manicured shrubbery and intricate-colored flagstone walkways.
The lawns were golf-course green with young oaks that would
one day turn into mighty trees to shade the winding streets.
The four-unit buildings were two stories high and painted a
pristine white. Green-and-white-striped awnings shaded the
front windows. Two matching rockers in Charleston green
sat on each small front porch along with a clay pot of bright
yellow chrysanthemums.

Abby shaded her eyes to see down the winding street. "I
never in my life thought I'd see a real Stepford community.
It's too damn perfect. Nothing is out of place. For God's
sake, there isn't even a leaf on the grass. Where are the trash
cans? There are no cars. The only thing missing is a bunch of
robots. It's spooky."

"I'll second that," Mallory said. "Shhh, here comes
Carol."

"What do you think?" she said, waving her arm expansively.

"Really tidy. Excessively neat. Everything seems . . . *perfect,*" Mallory said.

Abby was at a loss for words. Carol appeared to accept
their reaction as a compliment.

"Would you like to see the inside of the model? It's the one
Donovan is selling to Mrs. Lascaris."

"The raisin-cookie lady from New Jersey? How did that
come about?" Abby asked.

"Oh, he visited her a couple of weeks back, when Bobby
was in the hospital. You know Donovan, he felt sorry for her

because her children had moved away and she seemed low on funds."

"So where is she?" Mallory asked. "I can't wait to see her again after all these years. I wonder if she'll even remember me."

"She was supposed to have lunch with us, but she called and said she wasn't feeling too well. It's probably all the excitement. Donovan is going to have her picked up at her hotel and brought here for the dedication, then she officially moves in. She's going to be here all alone until the other owners move in the first of the year. Donovan engaged the entire security force just for her. Do you believe that? He says a gated community is a gated community, and that calls for top-of-the-line security. That was one of the major selling points. Every single unit has been sold."

Abby stepped over the threshold and was reminded of the day she entered her own house for the first time and saw all the perfection. She craned her neck to see if there was a green ceramic bowl with yellow roses in the dining room. There was, dead center in the middle of the table, just the way hers had been in the kitchen.

"It's so bright and light and airy," Mallory said. She dropped back a step, at which point she crossed her eyes and screwed up her face. "Oh, look, Abby, here are your books, just waiting to be read. That's a really nice touch, Carol."

"Donovan liked the idea. Do you think the silk trees are too much? I just couldn't make up my mind."

"They're perfect," Mallory said.

"Do the dishes match?" Abby asked.

"Match what?"

"The pots and pans and the carpet in the kitchen."

"Yes, why?" Carol said.

Abby shrugged. "I just wondered. What about the bathroom?"

"There are two. One is really a powder room. I did them in blue and white. Fresh and kind of powdery if you know what I mean."

"Did you fill her refrigerator, freezer, and pantry?" Abby asked.

Carol wrinkled her nose. "Donovan insisted. There must be a dozen boxes of raisins and four or five sacks of flour for her cookie baking. So, do you like it?"

"Very much," both girls said in unison.

Carol led the way outside. "I think we have time for a short stroll. Over there we have a movie theater, a supermarket, a drugstore, a gas station, an entire little village with one-of-a kind shops. We actually had to hold a drawing to decide which shops we wanted. We had a mile-long list of applicants. As Donovan said, this is the wave of the future. We have two churches and one synagogue. A person could move in here and never have to leave."

"Kind of like the Amish country villages. Remember that movie, *Witness*? A criminal could move in here and no one would ever know," Mallory said brightly. "Is that a pool?"

"Yes, and to your right is the park," Carol said, pointing off to the right. "There's also a tennis court and a clubhouse. Farther out is a nine-hole golf course. Donovan has certainly come a long way from those days when he used to drive that backhoe for that awful company he worked for in New Jersey. Moving here was the smartest thing he ever did. Of course, he was always a hard worker," she said, smiling. "We need to start heading back. The speeches are going to take a little while, and then everyone is going to want to see Mrs. Lascaris move in. She told me on the phone that she wears Depends. I hope she doesn't leak all over the furniture."

Mallory's tone of voice dropped to that of chilled milk. "Will it make a difference? I mean if she bought this place and it's hers, what business is it of yours or anyone else what she does with it?"

Carol whipped around, her face pinched with anger. "I'm trying, Mallory, I'm really trying. There was no need for you to make a remark like that. None at all. You haven't changed one damn bit."

"Neither have you, Carol. Guess that kind of makes us even," Mallory shot back.

"Which way is the clubhouse?" Abby asked.

"That way," Carol said, then pointed up ahead. "I have to lock Mrs. Lascaris's door. They're going to make a big production of her opening it with her key. I'll meet up with you at the clubhouse."

"You really had to set her off, didn't you? It's okay. You had the guts to say what I was thinking," Abby said. "If I didn't know before, I know now: She hates us both."

Mallory stared at her sister for a long minute before she fell into step with her for the walk to the clubhouse.

Arms swinging, Abby and Mallory walked to the clubhouse to find Donovan standing next to an elderly lady. "Ah, here you are," he said, watching them cross the lawn. "Mrs. Lascaris, these are those 'little tykes' you were wondering about. This is Mallory, and this is Abby."

"My goodness you girls are all grown-up. The last time I saw you both you were just little bitty things and so sad."

"And you baked us cookies and made us feel better," Mallory said. "Raisin cookies. They were the best cookies I ever ate."

Donovan put his arm around Mrs. Lascaris. "As soon as Estelle settles in, she's going to start baking cookies again, so you girls will have to invite yourselves over."

"Not a problem," Abby said. "I'd come even without the cookies."

"Here comes Carol," Donovan said. "You remember my wife, don't you, Mrs. Lascaris?"

Mrs. Lascaris's happy expression vanished, wiped away to

be replaced by what looked to Abby as astonishment. "Why, yes," she said. "I just didn't realize you were the one."

"The one what?" Carol questioned her.

"The one he married," she stammered. She reached for Donovan's hand. "I need to sit down. My goodness, I don't know what came over me. I just suddenly grew light-headed. Please, don't fuss. I'm fine. I think it's the excitement," she stammered, her eyes never leaving Carol's and Donovan's faces.

Donovan showed his concern for the fragile lady. "If you will all excuse me. I'm going to seat our guest of honor and get this show on the road."

Chapter Twenty-One

A bby took a step back from the Christmas tree, flipped on the light remote, and admired her handiwork. She'd always wanted a tree with a country look, and this year she'd accomplished just that. She and Mallory had worked for hours stringing popcorn and cranberries and baking gingerbread man cookies. The end result was everything she'd imagined and more.

"Umm, something smells good," she said, entering the kitchen. "Irish stew is Steve's favorite meal, and when he sees you made fresh bread, too, he's going to be beside himself." She glanced up at the kitchen clock. "I wonder where he is. He said he'd be here at five, and it's almost six. It's not like him to be late. Usually, if he knows he's going to be late, he calls or has one of his assistants call." Abby grabbed the long handled spoon out of Mallory's hand, dipped it into the pot, and scooped up enough for a mouthful. "That is soooo good, Mallory. You're a great cook."

Mallory flushed with her sister's praise. "Anything worth doing is worth doing well. Constance taught me that. She said that's how a person takes a measure of herself. Whatever I do, I give one hundred percent. When you exert yourself to do whatever it is you're doing, you have to concentrate. Total concentration was one of the hardest things for me to learn." She smiled. "You need to learn to cook, Abby."

"No thanks. I'll leave the cooking up to you."

"Listen, Abby, I didn't tell you this because I didn't want to spoil it for you when you decorated the tree. But on the way home from the grocery store, I had a flat tire and almost drove into a ditch."

Abby gasped, "What did you run over? Glass? A nail?"

Mallory shook her head. "When the auto-club guy checked the tire, he said there was nothing wrong with it, that it looked to him like someone had let the air out of it."

"Who would do that?"

"That's the question. *Who* would do that? And *why?*" Mallory stared at her sister, her eyes wide and shining. "I know you don't want to believe Donovan is a murderer but *if* he is and *if* he killed Constance for the reasons I already told you, then it would stand to reason that I'm next because I'm a threat to him."

"Then so am I," Abby said.

Mallory tilted her head and narrowed her eyes. "I'm not so sure about that. He loves you. He always has." Mallory turned her back to resume cooking, her shoulders rigid under her pale blue sweater. "When I started all this, I knew I would be taking a risk by letting him think I was on to him. I guess it never occurred to me he would kill again. I'm not going to lie to you and tell you I'm not scared because I am. Petrified would be a better description of my feelings right now. Especially after what happened today. I'm also frustrated. No matter what we do, we don't seem to be able to make any headway in getting the goods on him. He's either very clever or he's—"

"Not guilty," Abby cut in. "You've already convicted him, Mallory, and the truth is we don't have one ounce of proof.

Granted it looks bad for him. But looks can be deceiving." Abby walked over to the back door and made sure the porch light was on. "The guy from the fence company did fix the front gate, didn't he?"

"I don't think we need to worry about anything here. All we need is concertina wire at the top of the fence and we could pass as a maximum-security prison. We are wired, as the saying goes. Even if someone did try to break in, Beemer would get them and the others would back him up. They'd shred him to pieces."

"Our own personal Dog Squad." Abby laughed. "From now on when you need to go anywhere, I'll go with you. One of us will stay with the car."

"I have an idea," Mallory said. She held up her hand to forestall whatever it was Abby was going to say next.

"Please. I hate it when you get ideas. Ideas mean trouble."

Mallory waved her spoon. "No, no. You'll like this idea," she assured her. "Why don't we invite Mrs. Lascaris over for a few days? She could stay in the guestroom and have Christmas Eve and Christmas morning with us. We could get her a couple of little presents, perfume and powder, a book, a new nightgown. Feminine things. I bet she'd love it. It would be kind of like us having a grandmother for the holidays. She's going to be alone. What do you say, Abby?"

"I think this is one of your better ideas, Mallory. Let's call her and invite her."

"Good thinking, and speaking of phone calls, I'm getting nowhere fast with the receptionist at Argone. She must be new. Anyway, I've decided to fly up there after the New Year and get in her face. Legally, I am entitled to have copies of all my medical records . . . that is if they have them. While I'm there, I think I'll look up Dr. Malfore and see if he's enjoying his retirement." Mallory put the lid on the stewpot and turned the heat down to the lowest setting. "I don't suppose you've heard from Connor's brother about the autopsy?"

Abby shook her head. "I guess I should take his silence as a no."

"I'd call him again and tell him there has been another murder. Maybe that will help change his mind."

"I see headlights. Steve's here." A minute later, Abby opened the door for him. His face was paper white. Abby and Mallory said, "What's wrong?" at exactly the same moment.

He could only shake his head.

With Mallory's words about the car ringing in her ears, Abby panicked. "Are you all right? What happened?" She looked him over from head to toe, searching for anything out of the ordinary.

"I'm fine," he managed.

"Did something happen at the clinic? Are the animals okay? What, Steve? What's wrong?"

Mallory thumped Steve on the back. "Here," she said, handing him a bottle of brandy. "Take a swig of this. You're whiter than milk."

Steve took a swig from the bottle, then reached behind him and pulled a folded piece of newspaper out of his hip pocket. "I didn't see this until just a little while ago. Obviously you two haven't seen it either."

Mallory snatched *The Post and Courier* from Steve's hand. "Tragedy Strikes Mitchell's Paradise Setting." She glanced over the paper at Abby. "Eighty-two-year-old Estelle Lascaris, Donovan Mitchell's first tenant, succumbed to a fatal heart attack," her voice dropped to a whisper, "last night, only two weeks after moving into the exclusive retirement community. When Mitchell was contacted, he expressed heartfelt sadness and grief over Mrs. Lascaris's passing. He was quoted as saying 'she was a dear friend and will be sorely missed.' "

Abby collapsed into the closest chair, covered her face with her hands, and sobbed.

Mallory crunched the newspaper into a ball and tossed it across the room. "I thought it was strange that Donovan would be so good to someone he hadn't seen in over twenty years." She stared down at Abby. "I bet he brought her here to find out if there was anything she knew that could hurt him." She rubbed her cheek, thinking. "I remember Daddy calling her the neighborhood busybody, that she knew everything about everybody. Old people like to talk about the past. Donovan couldn't take the chance she might say the wrong thing to the wrong people . . . so he murdered her."

"I wonder why nobody called us," Abby said, only half listening. "Does the article list her next of kin?"

"A daughter and a son," Mallory said. "We need to get on the phone right now and find out where she is so we can get an autopsy."

"Listen, dammit," Steve shouted. "It's time to take your suspicions to the police. Forget the damn book and forget the damn party. This is dangerous stuff you two are messing with. One of you could be next!"

Both women ignored him.

"Carol will know where Mrs. Lascaris is," Abby said. "I'll call her and tell her I saw the paper and that we want to visit her at the funeral home." Abby picked up the phone and pressed the automatic-dial button for the Mitchell house. "Hello, Carol, it's Abby. I just read about Mrs. Lascaris's death. What happened? Why didn't someone call us to let us know?" Abby pressed the speaker phone button so everyone could hear the conversation.

"Oh, Abby, it has just been crazy around here. Donovan went off the deep end and took off in his truck. He's been gone all day. I have no idea where he is. He thinks the retirement community is jinxed now, which is silly, but I understand his thinking. He adored that old lady."

"What happened exactly? Who found her?"

"The security guard. Donovan had asked him to keep an eye on her and call her twice a day, once in the morning and again in the evening, to make sure she was all right and didn't need anything. Last night, when she didn't answer her phone, he went over to check on her. He found her slumped over on the couch. He said she appeared to have died peacefully watching TV. A death at Christmastime is just terrible, not that it isn't terrible at any other time, too. I'm just babbling, Abby. I'm sorry. Is everything all right with you?"

"Fine. We're fine. Maybe Donovan took the plane and went up to the cabin," Abby suggested.

"I tried calling, but the phone just rings and rings."

"He could be there and not answering. You could call the park rangers and ask them to go by and see if he's there."

"That's a good idea, Abby. Maybe I will."

"Carol, before I hang up, I'd like to know what funeral home they took Mrs. Lascaris's body to. Mallory and I want to pay our respects."

"I don't know, dear. Donovan took care of all the details and didn't tell me a thing."

"What about her son and daughter? Where can I reach them?"

"I have no idea. Donovan didn't say. I'm sorry I can't help you. You'll just have to wait until Donovan gets back from wherever it is he went. If I hear from him before you do, I'll tell him you called. Okay?"

"Yes, please. Oh, and . . . Merry Christmas, Carol." She hung the phone up. "Well that got me a whole lot of nothing. Hand me the phone book, Steve. I'm going to start calling all the local mortuaries and the coroner's office."

An hour later, Abby was no closer to finding Mrs. Lascaris than when she started.

Mallory put dinner on the table and insisted everyone eat.

"How can this be?" Abby asked. "It's like she just disappeared."

"Maybe her son or daughter came and got her and took her back to New Jersey," Steve said. "That's probably what happened. They could have called ahead to make arrangements and are on the way to wherever it is they sent her. They could also be shipping the body to where they live."

"She just died last night. They would have to be awfully fast on their feet to get all that arranged so quickly," Abby muttered.

"I say we try to track down Donovan," Mallory suggested. "Let's start with Bobby, then the cabin, then Steve Franklin."

The moment the meal was over and the dishes in the dish washer, Mallory took her turn on the phone. She called Bobby on his private line. She turned on the speaker phone. She told him Abby had just talked to Carol but had gotten so little information they thought they'd call him to see what he knew.

"All I know is that Dad got real upset. I'm not sure, but I think he was crying."

"Did he say anything to you or Carol?" Mallory prompted.

"Just that the security guard had found Mrs. Lascaris dead."

"Come on, Bobby, *think*. What else did he say?" she pushed.

Bobby groaned. "He said something to Mom that was kind of weird. He said, 'I hope you're happy now.' "

"Anything else?"

"He told her he'd see her later, that he was going to take care of this himself and didn't want her interfering."

"Thanks, Bobby. By the way, we've been meaning to talk to you about the urn in your closet . . ."

"Urn?"

Mallory hesitated. "It looks like a jar."

"Oh, you mean that ugly vase? I think Mom must have thrown it away. It's not there anymore."

Mallory opened her mouth to explain, then realized she didn't have to. Bobby had no idea what she was talking about. "Never mind. Thanks, Bobby. I'll talk to you later."

As soon as she hung up, Abby said, "You should have asked Bobby if Donovan was home yesterday afternoon and evening."

"I can call him back," Mallory volunteered.

"No. Let's call the guard station and ask the security guard to check the log. That will tell us."

But it didn't tell them anything. The security guard explained that Donovan and Steve Franklin came and went as they pleased without logging in or out. Their other phone calls, to the cabin and to Steve Franklin, proved just as worthless.

"I can't believe this," Mallory said. "We're like that little guy on the battery commercial who keeps banging his head against the brick wall. Nothing we do gets us anywhere. *Nothing!*" She paced the length of the kitchen.

Steve tapped his fingertips against the table. "Maybe the reason you can't get anywhere is that you don't have the right resources. Take what you know and what you think you know to the police and let them see if they can make anything of it. What can it hurt?"

"If Donovan is innocent," Abby said, "it could hurt a lot."

Steve raked his fingers through his hair. "All I do anymore is worry about you two," he said. "One or both of you could be next. You put too much faith in that electric fence and Beemer. If somebody wants in here bad enough, they'll get in."

"We aren't without protection, Steve," Mallory said. "I do have a gun, and I wouldn't hesitate to use it if the situation warranted it. For your own safety, I'd suggest you call from now on before coming over here."

Steve blinked up at Mallory. "Thanks for the warning."

"Enough of this," Abby said, pushing her chair back from the table. "Tomorrow is Christmas Eve. Let's get in the spirit. We put the tree up. Let's have some eggnog or something and stand around our handiwork and admire it."

Steve held back, his expression angry.

"Please, Steve, don't be upset with us. We have to do this our way. I know it doesn't make sense to you, but have some faith in us, okay? We aren't stupid," Abby said.

"Yes, you are stupid. All I can say to you, Abby, is that this had better not be about book sales."

The shock of his accusation hit her square between the eyes. "You know what, Steve? You can go home right now. How dare you say something like that to me! How dare you!"

"Fine. If that's the way you want it, I'm outta here."

"So go and good riddance," Abby shouted.

Mallory blinked when the kitchen door slammed. "Kind of hard on him, weren't you?"

"He deserved it. He knows me better than to think I would use people to promote my book."

"He just said that because he's upset. He's worried for you, Abby, for both of us. And he feels as helpless as we do. Call him back in here. You don't want to be mad at each other now. It's Christmas."

Mallory was right. Swallowing her pride, Abby ran to the front door and called out his name.

Steve grimaced as he twisted around to stare at Abby. She saw that he was scowling. "What?"

"I'm sorry I yelled at you," she said, closing the door behind her. A cold wind whipped around her, chilling her. "Come back inside and we can talk about this a little more."

"Okay. And I'm sorry I called you stupid and accused you of using all this to promote your book. It's just that all this is so damn upsetting. I don't want anything to happen to you, either of you."

"I know. And I love you for that. I love you for everything, Steve Carpenter," she said, reaching for his hand.

Christmas Eve

The morning was spent wrapping the Christmas presents. The moment all the foil paper, glossy ribbons, and tape were placed in the closet and the room tidied up, Abby and Mallory showered and dressed for the drive over to the Mitchell house to deliver their Christmas presents. The Christmas spirit had taken hold of them and they'd decided to make an all-out effort where Carol was concerned, to put the past behind them and try to build a new and solid relationship. If Donovan was guilty of the crimes they suspected him of committing, Carol would be left alone and would need all the emotional support she could get.

"Merry Christmas!" Abby and Mallory shouted the moment Carol opened the door.

Carol's face went white as she stared at them. "Come in, come in," she said. "I don't know where my manners are today. Donovan still isn't home."

She looks flustered, and why would her face drain of color at the sight of us? Abby wondered. "Carol, are you all right? You look . . . I don't know, strange, for want of a better word."

"I'm fine," Carol said as she stepped aside to allow the girls entrance into the foyer. "I'm just worried about Donovan. It isn't like him to go away without letting me know where he is. He knows how I worry."

Her words and her tone didn't compute, Abby thought irritably. She dismissed the thought a moment later and chalked it up to her imagination. This was supposed to be a pleasant visit. "I'm sure he's just upset and needed some time to himself," she said.

"You're probably right," Carol said, hugging each of them in turn. "I'm so glad you came by. I have presents for you, too. I'd intended to drop them off this morning but didn't want to leave the house for fear of missing Donovan." She ushered them through the foyer into the kitchen, her voice as jerky-sounding as her movements. Carol had a melodious voice most of the time and always moved with grace as she glided from one place to the other. Not so today.

Abby hung back, her mind telling her that something wasn't quite right. She felt herself shivering in the hallway that led to the warm, sunny living room.

The moment Carol turned her back, Mallory grabbed Abby's arm and squeezed it. "She hugged me," Mallory whispered.

Abby shrugged and continued to follow Carol.

The house looked like an ad for a Christmas issue of a home decorating magazine. Garlands graced each doorway. A nativity scene sat beneath the tree. Beautifully wrapped presents were piled high on the window seat behind the tree. Everywhere the eye could see there were bowls of red-and-white-striped candy, nuts, and chocolates. The tree was at least ten feet high, embellished with delicate ornaments, gathered from Carol and Donovan's world travels.

"I also have those two boxes of your parents' things," Carol said as she reached the kitchen. "Let me put on the teakettle, then I'll get them for you."

"That would be great," Abby said, looking around at the familiar surroundings. She used to love this kitchen. Especially the way it smelled. Carol was always cooking or baking something. It was also the place where they all gathered to eat, talk, laugh, and love. But all that was before she went off to college. Before she became independent. Before Connor.

The moment Carol was out of earshot, Mallory whispered, "There's something weird about the way Carol is acting. She seems nervous to me. Tell me you're picking up the same vibes I am, Abby."

"I know," Abby agreed. "She's probably just worried about Donovan."

Carol carried in one box and then the other and set them on the floor between Abby and Mallory.

When Mallory made a move to open one of the boxes, Abby stopped her. "Wait a minute, sis. Let's not do this now. Let's do it tonight when we open the other presents. It'll be our parents' Christmas present to us. What do you say?"

Mallory pulled a face that expressed her displeasure. It was obvious she wanted to open the boxes right then, in front of Carol. She gave Abby a long, irritated look before she returned to her chair. "If that's what you want, it's fine with me."

Carol set a tea tray down in the center of the table. Her hands trembled as the china cups clinked on the saucers. She immediately jammed her hands into the pockets of her sweatpants.

Seeing the Chintz tea set brought back memories for Abby. "I remember how Mama loved tea. Earl Grey was her favorite, I think. She liked herb teas, too. And . . . didn't she have a window herb garden that she used to make tea? Funny that I would suddenly remember something like that," she said quietly. "Actually, it's weird that I would think of that now after all these years."

"Donovan loves tea, too, but only loose tea, not the bagged variety," Carol remarked. She set a basket full of hand-labeled tea canisters on the table. There were fruit teas, flower teas, exotic teas, and herb teas in the pretty basket.

As Abby reached for one of the canisters, a vision of her mother pouring tea into two cups came to mind. Startled, she pulled her hand back and stared at the canisters, trying to make sense out of what she'd seen. She was about to mention her memory to Mallory, but instinct told her to keep it to herself, at least until she had time to think about what she had just remembered.

"I'll have whatever you're having, Carol," Abby said, deferring to her expertise.

"Are you sure? It's not the most flavorful tea. It's more for medicinal purposes than anything. A little rosemary, which is good if you're feeling low, and peppermint, which helps get rid of headaches. My favorite is green tea, but you pretty much have to acquire a taste for it."

"Whatever you suggest," Abby said as she watched Carol spoon tea leaves into a small sterling-silver strainer before she positioned it over her cup. They could have been crushed oak leaves for all she knew about teas and herbs. Next came the hot water.

"Let it sit for a minute or two before you drink it," Carol suggested. She then prepared Mallory's tea.

Abby's eyes narrowed at the kindness Carol was showing Mallory. She couldn't detect a trace of the animosity she knew Carol felt. The optimist in her wanted to believe Carol had meant what she'd said in her letter and was trying to make amends. But the pessimist in her couldn't help but think it was all an act.

They sipped tea and chatted like old friends getting reacquainted after a long separation. Two cups of tea later, Abby looked at her watch and made an excuse for them to leave. Carol helped them out to the car with their mementos and presents. She kissed each of them on the cheek and hugged them tightly. She stood in the driveway waving until they were out of sight.

"I can't believe how nice she was to me," Mallory commented on the drive home.

"I can't believe it either. That in itself is suspicious. I wonder what she's up to."

"See, now you're getting the hang of it." Mallory grinned.

"She is, you know. Up to something, I mean. We need to stay alert. We may not be the only ones who suspect Donovan. What else would make her so damn jumpy? That tea was really shitty."

"You can say that again. I was gagging as I drank it. Let's go home, Mallory."

"Yes, ma'am!" Mallory said smartly.

Chapter Twenty-Two

A bby had a delightful surprise waiting for her when she got home; Bunny stood on the front porch shouting, "Merry Christmas!" She waved wildly as she jumped up and down imploring Abby to hurry.

Abby turned off the ignition and jumped out of the car. "Bunny! I can't believe it! Why didn't you tell me you were coming? This is so wonderful! My God, I can't believe you're here." She ran up the steps into Bunny's waiting arms.

"I wanted to surprise you." Bunny laughed through her tears as they hugged each other. "By the way, just so you know, Steve let me in."

Abby broke away and stood back. "You look different somehow. What have you done? Changed your hair? Your makeup? You're absolutely glowing. Whatever it is, I want some."

Bunny grinned impishly. "Being in love will do that, I'm told. I hope you don't mind, but I brought someone with me."

Abby's expression turned to mock dread. "Please don't tell me you've brought me another dog. Seven is really enough. Did you say you're in love! This calls for champagne!"

"No." Bunny giggled. "I definitely did not bring you a dog. I think I'd be inclined to call him a fox." She turned and held out her hand. "Mike, I'd like you to meet my best friend in the whole world, Abby Mitchell and her sister, Mallory. Abby, Mallory, this is Mike Stone, my fiance."

Abby's mouth dropped wide open as she stared at the tall, blond, handsome, smiling man walking toward them. "Your fiance? When did this . . . How . . ." Realizing she wasn't making any sense, she clapped her hand over her mouth, her eyes sparkling with excitement.

"It's nice to meet you, Abby," Mike said, extending his hand. "I've heard a lot about you. All good stuff." He looked around Abby at Mallory. "I'm happy to meet you, too, Mallory. You're even more beautiful than Bunny described you."

Bunny snuggled against Mike's chest. "We made ourselves at home in your absence and whipped up a batch of really mean eggnog."

Abby put her hands on her hips and glared at Bunny. "How could you get engaged and not tell me? When did this happen? Where did you meet? Tell me everything and don't leave out anything. I feel so cheated."

"I'll tell you all about it, I promise," Bunny said, laughing. "But first take off your coat, sit down, and warm up."

In the living room, Bunny served eggnog along with a plate of cheese and crackers. "I just made myself at home. Hope you don't mind," she said, stuffing her mouth with a huge hunk of cheese.

"Not at all. My home is your home. Talk, Bunny."

Steve left Abby and her friend alone to renew their friendship. It was his job to carry in the boxes and presents from Abby's car while Mallory busied herself in the kitchen making dinner.

Abby listened raptly as Bunny explained that Mike was a

staff writer for *TIME* magazine and an aspiring male-adventure
novelist. He and Bunny had met three months ago at a party in
New York. They'd had a whirlwind courtship and decided to
become engaged on his parents' anniversary, December 22.

"Oh, Bunny," Abby cried, "I'm so happy for you. This is
wonderful. Can I give you a party or take you out to dinner?
I want to do something for you. Tell me more. I know there's
more. Share, girlfriend."

They talked nonstop for what seemed like hours until
Mallory called everyone into the dining room for dinner.

"My God, Mallory, you're a meal magician," Abby said,
when she saw the beautifully set table and a complete dinner
featuring chicken divan.

"Are you going to open your presents tonight or tomorrow morning?" Bunny asked as she helped Abby clear the
table an hour later. "Sit, Mallory. You cooked, we ate, and
now we'll do the cleaning up. It's fair."

"Mallory and I took a vote and decided to do it tonight so
we could sleep in tomorrow morning. Boy, it's a good thing
I'm as unorganized as I am or I would have mailed your
Christmas present off two weeks ago," Abby said, laughing.
"You'll never guess in a million years what it is. When I realized I'd forgotten to mail it, I thought I'd save it and give it to
you at my party in February, but since you're here now . . ."

"So you're finally going to have that party you've always
wanted, huh?" Bunny shook her head. "God knows you've
waited long enough. I can hardly wait to hear who's on your
guest list." She looked across at Mallory. "This girl always
said she was going to throw a fabulous party someday and
invite important people—the Pope, the president, the CEO of
General Motors, and all her friends. Is it *that* party?"

"I haven't made out the guest list yet. No, it's not *that*
party. This is a rehearsal party for the big one." She giggled.

"I thought I'd wait until after the holidays to get into the swing of it." She rubbed her hands together. "Let's get this show on the road and start opening presents. Mallory and I will do Carol and Donovan's presents first to get them out of the way. You did bring them in, didn't you, Steve?" When Steve didn't answer, Abby glanced around. "Where did he go?"

"Ho! Ho! Ho! Merry Christmas. Merry Christmas," a voice sounded from the hall.

For the second time in one day Abby's mouth dropped open in surprise as Steve stomped his way into the living room wearing a Santa Claus costume, complete with a shiny black belt, boots, and a bag slung over his shoulder. Abby giggled like a little girl when his long, white beard slipped down off his chin. He leered at her, then winked.

"Where are the children?" he asked, looking all around the room. "We can't have Christmas without the children."

Mallory jumped up and went to the French doors. "Here they are, Santa!" She opened the door and all seven dogs came bounding in. Beemer, wearing a red velvet Santa hat, led the pack, followed by Olivia, who had stuffed antlers tied around her head, then Woody, wearing a collar of jingle bells, Harry, prancing in patent-leather dog boots and the others, wearing Christmas bows on their collars.

"Sit, Beemer! Sit, Olivia! Sit, Woody! Sit, Harry! Sit, the rest of you!" Steve commanded, then waited patiently for the dogs to obey him. "I said *sit*, Harry!" When all seven dogs were sitting, he said, "Stay!"

Not wanting to interfere with Steve's commands, Abby muffled her laughter into a couch pillow. She wished she had a camera, when she saw a flash go off. She turned and saw Mallory standing at the back of the room. Mallory winked at her before she lowered her head to squint into the camera.

It was that wink that made Abby realize suddenly just how

much she loved her sister. And whether she was right or wrong about Donovan, she would still love her.

Steve retrieved a bag from beneath the tree and pulled out seven rawhide chew bones and passed them out. The dogs continued to sit, bones in mouth, until Steve gave the order. "Okay, outta here you guys. Go into the kitchen. This is now officially people night," he said, waving them away.

Abby clapped as Steve bowed low in appreciation of his canine prowess. "We've been practicing for a month, so don't go spoiling my performance," he said. When Abby started to get off the couch, Steve motioned her to sit back down. "Santa is going to pass out the presents," he said, "so sit there until I tell you you can get up."

First, he passed out the gifts Mallory and Abby had brought from the Mitchell household. A baby blue cashmere sweater for Mallory and a statement showing a generous investment into a blue chip stock fund. For Abby, there was a black Chanel purse and matching briefcase, which she knew had cost a fortune but would probably get very little, if any, use. From Bobby there were identical framed pictures of himself in his football uniform. They were even autographed.

Abby burst out laughing at how big and wide his shoulders looked with all the football padding.

With Santa's assistance, Abby and Bunny exchanged presents next.

"Since you can't have pets where you live," Abby said, "I thought you might like this." Bunny burst out laughing when she opened a fake fishbowl filled with battery-operated fish.

"And since you're a murder-mystery writer," Bunny said, "I thought you could use some more reference books."

Abby was delighted. One of the books was a guide to how criminals think and the second one was a guide to poisons.

"These are great. Grisly but great. I can't wait to read them."
She was inexplicably drawn to the guide to poisons.

Mallory and Abby exchanged their gifts next. They had
bought each other fun things, silly things. Mallory squealed
over her designer socks and shoelaces, and Abby laughed at
the studio photograph Mallory had had taken of the dogs.

"Now, Santa has a very special gift for Mallory," Steve
said, waving her over and motioning her to sit down. Using
both hands, he reached into his bag and lifted out a sleeping
puppy. "She lost her mama and needs a new one. I thought
you would make a good dog owner, Mallory. You have
heart."

Mallory gasped and steepled her hands beneath her chin.
"Oh, my God, Steve, she's the most precious baby I've ever
seen." Tears filled her eyes as she reached out to take the
puppy from Steve's gloved hands.

"All she asks is that you love her and take care of her.
She'll give you back everything you put into her tenfold, and
that's a guarantee."

"Oh," Mallory cried. "I love her already." She cuddled the
puppy under her chin. "Thank you, Steve . . . I mean, Santa.
This is the best Christmas present anyone has ever given me.
Are you sure she'll love me?" she asked anxiously. "You
know, *really* love me?"

"I personally guarantee it," Steve said, his eyes moist at
the rapturous look on Mallory's face.

Abby was equally touched by Steve's gift. It was everything she could do to keep herself from blubbering. Mallory
deserved something warm and loving. There was so much
love in Mallory, so much she had to give, and the little dog
was going to be the lucky recipient of all that love. How wise
of Steve to know and understand.

Next, Santa produced two bottles of chilled champagne.

"These are for Bunny and Mike and anyone they care to share it with. Hint. Hint."

Bunny bounded off the couch to accept the two bottles and to plant a huge smacking kiss on Santa's cheek. "Thank you, Santa," she said politely. Mike opted for a firm handshake as he grinned from ear to ear.

Santa turned his bag upside down and shook it to show that it was empty. He looked at Abby, and shrugged. "Oops, I must have left your present back at the North Pole."

Abby struggled to cover her obvious embarrassment. Was he kidding or had he really not gotten her anything for Christmas? In spite of her doubts, she forced herself to smile and pretend it didn't matter. "That's okay, Santa, but you're going to feel like a real bum after I give you my present." She put her hand under the couch cushion and pulled out an envelope. "Mallory and I wrangled this out of Donovan for the humane society," she said, handing it to him.

Steve opened the envelope. "Twenty-five hundred dollars!"

"He said there's more if you need it," Abby said.

Steve blinked as he choked up. "That is incredible, Abby. Do you realize how many animals' lives I can save with this? I can't thank you enough."

"Sure you can. Just keep doing what you do," she said, smiling at him, loving him with all her heart.

Steve smiled as he returned to his Santa mode and scratched his head through his hat. He started patting himself all over as if he was looking for something. "Wait a minute. I think I might have found your present, Abby." He moved over to where Abby was sitting, got down on one knee, and took a tiny red-velvet pouch out of his pants pocket. "Merry Christmas, Abby."

Her breath caught in her throat as she took the pouch

from his hand. With trembling fingers she loosened the draw-string. A beautiful solitaire diamond ring winked up at her from the velvet nest inside the bag.

"I love you, Abby Mitchell," Steve said, taking off his Santa hat. "Will you do me the honor of becoming my wife?"

Abby's eyes welled with tears. "Yes! My God, yes!" Abby squealed, then flung herself into his arms.

Abby and Mallory waited until Christmas afternoon, when they were alone, to open the boxes containing their parents' things. They couldn't have been more delighted with the treasures they found packed inside. There was a small jewelry box full of real and costume jewelry. They found their parents' wedding rings, an old watch, a pair of cuff links, and several antique pieces. There was an album full of old photographs, a couple of high-school yearbooks, a scrapbook, a china figurine, and their mother's diaries.

"I can hardly wait to read them," Abby said, flipping through one of them. Her mother's penmanship was beautiful, her letters elegantly formed with swirls and curlicues. Almost Victorian. "Maybe they'll help me understand her a little better. But let's wait until after Bunny and Mike leave, New Year's Eve."

"Okay," Mallory said. "If we're lucky, we'll find something in them that will shed some light on what we're dealing with now. But to tell you the truth, I imagine if there was anything, Donovan would have removed it. So let's be sure to look for crossed-out areas or torn-out pages."

Abby put the diary back in the box with the others. "I wonder if Donovan made it home for Christmas. I hope he didn't leave Carol and Bobby alone."

"Maybe you should call and find out," Mallory suggested.

"That's a good idea and while I'm at it, I'll thank Carol for the gifts. One less phone call to make tomorrow."

* * *

New Year's Eve dawned sunny and cold. Abby sat in the kitchen working on the guest list for the party. So far she only had twenty names, but each one had been carefully chosen. She'd contacted a company who would do the catering, the bartending, and the music. Mallory had volunteered to do the decorating, which included throwing out the old carpet, the drapes, and most of the living-room furniture.

Suddenly, the piece of toast Mallory was eating flew out of her hand. "Look! Isn't that Donovan pulling around the driveway?"

Abby rushed to the window. "Oh, my God! It is! How'd he get in? Where's Beemer?"

An earsplitting bark and vicious growl roared in their ears as the big shepherd came out of nowhere and hurled his body at the kitchen door.

Panic rivered through Abby. "Damn it, how did Donovan get through the gates? What are we going to do, Mallory?"

"Quick, run into the other room and call Steve. Stop standing there like a ninny and do it! Now!" She grabbed Beemer. "Easy, boy. Easy, boy. Sit!"

The police dog sat on his haunches, his ears flat against his head, his tail tucked beneath him. Olivia grabbed the opportunity to eat the remaining food in Beemer's dish.

Mallory sucked in her breath when she heard the knock on the door. Her movements were jerky as she undid the bolt and the dead bolt. So much for security. If he wanted to break in, all he had to do was smash one of the window-panes, reach in, and unlock the bolts. "Donovan! What . . . it is *you*, isn't it?"

Donovan looked down at himself. "I guess I do look a lit-tle out of character with this beard and these clothes. But, yes, it's me. I've been away, trying to get a handle on things. Is Abby here?"

"I'm here," Abby said, returning to the kitchen. "Would you like some coffee?" she asked for lack of anything better to say.

"I'd love some."

Mallory ushered him inside and closed the door behind him. "I was just making breakfast. I'll fix you a plate."

"No thanks," he said. "I'm not hungry."

Abby looked him over from head to toe. She'd never seen him look so rough-and-tumble before. Clearly, he hadn't been sleeping well. She motioned him to a chair. "I'm curious, how did you get in through the security gate?"

"It was ajar, so I just pushed it open," he said, taking his seat.

Abby and Mallory could only stare at one another.

Abby sat down across from him. "Have you been home yet, Donovan? Carol and Bobby have been worried sick."

"No," he said, shamefaced. "I just got back from Mrs. Lascaris's funeral and buying back the condo from her son."

"Mallory and I saw the newspaper article about her death. Why couldn't you have called us and told us what happened instead of letting us read about it in the paper, Donovan?"

"I'm sorry." He rubbed his hand over his beard-stubbled chin. "All I can say is, I haven't been myself. I just did what I had to do and didn't think about anything or anyone else."

"We would like to have paid our respects," Abby added sullenly.

"Again, I'm sorry. Her death really rocked me. She was a nice old lady." He took the cup of coffee Mallory handed him and gulped at it until the cup was empty. "I have something I need to say, and I want you both to listen to me." He looked from one to the other, his expression grave. "It took me a while to figure things out, but then it dawned on me what was up with you two. You've gotten it into your heads that your parents were murdered and you're going to use your book, Abby, to bring it all out in the open." He stared at them as if expecting them to deny it, but they didn't. "I can guess at how all this got started," he said, his gaze turning to Mallory. "And I can guess at the reason. Revenge. Right, Mallory? You want to get back at us for sending you away to Argone?" He didn't wait for her to answer before continuing. "I don't blame you. What Carol and I did to you was unconscionable. I know now there were other things we could have done to try to help you."

Mallory's eyes filled with tears. "Yes, there were," she said, her voice high and strained. "There were lots of things you could have done if only you'd cared enough to look into them. Instead, you dumped me, the same way people dump off dogs and cats they don't know how to care for or what to do with."

"You're right," Donovan admitted. "And believe it or not I've suffered for what I did to you. Guilt can be a vicious monster. It can eat you alive."

"Which is why you gave such large contributions to Argone . . . to assuage your guilt."

"Yes. But it didn't help. Nothing did, and nothing ever will. It's something I'll have to live with for the rest of my life. I can't change the past, Mallory, but I can shape the future, if you' ll give me a chance."

"And in return, I suppose you want me to forget that you killed our parents, Connor, Constance Oldmeyer, and Mrs. Lascaris?" Mallory touched the pad of her index finger to her chin. "Have I missed anyone?"

Donovan stared at Mallory in astonishment. "You can't be serious."

"I'm deadly serious," she said. "The only question I have is how did you do it? Other than my father, whom you shot, how did you kill them so they all appeared to die of heart attacks?"

Donovan's eyes dulled with disbelief. "When did Constance Oldmeyer die?" he asked, his voice shaking.

"How quickly they forget, don't they, Abby?" Mallory looked down at her sister then at Donovan.

"Was there an autopsy?"

"Yes."

Donovan nodded. "I'm sorry, Mallory, I didn't know. She was a kind, decent woman. She made you what you are today."

Abby felt the need to say something. "I didn't want to believe any of this, Donovan, but in every instance you had a motive."

"What are you talking about? What reason would I have to kill your parents or anyone else? Tell me," he demanded, looking from one to the other.

Mallory flipped the bacon in the frying pan. The six strips sizzled as she turned down the flame. "You killed our mother because you were angry that she had sex with Daddy and produced Abby. And you killed Daddy because he found out about you and Mama and me."

"Jesus Christ, Mallory. Listen to what you're saying. You're not making sense."

"Oh, yes I am, Donovan," she flashed back. "You had an affair with Mama for what, seven or eight years? On the nights John went bowling, I would watch you come across the lawn to the house, and then I would sit outside the bedroom door while you and Mama made love. Of course, back then, I didn't know that's what you were doing. Apparently I buried those memories, and they didn't resurface until Dr. Oldmeyer started hypnotizing me, which of course you knew and killed her to prevent her from talking about it. Did you destroy her files, too? Is that why no one can find them?"

Donovan stared at her, then closed his eyes. "It's true that I had a long-term affair with Harriet. I loved her, or at least I did until she changed and became such a shrew."

"When did she become a shrew, Donovan? When you told her she couldn't have sex with John? Or when you found out that she not only had sex with John but that Abby was his child and not yours?" She took the frying pan off the stove. "Blood tells, Donovan. And in this day and age, it tells the absolute truth," she said putting the bacon onto a paper towel to drain. "Let's take DNA as an example. You remember that key-man life-insurance policy Steve Franklin took out on you? The insurance company required you to give a blood and urine sample at the time you filled out the application. I had been working for the insurance company for more than a year by then, though you didn't know that, of course, because you so seldom inquired about what I was doing. Anyway, I'm the one who took the samples to the lab, and while I was there, I had the tech take a sample of my blood and asked him to run a DNA test on the two of them. And guess what? They matched . . . *Daddy.*"

Donovan's eyes narrowed as he studied Mallory. "I should have guessed," he said, staring at her as if seeing her for the first time. "I'm sorry, Mallory. I didn't know. As God is my witness, I didn't know."

"Why should I believe you? You're a consummate liar, Donovan. You even lied about Mama's ashes and told Abby you'd given then to me," Mallory charged.

"Carol and I went to the school and . . ."

"The *institution,*" Mallory corrected him.

Donovan threw up his hands. "We took the urn to Argone and tried to give it to Dr. Malfore. He said you were having a discipline problem and were being punished. He refused to take it from me, so we took it home, and Carol promised to take it another day." He stared at her as if expecting some sort of confirmation. "She never got it to you, right?" He leaned his elbows on the table, then dropped his head into his hands and took deep breaths.

It was Abby who answered. "We went into your house while you and Carol were in New Jersey visiting Bobby, and I found the urn hidden behind some other things on the top shelf of Bobby's closet."

Suddenly Beemer's ears stood at attention. He jumped up and ran to the door.

Steve stormed into the kitchen, his eyes wild, his body rigid. A clear indication he was looking for a fight.

"Who the hell are you?" Donovan snarled.

"This is . . . my neighbor," Abby said before Steve could speak. She didn't want to take any chance of Donovan knowing they were engaged. When she'd called Steve to come over, she'd taken off her ring and put it in a box in the great room. "Dr. Steve Carpenter. He's the vet I mentioned. I think it's time for you to leave, Donovan."

He didn't move a muscle. "Not until you two listen to reason. I don't know how I can convince you that I didn't kill anyone. You've made me out to be the killer in that damn book of yours, haven't you, Abby? There will be an investigation. Even though they will find me innocent, the publicity, the speculation, and the conjecture will ruin me and ruin everything I've worked my entire life to achieve. Please, I beg you to think about what you're doing. Please don't ruin people's lives for a few lousy dollars in book sales. I'll give you any amount of money you want. A million, two, ten . . . I don't care."

"But I do care, Donovan," Abby said.

"The truth will win out, Abby, and you'll be the laughing-stock of your profession. Why are you doing this to me?"

"For Connor, damn you," Abby cried out. "For Connor. He was too young to die. He had his whole life ahead of him, and you took that life away from him and from me as well. Don't ever ask me why again."

Steve walked over to the door. "Here's the door, Mr. Mitchell. I think you'd better leave."

Looking old beyond his years, Donovan marched out of the kitchen, down the driveway to his car, and didn't look back.

"How the hell did he get in here?" Steve asked, closing the door and locking it.

Abby melted into her chair. "The same way you did. Through the *open, broken* security gate. It's about as useful as Olivia being a guard dog."

"What'd he want?"

"You heard him. To stop us from publishing *Proof Positive*," Abby said. She felt so miserable she wanted to cry. She *was* crying.

Steve sat down and took Abby's hand. "The book can't really hurt him, can it, Abby? I mean you changed the names, the places, everything, didn't you?"

"Yes, but he doesn't know that. We wanted him to think the book would expose him, so he would make a stupid mistake and expose himself."

Steve frowned. "I may be out of my depth here, because all I really know are animals. I know what they are capable of. Like Olivia here. She's a lover. Her greatest love is Beemer. She's placid and lazy. You wouldn't think she's a scrapper, but she is. You put her in a situation where she has to fend for herself and she could do it, has done it. Now, Donovan, he's a rugged, whip-cracking kind of guy. You know by looking at him that he makes people jump when he gives orders. But underneath that rough exterior, there's a heart of gold. He could no more commit murder than I could abuse an animal. That's just my opinion, of course, for whatever it's worth, which probably isn't much if your expressions are any indication," he rambled.

"I wish I could agree with you, Steve," Abby said, then excused herself and went to her office to be alone. She kept to herself the rest of the day, reading her mother's diaries. The first one began the year after Mallory had been born, and the last one ended just days before her death. Donovan was mentioned often, though always with anger. She wrote that she thought Donovan had far too much influence over John and wished she could do something to stop it. She often told her diary how unhappy she was and how she wished she had someone to confide in.

Abby cried when she read the entries following her own birth. "She's a freak. I can't stand to look at her. This is God's way of punishing me for what I've done," her mother wrote.

Abby cried until there were no more tears, then went back to reading. She was determined to finish the diaries no matter what it cost her emotionally.

In the last diary, her mother wrote, "Donovan's new woman friend called on me today. I felt sorry for her, so I invited her in and fixed her a cup of tea. She seemed nice but naive, like I had been once. She told me how much she liked Donovan and that she hoped he liked her, too."

Abby read on; there were only a few pages left. "She came over for tea again today. It seems I have become her confidante though until today I never confided a single thing about myself to her. She told me she thinks Donovan is in love with her. I couldn't help but laugh. She wasn't amused and asked me why I laughed, and I told her . . ."

The writings ended with a bold, slashing line across the page, as if something had startled her. Abby sat looking at that line for a long time, wondering what she would have written if she had continued. Wondering, too, who Donovan's woman-friend was. Carol?

Chapter Twenty-Three

It was late afternoon before Abby felt confident enough to take a break and relax. She had spent the whole day working on a synopsis for a new book—a murderless mystery this time. She'd had enough murder, real and fictitious, to last her a lifetime.

She turned over the engraved invitation and smiled. "These really are pretty impressive-looking, don't you think, Mallory?"

Mallory gazed at her sister. "Not half as impressive as this guest list. There's a cool fifty names here: local book reviewers, the head chain store book buyers, the local bookstore managers, *Newsweek, USA Today, TIME* magazine, your editor and publisher. Wow!"

Abby set the invitation down on the kitchen table. "I'm also inviting all of Steve's staff, some of the neighbors, Bobby, Bunny, and Mike. Maybe Mike will get the assignment for *TIME.*"

"You're not planning on inviting Donovan and Carol, are you? Please tell me that's a no."

"I've been wondering what to do about that, then it occurred to me they wouldn't come anyway. I mean, jeez! We've accused Donovan of murdering five people. I can't imagine he would want to come. So the answer is no," Abby confirmed.

Mallory brushed her hand across her forehead. "I'm glad to hear that." Her relief was palpable.

"It's been over a month since Donovan was here, and as upset as he was about the book, I thought for sure he would call or come by or something. He gave up too easy. It's just not like him to do that. Donovan will fight till he takes his last breath if he thinks he's right. He just isn't the giving-up type, and that's what's worrying me right now."

Mallory's expression went from questioning to apprehension. "He knows the book isn't coming out until March. He's probably trying to establish an alibi for each murder. That's what I would do if I were walking in his shoes."

"Umm. Maybe so," Abby said, looking out the window to see Harry digging a hole. "Something's been nagging at me, Mallory. Remember the day we went to the dedication ceremonies for Donovan's retirement community? Both of us were looking forward to seeing Mrs. Lascaris and asking her if she would bake us her famous raisin cookies." Abby turned her gaze from the window to Mallory. "We went back to the clubhouse ahead of Carol, and Donovan introduced us to Mrs. Lascaris. She was so glad to see us, remember? She had a big smile on her face. Then Carol came and Donovan introduced her, and Mrs. Lascaris's smile disappeared. She said something to Carol like, 'I didn't realize it was you,' or 'I didn't realize you were the one.' Do you remember?"

"That doesn't stand out in my mind. What's the importance of what she said?"

Abby looked deep into Mallory's eyes. "I remember wanting to get her alone to ask her if something was wrong, then she turned to Donovan and told him she needed to sit down.

He spirited her away, and I never got another chance to talk to her."

"What do you think was wrong?"

"I don't know. I don't even know *if* anything was wrong. She just looked so . . . strange." Abby shook her head. "It was probably just all the excitement or maybe . . . Let's think about this. She was just fine until Carol came on the scene."

"Well, I was, too, until Carol came on the scene. Then I turned into Monster Mallory, the evil one!"

Abby waved her hand. "Would you be serious, please? I'm trying to play detective, and you're making jokes. Why would seeing Carol frighten, alarm, or unnerve that sweet old lady?"

Mallory pondered the question, then rattled off an answer. "Because she remembered Carol from the old days in New Jersey, didn't like her then, and was disappointed to learn Donovan had married her. That would also explain what she said."

Abby favored Mallory with a look of disgust. "Take it a step further and tell me why Mrs. Lascaris didn't like Carol."

Mallory looked up at the ceiling. "Because . . . Because Carol is controlling and manipulative."

"That works," Abby agreed. "And she said what she said because until Donovan introduced Carol as his wife, she didn't know he had married her."

"All right, now that we've got that settled . . ."

Abby waved her index finger. "There's something else. You said Donovan's motive for murdering Mrs. Lascaris was because she must have known something about our parents' deaths that could hurt him. You said you thought he brought her here to keep tabs on her. Come on now. *If* she knew anything, *if* she suspected him of something as sinister as murder, don't you think she'd be afraid of him? She wasn't afraid of him. She was *afraid* of Carol. And why, if she thought he was a murderer, would she let him move her here? She wouldn't, Mallory," Abby said, getting into Mallory's face. A moment later she sat back looking smug. "Now, turn all that around and look at it from Donovan's standpoint. If indeed Mrs. Lascaris knew anything about the murders, she'd kept it to herself for over twenty years. Why wouldn't he let sleeping dogs lie? Why would he want to visit her, bring her here . . . stir things up?"

Mallory squeezed one eye nearly closed. "So what you're saying here is . . . that you don't think Donovan murdered Mrs. Lascaris, that she died of natural causes?"

"I don't see a motive, Mallory."

"What about our parents, Connor and Dr. Oldmeyer? Do you see motives there?"

"Yes and no. I think there are a lot of ways of looking at a situation, and your anger toward Donovan has prejudiced you." She reached across the table and took her sister's hand. "Why don't you feel that same prejudice against Carol? *She* was the one who pushed Donovan into putting you in Argone. Why don't you suspect her?"

"Because she didn't have the motives."

"Are you sure? How long were Carol and Donovan an item before our parents' deaths? Weeks? Months?" She told Mallory about the last entry in their mother's diary. "What if Mama laughed in Carol's face and told her she was crazy to think Donovan loved her? What if Mama told Carol Donovan loved her, had loved her for years? And what if she told Carol about you? That would certainly explain why Carol hates you so much. It would also give her a motive for murdering Mama," she said, surprising herself that she was actually making sense.

"And Daddy?"

Abby shrugged. "Daddy got in the way. Carol shot him and made it look like suicide."

Mallory crossed her arms. "Okay. Fine. I agree you've presented a good case, Sherlock. But what about Connor?"

"All right," Abby said with more bravado than she felt. All she wanted to do was prove her point . . . that there was more than one way of looking at a situation. "As it stands right now, we have Donovan's motive for murdering Connor as jealousy. But we also know that Carol felt the same way. She admitted it." She took a deep breath and said the first thing that came to mind. "I remember Connor didn't like them, either. He was sure Carol hated him. He told me he had a gut feeling that something about her wasn't quite right." Her voice dropped an octave when she said, "He never did figure out what it was." She stopped to think and had a mental flash of the last time they'd all been together at the hotel cafe. She saw herself getting out of her chair to walk Connor to the door so he could get his cab. Donovan stopped him, handed him a small paper bag with a Danish and some coffee to take with him. Abby felt her breath catch in her throat. It was *Donovan* who gave him the bag with the Danish and coffee. If there was poison in the coffee, then it had to be Donovan, not Carol. Right? But wait a minute. Donovan never paid attention to who ate and who didn't. That was the kind of thing Carol did, always knowing who did what and what they needed. That was part of her controlling, her method for manipulating people. So even if Donovan gave the bag to Connor, that doesn't mean Donovan was the one who killed him.

"Mallory," she said breathlessly, "that day you told me Donovan murdered Mama and Daddy, you said you thought Donovan might have poisoned Mama . . . poisoned her with something that would simulate a heart attack." She got up, ran to her office, and came back with the two books Bunny had given her. The cover illustration on the writer's guide to poisons was of a hand dropping a teacup. Abby went to the back of the book, checked the appendix, and found a section that listed the poisons by the symptoms they caused. "Heart attack," she said, flipping pages. It wasn't there. She went back to the beginning and read, "Blood. Brain. Ah, here, Cardiovascular." She went down the list to find the symptom. "Cardiac arrest," she said, then in a column to the right were the poisons that could cause it. She read off the ones she recognized. "Cocaine, ergot, insulin, oleander, sodium . . ."

"Oleander?" Mallory cut in. "I didn't know oleanders were poisonous. What a shame. They're so pretty."

Abby looked up oleander in the index and turned to that page. "It says here it's a cardiac stimulator. All parts of the plant are poisonous, the leaves, the nectar from the flowers, even the twigs." Marking her place with her finger, Abby closed the book to look at the cover. "Would you know a dried, crushed tea leaf from a dried, crushed oleander leaf, Mallory?"

"No."

"But Carol would. She knows all about teas and tisanes. Doesn't it make sense she'd know which plants are poisonous?" She stared at her sister, her eyes narrowing as her thoughts compounded. "Donovan gave Connor a cup of coffee for the road the morning he died, but I'll bet Carol was the one who gave it to Donovan to give to Connor. And according to what we read in Mama's diary, Mama and Donovan's new woman friend had tea together at least . . ." She placed her hand over her eyes as she saw a scene out of the past . . . Mama and Carol sitting at the dining-room table sipping tea. "It *was* Carol having tea with Mama. It just came to me in a flash. I could see Mama pouring the tea and Carol looking up at her."

"If murdering someone is as easy as using oleander leaves

to make tea or squeezing the nectar of the flower into coffee . . ." Mallory took a quick breath. "Carol and Donovan have oleander bushes all over their yard. And when you and I were little, we had an oleander bush at our house in New Jersey."

"Where?"

"Under my bedroom window, on the sunny side of the house. Daddy had to cut it down so it wouldn't cover my window."

"My God," was all Abby could say.

Early the next morning Mallory caught the thirty-eight-minute flight out of Charleston to Atlanta's Hartsfield Airport. She didn't really expect to find her records, as she was sure Donovan or *someone* had taken them and destroyed them, but she had to know for sure. All she could hope for was that one of the staff would remember who they had been given to.

Abby spent the day puttering around the house, getting ready for the new carpeting that was to be installed the following day, along with the new draperies and furniture the day after that. Throughout the day, every time she thought up a new reason why Carol might want to murder anyone, she wrote it down. She also wrote down things Carol had said and done over time that now seemed suspicious.

At the top of her list was what Donovan had said to Carol on Christmas Eve before last . . . the night they'd broken into her house. Abby remembered his words verbatim. "You thought that damn birthmark of hers would tie her to you for the rest of her life, didn't you? You didn't think any man would ever bother to look beyond that birthmark to find out what kind of person our Abby was. When things looked like they were getting serious between her and Connor and that

Abby might move to New York, you started pressuring me to build this house."

Abby chewed on the end of the pen as another flash of memory rose to the surface. She committed it to the paper in front of her. Carol not delivering her mother's urn to Mallory and hiding it in the top of Bobby's closet. Then she asked herself a question: What kind of person would do something that mean and cruel? "A sick person," she jotted down in answer.

She scribbled, "Mallory's flat tire" and put a question mark next to it. And last, she made a note about the day she and Mallory had delivered Christmas presents to Carol's house. Carol had said she was upset about Donovan's absence, but she didn't act upset.

Did any of these things mean anything? Or was she doing the same thing she'd accused Mallory of doing—speculating and conjecturing?

By the time she was ready for bed she was exhausted.

"This is ridiculous, Donovan," Carol said. "Why you want to go to Abby's party is beyond me. Abby and her crackpot sister think you murdered their parents, and Abby is going to tell the world in that damn book of hers. Did you hear me, Donovan?" Her face contorted in rage, Carol threw a heavy cut-glass bowl across the room. She didn't blink when it shattered into hundreds of long, slivered shards.

"We have to go," Donovan said tightly. "I've never run from a fight in my life, and I'm not going to start running now. I'm going with or without you."

"This is all Mallory's doing. Plain and simple, all she wants is revenge. First, she wormed her way into Abby's house, then ingratiated herself into Abby's life, and now she's convinced Abby . . . Oh, God, how I hate that girl! There are no words to tell you how much I hate and despise her. We should have sent her to another continent. She's going to stand there in front of all those newspaper and magazine people and tell how she solved an old murder case. What the hell are you going to say to that, Donovan?"

"The burden of proof is on the police and the district attorney," Donovan said. He watched his wife out of the corner of his eye as she put on the diamond earrings he'd given her on their fifteenth anniversary. "Furthermore, we don't know she's going to do that, now do we, Carol?"

"This is going to destroy Bobby, not to mention us and everything you've worked for your entire life. Is it because Mallory is your own flesh-and-blood daughter that you refuse to see how evil she is?"

Donovan stopped in mid-stride before turning around to confront his wife. "What did you just say?"

"You heard me. Don't pretend you didn't hear what I just said, and don't pretend you don't know what I'm talking about either." The ugly look on Carol's face told Donovan his ears hadn't deceived him. "I've known about Mallory for years. When we first got married, you talked in your sleep," Carol stormed as she stomped across the room to her dressing table. She sat down at the table, her shoulders shaking with rage.

Donovan stared at her back, his thoughts ricocheting inside his head. He may have talked in his sleep, but not about *that*. He hadn't known about his paternal bond with Mallory until little more than a month ago. Finding out Carol had known from the get-go supported the conclusions he'd finally come up with. "You knew *all* these years and never said anything? Is that why you hate Mallory so much, Carol, because she's my daughter?"

"I won't even dignify that with an answer. Not now, not ever," Carol spit. "It's not too late to change your mind, Donovan. You said you've never run away from a fight in your life. So let's fight. We'll get you a lawyer and fight this thing tooth and nail."

"Carol, you don't think I killed John and Harriet, do you?"

"I don't know, and I don't care. But everyone who reads Abby's book will think you did. How are you going to fight that?"

"With the truth, that's how," Donovan said with more confidence than he felt. "The truth always wins out in the end, Carol." He started for the door. "Are you ready?"

Carol tore her gaze from the mirror. "Almost. You go down and get the car, and I'll meet you," she said, reaching for her evening bag. "Oh, and by the way, if I don't get a chance to tell you later, you look especially handsome tonight. I don't ever remember crashing a party before. It should be very interesting."

Abby looked around the living room with approval. Was there nothing this sister of hers couldn't do? "I like this combination of Laura Ashley and Ralph Lauren," she told Mallory. "It's country and comfortable at the same time, the kind of furniture and fabrics you want to cuddle up in on a rainy afternoon. I can't wait for a rainy day to check out if I'm right or wrong," Abby said, hugging her sister.

The party decorations, also à la Mallory, were simple but elegant. The focus was on low, dramatic lighting. Candles of every color and size graced the fireplace mantel and all the tables. A blue-flamed fire burned in the fireplace, giving the room a warm, cozy feel, which was Mallory's intention. In one corner, a tall, leafy ficus tree, studded with minuscule white lights, added a touch of romance. At least Abby thought so. Her gaze swept the room as she searched for Steve. She moved toward him, her arms outstretched. The man she loved. Only God knew how much.

A block of ice sculpted to resemble an open book sat in the center of the table. All around it, at various elevations, were more candles and finger foods: shrimp, lobster, ribs, caviar, as well as every canapé known to man.

"Everything looks beautiful, doesn't it?" Abby asked Steve as she turned on the stereo receiver. Piano music filled the room.

"Not half as wonderful as you look," he said, kissing her mouth lightly. "And that dress . . ." he winked ". . . is nothing short of spectacular." His eyes were riveted on her plunging neckline.

Abby wanted to tell him she had spent hours and hours looking for the perfect, long, black velvet dress and had finally found it in the last boutique, but she held her tongue. She knew she looked good. Her hair was just the right length, the cut perfect, and her medical makeup covered her stain without looking caked or theatrical.

Bunny and Mike entered the living room hand in hand, followed by Mallory, looking more beautiful than ever in a skintight red dress and an old-fashioned red snood to hold her hair in place.

The doorbell rang. Abby opened it to see Bobby, who looked adorable in his black tux and red tie. "You're lookin' good, sport," Abby said, hugging him. "I'm so glad you could come home from school to come to my party."

The doorbell rang again and from that point on a steady stream of guests poured into the house. Everyone was elegantly dressed, and the talk was lighthearted and flattering. It didn't take long for the party atmosphere to take over. A distinguished, white-coated bartender served Dom Pérignon and vintage wines from a bar set up in the foyer. Under other circumstances, this would have been the party of Abby's dreams.

An hour into the party, Abby caught sight of her sister. The lady in red, she thought, wondering if there wasn't a plot somewhere in that title. Mallory was holding court with the guy from *Newsweek* and a couple of book reviewers.

With Steve on her arm, Abby circulated among her guests, who thought they were Mallory's guests—or rather Bailey James, the mystery writer's guests. "Even on my best day I couldn't do what Mallory is doing," Abby said in a low voice. "Just the thought makes me shrivel up inside. Look at those media people, Steve. They're hanging on her every word. And look at Mallory, how cool and poised she is. She's eating this up. I'm so glad she agreed to all this."

Steve chuckled softly. "Yes, she is, and if you ask me, it's good for her. She needs to rebuild her self-esteem. I have to admit it's fun listening to the way people talk about her and the book when she's not in the conversation. If what they're saying right here in this room is any indication, you're on your way to being the Stephen King of the mystery set."

"*We're*—Mallory and I . . . are going to be the Stephen King of the mystery set. She doesn't know it yet, but I'm going to formally make her my writing partner. She will research, plot, and do publicity. I will write." Abby hugged Steve. "There's my agent and my editor. Let's go talk to them."

Steve held her back. "Are you sure you want to do that? What if they recognize your voice?"

"I've already talked to them hundreds of times, and they didn't. Amazing, isn't it? All those hours we spend talking on the phone, and yet they don't know me when they see me."

"Yeah, amazing," Steve agreed. A moment later, he put his arm around Abby's back when he saw Carol and Donovan Mitchell walk in. "Abby," he whispered, lowering his head to her level, "I think we've got a little problem."

Abby turned to see Carol's gaze sweeping her redecorated living room.

"My God!" Carol said, as Donovan helped her off with her coat. "She's changed everything . . . the carpet, the drapes, all the furniture. Everything! All my work . . . It was for nothing."

"It looks good. It looks like Abby," Donovan said honestly, earning himself a contemptuous snarl from his wife.

Abby saw and understood Carol's look but was determined to ignore it and make the best of a bad situation. "I didn't think he'd have the nerve to come here. Carol must have insisted. Stay here, Steve," she said as she started toward her adoptive parents. She hadn't taken two steps when Steve grabbed her hand.

"I'm going with you," he insisted. "I'm a big boy. You don't need to protect me. I can take care of myself."

"Carol! Donovan! How nice of you to stop by," Abby said with false cheer.

"Hello, Princess," Donovan said, stretching to give her a kiss. "You look absolutely beautiful tonight."

Without thinking, Abby put her arms around him and gave him a hug and felt him hug her back. When they broke apart, she looked into his eyes and saw only love and affection. "I want you both to meet Steve Carpenter, my fiancé." She lifted her left hand to show off her ring.

Steve reached out to shake Donovan's hand.

Donovan looked confused. "Haven't we met before?"

"Yes, sir. I'm the neighbor Abby called New Year's Eve."

"Right," Donovan said, nodding. "I remember now."

"Yes, sir," Steve said, looking embarrassed. "Before I forget, I want to thank you for your generous contribution to the humane society. I can't begin to tell you how many more lives we'll be able to save."

"Ironic, isn't it?" Carol spoke up, obviously offended at being ignored. "Here we are at a party where Donovan is going to be accused of taking lives, and the first person he meets thanks him for saving lives."

Abby flinched. She and Mallory had led Donovan to believe *Proof Positive* would incriminate him, but surely they didn't think tonight would be the night where they unmasked his guilt. She couldn't begin to imagine how he must feel. And, of course, now they were inclined to think the guilty party was Carol, not Donovan. But they couldn't tell him.

"Please, this is a celebration party," she said, looking from Donovan to Carol. "Nothing more."

"Celebration of what?" Carol asked.

"My engagement. My career. My life."

"*Your* life!" Carol spit venomously. "It's always about *your* life. What about *my* life?" she asked, crossing her hands over her chest. "The life you and that scum-ball sister of yours are bound and determined to destroy."

"Then why did you come here? I purposely didn't send you an invitation because I thought something like this might happen."

"Why? Because I happen to love Donovan, and I couldn't let him come here to face you and your hateful sister's charges alone."

"Ah, Carol," Mallory said, coming up beside Abby. "I thought I heard my name being mentioned. What brings you and Donovan here? I don't recall Abby sending you an invitation."

"Crashing the party was my idea," Donovan replied, accepting the blame. He was so flustered he didn't even react to Abby's reference to her engagement.

"I'm glad you could come. Two champagnes," she told the bartender behind them. He was doing an admirable job of acting oblivious to the family feud playing out in front of him. She handed Carol and Donovan each a glass and pointed them toward the food. "Enjoy yourselves."

Steve led Abby down the hall to her bedroom. The minute he closed the door behind him, he took her into his arms and held her tight.

"It's at times like this that I'm awfully glad you're around," Abby said, holding him close, absorbing his strength. "I don't know how Mallory gets through all of life's trials alone."

"She's not alone. She's got you." He lifted her chin and kissed the tip of her nose.

When they returned to the party, Abby watched Carol standing alone in a corner of the dining room, flipping through the bound galleys of *Proof Positive*. Her expression was intense and marked with loathing.

Abby walked past her and found Donovan in the kitchen talking to Mallory.

"I want you to know, Mallory, that whatever happens, I admire your courage and your honesty, and I'm proud of you for standing up for justice. I was wrong before when I accused you of seeking revenge. I was wrong about a lot of things. All those years I thought you were getting worse instead of better, and I thought that way because I stupidly believed everything Carol told me. It never occurred to me that she would lie about something so important."

"What makes you think differently now?" Mallory asked, a distant look on her face.

"The reports Argone sent to keep us aware of how you were doing. I found them a few days ago and read them. I'm so sorry, Mallory. I love you, honey. I've always loved you in spite of what you think. I wish I could take away all the pain I've caused you, but I can't."

"Leave me alone," Mallory said. "Please, just leave me alone." She tore herself away with a choking cry and ran outside.

Donovan turned and saw Abby standing in the doorway.

"Maybe it *would* be a good idea if you and Carol left," Abby said, smothering a sob.

Donovan put his hands on either side of her face and looked deep into her eyes. "I made a foolish mistake coming here. I thought I could make something happen that would clear all this up, but . . . I was wrong. Do me a favor though, will you, Princess? Believe me when I tell you I love you and that I didn't kill your parents or anyone else." He dropped his hands to his side and strode out of the kitchen.

Abby stared after him, her heart breaking into a million pieces.

Outside, beyond the patio, Mallory was literally knocked off her feet when Olivia, who had managed to escape being penned in the garage with the other dogs, slammed against the back of her knees. "Hey, you," she said, reaching down to pet the dog's big head. Other than her own puppy, Olivia was her favorite of Abby's dogs. All Olivia wanted was to be loved and petted and to be allowed to sleep next to Beemer.

Mallory walked across the patio and looked in the living-room windows at the party. Abby was standing next to Steve, her diamond ring winking every time she moved her hand. Mallory envied Abby and Steve's relationship, envied the love they'd known and shared. Never having loved or given love, she could only imagine what it was like. But from where she stood it looked wonderful.

Mallory walked to the pool. Candles, sitting on wax lily pads, floated lazily on the water. It was a particularly dark night, the moon and stars covered by clouds. "Come on, Olivia, let's go for a walk."

"Yes, let's do go for a walk," a familiar voice said behind her.

Mallory whipped around and saw Carol standing beside an azalea bush, a gun in her hand.

* * *

Abby reached for a champagne bottle from the bartender and threw herself into being the stand-in hostess. "More champagne?" she asked, approaching the buyers from the two major chain bookstores.

"Wonderful party, Miss Mitchell," the man from Barnes & Noble said, the galley of her book in his hand. "I hope *Proof Positive* is as good as your sister's last book."

"Oh, it is," she said, smiling.

"You must be very proud. She's a talented writer."

"Yes, I am." But not for the reason you think, she said to herself as she filled his glass. She was proud of Mallory because of the *person* she'd become in spite of the way people had treated her.

"I was hoping to talk to her, to arrange some signings, but I don't seem to be able to find her anywhere."

Abby glanced around. Mallory was nowhere in sight. "Maybe she's freshening up. I'll look for her and tell her you'd like to talk with her." She headed down the hall toward the bedrooms and ran into Bunny on the way out of the guest bathroom.

"Have you seen Mallory?"

"Not in the last fifteen minutes or so."

Seeing Carol holding a gun on her was as crazy as any dream Mallory had ever had. Only it wasn't a dream. It was reality . . . a frightening reality.

"Think about this, Carol. You don't want to do anything you'll regret," Mallory said in a voice she barely recognized as her own.

"Believe me, Mallory, I won't regret killing you. And it's not like I haven't tried before. You're just hard to kill."

It only took Mallory a moment to realize what Carol was

talking about. "So, it was you who let the air out of my tire, right?"

"How astute of you."

Keep her talking, Mallory thought. *The longer she talks, the better chance I have someone will wonder where I am and come looking for me.* "You know, Carol, if you shoot *me* . . . Bailey James, the famous mystery writer . . . it's going to be thoroughly investigated and . . ."

Carol aimed the gun and . . . *pop!*

It was the flash of light that made Mallory realize Carol had fired and missed. *The gun must have a silencer,* she thought crazily. Before Carol could fire a second time, Mallory turned and ran screaming toward the back gate. If she could outrun Carol, she might be able to make it around to the front of the house, to people, to safety.

A second shot whizzed past her as she opened the gate. She stumbled and bumped her head on the latch. Cars, dozens of them, blocked her way. Briefly, she thought about hiding among them, but she was so scared, she was afraid her ragged breathing would give her location away. The only clear escape route was toward the ravine at the back of the property.

The clink of glasses and hum of conversation surrounded Abby as she moved from the living room to the great room to the dining room. She found Steve standing by the table, filling his plate with food. "Have you seen Mallory?"

"She's probably getting her picture taken. She ought to be easy to spot in that dress she's wearing," he said as he picked up a cube of cheese.

"Don't eat or drink too much," Abby said, squeezing his upper arm. "We've got a long night ahead of us, and I don't want you getting sleepy." She gave him her sexiest smile as she sashayed her way to the kitchen before he could say anything.

"Mallory?" she called, the dining-room door swinging behind her. The kitchen was empty. The last time she'd seen Mallory was in the kitchen when she'd been talking to Donovan. She'd been upset and had gone outside.

Abby opened the back door. "Mallory, are you out here?" Only Olivia answered with a howl of distress. She trotted onto the patio, her ears flapping like soggy wings. "Oh, Olivia! You've been digging." Abby moved backwards to avoid contact with the dog's dirt-crusted paws.

Olivia danced around impatiently before she let loose with a second mournful howl.

"What's the matter with you, Olivia?"

As if in answer, Olivia waddled to the gate and continued to excavate her hole.

Abby ran after her. "No, Olivia, no," she scolded as she reached down for the dog's collar. "What's this?" she asked, seeing something red on the ground beside the hole. The instant her fingers came in contact with the item, she knew it was Mallory's knitted snood. "Mallory? Are you out here?" she shouted. The gate was closed but not latched. "Mallory?" she shouted again.

The second she opened the gate, Olivia barreled through, trundling off toward the back of the property, barking like a hound on the scent of a fox.

Icy fear twisted around Abby's heart. There was only one thing back there . . . the ravine. Abby reached down and picked up the hem of her dress and ran.

"Excuse me," Donovan said, cornering Steve in the dining room. "By any chance have you seen my wife?" He had her coat draped over his arm.

"No."

"Where's Abby? Maybe she's seen her."

"Abby went looking for Mallory."

Donovan's eyes narrowed to slits. "Shit!"

Steve's eyebrows shot upward as he watched Donovan take off like a flash for the kitchen.

Steve set his plate down and ran after him. "Do you mind telling me what's going on?" He took hold of Donovan's arm and wrenched him around until they were eyeball-to-eyeball.

"I'm not sure, but I don't want to take any chances. Get a couple of flashlights and meet me out in back."

Ignoring his concerns about Donovan, Steve raced into the pantry, retrieved two flashlights, and returned to meet Donovan outside. "At least tell me what you think might be going on," he demanded.

Donovan flicked the high beam of his light from one corner of the yard to the other. He made his way over to the edge of the pool and looked in. "Turn on the pool lights," he ordered.

Steve flipped the light switch and heard Donovan breathe a sigh of relief.

"It's Carol," Donovan said. "I'm worried she might *do* something to the girls."

"Carol?" It took Steve a moment to understand his meaning before he jogged over to the door leading into the garage. "Beemer, come!" He grabbed Beemer's leash from a hook just inside the door.

The big shepherd bounded out of the garage like a racehorse leaving the starting gate. "Give me something of Carol's for him to smell." Donovan handed him Carol's coat. Steve put the coat up to Beemer's nose, then attached his leash. "Fetch, boy. Fetch."

Beemer barked, sprang forward, and headed for the back gate. As Steve pulled the gate open, he noticed a freshly dug hole. When had that happened? he wondered.

Flashlights searching, the two men followed the ex-K-9 toward the ravine.

* * *

Abby ran as fast as she could, wishing she'd had enough brains to go back into the house to get a flashlight. She followed Olivia, who was barking as furiously as when they'd first started out. "Mallory," Abby called into the night. "Mallory!"

Olivia stopped when she reached the edge of the ravine and stood like a pointer with her tail sticking straight out behind her and her right paw up in the air.

"Abby!" a pained voice came back to her in a loud whisper. "Get help."

Abby dropped to her knees at the edge of the ravine. "Where are you, Mallory? I can't see you."

"Shh! I'm okay. Go get help."

"Don't be ridiculous. I'm not leaving you."

"Carol chased me out here. She has a gun, Abby."

Olivia gave up her stance and barked.

"Go, Abby. Now. Carol can't get to me here. You're the one in danger. Run back to the house. Get help, then come back for me."

"Such sisterly concern," Carol said.

Abby turned her head sideways and saw Carol standing just a few feet away, a gun pointed directly at her. Fear, stark and wild, shot through her as she struggled to get to her feet, only to have Carol kick her in the side. Abby rolled sideways and felt herself slide over the edge of the ravine. Frantic, she grasped for anything that would break her fall and caught hold of a protruding tree root.

"Abby?" Mallory called, her voice panicked. "Abby, are you all right?"

It took Abby a moment to catch her breath. "I'm okay," she answered in a breathy whisper.

Abby glanced up and saw Carol's silhouette hovering near the edge. She knew if she stayed where she was, Carol would be able to pick her off without any trouble at all. Mustering her courage, she swung around and let herself slide down the brush- and rock-crusted slope to the bottom. She landed with a bone-jarring thump that knocked the wind right out of her. Long moments passed while she tried to regain her breath. Once it came, she picked herself up and stumbled along the bottom until she was just below Mallory.

"Let go, Mallory, and slide down like I did."

"No. I'm afraid."

"Do it, Mallory! I'm here to catch you."

Mallory released the tree branch she'd been holding on to and slid down the rocky embankment. "Ow," she groaned, landing on her rear end.

"C'mon," Abby said, pulling her sister to her. "Let's get out of here. You can worry about your aches and pains later."

Beemer's bark echoed through the night. Olivia answered back with a bark of her own.

"Shut up, you stupid dog!" Carol raised her arm to strike the dog. Olivia growled, then lunged forward and sank her fangs into Carol's calf. "You goddamn . . ." Olivia let loose and ran toward the sound of Beemer's frenzied barking.

"Carol?" Donovan called.

Hearing her name in the distance, Carol ran into a stand of trees.

Abby wasn't sure where Carol was. Her only thought was to get as far away from her as they could. Though she'd never been down in the ravine before, she knew it curved around and crossed the road in front of her house. If she and Mallory could make it there before Carol caught up with them, they might have a chance.

"Hurry, Mallory," Abby urged.

"I can't go any faster in these shoes," she said, lifting her foot for Abby to see.

"Okay, okay, just do the best you can and get rid of the damn shoes!"

Abby's lungs were on fire by the time they climbed up out of the ravine to the road. She bent over, put her hands on her skinned knees, and gulped air.

Mallory reached the top a moment after Abby and held on to her sister for dear life. "If we live through this, we're going to start jogging. We are seriously out of condition," she gasped.

Abby straightened and looked around. She breathed a sigh of relief when she saw the house. "We're almost home free," she said.

"That's what you think," Carol said, appearing from out of nowhere, waving her gun threateningly. "Stand back, Abby," Carol ordered. "I want the satisfaction of killing Mallory first."

Abby clung to Mallory. "You'll have to shoot us both, Carol, because I love my sister, and I'm not going to let you hurt her. You'll never hurt her again. You're sick, and you need help."

"Why?" Carol screamed. "Why do you love her? She doesn't love you. She never did. She's a hateful, evil girl. Can't you see that?" She laughed then, an eerie, demented laugh. "All I ever wanted in the whole world was Donovan. Just Donovan. But there were always people standing between us. First, your harlot of a mother. Did you know she had an affair with Donovan the whole time she was married to John? How she loved to flaunt it in my face. And how she loved to flaunt her love child . . . you, Mallory . . . in my face. It was such a pleasure to watch her die.

"Then there was John. Poor, foolish man. I can't believe he put up with Harriet all those years. He really deserved better. You understand, don't you, why I had to kill him? He and Donovan were such good friends that Donovan didn't need anyone else as long as he had John. I wanted Donovan to realize he needed me."

"So you killed our parents," Abby ventured, "knowing Donovan would assume the responsibility for us and that he would need you to help raise us?"

"I couldn't have children of my own, and I foolishly thought I could make you mine."

"I loved you, Carol. I loved you like a mother."

"If you loved me, why did you want to leave me? Why did you want to live your life away from me?"

Tears welled in Abby's eyes as she began to understand Carol's motives. Really understand.

"Carol! Stop!" Donovan shouted as he wove his way through the azalea bushes off to Abby's left. Steve was with him, Beemer on a leash at his side, Oljvia on her own tagging behind. "Listen to me, Carol. Whatever's wrong I'll fix it. We'll go away, just you and me. It'll be like a honeymoon. We'll go to Paris, London, wherever you want. Please, just put the gun down." He kept walking, his step and his purpose confident as he headed for Abby and Mallory.

"Get out of here, Donovan. Don't make me kill you, too."

He kept walking. "Do what you have to do, Carol, but I'm not going to let you hurt my girls. I've made enough mistakes in my life where they're concerned, and I'll be goddamned if I'm going to make any more."

Carol fired off a shot. The bullet went high and wide. Realizing she'd missed, she fired again just as Donovan made a grab for Abby and Mallory.

"Go, Beemer!" Steve shouted simultaneously, sending the ex-K-9 into action. Beemer bolted forward, took a high, running jump, and knocked Carol to the ground. The gun flew out of her hand to land near Steve's feet.

Steve grabbed the gun and ran for Abby.

"I've got them, Steve. They're both just fine," Donovan

said, holding Abby and Mallory close to him, crushing them against his chest.

When the foursome turned around, they saw Beemer standing over Carol, his teeth bared. Olivia, panting from her exertions, waddled up beside Beemer, hoisted herself up onto Carol's chest, and sat down. Beemer licked at one of her long floppy ears as much as to say, good girl.

"I told you Olivia was a scrapper." Steve grinned.

Donovan called the police on his cell phone. They arrived in less than five minutes—one car, no sirens as per Donovan's instructions. After a brief explanation, Donovan slid into the police car next to Carol, who stared straight ahead of her.

Epilogue

Two hours later, Donovan returned to Abby's house just as the party was breaking up. Nothing in the comments of the departing guests indicated they knew anything about what had happened. He wasn't quite sure how Abby and Mallory had pulled it off, but he was grateful to them for their discretion.

At his questioning look, Mallory said, "We managed to sneak in through the back bedroom, cleaned up, and changed our clothes. We blamed the dog's hole-digging for our change of attire, and no one was the wiser. It worked."

The minute the door closed on the last guest, Donovan joined them in the living room. Mallory was trying to explain to Bobby what had happened, and he was shaking his head in disbelief. He reached out to Donovan, who wrapped his arms around the boy's shaking shoulders.

"I have a confession to make," Donovan said, sitting down in the closest chair. "I've known about Carol for some time now, but I didn't have enough evidence to take to the police."

"You knew? How?" Abby asked, incredulous.

"Mrs. Lascaris alerted me. Seeing Carol at the dedication

ceremony for the retirement village gave her quite a shock. Afterward, when I asked her what was wrong, she told me she'd always suspected Carol of killing John and Harriet. She said the day they died, Carol was at their house before she took me to the airport. Apparently she parked around the corner and went in the back door. She said she'd seen Carol go over there several times and had peeked in the window once and saw Carol and Harriet having tea. The houses were so close together she could see everything. I couldn't imagine Carol doing that. She *hated* Harriet with a passion. Anyway, it started me thinking, and I found myself asking some hard questions. Unfortunately, none of those questions had any answers."

Mallory rolled her eyes. "We know how that goes, don't we, Abby?"

"One of the questions I asked myself," Donovan continued, "was if you two could possibly be on to something. So I tracked down Connor's family, flew to Oregon, and asked them to exhume Connor's body and do an autopsy. Dennis, Connor's brother, told me you'd already asked him, Abby, but that he didn't take you seriously . . . you being a mystery writer and all. I told the doctor I suspected murder and asked that he cover all the bases. He determined that the cause of death was poison, specifically oleander. I thought about all the oleander bushes we have all over our yard, thought about Carol's knowledge of plants and herbs and tea, and remembered her having me give Connor a bag with coffee and Danish in it when he left for the airport."

Steve put his arms around Abby and held her.

"I called Mrs. Lascaris right away," he added, "and she told me Carol had called and invited herself over for tea. Mrs. Lascaris was another one Carol hated with a passion. She said she was nothing but an old busybody. I put two and two together and decided Carol must have realized Mrs. Lascaris suspected her of murdering John and Harriet and was planning on killing her now, too, to keep her quiet."

"And so she did," Abby said, disheartened.

"No, she didn't," Donovan said. "But she thought she did. Did you know Mrs. Lascaris used to be an actress? She did community theater." Abby and Mallory looked at each other. "I talked her into doing one more role, to play the part of a woman dying of poisoned tea. She said death scenes were her specialty." Donovan grimaced.

"Why did you bring Carol to the party?" Steve asked. Beemer was sitting beside him and Steve was petting him.

"Carol had been real edgy about what she thought was going to happen here tonight. She was also angry that Bobby was invited and we weren't. I thought she might do something to try and stop Abby and Mallory from telling what *Proof Positive* was really about."

"We let you think that, Donovan," Mallory said, "because we originally thought it might flush you out into the open. By the time we began to think it was Carol, after reading our mother's diaries, well, it seemed best to continue and hope *Carol* would make a mistake."

"Well, there you go. We were both trying to accomplish the same thing, and we both failed. So much for well-laid plans." He sat forward, hands on thighs. "I badly underestimated Carol. As I said, I figured her to try something, but I never dreamed she'd go after you with a gun. Christ, I didn't even know she had a gun. And not only did she have a gun, but a silencer, too." He shook his head and called himself seven times a fool. "I only let her out of my sight for five minutes . . . to talk to you, Mallory, and the next thing I knew she was gone. Anyway, this is all my fault, and I just want you to know how sorry I am for putting your lives at risk.

"I think I'll take my son home. We need each other right now." When he stood to leave, Mallory reached for his arm.

"She had to be stopped, Donovan."

"Yes, but there might have been a better way."

"Maybe yes and maybe no. The point is, you did stop her, and you risked your life to save ours."

"Where's Mrs. Lascaris?" Abby asked.

"At the moment, I believe she's enjoying the comforts of a first-rate Charleston hotel."

Abby looked at Donovan over the rim of her coffee cup. "Did Carol kill Dr. Oldmeyer, too?"

"I don't know," he admitted.

"We'll probably never know," Mallory said, squeezing her arms against her chest. "There's already been one autopsy. Her daughter will never agree to another."

"As for Carol," Donovan said, "I don't know what will happen. She's a sick woman. Being confined, locked up, is not going to be easy for her."

Abby looked up at Steye, who was sitting on the arm of the couch. "I can't imagine Carol in prison."

Donovan shook his head. "She won't go to prison. As much as I despise her for what she's done, there's a part of me that will always love her. I'm going to pull some strings, some really *big* strings, and bypass the court system if I can and have her committed to Argone for the rest of her natural life."

Mallory gasped and clapped her hand over her mouth. She wanted to laugh and cry at the same time. Ultimately, she could do nothing but stare at the coffee in her cup and thank God she wasn't the one going to Argone.

"Sum it up for us, Donovan, so we can sleep tonight," Abby said, pulling Olivia into her lap.

"I don't know if we'll ever know what was going on in Carol's mind, but I would guess that it all had to do with obsessive love." This time when Donovan got up to leave no one stopped him. "Come on, Bobby, let's go home. Oh, and Abby, I wish you the best on your engagement. I assume Steve is the lucky man."

They followed him to the door and waved good-bye. As Donovan started down the driveway, Mallory and Abby looked at each other, nodded simultaneously, and ran to him. "Hey, *Dad*, wait for us!" they shouted in unison.

Donovan turned, a look of disbelief on his face before he held out his arms to scoop them up and twirl them around until they were dizzy.

"What a great family," Bobby said, his eyes moist.

"The best," Donovan said.

"The best of the best," Mallory said.

"Better than that, almost perfect," Abby said.

Olivia waddled up to Abby, snorted, and sat down on her foot. Beemer cuffed her on the neck as he took up his position on Abby's other foot.

"We're a package deal," Abby chortled.

"Can I join in?" Steve asked hopefully.

"Damn right," Donovan said. "There's always room for one more."